THE THIEF AND THE WASTE

THE WOLF AND THE RAIN TRILOGY (BOOK II)

TANYA LEE

ISBN 978-1-7753929-5-8

The Thief and the Waste is a work of fiction. All names and characters are products of the author's imagination or are used fictitiously. Any resemblance to actual events or persons, living or dead, is entirely coincidental. Except for Frank the Cat. Frank is real.

Please note that this work contains mature themes.

Edited by Melissa Frain

Cover design by Lena Yang

For my mom

I thirst
But cannot hold the sea in me
Wandering this wasteland
Where your caverns
Used to be

Powerless to stop
As my youth peels and rots
I grow old
Mummified before motherhood

Am I doomed to drift
Begging for rain
To bring me solace
And soothe the thoughts
That plague me?
Though stricken
I stumble
Sickened by vertigo
I'll not mourn
The serpent skin
I shed

Better to bury this Sahara that has
Eaten all of me
Throwing daggers at the sun until
Stars rain into the sea
Sculpt a sepulchre from bone
To claim this crypt
As my own
I'll wait upon my morbid throne
For the Lethe to rise
Cloud my eyes
And carry me home

1

The North

An impressively foul string of curses cut through the hush of the forest. Sam glanced over her shoulder, back toward the camp. It sounded like Dot.

She grimaced and returned her gaze to the river snaking through the canyon below her feet.

The others were waiting. Five other girls to fill the cart, two men to guide it. Just like the last shipment. Except, of course, that this was a rescue mission instead of an abduction.

A badly planned rescue mission.

She leaned back on her hands and took a deep breath, filling her lungs with the fresh forest air. She wanted to bathe in it, store it in her pores for the dry days ahead.

The rain was gentler here, leaving shallow pools that disappeared by the time the skies grew clear again. It was nice, after the Barrow. The trees seemed to like it too. They grew thicker and taller south of the city. Perhaps the trees in the Barrow hadn't enjoyed drowning in dirty water. Sam certainly hadn't.

She picked up a stick and began peeling off the bark with her fingernails. It wouldn't be long now before the trees shrank to desert shrubs and the humid air turned dry. A few more hours on the road, maybe a day. She remembered the brittle, yellow grass that bifurcated the land. The North ended there, though the southern wall wouldn't be visible for another week, maybe two. Her memories of the Waste should be more precise. They weren't. There would be miles and miles with nothing but sand. Sand and ash and silence. That much she knew. Her throat felt dry just thinking of it.

Once she had stripped the stick bare, she laid it on the dirt beside her, parallel to the cliff edge. The area around the stick was cluttered, and for some reason this bothered her. She began clearing out the space, moving twigs and leaves and an old plastic bottle to the side.

There was a patch of grass behind her. Reaching back, Sam ripped out a handful and sprinkled it on the ground—not next to the stick, but north of it, after a good expanse of dirt. The world in miniature: grass to represent the north; then dirt for the Waste; and a stick to symbolize the wall.

The North, the Waste, and the wall. What was missing? Sam picked up a longer, thinner stick, and broke it into four pieces. She placed them down on the grassy earth—a rectangle, to represent the cart.

What next?

Sam dug around until she found eight small stones. She placed two at the front, to symbolize Adder and Jackal, the two men who would be impersonating guards. The other six rocks she placed inside her little rectangle: the six abducted women. Except, of course, that they'd rescued the women that the Vauns had kidnapped. And then Sam, Shale, Dot, Shya, Charis, and Skye had been foolish enough to take their place.

This meant that whoever was paying the Vauns to send women south would open the cart to find six armed and angry women who, along with Jackal and Adder, would assassinate the guilty party and rescue the kidnapped women. Including Raina, and Jackal's sister, Anna.

A Trojan Horse attack.

But less effective.

We might not all die. Perhaps we'll just be enslaved.

Ignoring the last thought, Sam reached into the symbolic stick-cart and removed four of the stones.

Much better.

One stone for Sam, another for Jackal, who she'd worked alongside for months. A third for Shale and a fourth for Adder. Technically it was Adder's grandparents that Sam had actually befriended back in the Barrow—but no matter. They were on the same team now. And she trusted Adder, which was more than she could say for the other half of the team.

Sam jiggled the four remaining rocks in her hand. The ones she didn't know, not really.

Dot at least had been with them in the compound tunnels. She'd been there when they'd buried Xenia.

Sam picked out one stone and placed it back inside the cart. Not such a stranger, she supposed. Plus, she liked Dot. They'd been on the road for over a week, and Sam found the other girl to be competent, honest, direct.

Sam glanced down at the remaining three rocks.

Nothing like three unknown variables to make a shaky plan even shakier.

One by one she let them fall from her hand to the dirt below.

"Miss it?" Jackal came to stand beside her, moving noiselessly as always. She glanced up at him out of the corner of her eye, still not used to the longbow that distorted the lines of his silhouette. Sam tensed one ankle, then the other, feeling the sheathed blades in her boots. She would have preferred a bow, had there been one to spare.

"The Barrow?" Sam got to her feet, accidentally knocking the plastic bottle over the cliff in the process. They watched as it tumbled down the ravine, bouncing off the trees that grew u-shaped up the sides of the cliff, coated in moss and half-shrouded by ferns.

"The South."

Sam shrugged, crossing her arms across her chest. "Some things."

"Some people?"

She hesitated, then nodded.

"Not expecting a warm welcome, then."

She shook her head.

They stood in silence for a moment. It was a comfortable silence, though. Unlike before.

Jackal flicked his head back toward the trees. "Our shadow's still following."

"He isn't very sneaky," said Sam.

Jackal chuckled. Jamming his hands deeper into his jean pockets, he leaned back, tipping his head to look up at the sky. A raindrop splattered onto his nose. It wasn't raining, not yet; just the wind blowing through the wet trees.

"Won't be giving him scout duty, then," said Jackal. "He ever decides to show himself."

"I keep expecting him to fade away one night, head back to the Barrow." She looked down at her half-mangled map, wishing she'd thought to add a ninth stone, lagging behind the rest of them and hidden underneath a leaf or behind a twig.

"I dunno. Cass lost his sister, his man, his job, his home..."

Sam swallowed. The image of Xenia as they'd last seen her was never far from her thoughts. Or her dreams. "Not much to go back to."

A second cry rang out. This time it sounded like Skye. Maybe. She didn't know the other girl very well yet, after all.

"They've started, then?"

He nodded. "Yep. Sent me to get you."

"You know, they used to do this to cattle," she said as they started making their way back toward the camp, kicking bits of plastic off their boots as they went.

Did people really come this far just to dump their waste?

Maybe it's from the people who used to live here.

"What for?" asked Jackal. "Folks couldn't remember what their own damn cow looked like?"

"Well, some people had a lot of cows." Sam had seen it in photographs, massive herds roaming the land. "Meat consumption was really high. It was big business." They'd sacrificed the rainforests to make room, destroying the world's best carbon sinks.

Sam lost sight of Jackal for a brief moment as they parted to skirt around a particularly thick and mossy tree stump. When he came into view again, Jackal was scratching at the black stubble that was beginning to take over his face. He looked puzzled. *Of course he's confused.* Animal husbandry in the Barrow consisted of a single dirty goat or cow tied up behind the owner's shack.

He caught her watching and a grin spread across his weather-beaten face. "Am I starting to look like a bear?"

Sam couldn't help but grin back. Despite grief, despite the imminent danger they were stupidly heading toward, Jackal seemed lighter. After three years of watching the Vauns for clues of his sister's whereabouts, she imagined it felt good to be going after Anna directly. She enjoyed it herself, in truth: being on mission.

Enjoy it? You need it.

"Not a bear," said Sam, stepping carefully over a tangle of tree roots. "Just a jackal."

He opened his mouth to reply and then closed it again, sniffing the air. A look of revulsion passed over his face.

"I smell it too," said Sam.

"I don't envy you."

Sam patted the scar on her stomach. "At least this time I won't get stabbed first." She cocked her head to the side. "Probably. Charis seems handy with a blade."

Jackal looked away. "Most of us are. Wouldn't be any good on this mission if we weren't."

Sam glanced around and then placed her hand on Jackal's arm, signalling for him to stop. "She's a huaina, Jackal. I've seen the tattoos."

He was looking at her hand. Flushing, she took a step back and crossed her arms.

"Charis and Shya—two of them been helping look for Anna since she disappeared," he said.

"But a huaina? We cannot have someone with us who is unpredictable, not where we're going. If we have any chance of getting through the border we need soldiers. People who can follow a plan. Not gang members."

“Not all huaina are bad people,” said Jackal.

“Really?” asked Sam. “Because all of the ones that I’ve met have tried to kill me.”

“Look.” Jackal’s hand twitched upward, as though he was going to put it on her shoulder, but then thought better of it. “You don’t know Charis yet, not well anyway. She’d do anything for her sister. The Vauns tried to kidnap Shya; someone down South thought to buy her. She’s pissed.”

“So, that makes her trustworthy?” asked Sam.

“It makes her aim here the same as ours.”

“I thought ours was a rescue mission.”

The smell of charred skin was getting stronger.

Sam looked in the direction of the camp, sighed, and marched forward.

They’d put it off long enough, as it was. The abducted girls were branded the night of the solstice, before the Vauns shipped them south. This meant that the scarring needed to look a few weeks old.

Though they weren’t sure whether anyone would even look inside the cart at the border. Or whether there would be other checkpoints. Or how they would be able to distinguish a checkpoint from the final destination.

These uncertainties were problematic. It wouldn’t do to jump out of the cart too early and murder the wrong person. If they killed some underling charged with transporting them, they might never make it to whoever was in charge. No vengeance to dole out. No grateful girls to rescue.

And what a waste of heroics that would be.

Sam and Jackal arrived back at the clearing to find the others crowded together near the fire. Only Shale stood away from the group, her face paler than usual. Sam looked at the inflamed “V” on the redhead’s wrist and winced.

There was a shuffling of bodies and suddenly Sam and Jackal had a horrifically clear view as Charis pulled a metal rod from the fire. As she turned back toward Shya, her heavy silver rings caught the light, making it appear for a moment as though her hand, too, was made of metal.

Dot and Adder were holding Shya between them, while Skye hovered in the background, muttering something about auras and energy and gods.

To their credit, no one looked away as Charis pressed the scorching metal against the inside of her sister's wrist. Once it was done, Shya wrenched away, stumbled, and fell into a crouch beside the fire, both her face and newly branded arm hidden beneath a sheet of long black hair. As they approached, Sam realized that Shya, usually so poised, was directing some very colourful language at her sister.

"Don't blame *me.* You asked for this."

After a moment, Shya straightened, looking down at her older sister. Despite being her junior by a good ten years, Shya was a head taller than Charis.

"True." Shya's voice sounded strained. "Want me to do you?"

In fact, while they shared the same light brown skin tone and black hair, Sam didn't think they looked much like sisters at all. Shya was elegant. Sam looked at her long, graceful neck and high cheekbones and pictured a heron.

Not everyone has to be a bird.

Well, Charis certainly isn't.

"Ouch, kid. So eager. And yeah. But first—" Charis pointed the metal rod at Sam, a disconcerting grin on her small face. "It's her turn."

Sam looked at Charis with her chin-up, shoulders-back, chest-puffed swagger and decided that she would have marked her as a huaina even if she hadn't seen the tattoos.

Careful to keep her expression bland, Sam stepped up to the fire. Dot took her right hand, giving it a quick squeeze before she flipped it over, exposing the soft skin above her wrist. Sam glanced up at the taller girl and wished she hadn't. Dot was so pale that her freckles had disappeared entirely.

Charis lowered the rod into the flames, her eyes on Sam. "Snake boy."

Adder rolled his eyes and sighed dramatically, though he produced the bottle of moonshine, which he tossed up into the air and caught one-handed before pulling out the stopper and passing it to Sam.

"You had to tell everyone what it meant, huh?" he asked, mock hurt in his bright blue eyes.

"I like etymology," said Sam. She took the bottle and choked back a mouthful, maintaining eye contact with Charis. It seemed foolish to take her eyes off the older girl. Even if they were on the same team. Supposedly.

Adder moved to hold her other arm, but she shook her head. "No, thank you."

"It's not just for you, sweet pea," said Charis. "You swing at me, I swing back. But with that," she added, nodding toward the metal rod.

"I'm good."

Charis lifted the rod out of the fire.

I embrace the pain. It is my choice to be branded. My sacrifice.

Charis didn't even have the grace to hide her smile.

Sam smiled back. *I embrace the pain. It is my choice to be branded. My—*

She kept her head up, her eyes on the huaina, as burning metal seared the Vaun "V" into her flesh.

Twice in four months. Ava would not have been impressed.

2

The North

They gave up well before sundown that night, making camp in a small clearing ringed by phragmites. It could have been the throbbing burns that the women were nursing, or the rapid consumption of alcohol that served as pain relief, or the annoyingly apologetic demeanors of the two un-branded men, or the drizzle of rain, but Sam didn't think they had been making particularly good time, anyway.

The cart didn't help. Not that they needed to push it, thankfully. While it looked like a simple northern pushcart, one quick shove actually kickstarted a silent motor, one that never accelerated beyond a walking pace. The subtlety of the technology, as well as the obvious absence of crude fuel, flagged it as Seiran-made to Sam's expert eyes, but only upon close examination. If the Vauns' guards had marched it down the streets of the Barrow she doubted it would even have registered in her brain. Except, of course, that she'd seen a cart like this before. In another life, on the other side of the Waste.

While the cart was not overly heavy, however, it was awkward.

Alternate routes often had to be found, when the trees grew too closely together to permit its passage.

At least they never feared losing their way altogether. The cart had come equipped with a primitive sort of porta, though of course only Sam recognized it as such. The others had been equally awed and baffled by the small screen with only one display function: a compass that didn't point north. Sam had explained it as best as she could, though the group had responded to even basic concepts like radio frequency and batteries with skepticism. They hadn't realized the obvious, either—that the porta was probably registering their coordinates as well. Which meant that someone in Seira knew exactly where they were.

Dot was the navigator, though she occasionally trusted the palm-sized device to Shya or Jackal. The delicacy with which she treated it was unnecessary, as they'd discovered before they'd even made it out of the Barrow. The compass had been dropped not once but twice that first day—the first time onto cement and the second time into an oily puddle. The experience had led them to three conclusions: the device was waterproof; the screen was shatterproof; and passing it from person to person was probably a bad idea.

The cart had come also equipped with one roomy, structurally sound tent, large enough for three guards. The two additional tents that Dot and Shya had scrounged before leaving the Barrow were of varying quality. One was dirty, but surprisingly resilient. The other was large but provided only the illusion of shelter—casting a shadow but repelling neither the elements nor the bugs. Out of fairness, the occupants traded tents nightly. The pairings, however, remained constant.

Dot and Shya always bunked together, as did Charis and her girlfriend, Skye. Sam, Adder, and Jackal were left with the third tent, though as the three of them took the lion's share of the nighttime watch, the arrangement was one of alternating rather than sharing.

Luckily, Adder's propensity for chatter and Jackal's tendency toward silence balanced out in something less awkward than she might have feared. Sam would take her scratchy blanket and curl up in the far corner, leaving Adder to flitter around Jackal.

Sam usually tried to grab first watch, if Jackal didn't. She was more comfortable around Jackal now, but enough tension—of what kind she chose not to explore—persisted to make the idea of sharing the silent moments before sleep less than appealing.

Why Jackal bunked with her and Adder, instead of with Dot and Shya, Sam couldn't determine. The three of them seemed very close. Dot and Shya had been his sister's best friends, Jackal had told her. They'd grown up together.

Perhaps it was a safety measure—Jackal keeping an eye on Adder, whom he hadn't met until the night of the solstice. Or perhaps it was her he didn't trust. Though that seemed less likely, considering they'd worked together for months. Maybe Dot snored.

Shya's very beautiful, isn't she?

Sam pushed the thought away. If Jackal was attracted to Shya he would seek her out, not avoid her.

Although, it was possible that he did have feelings for her but had chosen not to act on them. Maybe it was too complicated a romance to pursue. Or perhaps they had left other lovers behind in the Barrow. It didn't matter. It was none of her business.

As for Shale, Sam wasn't sure where the redhead slept. She disappeared every night.

No one ever spent the night inside the cart. They used it to store their tents, food and water, the fuel pucks that were so energy efficient that Sam was certain they must be Seiran-made as well, and a few other necessities. None of them ventured inside if they could help it. It wasn't something they had spoken about, but Sam suspected that she wasn't the only one who kept picturing the other women. Drugged and packed in neat rows. Like meat in an oven, someone had said, and the imagery had stuck in Sam's mind. She felt claustrophobic just thinking about it.

Sam was still awake when Jackal returned to the tent at the end of his watch. She had been keeping her arm elevated above her heart to lessen the throbbing pain in her wrist. It turned out to be a posture that did not facilitate sleep.

Judging from the low voices she heard coming from the other tents, the other girls were awake as well.

Jackal touched her arm as she slid out past him—a symbolic passing of the baton, nothing more, but the warmth of his fingers followed her out into the moonlight.

The air was humid, though the rain had finally stopped. Sam circled the camp silently three times, then stepped into the thick of the trees to relieve her bladder.

She was zipping up her jeans when she smelled it—smoke from a campfire. Two steps deeper into the woods, then she paused. Crept back to her tent.

She didn't even need to call out his name.

"Everything okay?" asked Jackal, stepping outside.

"Probably," said Sam, looking up at his silhouette, backlit by the stars overhead. "There's another camp close by. It's probably, just, well, you know who. But I want to check it out, just in case."

He nodded. "I'll keep watch."

"No, you won't." Even in the middle of the night, Adder was cheerful. He reached up and thumped Jackal on the back as he stepped past him, stretching his arms in an overly dramatic show of wakefulness. "You've done your time. I got this."

Jackal looked to Sam, shrugged, and headed back into the tent.

"I'll be back in a minute," she told Adder, and set off into the woods. It took her a moment to realize there were two sets of footsteps instead of one.

"Sure you don't want me to come?" asked Adder.

"Yes. The whole point of waking you—well, Jackal, actually—was to ensure the camp was being watched while I investigated. So, go watch."

"You might need backup."

"I don't need backup."

"But what—"

"Go guard the camp, Adder."

With a heavy sigh as though she'd wounded him deeply, Adder dropped back.

Sam continued onward, creeping slowly and lightly through the brush. At least the rain made it easier to sneak around undetected.

Which is important.

It might be.

It's probably just Cassio. Maybe he's ready to be found. Why else would he light a fire?

Warmth, comfort. Maybe he's too inebriated to remember that he intended to be secretive.

Or maybe he wants—

Sam hit the clearing and two things became immediately clear.

Cassio was not there.

Nobody in fact, was there. No person, no supplies. Just a fire.

Sam spun around and raced back to the camp.

3

The South

I watch the rest of my cohort file out of the dormitory on their way to the fifth-year examinations. They look prepared. They look excited. They look nervous. They look as though they might be sick. I smile reassuringly. Nobody notices. I understand, of course.

Soon only Ash and I are left. He rubs the sleep from his eyes and winks at me. I frown back at him.

"They'll be fine. We were." He leans heavily on the "i" in *fine*, as though we hadn't been just as terrified yesterday.

As Ash and I will be competing in tonight's contests, we, along with our teammates Oak and Juniper, were required to take our examinations early.

Our classmates have had one additional day for preparation, but I do not begrudge it. I had advance warning and prepared my study timeline accordingly. What is important now is that we are able to prepare for tonight's contests. And I do find it pleasant to be able to mentally focus on the task before us, without the distraction of examinations.

"I know they'll be fine." My voice is sharper than I intend it to be. "I'm merely being empathetic."

"Why? Nobody's watching."

I let out a sigh of exasperation.

Ash flashes me a grin. "Are you worrying about tonight?"

"A small amount of anxiety is natural. The whole country will be watching the contests."

I hadn't actually been anxious, though. Not until today. All of my nervous energy had been directed toward the examinations. For five years they'd been looming over us, and for good reason. Scores in both the academic and the combat portions are used to determine our designations. While it is technically possible to change designations later in life, from a P1 with general border duty to a P2 training master or librarian, or even a P3 specialist in engineering or medicine, it doesn't often happen. Certainly, nobody ever reaches the status of a P4 strategist or P5 base leader after a poor showing in the examinations.

The contests don't affect our career prospects—not in a tangible way. Winning would go on our permanent records, and we could gain popularity, respect, and glory for our base. But it wouldn't lift me from the mediocrity of a P1 designation.

So, while I have been training for the contests all year along with the three other selected cadets, it was the examinations that preoccupied my mind. I had prepared diligently and my performance in both the academic and the martial portions was flawless. I will rank well.

Yesterday I would have sold a victory in the contests for even a small advantage during the examinations. Today my stomach flutters with excitement and anxiety and something more primal. I want to win. It doesn't matter that winning won't affect my career. I want to win because I want to win.

Ash sits down beside me on my bed, shaking me out of my ruminations. I hadn't even seen him cross the room.

"So," he says. "We can't study. We shouldn't train before the contests. What do you want to do today?"

He's sitting too close to me. My stomach flutters again, though this time it is not the contests unnerving me. Ash nudges me with his elbow and I frown at him.

"Breakfast," I say. "Then we should review strategy and meditate."

"We could do that." He stifles a yawn with a hand and smiles at me. "Or we could get into trouble."

I do not need to express my disapproval verbally. Ash takes one look at my face and laughs. "Or we can meditate."

"The contests are in twelve hours," I say. "How can you be so flippant?"

He pats my shorn head in the careless, affectionate, aggravating way that he knows I hate, and returns to his station. "Dress, my future leader. We must break our fast."

"Don't joke about that." I turn around to change from my pyjamas into my standard-issue olive green uniform. It's hard to imagine that we are only days away from being able to choose our own clothing, to grow our hair long if we like, or wear makeup. The freedom is dizzying. "Grand Neilem has not taken an apprentice in fifteen years."

"Then it's time for some new blood."

"If it happens, it happens. I will not project my expectations onto her," I say, as I always do. We have had this conversation many times. I turn around. "Was Juniper—What are you doing?"

Ash has stripped down but seems to be in no rush to dress. Instead he is examining something on his thigh. "This thing's gone yellow. I like it. Purple and yellow."

I shift my eyes from the muscles on his bare chest and arms to the fist-sized bruise on his leg. "When did you get that?" I ask. "I have not seen anyone land a blow on you in months." For all that he is lackadaisical when it comes to schoolwork, he is one of the best in combat. It's why he is such an excellent training partner. Him and Linden and Fir. The four of us have been together since the first day of first year. When we were Sora and Vireo and Starling and Pipit. I shake my head, surprised at myself. Dwelling on past names is forbidden. We are the present. Only the present.

"Hmm? Oh. Nah, not training. Just me and Juniper." He grins at me.

"Oh," I say. "She kicks you during sexual intercourse?" It seems odd, but I have not yet looked into erotic norms and practices. There is a pamphlet under my bed somewhere. I will look at it later. After the contests, perhaps, when I can be distracted.

"It was an accident," he says. "I think. You can ask her about it at breakfast."

"I can. If you ever get dressed," I say, pointing at the heap of olive green clothes on his floor. "You're lucky Protector Nem didn't do an inspection this morning."

"It's examination day, there was no way she was going to do an inspection," he says as he pulls on a short-sleeved shirt.

"You're gambling again, Ash." I wait while he pulls on pants, socks, boots, so we can walk together to the canteen.

Only two others are still at our table when we arrive: two fifth-year cadets from the other dormitory, our teammates for tonight.

"Hi, Juniper."

"Hi, Sequoia." She greets me with a smile before turning to give Ash a kiss on the mouth. Juniper is tall and beautiful, with dark skin and long legs.

Oak waves a hello, his mouth full of breakfast. He is massive, a good head taller than Ash, who is not short. Oak is also a good teammate. We pair together sometimes, though he is the largest cadet in our year, and I am one of the smallest. *Sparrow.* The name floats by, untethered. I did not mean to think it. *Finch.* She is filling Ash's cup and mine with prickly pear juice.

I wonder why I cannot keep my thoughts in line. Perhaps it is because today is the last day that we are cadets. Tomorrow we become protectors, and another name will fall away. There will be a new Sequoia, and I will be someone else.

Have I grown attached? I swill the name around my mouth: Sequoia. Is it me? More than the other names? All fifth years are trees, just as all fourth years are canines, and all third years are chemical elements. And once I was a bird. *Sora.* The names are never ours to keep. Endings lead to sentimental reminiscing. I am sure I will be fine once we receive our designations and I know who I am again.

After breakfast we find an empty classroom and walk through our contest strategy. We cannot predict what tasks they will assign us, but over the year we have sketched out a variety of possible scenarios. For each scenario there are two predetermined strategies in place, based on our strengths and weaknesses as a team and as individuals.

I am the lightest, so if we need to throw a teammate, it will be me. We have practiced it over and over—the throw, the flight, the catch, the spot.

I may be the fastest in a footrace but Ash's arm is better in terms of throwing speed and accuracy. Oak is physically the strongest. Juniper's memory for movement and footwork is unparalleled. That we are the best in our cohort at the physical arts is clear. We can claim natural aptitude, but many cadets have a natural aptitude. We are also the most determined to excel. Most important of all, we work well as a team.

Time seems to be moving quickly, too quickly. Soon it is time for lunch. I force myself to eat, even though my stomach is knotted in anticipation.

After lunch I clear my dishes and make my way outside. Oak follows, but Juniper and Ash head off down the corridor together, hand in hand. To a coupling pod, probably. It makes me feel lonely, watching them. Ash has been one of my closest friends for five years —us and Linden and Fir. *Vireo, Starling, Pipit.* Stop it, I tell myself, though my mind goes one step further. I see our twelve-year-old selves running ahead of me, dashing across the dusty fields, laughing.

It is natural for Ash to be preoccupied with Juniper. We are biologically wired to prioritize sexual relationships over friendship at this age.

Still, I feel the loss. Then the irritation sets in. Meditation and visualization is a crucial part of our warm-up. More than that, it's Ash's weakest point. *Focus is a virtue.*

Sparrow—not Sparrow. Oak. Oak walks beside me, his tall, muscular body shielding me from the sun.

Why does my mind insist on slipping back to first year? An odd glitch. I haven't been Sora in four years. If I must endure errors of nomenclature, why does my brain not select from the recent past?

Perhaps it is because of the ending that draws near—the end of my time as a cadet. The ending of any story is linked to its beginning.

I frown. Feelings of nostalgia serve no useful purpose. Possibly they are linked to a hormonal change. I will make sure to visit the medical ward after the contests if my subconscious continues to prove troublesome.

We reach the meditation tent, the lone structure in an otherwise empty section of the field, far from the base. Oak tosses his water bottle into the air and catches it. I lean into a stretch and close my eyes. I need to quiet my brain. We will not win the contests if I am distracted.

"Sequoia?" The bottle thumps into his meaty hand as he catches it a second time.

I open one eye and peer up at Oak. The sun is behind him now, sending his face into shadow.

"Yes, Oak?"

"Have you submitted your rooming form yet?"

I raise my hand over my face, trying to reduce the glare. Oak looks pleased. *Why does he look pleased?*

"Not yet, why? Have you?"

He shakes his head. "I was, um, waiting."

I bend over and press my palms to the ground. "That is reasonable. We have been busy."

He nods, then switches back to shaking his head. "We have been, but that's not...I was waiting to speak to you."

My head snaps back up. I block the sun with one hand and examine Oak's face with the other. "Why..." My voice sounds antagonistic. I take a deep breath. *There is no need to be defensive. Perhaps he wants your opinion on his choice of a romantic partner.* I force a smile onto my face. *Better.* "What did you wish to speak about?"

"Would you want to? I mean for housing...the couple quarters. With me?"

"I—couple quarters? Oak, we've never..." I steady my voice. *Where is that smile? Courtesy is a virtue.* "I believe that the more harmonious dual-occupancy arrangements are typically those that are entered into after the individuals have already enjoyed a sexual and romantic relationship."

"I know, but...I thought maybe we could try? Or, okay. I see your point. If not couple quarters, then, would you be interested in beginning a romantic relationship? I could submit a request to use a coupling pod."

I swallow my impulse to reject him. I should consider it, of course. Sexual experimentation is natural, especially at our age. Most of my cohort have engaged in romantic or sexual relationships. Some people, like Ash, have already had several partners.

"Could I think about it? We have the contests tonight, and tomorrow we receive our designations." Even saying the words makes me shiver. *Our designations. The naming ceremony.* My entire future is on the cusp of being decided. Who has time to think about romance?

"Of course." He looks disappointed. "If not now, then maybe in the future."

This is why Oak is such an excellent teammate. He is good natured and persistent. *He would be a good choice for your first sexual partner.*

I look at his massive hands, picturing them on my naked body, and have to stifle a sudden urge to giggle. Of course, misplaced laughter and tears are natural reactions to discomfort. But I don't want to hurt Oak's feelings. He is kind. It is a kind offer. I'm not going to accept it.

We settle on the ground, legs crossed, eyes closed. The sun has grown stronger. I am grateful for the protection that the tent provides.

I imagine that I am on a mountain. *There is no earth beneath my feet, only rock. It is cold.* I visualize the peak above me, feel the wind threatening to tear me down. In my mind I take one step forward. Then another.

I look up at the mountain only occasionally, to keep my end goal in mind. Mostly I focus on the path ahead of me. It's a matter of balance. I need to keep the peak present in my mind without fixating on the future. It is the present that matters, the steps. *Find the path. Let it go. Advance. Check course. Repeat.*

I don't know how long we have been meditating when I feel Ash settle down beside me.

"See, lots of time," he whispers.

Even with my eyes closed my brows furrow. "I didn't say anything."

"I could feel your disapproval from the coupling pod."

I sniff. "No more talking. You're already behind."

"We have hours, still."

"And physical and mental preparation take hours. If we are going to win we must be focused." *Find the path, let it—*

"Of course. And since you can't focus when you're mad at me, you'll have to stop being mad at me."

Against my will, the corners of my mouth twitch. His eyes must be open still, because he pats my shoulder.

"You know I'm no good at visualization."

I can feel my shoulder burning where he touched it. "You would be if you practiced."

"Just lead it for me."

"No. You have to learn."

"Come on, Sequoia."

"No. It will be distracting to Oak and Juniper."

"Uh, guys?" Oak's voice rings out, loud above our whispers. "You're already distracting."

"Just proceed with the group visualization," says Juniper.

I sigh and let out a slow breath. "We are on a mountain. There is no earth beneath our feet, only rock..."

After meditation and visualization, we return to the dormitories, where a jug of prickly pear juice and four meal replacement bars have been left out for us.

We have just finished when a level one protector arrives with a large box. He pulls out scarlet singlets and loose black pants and hands them to us. I hold the singlet in my hands, rubbing the fabric between my fingers. I spent my childhood wrapped in beiges and tans and my years as a cadet dressed head to toe in olive green. This is the first bold colour I will ever wear.

Once we are dressed, the protector leads us to a small, empty classroom. He leaves and we wait in silence.

I hear boots in the corridor and soon four protectors enter. They too wear scarlet, though their uniforms are crossed with strips of gold.

One of them, a man with long blue braids, grins at us. "Ready?"

We nod, though none of us speak. I am glad that Protector Jheb is with us. The other three members of the protector team are familiar to me, of course, but Protector Jheb has been our training master for the past five years. He is kind and supportive, and I find his manner to be calming.

The click of boots once again. Three pairs this time.

Flanked by her seconds, Grand Neilem enters the room. We raise our hands automatically and press them palm to palm in front of our eyes in the sign of deference. From behind my fingers I watch her spiked red hair bounce with each marching step. She reaches the front of the room and stops. In unison, her seconds halt beside her. She nods at us and we drop our hands.

Grand Neilem's seconds remain motionless as she stares at each of us in turn. Even after all these years, I still picture a falcon when I look at her. Is it the straight, hooked nose? Or the intensity of her gaze? I can never decide. I should not think about such things. I straighten and struggle not to glance away when her eyes meet mine.

She smiles suddenly, abruptly. "The train has arrived to transport you to the contests. For the remainder of the day you will be acting as base ambassadors. Every word you speak, every action you take, both within the arena and outside of it, reflect on the virtue of this base. Comport yourselves honourably. Your successes are our successes."

Grand Neilem smiles once again. "Beholden, duty-bound, in gratitude."

"Beholden, duty-bound, in gratitude." We echo the state words as she turns and marches back out of the room. Only one of her seconds follows behind—P5 Protector Onyx. We all know who he is, though I doubt any of the cadets have ever spoken with him. He is striking—slim and fine featured, with dark blue hair dyed to match the blue of his eyes.

The other, Protector Jace, is a few years older than P5 Onyx—thirty-eight to Protector Onyx's thirty-five years. I know because I have looked at their public bios. Protector Jace is the opposite of his counterpart physically—being tall and bulky, with broad shoulders. He has dark skin and black hair flecked with gold. They do, however, seem to share an identical stoicism and taciturnity. Both seem more statue than man.

Protector Jace watches them leave, and then turns back to us. "Follow me, please." His voice is a deep, rich baritone. I stare at the P5 stitched onto the breast of his uniform as he strides from the room. The four protectors follow, then Ash, then me, then Juniper, then Oak.

We travel through the stark, cold hallways to an exit on the south side of the base and make our way across a dusty field. We have run this field and trained on it, but we have not strayed beyond it in five years. Ash turns back and looks at me. I try to suppress my excitement and fail. He grins and turns back around.

I do stifle the urge to look back at the base. Grand Neilem may be watching, and I want us to look unified, like soldiers. We are not children anymore.

4

The South

The train is empty except for an attendant. She holds out a porta and one by one we press our palms against the screen. *Sequoia* appears as soon as I remove my hand. I stare at it for a moment, feeling detached. I wonder if the others feel more sentimental, if they care that tomorrow someone new will wear their name.

I wonder if I will become attached to my new name. The one I will choose. The one I will keep for the rest of my life.

Once we are seated, the attendant passes each of us an orange sweet. The train starts up and the four of us turn to stare out the window. Nothing but sand and dirt, of course. Barren fields and dust. The landscape does not change and yet I cannot look away. A few rows over, the protectors chat quietly amongst themselves.

The train stops once, to pick up more contestants, I assume, though nobody enters our car. The train is long, though; there are other cars.

The remainder of the trip seems to take only minutes, though the movement of the sun tells me that an hour has passed. When we rise to disembark, it occurs to me that none of us cadets have spoken a word since we left the base. Even Ash has been silent.

A group of protectors is waiting outside the train. A middle-aged PI approaches us, porta in hand, and we are asked to press our palms to the screen a second time.

I look behind myself and see other contestants—cadets and protectors dressed in navy, emerald, and violet. All the cadets are shorn and all their protectors wear singlets crossed with gold. More PIs in olive green stand with each group, verifying identities with portas. They belong to the host base, I assume.

I inadvertently lock eyes with a tall, fair girl dressed in green. She grins at me and I smile politely back. I wonder if we will have the opportunity to interact with cadets from other bases.

Once we have been scanned, one of the host PIs ushers us across the field to a base indistinguishable from our own. Even the corridors are identical. Even the smell.

She then leads us to a small room, empty except for several mats that have been rolled up and leaned against a wall and a small table laden with jugs of date palm juice and millet bread. The screen of a Personal Communication Box flashes the time. *Not the time—a countdown. Fifty-nine minutes and seven seconds.*

Ash, Juniper, and Oak look at me. "Twenty minutes to refresh, twenty minutes for meditation, and twenty minutes for a physical warm-up."

I catch Protector Jheb, busy tying his long, blue braids back into a ponytail, looking at me, and flush. He grins. "We'll do the same. I'm leading imagery for the protectors. Did you want to join?"

I glance at my teammates for affirmation, and nod to Protector Jheb. "Please."

I take a glass of juice from Oak, who is passing them around, and watch while the others each ingest a small portion of millet bread. I could probably use some additional carbohydrates as well, but my stomach is tight and the sight of food is nauseating.

Ash passes me a tiny piece of bread.

"No, thank—"

"It's not for you. Throw it."

I stare at him. "Throw it?"

"Lob it. I'll catch it. See?" Ash tosses a second piece into the air and catches it in his mouth. Juniper applauds.

I glance over at the protectors and see that they are huddled together, not paying us the slightest bit of attention.

I look back at Ash, who is bobbing lightly on the pads of his feet, as though in preparation.

A laugh bubbles up, catching me off guard. "You are ridiculous."

"Just throw it."

I toss the bread in the air. My aim is off, but Ash lunges to the side and catches it in his mouth anyway. Both Juniper and Oak clap and I feel my shoulders drop as the tension dissolves.

I reach into the serving dish for a second piece of millet bread. "Two more. That's it."

Ash nods, still bobbing up and down. "If I get all three you have to let me pick your protector name."

"Absolutely not," I say, throwing the second piece.

He catches it easily, raising his fists in triumph as he chews and swallows. "Two down."

"Oh yeah?" I say and eat the third piece myself, earning a triumphant smile from Ash. Perhaps I misread the goal of the game.

After twenty minutes have elapsed, Protector Jheb leads us in team imagery. Instead of a mountain, we are branches on a tree, growing together in unity and peace.

We also accept his offer to lead the physical warm-up. Gentle cardio is followed by a deep stretch, after which we move slowly through our repertoire of kicks and punches. The contests do not always include martial aspects, but it is worthwhile to be prepared. And pushing through my full range of motion feels good. It makes it seem as though my body is wholly mine, wholly tethered to my will.

We watch the seconds count down in silence. Our silence has changed, though. Where there was tension now there is focus, calm. The blade ready to be drawn, the bullet waiting for the trigger. I want to move, and when Ash looks at me I can see it in his eyes too. Like a fever.

As the clock reaches zero the door opens. The same protector that led us here from the train escorts us across the base to a small room that feeds into the arena. It is pitch black inside, but I know where we are because even the floorplan of this base is identical to my own. We wait in the wings while she leads Protector Jheb and his team of protectors into the ring.

In a moment, more bodies fill the dark room. Other cadets, from other bases. We squint through the blackness at each other, but nobody speaks.

I hear familiar notes as a violinist and a pianist that I cannot see strike up the introductory melody. A voice booms loud on the amplobox: the words of gratitude. I repeat the lines that I am meant to repeat, but they feel distant. We are on the outside, still.

The notes die down and a new voice takes over. A female voice, rich and resonant. My ears don't register the words. They don't need to. The inflection, the tone—she is hyping up the audience.

Spotlights flood the far end of the arena with yellow light as the thunder of applause sounds. I close my eyes against the glare. When I open them again one of the spotlights is breaking away, growing bigger as it moves toward us. I reach out and touch Ash's hand, Oak's, Juniper's.

When the light touches the doorway, I sprint forward, Ash beside me, Juniper and Oak behind us.

I know to keep my gaze level. Vaguely, I register the roar of applause. *It doesn't matter. Find them.*

I spot it—the clump of red up ahead, the protectors from our base. We run to our position behind them and halt. Only then do my eyes flicker up to the stands. The faces, the noise, it looks fake, as though screens have been set up to give the illusion of a crowd. It isn't, of course. I pick out an individual face, then another. They are real. This is real. I am here.

The announcer is speaking again. *What have I missed?* A flourish of her arms, and I see it—the tent. I turn with my team and jog toward it.

Inside the tent there are eight benches, one for each of the cadet teams. A sign has been posted on one of the interior walls, under the red, blinking light of a camera. *A place for quiet reflection.* It says. In other words, no speaking. Also, *Help yourself to juice.* I look around until I spot the table that has been set up with pitchers and small glasses.

I hear a sound like the air being sucked away and look back to see that the tent has been sealed. The noise of the arena, even the voice of the announcer, are gone. Not only will we not be able to watch the protectors' match, we won't be able to hear it, either.

In the new silence, someone takes a deep breath and it is deafening.

Ash and Oak head to one of the benches and sit. Juniper and I follow, though we both remain standing. She taps her toe impatiently. I fold into a stretch.

I sneak glances at the other teams. They're watching us too. I wish we could speak with them.

A moment passes, then another. I wonder how the protector match is going. I wish we could watch, though I understand why we cannot. This is not the qualifiers, this is the contests. We don't get the advantage of watching what strategies the protectors employ. When it's our time we will have only seconds to decide how to act.

A minute later, or five, or ten—I'm not sure how long, really—the door unseals. In our teams, we exit the tent.

The floor of the arena is empty except for the announcer's podium. The protectors who just finished competing stand together with their teams along the back wall.

"Welcome again, cadets!" It is overstimulating to have all of that energy directed at us. "I am Protector Tayra. Are you ready for your first task?"

We are standing at attention: focused and silent. The question takes us by surprise. I push my shoulders down and back, straightening my spine and raising my chin ever so slightly in what I hope is a vision of competence and strength. In my peripheral vision I see Ash nodding, eager.

She laughs. "I want some noise, cadets! I said: Are you ready for your first task?"

It might be the excitement, or the nerves, or perhaps it is only fear turned loose, but the noise we release is monumental. It fills the arena and the air turns hot with potential.

"The first task is, well, it's not simple, is it?" Protector Tayra flashes the protectors a wide grin before tipping her head back to look up at the ceiling. " Let down the strings, please."

Harnesses descend on one side of the arena. I look up and see scaffolding.

"For this task, two members of each team will be situated on the platform above the arena. They are the puppetmasters." I frown at the word, not sure what she means.

"The other two will be travelling across the room, striking and defending in a simple 2-3-2 pattern. The cadets on the ground will control their own arms, but their feet will be controlled by their teammates." *Puppetmaster.* I look up again, the meaning clear to me now.

"Of course, it's not quite that straightforward...lights!" Colourful spots of light appear on the arena floor. "You must make your way across the room while remaining inside your spotlight. Step outside the spotlight or strike out of time, and a point will be deducted from your score. If five points are deducted, you will be eliminated from this round and receive zero points. Lose ten points and you will be eliminated from the contests."

A difficult task. I can feel the adrenaline pumping. I'm ready to start. Ready to win.

"You have thirty seconds to delegate roles amongst yourselves."

I turn to my teammates. "You and I," says Juniper, looking at me.

It is a good suggestion. When it comes to feats of balance, Juniper and I have always scored the highest. I nod to Ash and Oak and they jog over to the edge of the arena, where ladders will lead them up the scaffolding. We move to a set of harnesses and begin strapping them onto our legs. I try to kick forward, backward: nothing. My lower body is locked. I look up to the platform above me and see Ash looking down. He makes a move and my left leg shifts backward. I struggle not to lose my balance.

I look at Juniper. "Bend your knees," I say.

Cadets appear from the sidelines carrying wooden staves. We take ours and wait for the count to start. A light appears around our feet. From an amplobox somewhere comes a beat. A live, loud metronome. Four to countdown, as we do during practice.

"Don't look for the light," I whisper to Juniper. She nods, her dark eyes focused on mine. It's the only communication we have time for.

The 2-3-2 pattern is simple. Two strikes, followed by three strikes, followed by two strikes. Right-left; right-left-right; left-right. Then it is repeated, beginning with the opposite side. Left-right; left-right-left; right-left. It is designed to ensure that you develop your skills with both hands equally. The pattern begins and our staves connect midair. Twice. Three times. Twice again.

I feel the tug on my leg and bend my knees. Only then do I realize that I am the one who will be going backward. *Focus on the pattern. Juniper's face. Ash's lead.*

Despite my warning to Juniper, I find it difficult not to look for the spotlight. It is the wrong impulse. Ash and Oak are charged with direction; this is a dance, and every good dancer knows that only one party can lead.

I hear an off-beat strike, and then another. The tug at my legs grows faster. It jerks to the left, then to the right. I hear a shout as someone falls. I don't look away from Juniper's face until the drumming stops.

She wipes sweat off her brow with the back of her hand and grins at me. "Well done."

"And you," I say, looking past her to the damage around us. Only half of the teams have succeeded in reaching the end line.

I scan the arena until I find the amplobox. In front of it, a large screen showcases a set of scores out of twelve.

Three teams have received full points, including us. Another scored eleven. Of the four remaining teams, one scored ten, two scored eight, and one received zero points.

We slip out of the harnesses and jog back to the tent, where we're joined by Ash, Oak and the rest of the contestants that had been positioned up on the platforms. I must have been filtering out the sounds of the crowd, because it is only now that I register the applause.

Inside the tent, I grab juice and look for Ash. He grins at me and squeezes my shoulder. I want to speak this time, to talk through the task with him and learn how it felt from his perspective.

Instead we wait in burdensome silence until the door unseals a second time.

The second task is straightforward: an obstacle course. There are rings to swing through, a knotted rope to climb, a series of raised platforms to jump across, and a wall to scale. It ends with a fifty-metre sprint. Ash goes first, then Juniper, then Oak. I am the anchor. We lose the lead during Oak's turn, but I recapture it in the final seconds. We are the only team to receive full points this time.

The third task takes place in two stages. In the first, each team selects one cadet to deadlift weighted bars. The contestant who lifts the most bars is awarded twelve arrows, to be evenly distributed amongst his or her teammates. The team who wins second place receives eleven arrows, and so on. In the second stage, each arrow to strike the bullseye receives a point.

Oak wins the first stage. Juniper, Ash, and I each take four arrows. Eleven of our arrows hit the mark.

By the time the door unseals for the fourth and final task, we are flushed with excitement. With thirty-five points, we lead by five, and the third- and fourth-place teams are far behind with scores of only twenty-six and twenty-five. I barely glance at the bottom four scores. They cannot even be considered competition at this point.

A net has been strung across the arena. A hundred feet above the net two new rows of platforms have been erected. A rope swing with a metal bar for a seat hangs suspended from the wooden post above each platform. The extra height is needed for momentum, I assume.

"Your final task," Protector Tayra's voice booms out, filling the stadium, "will test for coordination, courage, and grace. Each team will position two cadets on one platform and two on the platform directly across from it. The mission is simple: one teammate from each side will swing out into the centre of the arena. If their movements are synchronized and their communication is clear, one of the cadets should be able to transfer to the other trapeze, and swing to the opposite platform. The first team to successfully transfer all four cadets to the opposite platform wins a dozen points. Second place will receive eight points, third place will receive four points, and the remaining teams, zero. No points will be deducted if a cadet falls before, during, or after a transfer. The cadet in question will need to complete the task a second time, however they may do so from either platform."

At her final word the stadium is plunged into darkness. Before I have time to catch my breath the lights have returned. Then darkness pulses a second time. A third. The darkness lasts longer the second time, and barely flashes the third. *Inconsistent. Interesting.*

Protector Tayra flashes us a wide, reptilian grin. "To further test your skills," she says. "You may begin on my count: Three. Two. One."

"Third set!" I call out to my teammates. While the first and second sets of platforms are closer, the possibility for competition with other teams could cause delays. "Juniper, Oak—go left!"

I reach the base of the third platform on the right half a second before Ash and begin climbing the rope ladder that descends from it.

Juniper and Oak had a shorter distance to run and are already standing on their platform when Ash and I reach ours.

"Knees to catch?" asks Ash.

I nod. It is the only possibility I have come up with, as well. Ash climbs up a ladder attached to the central pole and seats himself on the swing, which is secured to the pole with a large metal clip.

I look across to where Juniper and Oak are watching us, confused.

"Swing down," I say to Ash.

He lets his hands go until he is hanging by his knees. Across the room Oak is already following suit. Once he is securely seated on the second swing, I signal to them that Oak will be the one moving to our platform, and give the countdown signal.

In my peripheral vision, I see two other swings launch from their platforms. *It doesn't matter. Don't rush this.*

On my count, Oak and Ash unclip the swings and sail through the air. They lock forearms and Oak slides himself off his swing until his entire weight is supported by Ash.

I resist the urge to cheer, but do scan the room quickly. A cursory glance, but enough to note that one of the cadets from another team has already fallen to the net below. There is movement on the scoreboard. Our score has moved from zero to one—the first to do so.

The room fades to black.

When the lights flash on again, Oak and Ash are both swinging back toward me. Only then do I realize that I am going to need to catch them, somehow.

"Lift your feet!" I hear Ash shout to Oak as I look frantically around the platform and spy a harness. With no time to secure it properly, I wind one end of the strap around my right hand to tether me to the platform, and reach out to link my arm through Oak's.

His momentum pushes me backward, and then almost immediately we begin to slide forward. One foot. Then two. Then we stop. Ash looks down at me, a huge grin on his face. "Me next?"

"You next."

I look across to Juniper and see that she is holding the empty swing in one hand and a long metal pole with a hook on the end in the other. I search our platform until I find an identical hook strapped to the central wooden post beside the ladder. In case the empty trapeze doesn't have the momentum to swing back, I suppose.

The lights go out again. When they come back on, Juniper is climbing the ladder, the swing looped through one arm.

When she signals to me that she is ready, I count down a second time.

The lights pulse once, twice, three times. I watch Ash and Juniper swing toward each other and it doesn't quite look real. More like a series of photographs. Stop. Go. Stop. Go.

She catches Ash and swings back toward her empty platform.

Flash to black.

Light.

Ash jumps down onto the platform and grabs the metal hook.

Flash to black.

The darkness lasts this time. When the lights come on, Juniper is sitting up on the swing again, holding onto the wooden post. Ash stands at her feet.

"Did you want to catch?" Oak asks me. I shake my head. My upper body strength is good, especially for my size, but my hands are tiny. Out of the four of us my grip will be the weakest. "On my count," I tell Oak, as he climbs up the swing. "Delay a half second."

He looks confused for a split second and then nods, a smile breaking out on his face. "Mass. Gravity. Of course."

I give the signal. Juniper, tall but slim, floats down toward us. A half second later Oak, almost twice her weight, follows.

I check the competition. There are three cadets climbing out of the nets below. On the scoreboard I can see that most of the teams still have a score of zero or one. Only two teams have two points—and as I'm watching, one of those twos turns into a three. Our score.

Fade to black. Pulse on. Off. On. Off.

I help catch Juniper and wait for Oak to climb down from the swing.

I glance at the scoreboard again—one of the teams has caught up to us, but the others are still far behind. I bite down on my excitement. *Focus on the path. Not the mountain.*

I climb the ladder. Already seated on the opposite swing, Ash gives me the thumbs up. I signal the countdown: three; two; one. And let go.

The arena rushes past me, a blur. I focus on the figure swinging toward me.

Black. Light. The pulses speed up.

We collide. Ash's hands grab my forearms and I lock onto his. My heart pounding, I swing my legs off the metal bar. For a split second it feels like I'm falling. Then Ash's grip tightens and we're flying back toward his platform.

I jump down, pick up the metal hook, and turn to find Ash has managed to grab hold of the central pole without my help.

I look up at the scoreboard. Amidst a wash of ones and twos, our three changes to four.

I hear Ash land on the platform and turn to find him closer than I'd expected, eyes feverish with excitement.

Fade to black.

His mouth is on mine. Hot and insistent, though his hands on my face are gentle. I smell his sweat and lean in, closer. Then my mind catches up with my body and I shove him away as hard I can.

The lights flash on, and Ash is falling.

The sound of the crowd, again muted in my head for the duration of the task, cuts through as my focus shatters. I hear gasps of shock and screams of both disappointment and excitement. Across from me, I see Juniper and Oak staring horrified at the scoreboard. I turn to look but the lines are blurred. *There.* Our score of four has changed back to a three, and another team has won—the team that was in second place overall.

"We can still make the points!" I hear Ash calling, though my ears are pounding and it takes me a moment to decipher what he is saying. "If we come in second!"

I look for him and see that he is already climbing back up the ladder to the platform. I nod numbly, and move out of the way as he makes his way up to the swing.

Across from us, Oak is doing the same. They look to me, and I signal the countdown.

In one fluid, synchronized movement, they swoop down through the air toward each other. My eyes flicker over to the scoreboard. Most of the remaining teams have two points each, although a few have a score of three.

I cross my arms and look back to my teammates. Oak and Ash are swinging back to the opposite platform.

They land and our score moves to four, barely half a second before another team finishes.

The crowd erupts into cheers. We may have only come in second place with this task, but we just won the contests.

Across the arena from me, my teammates are hugging and shouting. I smile and wave back, though I feel sick.

5

The North

They were already surrounded when she arrived back at the campsite. Sam quickly put up her hands, a gesture of surrender to the people behind the half-dozen arrows that were strung and pointed in her direction. Twice as many bodies pointed their weapons at the others.

Keeping her head and body still, Sam eyed their captors. Primarily male, they ranged from adolescent to middle-aged, and each carried a beautifully made longbow.

Her fingers itched to inspect the weapons more closely.

Want to be on intimate terms with the bow that kills you, then?

The faces that watched her, however, were confused, wary, suspicious; not hostile.

"May we help you?" Sam asked, trying for calm. If you weren't actually fighting, it was always better to be calm around projectiles.

From the centre of the campsite Adder chuckled, and Sam thought she heard someone mutter "Southerner."

An older woman was starting to speak when more bodies crashed into the clearing.

A pair of men tossed first Cassio and then Shale in with the rest of the captives. They were much gentler with Shale than with Cassio, Sam noticed.

"Hey, man," said Jackal, as though they had met in the market buying eggs.

Cassio flicked black hair out of his face and started searching for something in his jacket pockets. Their captors moved in, weapons up.

"Drink, anyone?" asked Cassio, holding the bottle up toward them.

A teenage boy with large, clunky metal rings shining from multiple fingers reached out and took it from him.

"Hey, hey." Cassio stepped toward him, unaware of or at least uninterested in the weapons pointed at his person. "I was offering to share."

It was the older woman standing near Sam who responded. "None of that poison where we're going, child." Metal shone from her hands, as well. Closer up they reminded Sam of signet rings, the kind used centuries ago by wealthy families to seal documents and letters with wax. Glancing around, Sam realized that almost all of their assailants wore them. Some kind of gang insignia, she supposed.

"Now tie 'em up. We got a long march."

The man beside her gestured toward the cart with his longbow. "Should we destroy this first?" he asked, to a clamour of support from the group.

"Please," said Sam, her eyes on the woman, clearly the leader. "We need it. If there is any room to negotiate—"

"There isn't," the man said.

The woman held up her hand. "Something's off, Nero." She pitched her voice louder. "Pack it up. All of it. It's for the elders to decide."

Sam found herself feeling oddly relieved, when the group began marching, to find that they were continuing in a southward direction.

Well, you wouldn't want to be derailed from your suicide mission.

I just want to be prepared in case they don't kill us.

If you end up dead in either scenario, does it really matter? Or would you rather die in Seira?

Sam considered it for a moment. In all honesty, she thought she might in fact prefer to die in Seira. This realization was oddly comforting.

It took almost three hours to reach their destination. An hour in, their leader gave the command of silence, which Sam thought she did only in response to Adder's relentless efforts to engage her people in conversation. Not that Adder obeyed, and their captors seemed reluctant to use violence to enforce the order.

It wasn't a bad tactic on Adder's part, Sam thought. Emotional people tended to give away more information, and she firmly believed in his uncanny ability to talk someone into a state of frustration bordering on rage. Or laughter. He attempted both tactics, pursuing long after they stopped responding.

Eventually, however, even Adder was quiet.

With nothing to distract her from the pain, the throbbing in Sam's wrist grew from a rumble to a roar. She tried to focus on how they might survive the night. Instead she envisioned all the ways they might die. When she ran out of ideas, she thought about the Barrow.

She missed Ava. She missed her cat.

The flicker of firelight appeared in the distance, soon followed by the faint hum of human voices. As they drew nearer Sam began to catch fragments, not only of conversation but also of song.

It was—not a town, exactly. There were a half-dozen buildings made of tree trunks, large enough to sleep forty, fifty people each.

Men, adolescent boys, young children—all stopped to watch them approach, though it was the middle of the night. Why were they awake? Were they waiting for them? Though slim, they didn't look hungry or ragged, not so desperate that they would stay up all night in anticipation of the meagre fruits of banditry.

Without intending to, she started counting, calculating. Could the six buildings house all these people?

They could, and more people too.

She scanned the crowd again. Though she saw a multitude of hair colours and skin tones, there was something in the way these people moved, the way they watched the newcomers. If they had been children playing at war there would have been one clearly marked line in the sand. It was more than communal living. This was a clan.

The woman in charge and the man, Nero, ushered them into one of the houses. Sam counted the wooden poles as they walked. She wanted to touch them, see how the dry, rough bark felt against her skin.

There was a small fire inside, just large enough to provide a bit of light to see by. A small opening above the fire allowed most of the smoke to escape.

Around the fire sat three women and three men. They were old, older than most lived to be in the Barrow, with stooped backs and grey hair and loose skin. But they were powerful still—anyone could see that. They watched in silence as Sam and the others were lined up against the wall.

She saw their eyes flicker to the ropes at their wrists and back to the woman and Nero.

"We found them in tents," she said. "These two together, and those two. This one was guarding the camp, while the small girl there was scouting. He," she pointed to Cassio, "was sleeping half a mile away." She nodded at Shale. "This one was close by, tied up in a tree."

"He tied her to a tree?" one of the old men asked Nero, though his eyes were on Cassio, a look of disgust on his face.

Nero shook his head. "She tied herself to the tree. Made a hammock. Kind of."

"Didn't fancy waking up midair?" Cassio asked, turning to Shale.

The woman dumped their weapons onto the ground. "They were well-armed. All of them."

"Explain," ordered the old man who had spoken before, though this time he was addressing Sam and her friends.

"You attacked us, gramps," said Charis. She cocked her head at them, the challenge radiating up her body. As though she wasn't tied up. As though she was still a threat. "Explain that."

There was a rustle of discontent among their captors.

"Easy, now," said Jackal to Charis in a low voice. He looked across at the elders and held up his bound hands. "Not meaning any disrespect."

"But you did attack us," said Adder. "Sirs and madams, of high esteem."

The old man's frown deepened. "Are you all drunk?"

"Not anymore," said Skye, shaking her head emphatically. "Not really. And it was just the girls."

"Yeah," said Dot. She nodded toward Adder, her chestnut brown hair bouncing against her shoulders and casting shadows in the firelight. "He's just...he's just Adder."

"Hey, I take that as a compliment."

One of the other male elders stepped forward. "Enough," he said. "Why are you here? The cart—"

"Is none of your damn business," said Charis.

"Sh. Calm, my love," whispered Skye, turning to rest her chin on Charis' shoulder until her girlfriend was half-buried beneath her long black dreadlocks. "They're not going to hurt us. The stars told me."

The woman who had been in charge of their abduction sighed and addressed the elders. "Could be they found it, or stole it?"

A tiny, wizened woman stood and shuffled toward Sam and her friends, her eyes moving slowly from face to face. "We are the People of the Phoenix," she said after a long pause. "And we got questions for you. Answer honest, with respect, and we won't harm you."

Charis opened her mouth to speak but the old woman held up her hand for silence. Such was the power emanating from her that Charis actually obeyed.

The old woman turned back to her people. "Take them to the north pit," she said, gesturing toward Jackal, Adder, and Cassio. "The girls to the south. We will talk in the morning."

Sam glanced back as Nero ushered them out of the building. A trio of teenage boys were hauling Jackal, Cassio, and Adder to their feet, tightening their binds and stuffing something into their mouths. Amidst the smoke from the fire, Sam could make out Jackal's tall, thin silhouette, standing calmly as Adder's slight form ducked and weaved, trying to evade the gag. She wondered why he bothered. Another man moved in to help and Adder was bound tighter and silenced. Cassio, beautiful, electric Cassio, had slumped against the wall. Sam didn't know if it was the drink, or the exhaustion, or just grief, but there was no resistance in his willowy body. Nor grace.

6

The North

THE SOUTH PIT was as much a camp as it was a prison. Set about twenty feet in the ground, the sides were fortified with wooden stakes. They weren't quite vertical, but sloped upward and outward from the dirt floor like fingers from the palm of a hand. Even without the ladder, which Nero pulled up after them, it would not have been too difficult to climb out.

Which is probably why they left guards with loaded bows.

At least we're not gagged.

They'd even untied them and left a few torches, which Sam found odd. Somebody was underestimating somebody.

At the centre of the pit was a pile of ashes. Ringing the dead fire were animal skins and low tree stumps, laid out like seats and sleeping mats.

"Guess they don't keep a lot of prisoners," said Dot, surveying their surroundings with her hands on her hips. "That's...promising. I think."

"Yeah, this is going great," Charis said, eyeing her girlfriend out of the corner of her eye. Skye was walking along the perimeter stroking each hide and singing softly to herself.

"Here," a man called from above them. A moment later a basket swung down. Sam pulled out three small skins of water and a bowl containing tree nuts, berries, mushrooms, and some root vegetables.

Sam passed around the skins of water and then divided the food into six equal portions, examining each item under torchlight for rust as she went. She noticed Charis watching her, as though she thought Sam might sneak extra berries for herself. Sam struggled to keep the annoyance off her face. It was not useful to feel insulted. Even if she was.

Emptied, the basket began to rise back up into the air. Skye waved airily at the man pulling it up.

"Thanks for the snack, lover," she called out. "Too bad the mushrooms are just mushrooms, but I won't hold that against you."

"Lover?" asked Charis.

"Uh huh," said Skye, blowing a kiss upward. "So many boys. Clearly, they've been sent to distract us with lust. Get us to reveal our secrets."

She giggled when Charis' eyes narrowed. "It's not going to work, my love," she said in a loud whisper. "Wrong tree. Shya—toss your hair at them."

Tucking her long dark hair back behind her ears, Shya moved away from Skye and lowered herself gracefully onto the stump between Dot and Sam.

As though it were a throne.

Or a fancy chair, at least. Something high backed. With a good swivel.

"They're not trying to scare us, that's for sure," said Dot, her eyes on the cold, fireless pit as she ate a berry. "I wonder what they're doing with the boys?" Her brow creased with worry. "I doubt it's anything as fun as sending over pretty boys and girls to seduce them."

"There aren't any girls," said Shale.

Sam looked over at the redhead, who'd seated her petite form on a fur across the fire, away from the others.

"Well, sure there are, kitten," said Charis, settling herself on the stump beside Dot. "Who do you think dragged us back here? And sent us to this pit?"

Sam caught Shale's eyes as everything clicked into place. "Old women." She turned to Dot and Shya. "There are hundreds of people here. Did you see any teenage girls? Or young women?"

They shook their heads. Beside Dot, Charis rolled her neck back, looking up at the sky. "So, that's it then." She turned her head toward Skye, who seemed to be the only one who hadn't clued in yet. "They got missing girls too."

"Maybe missing," said Skye, swaying side to side for no obvious reason. "Maybe there were never any to begin with. Or maybe they sacrificed 'em to the Blood Goddess." She produced a flask from the folds of her long green skirt and took a long swig before seating herself on Charis' lap and passing her the bottle.

"How'd she hide that?" Dot asked Shya in a low voice. "That frisking was thorough."

"Mind you, I wouldn't mind being a sacrifice," continued Skye. "As long as it worked."

"No one's going to sacrifice you," said Charis, placing a hand on Skye's thigh.

"Imagine, my blood hits the ground and the storms stop. The quakes still. The fires turn to smoke." Skye snapped her long dark fingers. "They could name cities after me. Nations."

"The sky's not enough?" asked Charis, taking a drink before tossing the flask to her sister, who caught it one-handed.

Skye dropped her voice slightly, enough to convey the intention of, if not to actually assure, secrecy. "My real name."

"Sticks and stones," said Charis, her silver rings glinting in the moonlight as she waved at her sister to return the bottle. Shya took two smalls sips and then passed the bottle to Dot, who drank, coughed, and then reached across Shya's lap to pass it to Sam.

It was a bad idea. She might need to fight at any moment. Charis flicked her hand again, more impatiently this time.

Sam looked over at Shale, sitting by herself, her chin resting on her knees.

"Oh, she won't drink anything I've touched," said Charis, her eyes still on Sam. "Isn't that right, Red?"

Shale flipped a rude hand gesture at Charis, though she, too, was watching Sam.

It was the closest the two women had come to speaking since Sam had met Charis.

Tension there. History. Guess I didn't imagine it after all.

Congratulations. Are you going to drink or what?

Sam eyed the bottle again. *I should be in fighting condition.*

True.

But—

But what?

I should bond with my teammates.

Some team. There's no trust, no respect for leadership.

Don't forget the bickering.

Sam took a long swig, then held the bottle toward Shale, who shook her head.

"To me, Southerner."

Sam tossed the bottle to Charis without looking at her. There was a thud as palm met flask. The sound of drinking.

"Can I have a story, my love?" Skye asked her girlfriend in a low voice, her arms around Charis' neck.

Sam thought about going to sit with Shale. They'd become friends, in the Barrow. And yet, she was somehow the most unapproachable of the group. Since the solstice.

Since Xenia.

Sam started to stand, thought better of it and settled back down on her stump. She flipped her arm around and started tracing her finger around the "V" on her wrist. The skin had started to blister. Sam alternated between wishing she had a bandage to keep the area clean and wanting to poke it.

"What's that about?" Sam heard Dot ask Shya in a whisper.

"Another person who hates my sister, I guess."

"You know why, though?"

"Because they met her?"

Dot chuckled and whispered something in Shya's ear.

Sam shifted her attention over to Skye and Charis, wondering if Charis' story had begun.

"Does he eat the girl?" Sam heard Skye ask.

"Course not," said Charis. "If he wanted to eat her, he'da done it in the woods. No, he wanted to keep her."

It was the story of the wolf and the child with the red cape, Sam realized. She kept her eyes on the empty fire pit, pretending not to listen.

"Villain," whispered Skye.

"But she wouldn't be kept, so he sprang at her with his great big teeth." Charis nipped gently at her girlfriend's neck, eliciting a squeal. "But her sister had sewed—"

"Wait," said Skye, pulling away from Charis. "Her sister? Not her mother?"

"Nope. Mother was a lazy shint. It was the sister. Anyway, she sewed diamonds into the cloak, broke all the wolf's teeth."

"Serves him right," said Skye. "Though it's needles they sew into the cape, not diamonds."

"Well, in my story it's diamonds."

Skye considered that for a moment. "I guess maybe diamonds is better, anyway. And the grandmother? Was she okay?"

Charis shook her head slowly. "He ate the grandmother, remember?"

"Yeah," said Skye. "But the way my mum used to tell it, she was still alive in there."

"No," said Charis. "A wolf isn't going to waste good meat like that. He ate her right up."

"I like the other ending better."

"Well, I'm the one telling it, so I guess the ending's my choice."

Skye made a disgruntled sound.

"Kiss me and I'll change it," said Charis. Skye leaned in and the two women kissed as though they were alone and free, not being held captive in a pit with four other girls, including Charis' sister.

"Ugh," said Shya, looking up from her conversation with Dot.

"It's sweet," said Dot.

"It's my sister."

Dot grinned. "It's Charis. Snogging is hardly the worst thing she could be doing right now."

Sam noticed for the first time that Dot had dimples. She also realized that she could make out Dot's shoulder-length, chestnut brown hair in detail.

The sun was starting to come up.

She should do her morning exercises, stretch, prepare. The flask came around again and Sam took another sip.

I should talk to Shale, find out if she's okay.

She's not.

I know.

Just sit there, then. Feel guilty. I know, have another drink.

Good idea.

I was being provocative.

Sam fought the urge to stuff her fingers in her ears. Not that it would help. Her inner voice had been growing increasingly antagonistic ever since they'd left the Barrow. She tried to tune into Shya and Dot's conversation, but they were speaking about someone that Sam didn't know.

The darkness receded and Skye began to sing.

She was on the second verse when the People of the Phoenix came for them.

7

The North

The north pit was much larger than the south pit, large enough to hold the three hundred or so people who had gathered. At the nucleus of the group sat the elders from the day before. On a wooden platform beside them stood Jackal and Adder, no longer bound and gagged, though still closely watched by armed warriors.

Sam looked to the sides of the platform, her heart starting to thud.

"Over there," said Dot, nodding to the northwest side of the pit. Sam followed her sightline to find Cassio, wrapped in blankets and holding a bowl in his hands, steam visible in the hazy dawn light. An older woman and a few young children sat around him. Someone had placed a child's cloth bear on his lap. Even from this distance Sam could see that his eyes were red.

The people were silent as they approached. Men, older women, children, babies. She did spy a handful of young women, but fewer than might be expected. They sat together near the front of the group, a longbow beside each of them. Strong-looking men and middle-aged women stood nearby, bows strung and ready, their eyes flickering from the strangers to the girls, to the elders, to the top of the pit. Sam looked up and saw more fighters.

"What are you doing?" asked Dot from behind her.

"Counting," said Sam.

"It looks weird."

Sam forced herself to focus on Shale's hair in front of her, instead.

Didn't know you were that obvious, did you?

Criticism is helpful. I do not resent hearing it.

You're embarrassed.

Good soldiers use it to improve themselves.

You're not a soldier anymore.

A smart person uses it—

You looked stupid.

The women were brought onto a second platform. With a crowd on each side, they clustered in an awkward knot, facing the elders. Dot in front, between the two sisters. Shale, Sam, and Skye in the back.

The oldest woman, the tiny, wizened one who had sent them to the pits a few hours ago, stood, her eyes on them.

There had been whispers as they approached. Now there was silence.

"We have heard from the men," she said, bringing her hands together in front her shrunken body. "We would hear from you. Who is the leader?"

She could feel Charis bristling even before the older girl flicked a black eye on her, daring her to step forward.

Sam's lips itched toward a snarl. She breathed out slowly, relaxing her face. It wasn't as though she'd been about to raise her hand. The last thing she should have was a position of authority, she knew that.

In front of Sam, Dot stepped forward. In that moment, with her strong, rigid posture and her level gaze, she could almost have passed for a Seiran soldier.

The elder woman took in the display without so much as blinking. "We will allow you to speak until everything is told. You get one chance, girl. Leave nothing out."

The sky was turning gold as Dot began their story.

After Dot had spoken, the elders asked her whether any of the other women had information to add. Dot looked to Shya, Charis, Sam, Shale, and Skye. When they shook their heads, she glanced over at Jackal.

"We said our piece," he told her.

The elders conversed amongst themselves for several long minutes. Then they opened up the floor to the rest of the community, inviting anyone with concerns to come forward and speak. Some did. When they had finished, the elders conferred amongst themselves a second time.

"We have allowed the outsiders to speak," the old woman said at last, the hushed tones of her people fading to silence the moment she addressed the crowd. "We have allowed all present to raise their concerns. We are the People of the Phoenix." From all around them came the rumble of assent. "We silence no one." Muted voices rose; cheers spilled over. It was short-lived, though. Their enthusiasm did not threaten to disrupt her speech; these were two parts of a responsorial chant. "But we respect the decision of the elders. And we elders have decided."

She looked to Dot now, and Jackal. The mission leaders. "We will add warriors to your cause."

Adder shifted on his feet. Charis cleared her throat. But it was Dot who spoke. "We thank you, we do. But our only chance of getting through the border is fooling them into thinking this is a normal shipment. A band of fighters'll look suspect."

Silence.

"And how many women and men does a normal shipment have?"

"We got papers for six girls."

"And men?"

"Three guards at most," said Jackal. Sam looked at him standing motionless before them, tall and wiry and immovable, and was reminded of how he used to look to her in the mornings, when she would arrive early and alone at the Vaun compound.

Like a scarecrow.

The woman turned away and consulted the others. Seconds ticked by, then minutes.

"You will leave some of your people behind, then. Ours will take their place."

Sam felt the collective intake of breath. The clenching of fists.

"Funny," said Charis. "You don't seem to have girls to spare."

"Not with our skills, anyway, eh?" Skye added.

The elder woman glared at Charis and Skye, turning pointedly to look at Dot and Jackal. Sam understood. This community respected leadership. Sam and her friends had indicated that Dot and Jackal were the leaders. The others were expected to be silent unless called on. The other Northerners seemed to have trouble understanding this.

"We meant the men, obviously."

"This is a suicide mission," said Adder. "Do you really want to sacrifice your people?"

"Our people," the woman said, "were taken. We will take them back." A murmur of assent spread throughout the crowd.

"No disrespect," said Dot. "But our people were chosen for a reason."

"My grandparents lived in the compound, remember?" Adder looked from the woman to the elders around and behind her. "There might be questions that you can't answer, that I can."

Sam doubted that any identity verification tests would include information decades out of date, to which Geo and Jem had likely not been privy anyway, but she kept silent. Irritating or not, she wanted Adder on this mission. He was quick, resourceful, and good with knives. And she trusted him.

"It was my sister they took." Jackal straightened to his full height. His voice was calm, his expression pleasant, but Sam didn't doubt that the elders were seeing the same thing she had always seen in him—something steadfast and grim. If they left without him, he would follow. That much was clear. "I'm going whether—"

"It's okay, man." Cassio waved clumsily from where he sat. "They can have my place."

In front of Sam, Charis leaned in to Dot. "What place?" she whispered.

"Shh—"

"He's not even with us."

"Charis—"

Shya turned toward the other two, a slight frown on her face. "No, she's actually right this time."

Charis bristled. "This time?"

"Charis, if you can't keep your voice—"

"He's not one of us, Dot," said Shya in a whisper. "He doesn't have a place."

"Well, then it's an easy thing to give up, ain't it? Now shush, Jack's talking."

Whatever Jackal was saying, however, had been said.

"Since Xenia—" From his nest of blankets, Cassio swallowed, his voice breaking ever so slightly. "I want to help, Jack, but I'm fucking useless."

At Xenia's name, Shale let out a slow, deep breath. Sam wanted to reach over, take her hand, offer some semblance of comfort, but nothing felt right. Everything sounded worse. Sam clenched her fists and shifted her focus back to the elders.

The old woman was nodding her acceptance.

"So, uh." Cassio's attempt at a smile was so heartbreaking that Sam had to look away. Even as just one more face in the crowd she felt like an intruder. "If someone could just point me in the direction of the Barrow—or another city. Wherever. I'll, uh, leave you to it."

"You misunderstand," said the elder woman. "One of our warriors goes, you stay here. Until he returns."

"No way," said Jackal. *They're seeing it now. The steel.* "He's not your hostage."

"Of course he is," said the woman. "But you might have a different idea of what that means. He'll have the chance to be adopted by one of the families. They'll feed him, give him space in their house or one of the tents. He has to work, but he can take a partner who's willing. And when our warrior comes back, your Cassio can leave, or stay.

"And we have...ways...of dealing with grief." This she said to

Cassio directly, and for the first time Sam saw something soften in her face.

"Don't matter how you dress it up," said Jackal. "If he can't leave, he's—"

"It's okay, Jack. Not the worst deal. Besides, I was just going to drink until I stopped waking up. Guess this is better."

Jackal looked from Cassio to the elders to Dot.

"If we fail." Sam was surprised to find herself speaking. "Or if your warrior doesn't make it back, can any of us take his place?"

"You may."

"And what's the alternative? If we say no?"

"We keep all three of your men. Maybe we keep you six too." The old woman smiled, a reminder of who was the captor and who the captive.

"You need us, though," said Dot, voice even, friendly. It wasn't a threat or an ultimatum. Just honesty. "If you actually want to get your girls back."

"Yes," the elder woman said. "So, we hope you take this offer. A young, strong, fit warrior in exchange for your broken boy. And we'll mend him for you too. It's a good deal. You should take it."

"We do," said Cassio. After a moment, Dot nodded, then finally Jackal.

"Good. Now," the old woman turned to the three male elders, "bring out your best."

8

The North

THE THREE YOUNG men who stepped forward were beautiful. Tall and muscular, with smooth skin and shining hair tied back in ponytails. Beyond that, they bore the unmistakable signs of care. They'd had enough to eat, and clean water to drink. There might be scars on their bodies—though she suspected even these were few—but they hadn't had to fight, to struggle. Sam could see it on her people—Charis and Shya, Shale, Jackal, Dot, and Skye. All but Adder. There was something dark lurking behind their eyes. A whiff of fear. A readiness. They'd done ugly things to survive. They'd had to.

Sam wondered what they saw in her. Had months in the Barrow erased the calm of a lifetime in the South? She wasn't sure she wanted to know.

"Can you settle on one," the old woman asked the three male elders, eyeing the candidates, "or do we hold a trial?"

The men looked at each other.

"Trial," said one. The other two nodded.

Images of a bloodstained arena and men marked in blue and red for slaughter flashed up in Sam's eyes and she shivered. She didn't want to see any more bloodshed. Not yet. Not ever, if she could help it.

The trial, it turned out, was a game. There was a footrace, a wooden pole to climb, moving targets to hit with a bow and arrow, tree stumps to lift and carry. The atmosphere was calm, festive even, the three contestants joking with each other between events.

Sam quickly realized why the elders had been unable to select one man to represent them. Each race was won by a step, a point, a second. The winner was a man named Dash. He was slightly shorter than the other two, though still tall by Northern standards, with dark skin and black hair. He was fast, of course, and strong, but so were the others. In the end, Sam supposed it made no difference.

Dash would be an asset, that much was clear, though it felt like a knife to Sam's lungs when Cassio was ushered away before the trials had even finished. They weren't given the chance to say goodbye.

"He needs to rest. The rituals start at dawn," the elder woman told them. Rituals of healing, she said. They pressed to see him and were refused. They were no longer prisoners, though. Their bindings were removed and the strangers were invited to stay until the next morning.

"Bathe, wash your clothes, sup with us," one of the male elders said to them once the trial was over, clasping Dot's hands in his. "Tonight you are one of us. And tomorrow we'll bless you, as we do our warriors."

He was bent and wrinkled and half-blind and missing some teeth and had such a kindly, earnest smile that even Charis couldn't be ungracious.

"Kaya!" he called, and a young girl of about nine with long, sandy blonde braids ran over.

"Yes, uncle?"

"Take our visitors to the swimming hole, please."

She grinned. "Yes, uncle!"

The man was old enough to be the child's great-grandfather. Sam supposed that "uncle" was being used as a term of respect, rather than a familial label.

A group of children immediately swarmed over to join Kaya, who looked close to bursting with self-importance.

The children, led by Kaya, escorted them out of the pit. They walked sedately at first, eyeing the newcomers out of the sides of curious eyes. Sam expected to be peppered with questions but none of the children spoke to them, because they were shy, perhaps, or at the behest of the men and women who followed silently behind, their bows still strung though their arrows were no longer trained on the strangers.

Then they heard the crash of water falling into a pool and the children ran, shrieking and ripping off their clothes, to the cliffside. They plunged off the rock and into the clear blue water below.

Adder walked ahead of the others and peeked over the edge. "Uh, did they change their mind about murdering us after all?"

"There is a path," one of the guards called out, pointing with his bow to a gravel trail off the side. "That will take you down to the swimming hole."

Skye was already pulling off her shirt.

"Babe, there's a path, c'mon," said Charis.

Skye kissed her on the mouth, pressing her shirt into Charis' hands. "I want to fly."

"Use the path," the guard said, looking away from Skye, who had started unwinding her long skirt. "You must know the rocks below before you can jump."

"The gods will keep me—"

"I like the path," said Charis, as Skye passed her the skirt as well. "Maybe you can look for mushrooms."

"Oh." Skye brightened. "I like mushrooms."

"I know, baby."

"Did you know that most of them are poisonous?"

"Tell me about them," said Charis, slipping her arm around her girlfriend's waist and guiding her away from the cliff, toward the path.

The rest of the party followed, and most of the guards, though whether to keep them from running off or to protect them from eating toxic mushrooms, Sam wasn't certain. Both, probably. Theirs was the same mission now.

The path led them down through the trees, ending thirty feet above the water. Here they saw that it was actually a series of pools connected by narrow corridors in the rock; like beads on a string. A waterfall at the top pool, where the children played, created a current that rushed downward through the pools to the river below, turning the water white and frothy.

They picked their way down the boulders that stood between them and the water, Skye still wearing nothing but her underclothes. The sun was high in the sky now and without the shelter of the trees they began to sweat.

The rocks led to a smaller, shallow pool. Water from the upper pool spilled into theirs, where it slowed and flowed gently to the pool below.

Skye peeled off her undergarments and slipped into the cool water, wiggling her dark shoulders in delight. Charis and Adder were the first to follow.

Sam hesitated. Unabashed nudity was one commonality between the North and the South. So why had she always felt the need to hide? Even in the Seiran dormitories she'd slipped into a corner to undress or had changed piece by piece beneath the cover of her towel.

Keeping her eyes down, Sam sat on a big boulder at the edge of the water and began to slowly untie her boots.

"Here!" One of the children had climbed out of the upper pool and was rummaging around in the rocks. She pulled out a wooden washboard and two bars of soap and tossed them to Jackal, who was the closest to her.

Looking up, Sam realized with horror that dallying had had the opposite effect of what she'd intended. The rest of the party were now sitting in the water, looking around at the trees, the rocks, and their fully clothed friend, Sam.

At least the act of pulling their clothes into the water and scrubbing them clean afforded the group a distraction. Sam moved to the edge of the pool, turning away from the others as she pulled off her t-shirt and jeans, then her socks and her underclothes, everything but the cord around her neck, before slipping quickly down into the water. She kept her face away from the others, looking down toward the smaller pool below them. The water was cool, not cold, but Sam still found herself shivering. She bounced a bit, waiting to acclimatize. Two pools down she glimpsed a pale, redheaded figure and realized that Shale must have gone ahead.

As Sam watched, Shale lay her head back on the edge of the pool and closed her eyes, her auburn tresses pooling from the rocks into the water.

She looks tired.

We're all tired.

It was more than that, though. Where was the self-assurance and bravado that Shale usually wrapped around herself like armour? She'd been like a player with a dozen masks—all savvy, all beautiful, all adaptable. The collection showcased bits and pieces of the real Shale, but never the woman in her entirety.

Shale sat up as a young child approached her, holding something in his hand. It was a bar of soap. He pressed it into her palm and she smiled at him, only a flicker of her usual charm but enough to send him running back to his friends, his cheeks red and a big grin on his face.

Behind him, Shale's smile faded.

She's not gone. She's grieving.

A memory popped into Sam's head. What was it that the older girl had said?

"Wasted effort, lover, missing anyone."

Maybe it's more than grief.

Maybe it was love.

Someone was tapping her on the shoulder. Sam turned back around to find Shya holding out a bar of soap.

"Thanks," said Sam. She began scrubbing her clothes, half-listening to the conversations around her. When they were as clean as she could make them, Sam spread her clothes out on the hot rocks to dry.

She decided that she liked the rumble of the water as it poured over the rocks. Sliding down deeper into the water, she tipped her head back, blocking out the voices completely. The sky was a true blue today. Sam closed her eyes, enjoying the warmth of the sun on her face.

You know it's cooking your skin, right?

Sam sighed and lifted her head, turning away from the sun. She'd actually managed to forget for a second that she wasn't wearing sun-saving lotion.

Looking around, she realized that Adder and Dot were missing. They weren't in the lower pools or on the rocks, now strewn with clean laundry. She cocked her head, listening, but there was a definite absence of chatter.

"Clear the pool!" a familiar voice called from up above.

Sam looked up to see Adder and Dot standing on a boulder above the upper pool. Not the one the children had jumped from earlier—this one was only half so high.

A little boy was speaking to them, pointing at a spot in the pool as the other girls and boys pulled themselves out of the water and onto the rocks.

"Avenge me!" shouted Adder, throwing his arms out and flinging his head back as Dot got the jump on him and leapt down, one hand pinching her nose closed. Her chestnut brown hair lifted up behind her as she shot down, feet first into the pool.

"Hey!" Adder stared down, surprise on his delicate face. He placed indignant hands on his hips, unaware or uncaring how prominently this pose displayed his genitalia.

Dot surfaced with a splash and a gasp to the sound of Shya and Skye cheering. She swam across the pool to the rocks that separated the upper pool from theirs and grinned at them. "Worth it."

A mess of flailing light brown limbs flew down behind her. Adder hit the water with a louder splash. He surfaced with a gasp and then swam over to join them as well.

"Who's next?"

Skye and Charis were already climbing out of the pool.

"Sam?" asked Adder.

She clenched her teeth and shook her head. "No thank you." She liked the shallow pool. It was warmer and there was no chance of drowning.

Unless someone drowns you.

Thank you for that.

"Jackal?"

Jackal shook his head. "Leave that for you'uns. I'd rather sit a spell."

"Suit yourself, tall man." Adder looked at Dot. "Again?"

"Oh, yeah. Shya?"

Shya had slipped out of the pool and was settling onto her stomach on a smooth shelf of sunlit rock behind Jackal, her face away from the pool. "Nah," she said. "I'm working on my base tan."

"You already have a base tan," said Dot, gesturing at Shya's long, brown legs.

"Improving it, then." She flicked her fingers in dismissal. "You go."

Dot and Adder climbed past her up the rocks and onto a secondary path that Sam hadn't noticed before.

Sam caught Jackal's eye. He gave her a slow smile and she was suddenly very aware of how naked the two of them were. And how alone in the water.

"Is your sun like this, in the South?" Shya asked, turning her head to face them.

Sam looked over, grateful for the interruption. "It's stronger. And we don't have shade. But we have a—a sort of salve that we put on our skin to avoid sunburns."

"I don't burn," said Shya.

Sam snuck a peek at Jackal, wondering what he was thinking about. "Everyone burns in Seira."

"Hmm. In the North it's mostly the fair ones who have to watch out. The blondes, especially."

It was instantaneous—the empty feeling in her gut, the shift in Jackal's face as a shadow fell over his dark features. Shya was astute enough to feel it.

"I'm sorry," she said, sitting up. "I didn't mean to make you think of your friend."

"Don't fret on it, Shya," said Jackal, though he sounded tired as he said it. "We're always thinking of Xenia. And if we weren't, well, I'd wanna be."

Sam nodded her agreement, though neither of them were looking at her.

Shya reached out a hand and smoothed Jackal's hair, which had fallen loose from its ponytail, back from his face. "Like we think of Anna."

"Every damn day."

"Only we're getting her back."

There were so many circles of grief. She bound them together, Anna: Dot, Shya and Jackal. She connected them.

Then there was Xenia. They carried her ghost now, Sam and Jackal, Cassio and Shale.

Sam turned away from the others, resting her arms on the rocks and gazing out at the trees.

There was no circle for Corvus. How could anyone else mourn him when the Administration wouldn't admit that he was dead? There had been no candles lit, no ashes for her to spread, not even a shallow grave dug by hands that loved him. It was a void. Like he'd never existed.

Because of you.

I loved him. I love him still.

And what shit luck for him, that you did.

Shya and Jackal were still speaking—she could register that much. But she'd stopped processing the words.

She laid her head on her arms and closed her eyes against the glare. What did sun-saving lotion matter anyway, if you weren't likely to live out the month?

As though from miles away, Sam heard the shrieks of manufactured fear and the splash of bodies hitting the upper pool.

The water surged around her. Without lifting her arms off the rocks, Sam opened her eyes and craned her neck to see Shya slipping into the pool, one hand held high, her fist closed around something Sam couldn't see.

Shya's mouth parted slightly into the foreshadow of a smile and she opened her fingers to reveal a handful of indigo berries.

Behind her a child was scampering back over the rocks to the main pool, laughing wildly at his own daring.

Shya was so close to her now that the sun's rays danced behind her head. Sam blinked and looked back down at Shya's hands, still outstretched, and took a berry. It was fresh and juicy and tart, not sweet like she'd been expecting.

"Where's Jackal?" asked Sam, noticing his absence for the first time.

"I convinced him to go for a jump," said Shya, maneuvering until her back rested on the rocks beside Sam.

"Oh." Jackal had always struck Sam as immovable. But then, most of the time she'd known him, he'd been playing a part. Someone who worked for the Vauns because it was the best coin around. Someone who didn't worry overmuch about the ethics of the work itself. Someone without an agenda, without a sister.

"How did you get him to do that?"

Shya ate a berry and then placed the rest gently on a smooth bit of rock out of reach of the water. "I told him he owes it to Anna, to have some stories to tell her when we see her." She gave another faint smile. "So she doesn't think he's gotten boring."

Sam flipped around so that her back rested on the rocks, too. Shoulder to shoulder, the two girls sat in silence, the water rocking forward and back, forward and back, until it slowed, though it never quite stilled.

"There's nothing between me and Jack," said Shya, taking Sam by surprise.

"I—why do you—"

"I saw your face. Thought maybe you misunderstood. Jackal's big brother for us lot, he has been ever since we were small. That's all he's ever wanted."

Sam squirmed, wrestling with the question she didn't want to ask.

"All I wanted, too," said Shya.

Sam felt her shoulders drop.

"It's Dot, actually," said Shya.

"Dot?"

"For as long as I can remember. But Jack's never seen her that way."

Sam looked down at the water, wishing Shya hadn't told her. This was Dot's secret, what right did Sam have to it? "You didn't have to... It's none of my—"

"No?" asked Shya, looking over at Sam, her eyebrows raised. "My mistake, then. Thought I caught a spark."

Sam felt herself flushing. "I don't—I mean, maybe. But that wasn't jealousy."

Shya nodded, but Sam felt a door closing. For some reason she wanted to keep it open.

"I was just thinking of somebody I lost," she said at last.

"Funny, ain't it." When Shya finally spoke her voice was low, barely audible above the rumble of the rushing water. "It's beautiful here. Really beautiful. And all we can think about is our dead."

Sam nodded, though she felt oddly like weeping. Shya's fingers gripped hers under the water. Just for a second.

"Now, let's watch this tree of a man cliff jump," said Shya. She beckoned to Dot, swimming in the upper pool, and then pointed up to the boulder above.

Dot laughed, choked on a mouthful of water, and pulled herself onto the rocks that divided the two pools. "Let's go, old man!" she called out as the tall and wiry frame of a very naked Jackal stepped to the edge of the rock.

Adder climbed up beside Dot, shaking his wet black hair and letting loose a howl. Something moved behind Jackal. Before they could so much as cry out a warning, Charis and Skye ran forward, grabbed his hands, and jumped, pulling him with them off the cliff and into the blue, blue water below.

And despite the tears, unspent, that burned her throat, Sam found herself smiling as Jackal popped up from the water to the cheers of the children.

9

The North

THE EVENING STARTED WITH MUSIC. A pan flute, at first; played by a young boy as the sun set behind him. They were back in the north pit, and their hosts had indulged in a bonfire. The erstwhile captives had been seated closest to the flutist and the fire, a spot of honour, according to their hosts. In actuality it wasn't particularly close to the fire considering that the bonfire had been lit within six rings: a ring of stones; a ring of sand; a trench; another ring of stones; more sand; and some kind of powder.

What does it symbolize?

That fire safety is important.

Six is the first number that is neither a prime nor a square number.

Probably not what they were thinking.

Or maybe the fire itself makes seven.

Sam frowned. She didn't like the number seven. A few feet to the right of her, Charis yawned loudly and muttered something to Skye about music being better in the Barrow. Sam had to fight the urge to shush her. Charis had been particularly disagreeable that evening, even for her.

Unwittingly, Sam's eyes moved past Charis to Jackal, and Dot beside him. Their leader. Instantly likable because she was kind and fair and reasonable. Jackal cocked his head to the side as Dot leaned over and whispered something in his ear. He nodded and Dot looked up at him and smiled and Sam wondered how she could have missed it before. Flushed cheeks, shiny eyes—Sam could practically smell the dopamine, adrenaline, and norepinephrine swelling up inside the other girl.

"Are you into Dot?" asked a low voice in her left ear.

Sam's head snapped back around. Adder's bright blue eyes were two inches from her own.

"What? No," she whispered.

"Oh, good." He winked at her. "Not that I mind a little competition, but it's just—I didn't bring my fiddle. How can I battle for love without my fiddle?"

She stared at him. "You are very dramatic."

"It's called courtship, Sam," said Adder. "And I happen to be very good at it."

Rolling her eyes, Sam turned her eyes back to the musician. She needed to clear her thoughts. Taking a deep breath, she tried to listen —really listen.

The melody was simple but the child, who couldn't have been more than ten, played it beautifully. It was slow and sweet and tinged with sadness. After several minutes a second flutist joined him, and then a third. The music rose to a crescendo and then came to an abrupt stop.

The original flutist returned with the main melody, stripped down to its simplest form. Looped it once, twice. On the third loop the second flutist began playing the same line, but with a delay. Then the third flutist, after a second delay. The musical term was a canon: the same piece, but with a temporal difference. Three different points in time, overlapping, like a word or a glance and its echoes.

Sam's eyes slid from the child to the flames, watching them dance as her mind started to drift.

The memory was blurred—a feeling rather than a linear narrative, half-remembered like a scent or a flavour. They might have been in music class, or perhaps they'd been practicing in one of the soundproof rooms. How old had they been? She wasn't certain. Perhaps twelve or thirteen. She couldn't remember her name at the time, or his. What she remembered were his eyes, roguish as he looked at her over the flute he was playing. Or perhaps it was a clarinet. Or maybe an oboe. The prescribed melody had ended, or perhaps it had been scales they'd been practicing. Either way, he'd continued playing; an improvisation.

When it came to music, Sam had always scored higher than Corvus. Her technical skills were stronger, and her memory was better—she'd had more songs in her repertoire than any other cadet in their year—because she'd practiced until she was flawless. But Corvus, he could play with music. He didn't need to plan it out beforehand, trace back the key, look up harmonious intervals. It came naturally to him. She remembered being vexed. Or did she? Sam saw his eyes again—dark blue with a ring of gold around the pupil.

He smiled at her, in this memory that was not a reliable memory, and her breath caught.

Sam blinked, refocusing her eyes on the scene before her, and found that the song had ended. More children were joining the flutist, sticks in their hands.

They sat in a row and began to tap out a rhythm. Not too fast, not too slow. More like a metronome keeping time in someone else's song.

The tiny old woman who had presided over their trial came forward and knelt, a small bowl beside her. From the row of children, a little boy who couldn't have been more than four or five years old ran up, dipped his hand into the bowl, and began drawing lines on the woman's face.

At first Sam thought it was blood. But even in the dim light she could see that the colour was too dark. Then she wondered if maybe it was mud, but the consistency didn't seem right.

The tempo changed—from a steady pace the children began

playing faster and faster until the old woman raised a hand and they stopped, their sticks raised to the night sky.

She climbed slowly to her feet as the little boy ran back to his spot and picked up his own set of sticks, holding them aloft like the others.

"One day, the door between our world and another got left open," she said into the new silence. "How it got left open and why and by whom, we don't know. But it did. And not just any door, either. It was the door that led to the world of fire."

As if on cue, a gust of wind blew through the crowd and the bonfire crackled higher.

"It was midday when they heard it coming. But it's always night in that other world, and the sky soon darkened to an orange glow."

She lowered her voice and the audience stilled.

"The firebrands came ahead of it, like children skipping before a bride. They hit the homes of our ancestors, their schools, their gardens, and gave birth to a million little fires.

"Then came Hell itself. Flames as high as the tallest trees you ever saw, and above that, clouds, thick and swirling with wind. And though there wasn't a drop of rain, lightning cut the sky.

"The fire came faster than a body could run. But run they did—the young and strong carried the old, the weak and sick, the babes in arm."

Movement drew Sam's eyes to the fringes of the fire, where young, lithe bodies were dancing. Not measured steps but wild undulations. More dancers appeared, carrying wooden slabs.

"They all ran. Didn't matter if you was rich or poor, godly or sceptic, wicked or kind. The deer ran with the bear and up high the birds raced to fly ahead of the smoke."

The masked dancers spun around the fire, wooden props becoming antlers and wings and ears.

"Because even if you escaped the fire, the smoke would find you. It crept in when you thought you was safe and stole your breath."

Sam felt the collective shiver of the crowd. Some of the children squirmed and cuddled closer together. It was the end of the world. It was a ghost story. It was their history.

"Only the snakes didn't run. Instead they burrowed deeper and deeper into the ground. So deep that the fire couldn't follow.

"The rest of the living, though, they ran until the seasons changed and the rains came. It was only then that they stopped and looked at each other, at their bodies all burned and bloodied and scarred and smeared with char. And as one people they thanked the rain and wept for those they'd lost and watched the water turn grey at their feet."

At this word, the dancers all froze. They straightened from their last pose and stood still and straight, masks and props falling to the ground.

"They went back. After all that running they turned around and went back. They had to see with their own eyes if their whole lives had burned away.

"Some thought they walked through another door, then, not to Hell this time but to the land of the dead. It was the silence, partly. You never been somewhere so quiet. And the air smelled of char and dead wood and though the trees were still standing they were black and grey and dead. Dead but standing. They couldn't understand it.

"Others thought maybe they'd travelled through space, not worlds. That they were on a moon somewhere. Maybe not our moon, because they could still see its lonely face in the sky at night. But another moon."

"It was the ash, see, it covered the ground a foot thick, even more. They kicked it when they walked and it floated up, up, up. Settled on their eyelashes, their hair. And once again they were the same colour: the colour of ash.

"The houses were gone, mostly, though Hell spared some. 'Cause the people who lived there were good, they said. Or evil. Or lucky. Or built their homes of tougher stuff. Nobody knew. The people were all gone, though, those that had been left behind, and most of the animals. Not black-backed woodpeckers, though, nor hawk owls. They were queens of the sky. And with the people came deer, and rabbits, and coyotes.

"Soon some green began to poke through."

At this the children began banging their sticks together again.

"The dead trees started to fall and the grass began to grow again. Wildflowers came up, the colours so bright you'd think the gods had planted them. And the trees—now, that was best of all. So, the people got a feeling of hope. They started to build." The dancers began to move again, arms stretching out slowly toward the sky.

"But then the fires came back." The dance changed, became frantic and wild as the tempo grew faster and faster. "They came back again and again. Until came the time..." The children dropped their hands and the dancers stopped, melting away to the sidelines until only the old woman stood before them. "Until came the time when the trees didn't come back. And the people that were left, the few that had survived fire after fire after fire, they rose from the ashes and made a new home."

From the periphery the children began to hum.

"We are the People of the Phoenix. Our ancestors survived the flames. And when they finally left the Waste behind they came here to make a new life."

Around them, other people began to hum, too. "We are the People of the Phoenix and we honour them by being strong. We support our people. We protect our people. We respect this land for nourishing us. For giving us a place when we had none."

The old woman paused. She looked over at the children, then back to the fire. "And one day the land we left behind will wake from its slumber. The trees will take root again and the animals will come back. And then we, my friends, my family, then we shall go home."

The power of the old woman's voice was such that Sam had forgotten how frail she was. At this moment, however, the old woman faltered, and for a second Sam wondered whether she might collapse. A man stepped toward her from the sidelines but she waved him away. Pulled herself together.

"Two years ago, men came to our land. They took our daughters. They took our sisters. They took our granddaughters!" The woman began to shake, not with weakness but with rage and grief, and Sam knew from the way she screamed the words that these traffickers had taken someone from her personally, someone that she loved.

The old woman took a deep breath, and waited. When she was

calm she spoke again. “Now these strangers here have come to tell us that they know where our people have been taken. That they were brought back to the burned lands, to the Waste, and through it to the southern land beyond.” She looked at them now, her fears and hopes pulled tight into every crease on her tiny face. “You speak of your worries, but you must speak of your strengths. You will find our people and bring them back to us.” She looked back out over the crowd and raised her voice higher. “They will find our people and bring them back to us!”

A roar tumbled out, pulled from every woman, man, and child. Even Sam and the other strangers were swept along, helpless against the force of this woman’s conviction.

“Come,” she said. “We will bless you. For this day and the days that come you will be one of us.”

They stumbled forward, all of them, to kneel at her feet. The little boy with the bowl came back and stood beside the old woman, holding the bowl steady as she dipped her wizened hand into the mud-like substance within.

It was soot, Sam realized, the last to be blessed, as the woman pressed her thumb into Sam’s forehead; soot that had been mixed with oil and something that smelled floral and alien until it formed a thick, greasy paste. The old woman peered down into Sam’s face and then pulled her up and kissed both her cheeks.

“Now we must feast them!” she cried.

The crowd cheered, and someone began playing a light, lively tune on the pan flute as baskets of tree nuts and berries and more root vegetables were passed out. People came forward to where Sam and her friends were standing, to take their hands and pull them over to sit with them and their families. To tell them more stories. To give them tokens for luck. To tell them the names of the girls who’d been taken. Twelve girls. It was their burden, now, too.

Twelve more ghosts to carry.

10

The South

"CAN'T *BELIEVE* YOU TRIPPED. You! You're never clumsy." Juniper shakes her head at Ash, who shrugs lazily.

"It was the lights. Or maybe I just wanted to see how it felt to freefall."

He tries to catch my eye but I turn away toward the window, though in the dark it only reflects my own angry face back to me.

I have acknowledged my anger and gone through a set of relaxation breathing exercises, but I am still angry.

"Sequoia?"

I turn to find Oak watching me. "Yes?"

"Are you okay?"

I force a smile. I feel as though I have been doing nothing else since we won. "Yes, thank you. I am just tired."

He smiles back at me and reaches for my hand.

I pretend not to see, and tuck my hands under my thighs.

I hear the aircraft the moment we disembark from the train. A figure in silhouette is climbing into the back of a sleek, powerful

Lacewing—they wave in our direction and we make the sign of deference in return. The wind pushes dust into the air, and I am left to dig the grit from my eyes as the jet rises above us and takes off southward. Blinking repeatedly, I turn my head to watch it pass. The familiar symbol glows, as though we need the Administration's mark to tell us who rides inside. As though anyone besides the Administration would have access to a Lacewing.

Juniper cocks her head at me and I shrug. We can't know why they are here. I should not waste time speculating.

Though the hour is late, the corridors are crammed full of cadets and protectors. They clap as we walk past them, and Protector Jheb and his teammates are quietly pulled away by friends eager to wring their hands and hear their stories.

All of our year-mates wait together in one of the corridors near our dormitories. They run forward to meet us, shouting and cheering. Linden tackles me in a hug, her slight frame somehow managing to knock me off balance. A hand reaches out to steady me, and I turn back to find Ash smiling down at me.

"So clumsy, for a champion."

"Her?! After you fell off that platform?" Fir claps Ash on the shoulder, prompting five other cadets to do the same.

"Oh, you leave him alone." Linden waits for a gap in the congratulatory shoulder and hand clapping to give Ash a hug. "You were amazing, both of you," she says, her big grey eyes bright with excitement. "All four of you," she corrects herself, looking past Ash to Oak and Juniper.

"But really, how did you manage to fall?" asks Fir. "You landed perfectly!"

Ash shrugs. "Tripped over my own feet."

Fir gives an incredulous sputter.

"We've been training together for five years," says Linden. "I've never seen you miss a step."

Ash shrugs his shoulders and gives a lackadaisical wave of dismissal. "Maybe my luck's running out." He looks up at Fir, who stands almost as tall as Oak, though only half as wide. "And we never trained with flash lighting."

"It was unusual." Fir looks excited, and I know that he is about to bring data into the conversation. "In the transcripts of past contests, I didn't find any mention of it. I would have told you, obviously."

Linden turns to Fir, hands on her hips. "We did talk about visual impairment, though. I think the conclusion we came to is that in order to ensure the best possible experience for the audience, the preference seems to be to use blindfolds on the contestants, rather than using diminished or inconsistent lighting or anything that might limit the viewer's ability to properly see what is taking place in the arena."

"So, it was our presumptions at fault, then. Some research team, huh, Sequoia?"

I feel Ash moving closer to me and pivot to the side. "Actually, your suggestions were really helpful, as you saw. We couldn't have done it without your help."

"True." Linden winks at me. "We're basically champions too."

"Right," says Fir. "Just, you know, unofficially."

"So, I am pretty tired. Goodnight, everyone," says Juniper.

I start and look past Ash to see that Juniper and Oak are still standing behind us.

Juniper's tone of voice suggests irritability. I wonder if they felt excluded from the conversation. Even though Juniper is Ash's romantic partner, she still always seems outside of our foursome.

"I'll come too," says Oak, whose smile is certainly genuine.

"Goodnight," I say to Juniper and Oak as they pass us. "Linden's right. You were both amazing."

Juniper gives me a smile that doesn't quite reach her eyes. "You too, Captain."

"I'm not—"

"Goodnight, Sequoia." Oak reaches out a meaty paw and gives me what I assume he imagines to be a friendly pat on the back, though it feels more like someone trying to help me dislodge food from my windpipe. "See you in the morning."

They walk toward the corridor that leads to their dormitory, and half of the cohort breaks off to follow them. The other half start filing into our dormitory.

"Night night, Captain." Ash squeezes my arm as he follows our year-mates. I shrug off his hand, frowning, and turn away to see Linden and Fir watching me with raised eyebrows.

"I'm going to turn in too," I say. "Big day tomorrow, I—"

"Oh!" Linden's voice is so loud that Ash turns back. "You'll never guess who was here. Councilman Naru. Can you believe it? He was here meeting with—"

"We don't know for sure." Fir crosses his arms, his usual defensive position. "We shouldn't share what is only conjecture. We only know that Cedar thinks she heard one of Grand Neilem's seconds saying that he heard that she—"

"She's taking an apprentice." Linden's voice is nothing but a whisper, as though the truth is so fragile that a spoken word could shatter it.

"She's...not. She never..." I stare at her, seeing the same feeble hope in her eyes that I am certain she is seeing in mine.

"Not for fifteen years," says Linden. "The councilman—"

Fir crosses his arms so tightly that his shoulders jut forward, making him look even more angular and skeletal than usual.

Linden rolls her eyes. "Sorry, the unsubstantiated rumour—is that better?—is that the Administration had to step in and force the matter."

"So then tomorrow..." I can't seem to say the words aloud.

"Someone becomes a P5."

11

The South

I STARE AT MY WORN, olive green uniform before pulling it on for the last time. I wish I had something special to wear, something different, something to signify that I am about to become a protector and an adult.

I sit down on my bed and watch the others flit around, dressing and chatting, though my eyes keep flickering over to the Personal Communication Box beside the door.

Rooming assignments are due by noon. I don't know why I have been delaying. I will request a single room, of course. That is the only sensible thing to do.

"What is the plan for today?" Linden asks, plopping down on the bed beside me. Fir hovers beside her. "No exams to study for, no contests to train for."

"We could go to the library," suggests Fir.

"Sure," I say. "And then maybe afterward we could go check out one of the archaic weapons from the armoury."

Fir nods, though rather unenthusiastically.

"Neither of your ideas are fun," says Linden. "You are both terrible at free time."

I shrug. "When else are we going to work on our IDPs?"

Linden rolls her eyes. "Individual development plans are important, sure. But it's a whole free day. You could train for an hour and then do...nothing. Or something different. Something we don't always do."

"We could laze." Ash crawls onto the bed behind us, sprawling out lengthwise. "Starting tomorrow, we can shop."

I scoot forward so that there is space between myself and Ash.

"Um, I don't think we actually receive the first installment of our stipend tomorrow," says Linden, turning to face Ash. "I think it takes —Sequoia? How long does it take?"

"We get paid at the end of each week."

"Well, we can scope it out," says Ash. I hear him dig my pillow out from underneath the tightly folded sheets and punch it into submission. "Maybe we can write a note. Promise future wages."

I cannot contain myself. I turn and stare down at him.

"I cannot—how can you—why—"

Ash crosses his hands behind his head and grins up at me. "What could possibly go wrong, Captain?"

I take a deep breath and turn back around, suppressing images of myself yanking my pillow out from under his head and beating him with it.

"You are being intentionally vexing." I look to Linden. "He—"

But she is looking toward the door, her head cocked to one side. I hear it a second later: the familiar cadence coming from the Personal Communication Box. We have a message to retrieve.

As one, the cadets in the room rise and file over to the PCB. I wait behind Linden, trying not to watch as the cadets in front of us press a hand each to the screen and receive a message in return. The information could be sensitive.

My heartrate increases. *What if it's our examinations results? Or our designations?*

It won't be, of course. Our marks will be broadcast on the screen in Tranquility Square at noon, and we will receive our designations in front of the entire base during the ceremony immediately after. This is how it is always done.

Linden lowers her hand and stares at the screen for a moment. "Oh. Obviously. Medical ward."

"Is it a full assessment?" asks Fir from behind me.

"Looks like," she says. "Two hours each. Yup. Full physical. So much for free time."

She steps aside as I sign in to the PCB. My message is the same, though I note my personal time and the room number.

A housing request order flashes at the bottom of the screen.

I ignore it. I will need to hurry through breakfast to make my appointment.

I HAVE MET with the P3 who ushers me into the examination room before. Her name is Mina. It is a pleasant-sounding name, and not uncommon. There have been other protectors named Mina. I can picture their faces, so I must have seen their biographies flash across the screen in Tranquility Square. I wonder if that is how this Mina chose her name. Or perhaps it was in a book, although I am up to date on the nation's recent fiction and have not encountered any characters named Mina. From an older novel, then, or a textbook, perhaps. There are more textbooks in the library than even Fir could read in a lifetime.

Mina's hair is blonde and tied back from her face. "We'll begin with a full physical assessment," she tells me as I change into a paper dressing gown. "Then I'll ask you some questions, and then we'll talk about your sexual health." She smiles at me. It is a nice smile.

The physical assessment is routine. She looks into my eyes, my ears, and my throat. She listens to my heart and my lungs and checks my breasts for lumps. She tests my eyesight and my reflexes. Then I lie down on the table and she places a mask over my face and counts down as I breathe in. The air tastes sweet, somehow.

I wake to an empty room and a dry, itchy throat. There is a glass of date juice beside my clothes. I dress and then settle onto a metal chair to wait, sipping slowly at the juice.

P3 Mina returns shortly, a mess of wires and cords in her hands. She fits the headpiece snugly over my ears and my vision is momentarily blocked by the eye scanners, though they adjust quickly and soon I can see through them to Protector Mina. She fits sensors to my heart and my fingertips and settles down into a padded chair across from me, a porta in her hands.

I am always surprised by how light the headpiece is. It looks heavy and clumsy, like antiquated armour.

I picture myself donning this in a sparring match, and have to stifle a giggle.

Protector Mina smiles at me, and begins asking questions. These too are routine. *Do you feel rested when you wake in the morning? In the past six months, have you had moments when you felt unhappy for more than an hour at a time? How do you feel about your dormmates? Your training masters? Grand Neilem? How do you feel about the Administration?*

The questions come quickly, and even so, I have to stop myself from answering before she has finished speaking. As though I have not gone through this process a dozen times in five years.

We finish. She pulls the cables gently from my body, and for some reason this leaves me feeling oddly naked.

She begins flicking through screens on her porta. "Ah, here. I noticed that you have not responded to a rooming request."

I swallow. "My apologies, Protector. I only saw it this morning, and did not want to be late to this assessment. I will respond as soon as I return to my dormitory."

"I see."

"I—I already spoke with the cadet in question."

"You intend to reject the rooming request, then?"

"I do, Protector."

She nods, her expression pleasant and free from judgement. "Please ensure that both you and Cadet Ash indicate on the rejection form whether a different cohabitation assignment is desired or whether single rooms are preferred."

"I—what?"

Protector Mina's eyebrows raise ever so slightly.

I can feel myself flushing. "Yes, Protector." I swallow. "I—*we* will complete the appropriate forms immediately."

She smiles at me again. "Thank you, cadet. You are dismissed."

I trip slightly as I exit the room, though I regain my balance in time to avoid actually falling. I look around the waiting room and spy Linden.

"Are you alright, Sequoia?" she asks.

"I—where's Ash?"

"Ash? He just left. Maybe the dormitory?"

I nod and make my way out of the medical wing.

I think Linden is calling after me, but I cannot make out her words, and keep walking.

Ash is not in the dormitory, nor in the cadet training ring. *Outside.*

I step out onto the empty training field, squinting in the mid-morning sun. By the time I cross to the second field my entire body is flushed with the heat and I can feel my skin starting to burn.

This field, too, is empty, except for a handful of protectors in the meditation tent.

I start to head back into the base, and then stop.

It will be quick to check.

I start jogging.

My lips are starting to burn. *I really should have grabbed my sun-saving lotion.*

The obstacle course is empty.

Of course it is. It's too hot to train outdoors right now.

I am turning to leave when I notice that one of the knotted ropes is swaying slightly.

Lifting my hand to shield my face from the sun, my eyes follow the rope up to the platform above, and a backlit figure.

"Hey, Captain."

"I need to speak with you."

"Come on up, then."

"Could you come down here, please?"

"It's better up here."

I let out an exasperated sound. This does not improve the situation, so I start climbing the rope.

The notes to our national words of gratitude drift over. *Is he whistling?*

My head has just breached the platform when I see a pair of boots lift off the ground. I look up to see Ash, with a second rope in hand, swinging himself over to the next platform.

"What are you doing?" I ask as I pull myself to standing.

"Just making sure I don't get pushed off a platform again."

"I am—I am really sorry about that. It was irrational and dangerous. And we almost lost."

"Almost."

I study Ash's face, the feigned solemnity. "You're not even upset about it."

He breaks out into a grin. "It was worth it."

I grab the rope. "I cannot—how can—you are in a sexual relationship with Juniper! It is irresponsible and dishonest and—" As I swing toward him, Ash moves to the next platform.

"And this—this rooming request? We have never, I mean—"

Ash pulls himself up onto the bar above his new platform and does a one-handed chin up. He then swings his legs through and flips himself upside down. "Come on, Captain—"

"Stop calling me that."

"Why? You are."

"I'm not."

"Of course you are. You're the best, and we're a team."

"The contests are over."

"I don't mean the contests," he says. I am starting to feel nauseous, staring at his upside-down face. "I mean us. We're a team."

"Well," I said. "Us and Linden and Fir."

"Sure. But also, me and you."

I can feel myself starting to turn red again. "Sparring partners."

"And study partners."

"Really? How have you helped me?" I cross my arms across my chest.

He copies me, and I grab the next rope and swing across to him.

He is faster, though, and somehow manages to get to the next platform before I catch him.

"I hear teaching is the best way to learn."

"This is stupid. Stop being elusive."

"Am I being elusive?"

"I don't know what you're being!" I clap my hands over my mouth, and glance around. Luckily the course remains empty. "I don't know if you're being funny, or if you're treating Juniper disrespectfully, or—or—"

"Why do you keep worrying about Juniper?"

"You chose a monogamous sexual contract, Ash. She told—"

"I ended the contract."

I stop and stare at him. "What? When?"

"Last night."

"I—why? I thought you liked her."

"Juniper's great," he says, swinging to the final platform.

"So why end your contract?"

Ash lands on the balls of his feet and turns to face me. "It's time for me and you."

I could catch him—there is nowhere for him to go—but I find myself hesitating. He takes the rope and swings back over to me. He is too close, suddenly. I look back at the platform behind me. Should I retreat?

"It's always been me and you," he says. "Now don't throw me off the platform this time."

He leans toward me and the world shrinks to his body and mine, and the hot dusty air encircling us, and the midday bell....

I step back. "Our marks," I whisper.

12

The South

I GRAB the rope and slide down so quickly my hands burn. My feet hit the ground in a puff of dust, obscuring my vision as I race across the obstacle course, making for the closest entrance to the base. I move to fling open the door and am met with solid resistance. Wrenching at it a second, and then a third time, I scream in frustration before it occurs to me that the door is probably locked. The next door I reach opens easily, smashing into the wall as I throw it open and dash through the corridors to Tranquility Square.

It is crowded inside. All of our year-mates are there, of course, but so are various other cadets and protectors. A few heads turn as I enter, breathless, but most eyes are locked on the screen.

The base map disappears and names start to appear. I can feel my heart racing. There is motion at the door opposite me. Out of the corner of my eye I see Ash enter the room. Our eyes meet for half a second but I break the connection, looking back to the screen.

It is my name at the top of the list. And the score—

"Perfect marks." Linden is beside me. "Of course you did."

Perfect marks. The top score. If Grand Neilem has to pick an apprentice...don't think about it. Don't think about it yet.

I stare at the number for one second—two—and then scan down the list. Linden's score is below mine—the second highest mark overall.

I reach down and squeeze her hand. "Well done, you."

Fir's academic score is equal to hers, but his martial score is much lower. And Ash—my heart sinks.

"Well, it's as good as could be expected, I think." Fir has joined us. He smiles crookedly at me. "Guess all of those nights studying paid off."

I nod, trying to keep the pity off my face. "Your academic score is excellent."

"I'm okay with my martial score, Sequoia," he says, stumbling as Oak claps him on the back. "I wasn't last, was I?"

"Amazing, Sequoia." Oak pulls me into a hug. I feel myself stiffen, and reach out and pat him awkwardly on the back. "You too," I say, although I have no idea how he placed. His hulking frame is now hiding the scoreboard from view.

The crowd is building around us. Protectors and cadets are congratulating the other fifth years, congratulating me. It is a joyful, celebratory moment—and yet I want to leave. I feel like I am suffocating.

Protector Nem appears, calling us to assemble in an adjacent classroom. We follow her, and I am grateful to leave the square.

We file into the room and seat ourselves at the desks. The illusion of normalcy on the most abnormal of days. Protector Nem reaches the front of the classroom and stops, locking her hands behind herself. It is just as though she is about to begin a lecture—a lesson on virtues, or health.

I find myself staring at the streak of white hair that has recently appeared on the side of her head, the white in stark contrast with her shiny black hair, and at odds with her trim, muscled physique and the smooth, light brown skin that has yet to permit a wrinkle. Were Protector Nem to dye her hair, she would look exactly the same as she had the day we arrived at the base, five years past. Perhaps this is why she allows it: tangible proof that time is, in fact, passing. I can think of no other reason. The fact that the rest of her hair is black instead of violet or turquoise is already peculiar enough.

She informs us that we will take our midday meal here, and that she will return for us when it is time to enter the ring for the designation ceremony. She leaves, and I find myself feeling oddly disappointed. As though I had been anticipating a speech, perhaps something inspirational. I don't know why I would think so. Inspiration comes from the council, and from Grand Neilem at this base. Protector Nem, though the leader of us during our tenure as cadets, is in the end only a P2. It is strange to think that after tomorrow I won't report to her.

You might even outrank her.

I push the thought away. I do not want to raise my expectations.

You know you'll at least make P3 or P4, even if the Grand doesn't choose—

Enough.

Two third-year cadets appear pushing carts laden with prickly pear juice, flatbread, mesquite cakes, okra, and a large pot of squash stew. I am pleased that we will not need to eat in the canteen. My year-mates are not quiet—but the sum of twenty-three voices is paltry compared with the volume of the entire base.

I sit beside Linden, who is chatting with Fir and Cedar. Ash sits on the other side of them, and I find myself grateful for the distance.

I try to swallow some flatbread but my throat is too dry and I end up coughing. I settle for juice and a small bowl of stew. I make an effort to appear as though I am interested in the conversations around me, but my ability to process words seems to be blocked by the enormity of the moments before and after me.

My marks. The designation ceremony. The rumour of Grand Neilem taking on a P5 apprentice. Ash. Ash's marks. Winning the contests. The examination. Pushing Ash off the platform.

This is cycling—I am not learning or resolving. I breathe deeply and slowly and try to work myself back into the room. Training Master Jheb's techniques: see; hear; taste; touch; smell. From the body to the brain—reverse the flow.

Smells? The stew in my bowl. *Taste.* The sweetness of the juice in my mouth. *Sound.* Linden's voice. I look over, and see that her arm is wrapped around Cedar's hips. It makes me wonder if I am losing her.

Of course you are. Everyone is moving into monogamous, sexual relationships.

Everyone but me.

Why not you? What are you scared of?

It's not fear. It's a decision.

It is fear. Fear of being distracted.

Touch. I pick up the piece of flatbread again and squish it in my hand.

Now, focus on the conversations around you.

I DON'T KNOW how much time has passed when Protector Nem returns. She leads us through the empty corridors to Ring 2. We enter the arena through a side door.

Like last night, the stands are packed with every cadet and protector in the base. Unlike at the contests, however, this audience is silent, and the room over-bright. The occasion calls for sobriety, transparency.

A platform has been erected and on it stands a small group of protectors—those who have selected a C5 apprentice this year.

I spy a P2 unit commander. Unit commanders lead the P1 protectors, those assigned to general border duty—though in an emergency, the P2 unit commanders would report directly to the P5s.

The bulk of the base protectors are P1s and I know that most of my year-mates will join their ranks. It is reputed to be a pleasant career. Daily patrols, ample time to exercise and train. Like all protectors, they receive two free days a week and a weekly stipend. They never seem hurried. I do not see them exhibiting stress.

It would be a good life, if I wanted it.

Also among the P2s I see Training Master Tila and Professor Hurst. The significance is clear. Only the P2 unit commanders, training masters, and professors are recruiting cadets from amongst my year-mates.

Although, the P2 unit commander might not only be here to welcome the new P1s into their ranks—they could also be recruiting a P2 unit commander apprentice.

Who are you here for?

There are few representatives at the higher levels: P3 Protector Zaphyr, head of the medical ward and medical training; and P5 Grand Neilem, flanked as always by her seconds, Protectors Jace and Onyx. My heart skips a beat. I try to steady it. Like the unit commander's, her presence is unclear. She always officiates the designations. That she is standing on the platform confirms nothing.

We line up in three rows, facing the platform. Protector Nem taps gently with the toe of her boot, and as one we raise our hands, pressing them together in front of our eyes.

Up in the stands, in an amplobox, musicians strike up the opening notes to the words of gratitude and we lower our hands.

A massive screen, positioned high above us, lights up with an image of Grand Neilem's face. She begins the words. Her mouth barely moves—she does not need to shout, or even project. The platform has been amplified for her.

The rains pulled back
From our lands
Drought swept sea to sea
We would have perished, all
But you delivered us

The words course through me. I want them—I want their truth, their familiarity, their ritual. I wish I could speak them all with her, but we repeat only the final line of each stanza.

Fruit withered on the tree
Crops failed one by one
From the brink of famine
You delivered us

I close my eyes and try to breathe them in. Make them part of me. *I am the nation. The nation is me.* My own, silent mantra.

Generation zero
No child was born until
You pushed the bounds of science
And delivered us

Fear led to violence
As rule of law grew weak
To a greater order
You delivered us

Beholden, duty-bound, in gratitude

I whisper the final words. The beautiful words. I have heard them roughly six thousand times but today they become a part of me. I am no longer a child. No matter what designation I receive, I am now a protector of Seira. I could almost weep.

"Duty," Grand Neilem repeats, looking down at us. "Such an important word. We have nothing, if we do not have duty. Without duty we are animals. Or worse, we are savages, like the barbarians in the North. We have survived, grown, evolved in Seira because of duty. The duty of each citizen to the planet, the duty of each generation to those who came before them and those who will live after them, the duty of the Administration to children, cadets, and protectors, and the duty of each cadet and protector to the nation."

She looks up at the crowd, a slow smile warming her face. "It has been our duty and our pleasure to nourish these young cadets. To teach them and mentor them, to care for their health—both physical and emotional.

"I am so pleased today to be able to lead them up onto the platform and into our ranks as protectors. May they fulfill their duty to us, to this base, and to Seira."

She pauses, letting her words sit in the air, giving us time to breathe them in, before looking down at us, expectantly. I am ready. We are ready. She smiles and looks back up to the crowd.

Juniper is called first. The camera cuts to her face. Her examination marks, both academic and martial, flash at the top of the screen, along with the laurel marking her as a contest winner.

Grand Neilem repeats Juniper's accomplishments and invites Training Master Tila forward. The applause drowns out P2 Tila's words of welcome, but the words are unnecessary, anyway. The message is clear. I raise my voice and shout along with my yearmates. Training master is an excellent designation—one that Juniper has well earned.

Perhaps the training masters have recruited additional cadets, perhaps not. There is no visual cue. Juniper and Training Master Tila remain on the platform, as is tradition.

It doesn't matter.

It's not what you want.

True. But it's better than being a P1.

Grand Neilem turns back to the crowd and we fall silent. "Congratulations, C5 Juniper, for all of your hard work. Now, as you step into your role as a protector, you are invited to select a permanent name. Have you chosen a name, protector?"

"I have, Grand Neilem." Juniper's chin is lifted, her voice confident. "With your permission, I will be known as Raya."

"Thank you, P2 Raya. Let us welcome her."

The audience applauds again, and Juniper breaks out into a smile. She is beautiful. I wonder how Ash feels about terminating his relationship with her. I glance over at him, examine his face as he cheers for his ex-lover. I see no regret there.

But then, Ash is not a terribly regretful person.

P1 is the ranking given to the next five cadets who are called forward. The unit commander welcomes them. We applaud. They look pleased. It is as I would expect. I try to keep the new names straight in my head, but already I have forgotten a few. I assume someone has made a list; perhaps it can be shared upon request.

Linden is called. She squeezes my hand before she walks up to the platform. I watch her go, wondering if I am losing one of my best friends—to Cedar or another girl, to a different career path.

Change is good. Change is growth. Be grateful for change.

I swallow and dig my nails into the palms of my hands.

When P3 Medic Zaphyr steps forward I have to clap a hand over my mouth to prevent myself from shouting out. I needn't have bothered—the audience is screaming with excitement.

I add my voice to theirs. The joy on Linden's face is incredible to see. A P3 designation is highly honourable. She will learn so much as a medic. I only hope that if there is no P5 apprenticeship, that I will be able to join her.

"Have you chosen a name, protector?" asks Grand Neilem.

"I have, Grand Neilem," says Linden, her slim, willowy form oddly stiff with the formality of the moment. "With your permission, I would be known as Lyra."

"Thank you, P3 Lyra. Let us welcome her." I clap along with the audience, repeating the new name to myself. *Lyra, Lyra, Lyra. Not Linden anymore, not Starling. Lyra.*

"Now, we have an unusual situation this year," says Grand Neilem, once the clamour has faded. I feel my heart begin to pump faster. I wonder if the cadet beside me can hear it. I wonder if I am vain, or arrogant.

"A record of academic excellence, a humble attitude, and a willingness to put maximum effort into all ventures has resulted in a dual designation request for one of this year's graduating cadets."

A dual request? I have never heard of this happening before. I shift slightly on the balls of my feet. *What does this mean?*

"C5 Fir, please join me onstage."

My body stills. Fir, of course. His academic test scores almost rivalled mine. He must be wanted by the professors, and....

Both Professor Hurst and the P3 medic step forward.

Fir looks taller and skinnier and more awkward than usual. His ears are glowing red even before he steps up onto the platform.

"C5 Fir," says Grand Neilem, sounding oddly gentle. Perhaps she has noticed how uncomfortable he is with all of the attention. That would be intuitive of her. "We invite you to make the choice."

Fir looks at Professor Hurst, and then the medic, then back to the professor.

"I—um." He swallows and his eyes shift down to us—to me and Ash, and then over to Linden, standing behind P3 Medic Zaphyr.

"Thank you for the—the opportunity. I think I would like to be a medic."

I cheer alongside the crowd, though my heart is sinking. Apprenticeships to the medical ward are rare. The fact that they have requested two this year...there is no chance that they will take a third.

A professor then, maybe, or a training master, or a unit commander.

Or just a P1.

Or maybe Grand Neilem...

Fir gives his new name as Elium. It is a good name. I have not heard it before, but then Fir—Elium—probably found it in an obscure book that nobody else has read.

Oak is called next. He receives his designation as a P1, as do the next several cadets called after him.

Then it is Ash's turn. I watch him stroll onto the stage with—not arrogance, exactly—more like buoyancy. Luck and an oversupply of physical grace have given Ash the dangerous impression that everything will work out in his favour. I only hope that the recruiting teams have looked past his academic marks to his perfect martial score, to his status as a contest winner, to his brain that is brimming with potential.

When the Unit Commander steps forward I wait for him to claim Ash as a commander, as a P2, as someone who can lead.

But the words never come. Ash accepts his designation as a P1 cheerily, and I am so distracted that I almost miss his new name.

"With your permission, I would be known as Corvus."

I start to clap and then stop. *Corvus—Corvus. I know this. It's—*

No, no he wouldn't. Bird symbolism is for first year cadets.

Ash—Corvus grins and takes his place with the other P1s.

Why would he choose such a name? How can they allow it?

How can they forbid it?

I barely watch the next designation, or the one after it. When my name is called, I realize with a start that I am the only one left.

I fix a pleasant expression on my face and march up to the platform.

A P1 or a P2 is an honourable career. I can excel no matter where they put me.

Perhaps. Watch your face. Do not disgrace yourself.

Grand Neilem smiles as I approach, but I can detect no warmth from her. If anything, she seems as though she is unhappy with me.

More than that. It's as though she dislikes you.

That's absurd.

"C5 Sequoia," Grand Neilem says, speaking to the audience, "has an unparalleled history as a cadet. As you witnessed last night, she led her team to a first-place victory in the contests. I say led, because although there are no formal leadership positions among cadets, every single one of her professors and training masters has identified her as a natural leader. She has earned perfect marks on both her academic and martial examinations, an accomplishment which has not been achieved in over two decades."

I want to look down, but force myself to gaze forward at the audience, my expression bland, pleasant.

Humble, you should be humble.

My mouth is dry and I want to clear my throat but I am worried that if I cough once I will not be able to stop.

"It is only fitting that we nourish this young cadet. That we give her opportunities to continue to grow as a leader." Here Grand Neilem pauses and I sense...reluctance?

Stop it. Just stop.

"I am so pleased to announce that C5 Sequoia will be joining me as my personal apprentice, to train as one of my seconds, so that she may one day step into the role of Grand, if needed."

She stops speaking. I wonder why, until I realize that the audience is cheering. More than cheering. They are screaming for me as they screamed for me last night.

"As is tradition," says Grand Neilem once the clamour finally fades, "P5s take on the names of our honoured past council members, as selected by the current Grand." She turns to me and smiles. My face feels frozen. I do my best to smile back at her but suspect it looks forced and possibly lopsided. “Please join me in welcoming P5 Sierra.”

Sierra.

The audience is too much for me. I look to my year-mates. Ash—*not Ash—Corvus. What a stupid name.* Corvus catches my eyes and I feel something come unstuck.

I turn back to Grand Neilem. “Thank you for this honour.” My voice is strong and clear. It fills the stadium. “I will not fail you.”

She smiles again. I study her face, but all traces of resentment have disappeared.

If they were ever there to begin with.

13

The South

I AM USHERED off the platform by Grand Neilem's seconds before the applause has even ended. I glance back once. Though organized by rank, my year-mates still stand as a unit, as a team. They are beginning to celebrate—hands clasping hands, arms around shoulders. Their voices are raised, but I am soon too far away to make out what any of them are saying.

I stumble slightly on the last step. I catch myself, shift my eyes forward.

It is only Grand Neilem, her seconds, and me now. They lead me through the maze of corridors. Eastward, through a set of doors that I have entered only once before, to a second hallway. P5 Onyx presses his hands to a small screen and the doors open: the east wing—an area forbidden to cadets, P1s, P2s, and even P3s.

We climb a short flight of stairs to reach a door with a second security screen beside it. "Iris scan, please," a pleasant, automated voice says. I stare at the large, golden number five that has been mounted on the door, as Protector Jace steps forward and allows the laser to scan his eyes.

I hear a click, and Protector Jace swings the door open.

It is my second time entering Grand Neilem's office. I am four years older than the last time, and yet I feel equally as small, as young, as unqualified as I did standing in front of Councilman Naru that evening at the end of first year.

Perhaps it is the shards of sky shining down from the scattering of skylights that speckle the ceiling —perhaps they are intended to encourage humility, to remind us that we are insignificant.

Or perhaps it is the luxuries—the tech, the elegance—as far removed from the concrete floors and thin mattresses of the cadet dormitories as I am from the P5s beside me. The walls, where not punctured by windows, are covered in screens that I know can act as mirrors when needed. The furniture is heavy and dark, and unblemished.

Grand Neilem settles herself behind the desk. Her seconds stand on either side of her. I glance from Protector Jace to Onyx, but neither one looks at me. Though they couldn't be more dissimilar physically —the large, muscular Protector Jace with his dark skin and broad shoulders, and the delicate Protector Onyx with his blue, blue eyes and hair. Yet, there is something uniform about them.

Identical stony expressions?

Synchronized stoicism?

I feel a horrible, irrational desire to giggle and look down at my feet. Where are these thoughts coming from? It's suggestive of a lack of mental discipline. Unbecoming in a cadet—shameful in a protector.

Not just a protector. You're a P5.

"Please, be seated." Grand Neilem gestures to the armchair across from her, on the other side of the desk.

Same seat as last time.

I cannot seem to keep my mind from flicking to the past. *Focus on what is at hand.* I am just tired. It has been an eventful day.

Grand Neilem reaches into a desk drawer and unearths a porta, which she passes to me. It is larger than the ones our instructors permit us to use during our lessons. I hold it gingerly in my hands, unsure of what she wants me to do with it.

Grand Neilem folds one hand over the other and smiles me. "In order to run the base, it is imperative first that you understand the base."

She seems to be waiting for me to speak. "Yes, Grand Neilem," I say, and feel immediately irritated with myself. I am the first cadet selected for apprenticeship to a Grand in fifteen years. Surely, I should have something more impressive to say. "I am—I am eager to begin learning."

Well, that wasn't any better.

She nods, as though I don't sound like a particularly slow first year. "And how would you go about it?"

I stare at her for a moment. *It's a test. Of course, it's a test.* I look down at the porta in my hands, as though it might provide me with answers.

A porta that can read my mind—that is what I need. Of course, no such thing exists.

Perhaps that's one for the engineers.

I frown, and look back to Grand Neilem. "I know so little about the engineers, or the medics, or the P2 unit commanders, or the strategists..."

She nods, and this time I catch something in her expression.

She's pleased, despite herself.

Don't be ridiculous. She chose you. She will want you to succeed.

The desire to prove myself is so strong I find that I am actually leaning forward in my chair.

"I should shadow each team."

Protector Neilem leans back in her chair, her eyes appraising me. "Propose a schedule. Send it to me by tomorrow."

The dismissal in her tone is clear. I stand and try to pass her back the porta.

"That is yours to keep. Your required reading is included, as are some suggested assignments. Drag anything you've completed into the red folder, and I will be able to access it."

"Oh, I—uh..." I place the porta gently on the table so that I can make the sign for deference. "Thank you, Grand Neilem. Protector Jace. Protector Onyx."

Protector Jace gives the barest of nods, while Grand Neilem and Protector Onyx do not respond at all.

I pick up the porta and make my way out of the office. My arms feel suddenly too heavy, my footing clumsy. I wish they weren't watching me.

It's just a test.

You can do this.

It's just another test.

IT'S LATE. I am the last one in the dormitory; the rest of my year-mates moved out while I was meeting with Grand Neilem. I should have left an hour ago—it is not as though it took me long to gather up my belongings. I came back to find that a box of clothing had been delivered to my station—my new uniforms. To this I added the porta; my toothbrush; a novel from the library that I've finished; an autobiography that I haven't; and the scarlet singlet and black pants I wore during the contests. I don't imagine that the costume is mine to keep, but no one has come to request it, and for some reason I have been loath to bring it to laundry and bury it in the mess of olive green training uniforms.

I look down to my feet, dangling over the edge of the bed, and to my box, pressed neatly against the side of the bed, as though Protector Nem is about to conduct an inspection. I count the empty beds in the dormitory: eleven, plus the one I occupy.

I really should leave—first years will be arriving shortly to clean the dormitory.

I look across to the PCB, blinking brightly beside the door, then back down to my feet. Then the box. Then the beds again.

I hear footsteps. Fir is almost at his old station before he notices me. *No. Not Fir. Elium. Not Pipit, not Fir. Just Elium.*

"Sequoi—uh, Sierra, um...hang on." Elium drops to the floor and searches under his bed for a moment before emerging with a gigantic textbook under each long, skinny arm.

"What are you still doing here?" he asks, taking a seat beside me on the bed. "Did you just get back?" Suddenly he jumps back up and begins fumbling with the books. "Wait, you're a P5 now, I should be, the sign..."

"Oh," I say, realizing what he's doing. "No, please. Don't. That's for Grand Neilem. I'm just—please don't."

"Um, well. I guess. If you—if that's what you request." His ears flushing red, he seats himself back down beside me.

Side by side, we stare around at the empty dormitory for a moment.

I should make conversation. "Where, um, where are your quarters now?"

"Oh!" He turns to me, a smile on his face. "I'm at 62A. Right down the hall from Linden and—er, I mean Lyra and—and...Cedar—I can't remember her new name."

I nod. I cannot remember her new name either.

"And you, your new quarters are...?"

I cross my arms over my chest and shrug.

"Oh." He looks down at the textbook in his arms. It looks to be advanced chemistry. "I thought maybe Ash—I mean Corvus, asked..."

I shift on the bed, wishing my feet reached the ground like Elium's did.

"He did."

"Oh. You said no, then?"

I shrug again, and go back to counting the beds. "Congratulations, by the way, on being recruited to medic," I say, when the silence begins to stretch on too long. "That's a wonderful accomplishment."

Out of the corner of my eye, I see Elium straighten. "Thank you. It's such an honour—and there's going to be so much to learn."

"There will be. And you'll get to study with Lyra."

He nods emphatically. "I'm grateful, to have her with me."

I suspect it is more than gratitude—that perhaps he needs her, that perhaps she was even the deciding factor in his decision to become a medic over a professor.

"I'll actually be with you too, for a bit," I say. "I'm going to be shadowing the other teams."

"Oh! That'll be great. And it makes sense, of course."

"Yes. I'm excited to learn." My voice sounds hollow, which is strange. I *am* excited.

I glance down to the box. Elium's eyes follow mine.

"Have you finished Grand Septir's book?"

I shake my head. "I haven't started it, to be honest. The fiction was —I finished the fiction first."

Elium snorts and then quickly covers his nose with his hands.

"I skimmed a lot of parts." The Administration's newest fiction writer seems inclined toward erotica—no matter the genre, scenes of sexual exuberance seem to pop up everywhere, distracting from the plot.

He nods and gets to his feet, the textbooks cradled in his arms. He is so tall now it strains my neck to look up at him. "I should get back —there is some reading I should do before tomorrow."

"Of course."

He makes it to the door, and then turns around.

"I—if you read Grand Septir's autobiography...she, I mean, her accomplishments are outstanding, but..."

I wait a moment, but Elium seems to be struggling to find the words. "But?"

"But she seems, well, a bit unhappy, perhaps." His ears are bright red now. "I think it's lonely, being a Grand."

I swallow, but before I can respond he has slipped out of the doorway—back to his new quarters, single quarters. *Single, maybe, but awfully close to Lyra.*

It's his choice. Room assignment, name—we get to make choices now.

Except that you didn't get to choose your name.

I wait while another minute passes. Then five. Then ten. And then the decision is clear.

After looking around the empty dormitory one last time, I heft the box onto my hip. I only need one hand to sign into the PCB and use the touch screen. *36C.*

I leave my box in the hallway and cross to the lavatory. It is empty, of course. I splash my face with water and stare at myself in the mirror. Light brown skin; black stubble on my scalp; eyes wide and frightened, like a child's. I straighten my spine, tuck my chin.

Better.

The shavers have been packed away. We will not need them again. I suppose a protector could choose to shave their head—but I have never seen it. Perhaps they fear looking like a cadet. Or maybe seventeen years of being shorn is simply long enough for anyone. I wonder what I will look like, with hair. Will it be straight? Or curly? Will I dye it red or blue or green? I have not given much thought to aesthetics before. It all seems silly to me.

I give myself one last look. Lower my shoulders. Smooth a nonexistent wrinkle in my uniform.

Stop dawdling.

As I make my way out of the deserted corridors outside my dormitory and into the busier sections of the base I am stopped by protectors offering their congratulations, calling me by my new name and title. The cadets I pass stare wide-eyed and whisper. A few make the sign of deference.

I smile back and give standard courteous replies, but my face feels frozen. I long to hide.

I find the door and punch in the code that the PCB gave me.

Corvus is changing into his nightclothes when I enter, his back toward me.

"I—uh."

He turns toward me, the expression on his face so hopeful, so full of joy that I feel oddly like weeping. "I saved you the side near the window."

"Thank you," I whisper.

"It's a fake window."

"I like it anyway." It's actually a luminescreen, programmed to colour-match the exact hue and brilliance of the natural sky, so that we can wake up to sunlight and fall asleep to moonlight.

"I even put my clothes away in the wardrobe, though there's no Protector Nem to inspect our room in the morning."

"You should always put your clothes away," I say, still whispering. *Why am I whispering?* "Protocols are meant to be followed regardless of whether anyone is watching."

He takes a few steps forward and kisses me on the mouth. Just once, and just for a second. I barely move.

"I—I've never...from medic, I just didn't have time—"

He takes the box from me, and suddenly I'm not sure what to do with my hands. I almost reach out to take it back from him.

Corvus nods toward the desk, where a dozen pamphlets on sexual health have been stacked, almost neatly. He must have picked them up from the medical ward for me.

"We can even go module by module. When you're ready."

"That was very thoughtful."

Corvus breaks out into a grin and pulls me forward—not for a kiss this time. Just an embrace. Just like we've always done. I feel something drop—something in my ribs or my stomach. Something I hadn't realized I'd been holding.

There's an odd sound, and I realize that I'm laughing.

14

The North

THEY BREAKFASTED IN SILENCE. Kaya had been sent to fetch them at sunrise, though the festivities had lasted long into the night. They were so tired that it wasn't until halfway through their berry-smothered root cakes that Dot lifted her head, looked around, and said: "Hey. Where's Charis? And Skye?"

It turned out that nobody had seen them since the night before. Sam and the others quickly finished eating, and were getting ready to go search for the two girls when Skye appeared.

She ran toward them, tears mixing with the kohl that lined her eyes and racing down her face in black ribbons.

"Has anyone seen Charis?" she asked, her fingers twisting and untwisting the ends of her long black dreadlocks. "I looked in the pits and down by the pools."

The others shook their heads. "We'll find her," said Dot. "She probably—"

"I think they sacrificed her," Skye said in a whisper, before giving a deep, shuddering sob and falling into Dot's arms.

Dot held Skye, making comforting shushing sounds though she raised her eyebrows at the others behind Skye's back. "That doesn't sound right," she mouthed.

Shya rolled her eyes. "They didn't sacrifice her, Skye, she's probably just off challenging someone to a fight or trying to loot—"

Skye shrieked, cutting off the end of Shya's sentence, and pointed at something behind them.

The others turned to see the tribe elders walking toward them, a dozen warriors at their heels. In the midst of them stumbled a single, slight figure.

The elders stopped when they were ten feet away. One of the warriors pressed an arrow to Charis' neck, forcing the huaina to her knees. When Skye shrugged off Dot's arms and ran forward, though, the People of the Phoenix made no move to stop her.

Skye knelt and threw her arms around Charis, sobbing. "What did they do to you?" she asked.

Jackal looked to the elders. "What happened?" His tone was respectful, not accusatory. From behind him Dot stepped forward, her hands on her hips.

It was the wizened old woman who spoke. "This one," she said, pointing back at Charis without looking at her, "thought to cut a deal."

"A deal?" Jackal looked from the old woman to Charis. "What do you mean, a deal?"

The old woman held out a closed fist. Jackal stared at it for a moment, confused, then stretched out his open palm. Three heavy, silver rings fell from her hand to his.

"Asked us to poison that one," the old woman said, pointing a shaky hand at Shya, then at Skye. "And that one."

"What?" Skye pushed away from her girlfriend.

"Bav taow, Charis!" cried Shya.

Dot stared blankly at the old woman. "She wanted you to...what?"

"Not really poison," the old woman clarified. "Just a little. Just so they'd be sick enough that you'd leave them behind."

All around Sam, the sounds of anger and denial broke out.

The old woman held up her hand for silence.

“What are you intending to do with her?” asked Jackal.

The old woman shook her head. “This is your tribe, your mess. We can keep her here, for you, a prisoner. Or you can send her back where you came from. Or you can put an arrow in her.”

At this, Skye, who had gotten to her feet, covered her face with her hands and let out a strangled cry.

“Calm down, Skye,” said Dot. “We’re not going to shoot her.”

Shya walked slowly to her sister. But it was a forced calm, Sam could see. Shya looked down at Charis. “You think I can’t handle myself?” she asked in a quiet voice.

With a nod from the elder woman, one of the warriors began loosening the ties on Charis’ gag.

“If I’m willing to die for the cause,” continued Shya, “that’s my call. Not yours.”

The fabric came loose from Charis’ mouth and fell to the sand. Charis spat, but when she looked up it was Jackal’s eyes she sought, not Shya’s.

“What cause?” she croaked, and spat again. “Anna’s dead, you shint, she’s been dead for years! Now you wanna get my sister killed? And Skye?” She looked back to Shya. “I woulda stopped you in the Barrow, knocked you out and tied you up until these jits left town.” She turned to Skye, and her face fell. “But I couldn’t stop both of you. Not then.”

Charis looked up at Jackal again, and then Dot. “You’re idiots, both of you.”

Sam snuck a peek at Jackal’s face, and wished she hadn’t. He alone didn’t look angry. Only sad, and tired.

He walked forward until he stood beside Shya. “Might be you’re right, Charis,” he said, placing the silver rings on the sand in front of her. “But I’m going anyway. And it’s not my place to choose what Shya here does, or Skye, or anyone else.”

“And if it was Anna?” she asked.

“Be her right to choose.”

“Bullshit.”

Dot looked at the elders. “Can we talk, in private?”

“Of course,” said the old women.

"Shya, Skye, Jack, c'mere," said Dot. She looked at Sam, Shale and Adder. "Sorry, but this is a family matter."

Shya helped Skye to her feet, and the two of them walked off with Dot and Jackal, while the rest of the group watched them in silence.

"Bet you're loving this." Sam looked over to see Charis glaring at Shale.

Shale's face was closed and unreadable. "If I'm getting knifed in the dark, I'd rather get it over with quick," she said in her low, throaty voice. "Have a nice walk home, Charis."

It was several long minutes before Dot, Jackal, Shya, and Skye rejoined the group. They approached the elders together, but it was Shya who spoke.

"Hold her for a day, so she doesn't try to follow us. Then send her back to the Barrow." She turned to her sister. "We'll pack you enough food and water."

"I did this for you," said Charis, looking from Shya to Skye. "Both of you."

Sam watched Charis' jaw clench and unclench, and realized that the older girl was fighting tears.

Guess she's softer than she looks.

"Come back with me," said Charis. One last, desperate plea.

"We'll find you, after," said Skye. "We won't be mad anymore." A tear slid down her face.

Charis swallowed. "Thanks baby. Shya?"

But Shya's face was stone. She was the first to turn away, though the others soon followed. Northerners didn't believe in goodbyes. And sometimes there was nothing else to say.

15

The North

THEY PACKED the cart in silence, speaking only when Dash arrived with a half dozen other tribespeople laden down with supplies, including Nero and the woman who had led their abduction.

In addition to Dash, the People of the Phoenix had provided them with medicinal plants, spare bandages, and extra food and water.

They couldn't make them bows, the elders explained. The trees they used had been destroyed by pests the previous year; the old and the saplings both. They were sending fighters to the east, the west, and the north to find more, they told them, but they weren't hopeful of what they would find.

What they supplied instead for weapons was impressive even by Sam's standards. It turned out the rings they wore contained a hidden compartment filled with a poisonous powder.

"Don't wear them until you need to," Nero told them, a wry smile on his face. "You don't want one of 'em slipping off while you're washing rice."

When inhaled or ingested, the powder, which Nero refused to

identify, could lead to sleep, a coma, or death, depending on the quantity consumed and the size of the person.

There were necklaces and bracelets as well, the powder twisted up inside colourfully dyed paper beads. They weren't often worn, according to Nero; too high a risk of being caught in the rain or accidentally catching one on a stray branch.

Dot took the well-disguised arsenal and packed it away with the festive solstice clothing the girls would wear when they neared the border.

"We'll need these soon, I guess," Dot said as they readied to leave, passing out the strips of cloth and extra hats that had been stowed in the cart. At Sam's behest Dot had purchased extras before they left the Barrow. The Vauns had only packed enough for the guards.

"Um, thanks," said Adder, reaching out to take one of the bands of fabric. "What are these for, exactly?"

"For the dust," said Dash, who was storing extra arrows in the cart. A length of fabric already hung loose around his neck.

Adder raised an eyebrow. "The dust?"

Jackal accepted a strip of cloth from Dot and tied it over his mouth and nose. He looked down at Sam. His grey eyes creased to give away the smile, though half of his face was hidden.

A half-smile, probably, something feigned or polite, given the heaviness of the day. But Sam felt her pulse quicken anyway. Then she reached out to take a kerchief from Dot and felt instantly guilty.

Unnecessary. You have no intentions regarding Jackal.

"Like ash," said Dash. "But finer."

Sam tied the band of cloth around the lower half of her face. It felt like a disguise. She liked it. The hat she selected was too floppy—it wouldn't stay on in windy weather—but at least the brim was large.

The People of the Phoenix walked with them, at first. Many were silent; others sang; some prayed. Or at least, Sam thought they did. They used languages she didn't know. The elders were the first to turn back. At their behest, the children soon followed. The warriors faded away last of all, until Sam and her friends were alone.

The air grew dryer as they travelled south, the moisture leaching from the world like a photograph fading from vibrant hues to greyscale. The trees disappeared altogether, leaving only low, brown shrubs. Though these, at least, were plentiful.

Soon they were picking their way across the dead, brittle grass that bifurcated the North and the Waste.

A harsher, hotter sun reigned here, desiccating the air. It was windier, too, and a cloud of dust soon floated up like an unwelcome honour guard. It coated their clothes, their hair, their faces. Dash pulled up his kerchief to cover his nose and mouth and the others followed suit until only their eyes were visible above the bands of fabric.

It was nothing like the drylands of Seira, this dirty, burnt earth. As a child, when Sam had pictured the wildfires she'd imagined them razing cities, undoing centuries of human activity to return the land to how it used to be. But this wasn't just sand and earth they were wading through; it was a nation's worth of plastic and polyurethane, formaldehyde and asbestos, lead and silica, reduced to powder.

And there was something else, too—maybe it was the charred logs that lay strewn across their path, or perhaps it was the dust devils that swirled around them like angry spirits, but it felt like they were picking their way across a graveyard.

Because of course, they were.

Every so often they passed the ruins of a building. A bit of wall or some roofing or a corner of a house that hadn't burned. Sam avoided looking at these, when she could. She didn't want to wonder about the people who had lived here, died here. Were their ghosts watching? Did they still mourn the cities that burned?

Ghosts are a myth.

In Seira, maybe. Here, I'm not so certain.

The sun was relentless. Flimsy hats and kerchiefs weren't enough to protect them, not with the wind pushing them onward and backward, hurling sand and ash and then disappearing only to reappear with renewed animosity. It was deceptive too. As hot as they felt, with the wind cooling their skin, Sam knew that the actual temperature must be much, much higher.

Despite the risk of heat exhaustion, they couldn't travel at night as they'd planned—not according to Dash. When the wind picked up, he'd warned them, they'd have trouble enough seeing and hearing one another during the day.

The desert wasn't as placid as it looked, either. Though they weren't plentiful, every so often a dead tree towered up overhead and Dash led a wide detour around it. They were unstable, he explained, due to the soil that had burned away and the loss of structure at root level. His people called them widowmakers, for obvious reason.

They also had to skirt around the little wooden spikes that stuck up out of the ground—the deadly remains of trees and shrubs that had burned, leaving only a bit of stem or root behind.

Sand hid rocks, crevices, and the fallen remains of tree trunks, making it easy to sprain an ankle or break a leg if you weren't careful. Which was a best-case scenario. Apparently, the venomous snakes that slept in these holes weren't keen on being stepped on.

The first time the wind died down, Sam was struck by the absolute quiet of the Waste. Not the deep, muddled quiet of the forest, but the stark emptiness of dust, of a sky without a single bird to break the horizon. Was she expecting crows? Dogs? Cats? Perhaps she'd gotten too used to the Barrow. But the South wasn't quiet either, not like this. There was always the hum of electricity in Seira. This was the silence of a void.

In places the ash had hardened into a thin, grey crust. Their feet broke through it like ice, leaving splintered footsteps behind. As pleasantly tactile as she found the experience, Sam hated the noise it made, and the trail it left behind.

Here we are, it seemed to scream. The lone prey in the dead land. *Come and find us.*

They couldn't even send scouts ahead or outward from the cart to watch for danger. Not when a sandstorm could blow over at any moment.

Instead they marched in tight formation: Jackal at the front, Shya and Shale at the sides, and Sam at the rear, nobody more than fifteen feet away from the person closest to them. At the centre was Adder, guiding the cart, and Dot navigating. She and Skye also helped Adder to move rocks out of the way and dig out the cart when the wheels became stuck in the sand. In theory, anyway. In practice Skye helped pick smaller stones from their path while Dot, who was taller and stronger than most, cleared away any larger obstacles that couldn't be easily avoided.

Between the cart and Sam came Dash.

With a dozen feet between them, Sam could keep an eye on the newcomer without the inconvenience of polite conversation. Not that Dash seemed particularly prone to it. He didn't come across as shy or arrogant, simply observant. She wondered what he thought of their motley crew, their doomed mission. She also wondered who they had taken from him. A sister? A lover? A friend?

He glanced back, as though he could feel her watching him. Sam pulled down her kerchief to smile politely at him, wincing as her lips split and bled.

The situation worsened as Sam, her eyes on Dash instead of the terrain before her, walked shin-first into a fallen log.

At least she didn't cry out as she tumbled face first into the dust. And Dash had already turned back around, so there were no witnesses.

Something to be grateful for.

She shook out her legs and hurried after the others, tracing the three points of pain as she limped along—her wrist, her lips, her shins. A morbid marching song.

When she wasn't watching Dash or scanning for hazards Sam found herself sneaking glances at Shya and Skye. Not that Sam could see their faces from her position at the back of the party, but then she didn't need to.

Skye had moved past her initial anguish to exhaustion. Her steps were slow and heavy; she stumbled over the ground as though her body was disconnected from her brain.

Shya, on the other hand, moved like a soldier—stiff and silent, her eyes fixated on the land before her. Though there were logs to scramble over and pits to skirt, her feet never faltered, but her usual fluid grace was gone. There was no grief in Shya, not yet. Only rage.

Sam couldn't quite understand it. Charis' plot had been misguided, but not malicious. It actually seemed to be an act of love. Not that Sam was doubting the decision to leave Charis behind—

from a leadership standpoint, Charis was dangerous. Anyone who pushed their own agenda at the expense of the mission posed a risk. She was glad that they were continuing south without Charis. It wasn't the decision that troubled Sam, but the anger.

Over the idea of freedom, and its violation.

Was that it? The Northern obsession with freedom of choice?

Some freedom they have, in the Barrow. The choice between starvation or sex work. Between being beaten and robbed or joining a gang. Between abstinence or pregnancy. We have more freedom than this in Seira.

No, there is less freedom in Seira. But the choices are better.

Midday they stopped for a meal and to wait out the worst of the day's heat.

Sam watched longingly as Dash loosened the long swaths of cloth from his head and shoulders, pulled off his kerchief and shook out the dust that had accumulated. From the way the skin on her face and arms was tingling, she could only fear the worst. At that moment she would have traded her midday and evening meal rations for a glob of sun-saving lotion.

Dash took a swig of water and picked up his bow. "I'll take first watch."

"Before eating?" asked Adder. "Don't be a martyr, new guy." His skin, light brown like Sam's, showed a definite reddish tint.

Don't worry, you won't live long enough to develop skin cancer.

"You're still the new guy, Adder," said Dot, stepping down from the cart with a basket of the food Dash's people had gifted them. Sam winced when she saw the bubbling, blistered skin on the taller girl's pale, freckled face, chest, and arms. "And I'll join you, Dash. Time to double up. Don't wanna get caught unawares again. Not that it was your fault, Sam."

"It was my fault," said Sam. It felt clumsy, speaking after hours of silence. Or maybe it was the dust in her teeth.

"Hey, don't blame yourself," said Adder. "You could just as easily say it was my fault."

Sam considered it for a moment. "Well—"

"Hey, hey." Adder placed his hand on her shoulder, either oblivious to or unfazed by the glare she gave him. "Let's not fight in front of the new guy."

Dot rolled her eyes at Adder, picked up her crossbow, and positioned herself on the opposite side of the camp from where Dash stood, only a stone's throw away from the group. Close enough to make it back if a sandstorm blew in unexpectedly.

Sam took her rations—a few tree nuts and a large tuber, as the People of the Phoenix called the root vegetables they grew in the forest—from the basket and settled down on the ground beside Jackal. Closer than she'd been wont to. Farther than she wanted to.

"Hi."

"Hey."

Sam took a bite of her tuber, trying to think of something light to say, something pleasant, maybe even something witty or charming. Anything that belied their dismal situation.

"No such thing as demons," Shya was saying to Skye, on the other side of Sam.

"Explain the head, then. And the red necks."

Sam finished the tuber and moved onto the cooked tree nuts, wondering whether Skye actually suffered from psychosis. She didn't seem to be intentionally lying—there was too much conviction in her voice.

"I wonder how they're treating—" started Sam, just as Jackal spoke.

"I just keep thinking about—"

They both stopped. Jackal smiled, but worry hung heavy in his eyes.

"Didn't relish leaving Cassio behind."

"Me neither," said Sam. "But it was—"

"Yum, more nuts!" Adder grabbed his rations and settled himself down between Sam and Jackal. "I love this stuff—the way they cook them with spices, you know? Cannot get enough of it."

Jackal grunted.

"Hey Sam, trade you one of my tubers for the rest of your nuts."

With a sigh, Sam passed over what was left of her tree nuts. She could have used the protein, but it probably wasn't worth the calories she would burn arguing with Adder.

"Aw, really?" said Adder, balancing them on the palm of his right hand like he was weighing the balance of a gun. "Thanks, friend. But did you actually want more tuber, or are you just being nice?"

"It's fine."

"I don't want to steal your nuts, Sam."

"Adder, I don't care."

"So surly. Is that a southern thing?"

"Southerners are cheerful and obedient. Now give me the tuber."

"Yikes," he said, passing one of his tubers over. "You must be a bad Southerner, then." Adder popped a nut into his mouth and then turned to Jackal. "Do you know what keeps getting to me? It's the smell."

Jackal sniffed the air, coughed, and shook his head. "I don't smell anything."

"Exactly. It's weird, you know?"

Jackal frowned. "I guess, I mean it's better—"

"Than the Barrow? Yeah. But still. I feel like someone's amputated my senses. What do you think, Sammo?"

"I was a great Southerner," she said, glaring at him.

"What? Oh, well, you can tell us all about it, then."

Sam took a bite of tuber and continued to glower at him.

"No, really though. You should start teaching us all your secret handshakes and stuff. It might help us to not die. Or at least, to not die so quickly."

Behind Adder, Jackal was getting to his feet.

"We're not impersonating Southerners, Adder," said Sam.

"Maybe not, but the more we know about the South the better."

Jackal pulled off his hat and shook off some of the dust that had settled onto the brim, then retied his ponytail. "He's right."

Sam dragged a hand through her own hair, wishing irritably that she had an elastic. Better yet, shampoo and a bucket of water. "I know."

"We just never know what'll come in handy, you know?" said Adder.

"I know."

Jackal pulled on his hat again, and then looked down at her. "Doesn't need to be anything too personal." His grey eyes were a little too understanding.

She looked away. "Fine."

"Peachy!" said Adder. "Tonight? Storytime with Sam?"

"Not tonight," Sam said, chewing angrily the last of Adder's tuber. She was being petulant. It was counterproductive and unbecoming. She didn't care. "Later."

"See? Surly." Adder popped the last of the tree nuts into his mouth and then stood up and surveyed the sky. He pulled absently at his black hair until it stuck out from his head in half-hearted spikes. "At least it won't rain on us tonight."

"It'll be a while until we see rain again," called Dash from where he stood sentinel.

"How long?" asked Jackal, looking up as well, his lips tight.

Dash didn't take his eyes off the horizon. "Until we walk north again."

Skye looked up, a bit of spark reigniting in her tired, swollen face. "Should we dance for rain? I have a song—"

"Pray to your northern gods if it makes you happy." Dash frowned. "But I don't think they'll hear you here."

"What I hear, there's still some water in the waste, if you can find it. If not..." Jackal shrugged. "We can handle scarce."

"Yeah. Problem is, so can they."

"They who?" asked Adder, turning to look at Dash.

"The skags."

"Right," said Adder, looking back up at the sky. "Wait, who?"

16

The Waste

THE WIND CAME AND WENT, but the dust continued.

It was better than the polluted stink of the Barrow, Sam told herself, unconvincingly. Maybe it was. But unlike the Barrow, the rain never came to offer respite. She wanted a moment to collect herself. A moment of cleanliness. A moment to breathe.

The dust settled on their bodies like a second skin. It got into their food. It was in her throat when she spoke and her nose when she sneezed. The heat didn't help. Rivulets of sweat carved lines of grime onto their bodies until Sam felt like she was being buried within her own skin. She existed beneath the layers of dirt and ash. It was something separate, her body, as though the Waste had claimed it. She'd claim it back later, she figured.

Not the Northerners. It was darker and messier than it had been in the North, but the ritual of the toilette persisted. In their tents that night, they worked combs through their gnarled, dusty hair. Deft fingers forced braids, or ponytails. The men used Adder's knives to shave. Without the broken shards of mirror so prized in the Barrow, the process yielded unimpressive results. Eventually they gave up and took turns shaving one another. Shya, Skye, and Adder retraced the lines of black kohl that contoured their eyes. They shook out their clothes in a futile effort to beat out the dust. They used sticks to scrub at the gunk that collected on their teeth.

Sam tried to emulate them, but her efforts were half-hearted and she gave up sooner than they did. Except when it came to scraping her teeth. She took her time with that.

Sam wasn't the only one—Shale seemed to have given up, as well. But this wasn't new. Sam hadn't seen Shale take an interest in aesthetics since the solstice.

However, while appearances were, for the most part, maintained, conversation sagged. Whether the silence stemmed from collective guilt over Cassio and Charis, or fatigue, or the stress of knowing they had no real plan of attack, Sam didn't bother to speculate. All of the above, probably. The persistent throbbing of their burn marks didn't help.

And the skags?

Though a tangible threat, the probability of encountering skags was low, according to Dash. Nobody lived in the Waste, not even bandits. The skags lived north of the line, west of the People of the Phoenix, which meant Sam and her friends were unlikely to stumble across them in the middle of the desert.

Unless they followed you down.

We would have seen them. Someone would have seen them.

Sam was trying and failing to fall asleep. She shifted, trying in vain to find a comfortable position. With a sigh, she looked toward where Jackal was lying and wondered if he was asleep. If he slept, did he dream as she did?

She hoped not. She wished him rest. And peace.

You make it sound like he's dead.

He probably will be, soon. We all will.

Well, that's some lovely, positive thinking. Great visualization there.

I'm just tired.

Then sleep.

What she wanted, though, was not just sleep but dreamless sleep. Beautiful, pharmaceutically induced nothingness.

Her dreams had changed since they left the Barrow. She'd lost the narrative, and one storyline spilled into another as though there were simply too many threads for her mind to hold.

Sam usually started the night with Xenia. Fragments of moments from the solstice, but warped. Like someone had gone through Sam's memories and edited them. Made them brighter, harsher. Death permeated the moments that had been alive.

And then there was Raina. Sam had been worried at first that the other girl might simply fade away as they crossed out of the flooded city. But all of Sam's ghosts had followed her south, characters flitting in and out of her dreams until Sam didn't know what she wanted or who she was looking for.

Most nights she ended up at the Vaun compound, alone in the tunnel, watching the bolt hit Xenia's body. Over and over, she saw Xenia crumple to the floor. Sometimes it was the faceless guard who pulled the trigger. Sometimes it was Raina. Sometimes it was Sam.

Then it was Cassio sitting in a pool of blood, his sister's head in his lap. "I can't leave her," he'd say, as he had in real life. The words hit, rewound, echoed over and over. Then a grave, a ribbon, a leather choker and a silver ring.

Sometimes, closer to dawn she dreamed about Corvus. Not his death, but him. Small moments, ordinary days. Teasing moments. Tenderness. Unimportant rules he'd flaunted and the ineffective scoldings she'd given him. His arms around her at night.

One a nightmare she woke to find true, the other a fantasy she woke to find a lie. She wasn't sure which was worse. It didn't matter. She grieved both times.

With a sigh Sam rolled onto her left side, felt her knees knock together, and flipped back onto her back. Side sleeping was useless without an orthopedic leg pillow. Or at least a bunched-up blanket. Also, a mattress.

Sleeping on your back has been shown to be the best—

Oh, shut up.

17

The Waste

SAM KNEW that she should start telling the others about the South: how the government functioned and the state creed, cultural norms and expectations, the education structure. Knowledge was power. She believed that, truly she did. But she was so tired. Sam found sleeping on the ground to be a challenge even when she wasn't woken twice a night to stand sentry. She seemed to wake most mornings with a headache now.

At least you're not hungry.

It was true. The food and water, though rationed, were sufficient.

"Dot took care of it," Jackal told her when she asked.

They'd stopped for their midday meal in the shade of a blackened but strangely intact building. Well, half a building. At least it stood tall enough to cast a shadow. It wasn't the right shape for a house or a school—a storefront, perhaps. Sam wondered what they'd sold. Clothing? Cars? Bathtubs?

"The Vauns didn't pack enough?" asked Sam, her eyes on his. She was scrutinizing him. She recognized it but couldn't seem to stop. It was as though she wanted to prove Shya wrong—to find clues that Jackal felt something for Dot after all. Something beyond friendship. Some proof that this was his love story.

Maybe she wanted to sort out the narrative of their last days. Once she knew the ending she could construct the history in hindsight—work backward, collecting bits and pieces that fed into this new Dot-Jackal storyline. Because it was a grim story, without a bit of romance.

Or maybe you want to create an obstacle.

Jackal's face was impassive. "Enough for the guards. Half rations for the...the women."

"They wanted them hungry." An ugly realization poked through. "Weak."

"Seems so." He looked at his bowl, about to take a bite, and then put it down. He was imagining his sister, Sam realized. Drugged, branded, close to starvation.

"Or maybe the guards were planning to pick up more supplies on their way out of the Barrow." She tried to picture it, but could only think of the guards as she'd last seen them in the tunnels. Shot to death, their bodies facedown in the water.

"Might be."

They sat in silence a moment. Not talking. Not eating.

Distract him. "So, the group you had back in the Barrow...was Dot always the planner?"

"Dot figures out the big details." Jackal's voice was casual, but a line of tension bulged from his temple to his jaw. "Shya makes it happen."

"She's in charge of coin?"

"Yep. Don't read and write letters, but she's good with sums. And better with bargaining."

"I'm surprised Charis..." Sam let the sentence hang.

"I'd have trusted Charis with my life. But not with my xots."

They were already speaking about her in the past tense. "That's odd, isn't it?" asked Sam.

Jackal shrugged, pushing his hands down into his pockets and kicking up a cloud of ash with his boot. "Could say the same about Shale, couldn't you?"

"Maybe. I don't really know." Sam watched a bead of sweat make its way down Jackal's face. She wanted to dust him off. Not that he was any dirtier than she was. "Speaking of, I noticed a...a tension."

"With Shale and Charis?"

"Yes. Were they...I mean, did they used to be..."

"Lovers?" Jackal's broad shoulders dropped, the absurdity of the suggestion kicking his worry to the background. "Naw. I knew Charis a good long while, ever since Anna and Shya were kids. Not well, maybe, but I always saw her around, often enough that I woulda noticed Shale."

Sam nodded. Shale was not someone that you forgot easily. "Maybe before that, then?"

"Maybe. Probably not, though." Jackal paused, squinting up at the midday sky. "She's not Charis' type."

"I thought Shale was everyone's type."

Jackal grinned down at her. "Not everyone's."

Sam flushed as Dot called for the march to resume. As they packed up and started moving, someone began to sing.

It was Skye, walking alongside the cart. The melody was low and haunting—a sorrowful song, Sam thought, though she couldn't make out the words. It wasn't a language she knew.

The ground began to slope downward. They followed a makeshift path snaking down the side of a massive mound of rock. The group tightened, moving closer to the cart. The wind had picked up and sand and ash swirled up, blinding them.

It wasn't enough, the fabric over their mouths and noses. They needed goggles, face shields.

Ask for some prickly pear juice while you're at it. And a porta.

Her mind must have drifted, because it took her a moment to notice when the music shifted.

Sam squinted through the dust at the others. Dot stopped and hand signaled to Jackal to do the same.

Not a shift—an overlap. A scream, almost. But not human.

Something flashed by overhead. It was fast, too fast. Sam saw the glint of steel. A bloody shoulder. Fragments of an impossible silhouette.

"Don't suppose these are your people again, coming to check up on us?" Dot shouted through the wind at Dash as she pulled out her crossbow.

His longbow was already in his hand. "Skags," he said, his arrow trained on the hilltop above them.

Then, as quickly as it had come, the wind died and their world fell silent. Sam strained her eyes, trying to see through the dust that still floated, unhurried. One second. Two. Then she heard it again, the scream that wasn't a scream. Then chanting.

"Wait!" said Dot, crossbow pointed at the hillside though her eyes were on Dash. "We have to be sure. They might just be—"

An arrow cut through the dust, missing Dot's head by a few inches and ricocheting off the side of the cart.

"Get cover!" she shouted, just as Sam caught a clear view of one of their attackers. His head was encased in a cage of bones. It covered his hair and the sides of his cheeks and protruded forward, morphing his face into an open mouth; wider than it should have been, and longer. Swaths of red fabric shone through the bone, like a tongue pressing against teeth. More red shone from the skag's arms—blood dripping from shallow cuts. Self-inflicted, if she had to guess. It was an old intimidation tactic, used to demonstrate fearlessness. Horribly unhygienic, and dangerous, considering the lack of antibiotics in the North. Not that antibiotics were the solution—not when there weren't trained medical professionals to administer them. The world did not need more superbugs.

He stopped chanting to scream at the sky. Sam couldn't make out the words. The wind pulled his voice westward, away from them.

The beast beneath him reared up, a sharp, high screech mimicking the madness if not the sounds of the man who rode him. And suddenly the bones made sense.

Somebody grabbed her and pulled her behind the cart. Sam looked over to see Dash beside her.

"Are they, are those…horses?" Sam asked him as the others scrambled to find space behind the cart. He leaned out, chose his mark, shot once, and slid back behind the cart. "Yep." There was a shriek, and something tumbled from the cliff above them.

"I didn't think anyone…I mean, I thought they were all gone."

"Nope." Dash poked his head out and loosed a second arrow. Another shout, but whoever was hit this time managed to stay mounted.

Sam slid a knife from the sheath in her boot. Not that she could use it. The bandits were far out of range.

"What are they saying?" Adder asked as he loaded his crossbow.

Beside her Dash took another shot. "They're praying to the wind gods."

"Wind? Why the jit would anyone pray for wind?"

"My mother said they used to pray for rain," he said, nocking another arrow. "Guess they wanted a god that would answer."

Jackal had his longbow out as well, an arrow trained on one of the moving clouds of dust. Beside him, bolts flew upward from Dot and Adder's crossbows. Sam looked over at Shya and Shale, their knives sitting uselessly in their hands like hers were.

Skye, on the other hand, was still singing, her eyes closed, tears on her face as she leaned back against the side of the cart.

"Um, Skye?" Dot fired off a bolt and then ducked back down. "That's not really helping."

"I'm praying."

"But—"

"It's demons; we have to pray."

Shya looked over, her eyes wide. "Jit taow, Skye, is this what you meant when you said you saw—"

Something bounced off the top of the cart and landed at Skye's feet.

"Oh," she said, leaning over. "A present."

Sam already had the grenade in her hand. She stepped back, out of cover but needing the distance, and launched it back toward the bandits.

It detonated before she had time to hit the ground.

"Quick hands," said Adder, who looked to be the only one who'd thought to cover his ears when he dropped. He turned his head to spit out a mouthful of ash and screamed as he noticed the sharp little spike of tree stump that thrust upward scant inches from where he had faceplanted.

"Yeah," said Dot, far too loudly. "That was really good—"

Beneath the ringing in Sam's ears, something rumbled. Like a summer storm but without the release. The momentum built, intensified, spilled over. As Sam squinted up at the hill above them, a rock hit the cart. Then another.

"Move! Now!" Dash was already sprinting away from the cart.

Sam took a few steps forward, then stopped when she realized that not everyone had followed.

"Jackal!"

He had moved to the back of the cart and was trying to push it forward. When nothing happened, he tried to pull it back the way they'd come. The wheels, already half buried under sand and rock, didn't move.

Sam hesitated for a second, then raced back to the cart.

"Come on!" Sam said, grabbing his arm.

He shook her off and then reversed course and dove toward her as a boulder the size of a tire crashed down onto the dirt where he'd been standing.

"Jackal, come on!" Sam choked on a cloud of dust and broke into a coughing fit.

"I can't!"

Sam saw it again, the look she'd glimpsed in his eyes their last night in the Barrow. If their mission failed and they somehow didn't die in the process, the rest of them would go home. Jackal wouldn't. Sam knew that without a doubt. He'd howl at the wall until his sister appeared. Or they shot him down.

He struggled to his feet and ran toward the back of the cart.

This time she managed to grab and hold onto his arm. "We can fix a cart, Jackal! We're not rescuing anybody if we're dead!"

The thud of boulders landing on the roof of the cart drowned out the end of her sentence. Jackal lunged forward, but too slowly. Sam barely got her arms up in time to shield her head as a half dozen rocks rained down on her.

Jackal grabbed her by the waist, panic in his eyes, as though he expected her to fall limp into the sand.

"I'm okay." She wasn't, but she would be. Just as soon as she regained feeling in her arms and back. And stopped seeing multiple Jackals.

"Jack!" Dot was running back toward them now.

Jackal looked at the two women, then back to the cart, and Sam knew she'd won. His hand still on her waist, they half ran, half stumbled away from the cart and toward Dot.

She didn't say anything when they reached her, just looked from Sam to Jackal and then turned and ran with them back to the others.

"Sammo, you made a rockslide," said Adder when they caught up to the group.

Sam ignored him, fingers already probing her forearms, her shoulders, her back. Nothing was broken, though she'd be dark purple within a day or two. She looked to the others. Jackal had a cut on his cheek and Dot was already sporting a nasty-looking bruise on one shoulder, but overall, they looked generally intact. Bruised and dishevelled, but intact.

"Shut it, Adder," said Shya, her beautiful face flushed with anger. "It's better than being blown up."

"Well, yeah, of course," said Adder, looking taken aback. They all did, Sam realized. Shya never shouted.

She must have been terrified.

Adder held his hands up in submission as though he expected Shya to deck him, and then glanced over at Sam. "Not criticizing, Sam. But next time maybe toss the bomb away from the deadly pile of rocks, eh?"

"Then we'd still have skags shooting at us!" Shya was shaking, her hands clenching and unclenching.

"Shya..." Dot stepped toward her, but Shya spun and stalked off.

Or it's all that anger she's been bottling since we left her sister behind.

Adder looked to the others. "We'd have taken them out."

Dash snorted and turned back to watch the rockslide.

The cart had been knocked on its side and was being slowly buried under ash and rocks.

"Well," said Adder, when the dust finally settled above them. "Who wants to pick some pockets?"

Once Dot and Shya had returned and they'd ascertained that the bandits were, in fact, all dead, Dot tasked Shale and Shya with searching the bodies for usable weapons or supplies, while the rest of them got to work unburying the cart.

When Skye, who had started crying about Charis again, began naming the boulders, Dot sent her off to find water.

"We should have more than enough," said Adder, straightening up from the rock he'd been struggling to lift with Sam. He brushed a hand through his dark hair, knocking out some of the dust. "Once we dig out the cart, anyway. I mean, I suppose the canteens could have been damaged, but I doubt—"

Dot gave him a look.

"Ah, I see. Sneaky ladki." He crossed his arms over his chest and gave Dot an appreciative nod.

"Adder," said Sam, pointing to the boulder.

"What? Oh. Well, come on then."

The cart, though dinged and dented, was mostly functional, although it was now harder to pull and kept trying to lead them westward. The food, water, and supplies inside were likewise in disarray but undamaged.

Shale and Shya came back with four ancient crossbows, nine bolts, two rusty knives that looked better suited to spearing an apple than an enemy, four water canteens, and several strips of dried meat. The only ornamentals they'd pilfered were a handful of heavy metal rings, silver in colour if not made from the actual element.

"Not the richest of men," said Shya, settling gently down on a charred log beside the newly dented cart and taking a sip out of one of the canteens, her characteristic poise regained. She stopped, an odd look on her face, swallowed slowly, and coughed politely into one hand. "And that's not water."

"What about the horses?" asked Jackal.

"Dead or gone."

Sam looked at Shale, who was stuffing long strands of something into one of the supply packs.

"Horse hair," she said, with the shadow of a smile. "Thought it might come in handy."

"Ooh, we can make a fiddle!" said Adder.

"You want the rest of them skags to find us?" asked Dot, striding over.

"The—the rest of the skags?"

Shya passed the canteen to Dot. The taller girl took a big gulp and choked, spraying liquid onto the dust in front of them. "Jit taow, Shya! Warn me next time."

Shya had begun untying her dusty braid and did not reply.

"Ooh," said Adder, reaching to take the canteen from Dot. "Good find, ladies." He took a good long swig and let out an unnecessarily loud sigh of satisfaction. "Anyway, what were you saying?"

"Well." Dot stopped to cough again. "Four bandits, no bedrolls, no tents. We're too far to pop back over the line for food and a kip. Means they have a camp nearby. My guess is that if they do, they don't leave it unattended."

"You'd be right," said Dash as he and Jackal joined the group.

Dash reached into his back pocket and pulled out one of the red bandanas the bandits had worn. There were black marks on it: a skeletal smile. "They have a camp west of my people, a big one."

"Maybe they've been following us," said Adder.

"Maybe."

"Oh," said Adder, taking another sip from the canteen. "I thought you were going to disagree with me."

Dash shook his head. "They don't make anything, skags. Just take what others have." He nodded toward the cart. "They want what's in there."

"There's nothing in there," said Dot. "Nothing of worth, anyway."

"They'll take it anyway. Then they'll take us."

"So—"

"Hang on," said Adder. He tossed the canteen to Jackal, then gestured toward the bandana. "This is the identifying insignia? Not the freaky horse skeleton-helmets?"

"They don't all wear horse bones," said Dash. "Only the leaders."

"Their—oh. Goody," said Adder. "So, we didn't just kill their friends, we—"

Dash tossed the bandana onto the sand and pulled out his longbow. "We should move before they come looking for their chiefs."

18

The South

We always eat breakfast together. Not officially, of course. Officially I sit at the head table with Grand Neilem and her seconds, facing the room. Corvus sits with other P1s, our year-mates sometimes, or other protectors he has befriended. He makes friends so easily.

I envy him at mealtimes, laughing and relaxing at his table, so far from where I sit, eating in silence. All eyes and no conversation at the head table. It makes it difficult to swallow my food.

My first morning as a P5 I chewed and chewed until the juices leeched out and I was left with a gummy clump hidden in my cheek.

A silly, psychosomatic response, I told myself, and tried again at the midday meal. It was easier, then. There was more conversation at the lower tables, fewer eyes watching me. Or maybe I was over the initial nerves.

Except that breakfast began to follow a pattern. Perhaps my stomach was weaker in the morning, but I managed little more than my vitamins and some juice. I left hungry and nauseated.

At the end of my first week I woke to find a meal tray with sorghum porridge, date flakes, and prickly pear juice. Apparently, it had been easy for Corvus to convince the C2s in the kitchen that the base's newest P5 needed to consume the bulk of her breakfast in private. Of course, Corvus has lots of conviction. And charm. They even installed a box beside the door, so that the C2 who delivers it does not need to knock on our door.

I eat in uniform. Corvus is usually nude or close to nude. We talk about books, surprisingly. Corvus brings them back from the library. They cover all manner of topics—historical texts about caves in some country that is now underwater or a specific type of boat our ancestors used or animals so obscure that it is hard to believe that they ever ate and drank and mated and survived the cold season: the Amur Leopard; the Black Rhino; the Malayan Tiger; the Sumatran Elephant.

Sometimes, he starts by reciting absurd bits of trivia on the topic. Then he'll watch me look skeptical and call his facts into question. Sometimes he lies, to keep things interesting. I've told him that invented facts are not scientific and he has begun to call himself the Fake Historian.

Today is Corvus' free day. Mine too, technically, but in all the years that I have been a P5 I have never taken a day off. It seems unnecessary. The base doesn't stop running two days a week, so why should I?

My schedule has a gap in it this morning, though, so I decide to wander by Ring One. I enter through the stands, hoping to remain unnoticed.

Corvus is surrounded by cadets. They crowd him as he draws something on the floor. I see this year's C5 contest hopefuls along with a scattering of onlookers. Corvus never turns anyone away from these informal training sessions.

They break from the huddle into groups of four and begin practicing basic throws, three cadets tossing the fourth into the air, while some of the onlookers act as spotters. I can see Corvus now, though his back is toward me. A young cadet reaches up and tugs nervously on his sleeve. I can't hear the question that he is asking but the worry on his face is clear even from the stands. Corvus bends over to whisper something in the boy's ear. Something ridiculous, I assume, for the boy turns and lets out a peal of laughter.

Corvus turns to the group of cadets behind me and I catch sight of his face—the easy smile that still lingers. Something buzzes in the back of my jaw as though I have just bitten something sweet and rich and dense.

Several C1s are copying the older cadets. Corvus moves in, adjusting stances, demonstrating proper holds. He acts as their spotter, then pulls in another cadet to take his place as he checks in with the C5s.

I watch him moving back to the C1s a moment later. He jokes with one of the cadets, and I wonder for a split second what he would be like with a young child. I picture him training a bunch of round-bellied three-year-olds and the corners of my mouth twitch. It's a floating thought. Untethered and unnecessary.

Then the training masters move in. A whistle is blown. The morning's official lessons are beginning and Corvus makes his way out. To relax in Tranquility Square, perhaps.

I consider joining him—just for a moment. Just to say hello.

But there is work to be done, so I head to Grand Neilem's office.

I SPEND the day with the P4s who specialize in base strategy, leadership, and recruitment. Every quarter they report to me on any current or anticipated gaps in human or physical resources.

It is a busy day, with only a quick break for meals. It isn't until I check the calendar on my porta during the evening meal that I remember about our training session.

Even so, I arrive at Ring Two before the others, with ample time to do a light jog before the familiar figures of Elium and Lyra appear in the arena.

I cannot help frowning as I watch Elium approach. Where Corvus has filled out, becoming broader and more muscled, Elium is just as skinny as ever. I wonder if he's training at all anymore, outside of our weekly sessions.

Weekly is all we have been able to manage for the past two years, since I passed probation. As a P5 I'm expected to train with different groups of protectors throughout the week, to ensure consistency of training practices and to report any lapse in self-discipline or change in mood or attitude among the protectors. The wellness check-ups in medic are thorough, but it is always best to triangulate.

Even medics like Lyra and Elium are expected to be in combat condition. I'll have to ask Corvus to plan some additional group sessions. If necessary, I can train twice in one day. The three of them could also train without me, or bring in an additional fourth, but we have been a team since we were first-year cadets, and I am reluctant to delegate away my place within the group. Social support networks are important for mental health—the data is unequivocal. A better option would be to invite them on my and Corvus' daily jog, and end with some drills or sparring. I consider the possibility and then dismiss it immediately. I enjoy it too much, the time I spend alone with Corvus, even when it is cardio-focused. I would rather add in another training session, I decide, than give anything up.

"Good evening, Sierra," says Lyra, bouncing over and pulling me into a hug. I can tell from her toned arms and legs that she at least is finding time to train regularly, despite her busy schedule. "How are you?"

"Well, thank you," I say. Her hair has changed since the last time I saw her, the amber highlights she has chosen so subtle they look almost natural. I have been seeing more muted tones lately—I wonder if it is a new trend.

Elium's hair, which he has started wearing pulled back in a ponytail, is dark blue, as usual.

"Elium, hello. What have you found for us?" I ask, gesturing at the book.

"Oh!" He turns it over, showing me the cover. Over a vibrant red background the illustrator has painted men and women flying through the air, legs extended in impressively high kicks. "It's a late Pre-Decline take on a fighting style called Muay Thai."

"Wonderful," I say, taking the book from him to look at it more closely. We have worked our way through several of the traditional fighting styles. Muay Thai was one of our favourites, but the other texts we'd found had been limited. "Are there more combs?"

He grins and takes the book back from me, flipping to a spot halfway through. "Yes, and not just one-on-one. The author has several scenarios with multiple assailants."

"Excellent." I smile up at him. "Where did you find it?"

"It was misclassified as art, likely due to the title."

I peer at the cover again. "*The Colours of My Life in Flight*."

Lyra comes and peeks over my shoulder. "I can see why."

Elium looks at her, his face brightening as she takes the book and begins flipping through the pages. She is oblivious to his admiration. But then, she always has been.

"There's one I think would be really interesting to work on once Corvus—Where is Corvus?" Elium glances around us, then over to the door.

Corvus is late, as usual, though his schedule is the least demanding. Especially today—on his free day.

"Oh! He's probably preparing for the competition," says Elium, looking over at me.

"The competition. Of course. That's tonight." Corvus had forgotten to book it in my calendar, again. "But wait—" I look at Elium. "How did you know it was tonight? Did he solicit your assistance?"

Elium lifts up his hands in an overt display of innocence. "Only with a minor, minor detail. He did the majority of the planning."

"I'm here!" Corvus jogs over, a grin on his face. He pulls Elium into a one-armed hug, and then Lyra, before taking my hand and spinning me once, twice, and then swooping in for a kiss.

"You're late," I say, pushing him away gently.

"I am distraught with my shortcomings," he says, bowing low. "And will strive to improve."

"Oh, you will not."

Corvus winks at me. "Not if you don't believe in me. Ooh, new book." He holds out his hands and Lyra passes the textbook to him. "I hope this one has pictures."

"Tons of pictures! But go to page 81," says Elium. "These are a few multiple assailant scenarios I thought we could work on. I figured you two," he nods toward Corvus and Lyra, "could attack Sierra, since she's the—well, I mean..."

"You are a tiny human," said Corvus.

"Lyra is barely taller than me."

"Taller is taller," she says with a grin.

Elium looks apologetically at me. "To test how effective these combinations are, I thought we should go with the largest size differential."

"Which would be you, instead of Lyra," I point out.

Elium looks alarmed at the suggestion. "But I thought I could use the book to give direction...besides, Lyra is better at combat."

"Much, much better," says Lyra.

I think about pointing out that if skill and effectiveness are the overriding criteria then we should be attacking him, but think better of it. Truthfully, I want to test out the moves, and Elium wants to guide us using the textbook. There is no reason for me to disturb his plan. The base flourishes when everyone contributes.

Outside of combat, a virtuous leader encourages innovation and initiative from the lower ranked members.

"Of course," I say, ensuring that my face is pleasant. "Let's warm up with the pads first, so that we can all meet our physical goals for today's session."

Elium sighs, and places the book gently on one of the benches that lines the ring.

"Are you going to make us run too?" asks Corvus.

I turn to glare at him but he has already started off at a jog. "Catch me, friends!"

The first few scenarios are simple; minor variations of combinations we have previously mastered. Only the final scenario presents a challenge.

Elium positions Lyra and Corvus on either side of me, an equal distance apart. "All the previous combinations," explains Elium, "assumed that the two assailants would attack in sequence." He grabs a full-body pad and passes it to Corvus, and brings a smaller kick-pad to Lyra. "The author here suggests a forward reverse attack. It requires a very strong push kick against one assailant," he points at Corvus, "using the momentum from the push kick to attack the second assailant," he gestures toward Lyra, "with a swing kick."

I raise my eyebrows and glance at Lyra and Corvus.

Elium notices our skeptical expressions. "Problematic?"

It's an odd combination of moves, one I doubt will be effective. I look over at Corvus and Lyra and can see that they're thinking the same thing. But we also know that it's a poor use of time to discuss hypothetical obstacles during training.

"Count it down, please," I say to Elium.

Corvus and Lyra sprint toward me from opposite directions. I ready my push kick—and get knocked to the ground by Corvus.

"Hmm," says Elium, frowning down at his book while Corvus and Lyra help me up.

"Maybe try it without the running start," says Lyra.

"But the book—"

"Come on, El," says Lyra. "If he was running full speed we'd do a bailout kick."

"Well..."

"Or we'd move off line to disrupt their momentum."

"Or we'd just shoot them," says Corvus.

"Let's try Elium's move," I say, shaking out my trampled limbs. "With a shorter timeline." I point to a spot five feet away from me. "Take it from there, Cor."

This time the push kick is smooth. But as quick as I am, I only seem to be able to catch Lyra with the swing kick once in every four or five attempts.

"I think—I think this combo is still problematic," said Elium, looking with a puzzled expression at the book.

I lean over into a stretch, gulping air and watching my sweat drip onto the training room floor. "Agreed."

"Are we missing something?" asks Corvus.

Elium shakes his head. "No, no we're following the author's instructions."

"And these...these were tested combinations?" I ask, accepting water from Corvus. I take a small sip and try to slow my frantic breathing.

"Oh!" Elium begins flipping through the pages. "Actually, I'm not certain. It simply says that these are Muay Thai inspired." He lets out a low whistle. "You should see the illustrations at the back."

"Maybe it is an art book after all." Corvus takes the water back from me and sets it on the bench.

"Why don't we just do a bailout kick?" asks Lyra.

"Because we always do bailout kicks," says Corvus. "Also, I still don't see why we wouldn't just use a weapon. Hey El, is there a weapon that can shoot in two directions at once?"

"What if we needed to be silent?" asks Lyra. "Or our weapons have been lost or damaged?"

"A sneaky weapon, then."

"And why can't you just deploy two weapons at the same time?" asks Lyra. "Or in close succession?"

Corvus wiggles his fingers at Lyra. "Maybe you only have one hand free."

"This—this isn't the point of the exercise," says Elium with a slight frown on his long, angular face. "Aren't we supposed to be broadening our repertoire of hand-to-hand combos?"

Lyra laughs. "Oh, you just want to follow the book because it's a book."

"I—well..."

"Your book has inspired innovation." Corvus looks at me. "You love innovation," he whispers loudly.

"A covert weapon that fires in two directions simultaneous does actually sound interesting," says Lyra. "I'll pop by Tarik's tonight."

"Oh, it's not urgent," I say, beginning my cooldown stretches. "You can speak with weapons engineering in the morning. Or I can, if you like." I sit down and reach forward to grab my toes.

"Oh, well..." Lyra tries and fails to hide a grin.

"Oh." I lift my head up and look at her. "Never mind."

"Are you propositioning P3 Tarik?" asks Corvus, kneeling in front of me. He applies counterpressure as I stretch my toes forward, backward, then to each side. "I like her."

So do I. "She's very energetic," I say. "I'm sure she'll make for an enthusiastic sexual partner."

"That's what I'm hoping for." Lyra looks up at the clock. "I had better get going then. Thanks for the training session!" She smiles at me and Corvus and then waves at Elium, who pastes on a smile and waves back.

As she turns and jogs for the exit, Elium's smile starts to fade. I look away, but not before I catch sight of his face. He looks crestfallen, as he does every time Lyra begins a romantic relationship.

Corvus catches my eye. I shrug and then signal that he may as well proceed.

"Are you ever going to proposition Lyra?" asks Corvus.

His tone of voice is excellent—empathetic, understanding. There is no hint of judgment or impatience. If Elium has need of emotional support, I'm certain he will have no qualms in sharing his feelings with Corvus.

"I think—I think I will not," says Elium, after a moment. His expression shifts into something more neutral. "Thank you for...for indulging me," he says, gesturing toward the book. "Enjoy your competition. I look forward to our next session."

I watch him leave, wishing I could inspire him to act on his feelings as he once convinced me to act on mine. I want to, but I am not sure how to proceed. He has entered into several relationship contracts over the years—why is it so difficult for him to broach the topic with Lyra?

"Well," says Corvus, once we're alone. "Are you ready to lose?"

As USUAL, I dawdle in the bathroom after showering to ensure that he has ample time to set up. Out of boredom I pull out my supply of cosmetics. We are expected to follow aesthetic trends—it promotes unity. But I can't seem to remember if this month's hero and heroine had gold eyelashes or silver. I read the state fiction when it came out —I always do—but this last story was particularly formulaic and unmemorable.

What cosmetics were Lyra and Elium wearing? I close my eyes and try to focus on their faces, but it's no use. Other than a general sense of shine and glitter, I cannot bring the details to mind.

It doesn't matter, anyway. Only Corvus will see me. And he uses off-trend cosmetics intentionally.

In the end I paint one set of eyelashes silver, the other gold. Then I pour too much glitter in my hair. In an effort to reduce it to an appropriate amount, I hang my head upside down and vigorously rub my scalp with my hands. When I look at myself in the mirror afterward I find that I have only succeeded in redistributing the glitter from my hair to my skin and clothes. I check the floor and realize that it, too, is now sparkly.

"So, I present to you—oh—" Corvus stops and cocks his head at me. "What a shiny face you have." He peers past me toward the bathroom. "Should we make glitter clean-up a bonus penalty to tonight's loser?"

I cross my arms. "This is why I don't bother with cosmetics. They are unnecessary and time consuming."

"Isn't that the point?" Corvus asks, passing me a glass. "And is that a yes?"

"Of course." I have no intention of losing, after all.

He picks up a long, skinny bottle and pops the top. It fizzes over as he fills first my cup then his own. "For tonight's refreshment I give you...lemon kombucha."

"Lemon?" I saw the pair of lemons at the outpost earlier this week, perfect yellow ovals sent directly from Ankev. Twice in one year—they must be making progress with the rust-resistant varieties. "How could you afford a lemon?" Corvus typically operates at a deficit.

"Well," says Corvus, "it turns out that I'm not the only one interested in citrus..."

"Did you convince the kitchen master to incorporate lemon into this week's flavour profile for your own personal gain?"

"It's not about flavour, Sierra, it's a nutrition-based experiment: we're investigating Vitamin C retention in fermented products."

I frown at him. "When you say experiment..."

"Oh, well..." Finally, he has the decency to look sheepish. "We each have to submit a urine sample. But the lemon was free! Come on, Sie. Try it."

Before I can argue with him, he links his arm through mine and tips his glass toward my mouth. The fizzy kombucha hits my tongue and it is sweet and tart and unbelievably delicious.

I purse my mouth at him, but he's grinning at me now.

"A delicious beverage and a contribution to science; what more could you want?"

As usual, Corvus has laid down a blanket on the floor. I sit cross legged and watch as he sets up the projection.

"For music, I have borrowed two options from the library. Would you prefer Mendelssohn—"

"Op. 44?"

"20."

"Hmm." I like Mendelssohn. "What is the second option?"

"Chopin."

"Polonaises?"

"Of course."

I take a small sip of my drink and consider it. "I would like Op. 20 tonight, please."

"Excellent choice," he says, as the sounds of a string octet fill the room. "For video, would you like the accompanying live performance or a nature gallery?"

I look up at Corvus, standing there with a goofy grin on his face, and there is a tightness in my chest that makes me want to preserve this moment. "Nature gallery, please."

The image of an enormous, moss-covered tree flashes against the back wall. Then a bird, bright and fat and feathered.

Corvus plugs in our tiny diffuser. A moment later the smell of sweet orange fills the room.

I close my eyes and inhale slowly. It feels like the first true breath I have taken all day.

With my eyes still closed I hear him pulling the slate out of the bookcase and propping it up on the desk. He isn't careful enough with how he positions it and it falls, once, with a resounding crash, before he corrects it.

This too is part of our ritual, though, so I am braced for it.

It isn't until he sits down across from me, a white box on his lap, that I look over at the slate: one hundred twenty-two for Corvus; one hundred twenty-three for me.

"What did you borrow today, Cor?"

"It's a building game," he explains, laying down the pieces. "Whoever builds the biggest city wins."

"Modern or Pre-Decline?"

He picks up the box, flipping it around until the standard, white label is visible. "It gives a range: PD-20 to PD-50."

The only other information is a white piece of paper with a list of instructions.

I watch him as he reads through the information, once then twice. I'm still amazed at how uncharacteristically fastidious he can be when it comes to these games. Almost as amazed as I am by how much time and effort he puts into our evenings together.

After the first competition I offered to organize the subsequent one, but Corvus refused. I was busier than he was, he insisted. My contribution would be to show up and play.

He wins tonight, tying our scores at one hundred twenty-three. But I don't mind. I'll pull ahead again soon. By this point I'm used to winning.

19

The South

I STAND outside Grand Neilem's office the next day, waiting to be called. In all the years that I have worked under her, I have never once tried to gain entry on my own. I might have authorization—after all, the inscription on the door does not say "Grand Neilem" or even "Base Grand." It is simply the number five.

I trace the number five with my eyes—once, twice, three times. I am a full-fledged P5. I am one of Grand Neilem's seconds. There is no difference in ranking between myself and Protector Jace or Protector Onyx.

So why do I still feel like I'm on probation?

"Sierra, come in." P5 Jace doesn't quite smile—but his manner is at least pleasant.

"Thank you, Protector Jace." I step past him into the room.

"Hello Grand Neilem, Protector Onyx."

Protector Onyx nods at me, but as usual says nothing. I have long since stopped thinking of him as a person. He is the stone lion that guards the Grand.

"Welcome, Sierra. Please have a seat." Grand Neilem is cordial, but nothing more. It's fine. I stopped expecting to connect with her long ago. Despite my rank I am outside the inner circle—I expect I always will be.

"Thank you, Grand Neilem." I still have to fight the urge to make the sign for deference when I see her. It is unnecessary between P5s, I have been told. The only pretense of equality that exists among the four of us.

Of course it's not equal. Why would it be equal? She's the grand, and they each have twenty years of experience on you. Their value surpasses yours in every way.

Protectors Onyx and Jace leave shortly. For an inspection, perhaps, or a meeting. They don't share this type of information with me. Grand Neilem remains, sitting behind her desk, scrolling through something on her porta.

A small section has been set up for me along the back wall between a set of cabinets. I place my porta on the desk and walk quietly to the drink tray beside the door for a glass of water. As I cross the plush carpet, movement catches my eye outside one of the windows.

For a moment I wonder if the screen function has been activated. The scene in front of me makes no sense: two men in ragged clothing with long, unkempt hair, leading a brown metal box on wheels. It is out of place, like something from a historical film.

My body tenses, feeling the call to action. "Grand Neilem, there are men approaching the wall."

"Not to worry, Sierra." The Grand doesn't look up from her porta. "Protectors Jace and Onyx are handling the situation."

"I—they are—"

"Handling it, yes. Please continue with your morning's work. I believe you are processing this year's C1 recruits."

She smiles as she speaks, though her eyes are cold. I relax my hands, which have clenched into fists, and wipe the incredulity from my face. I have forgotten my place.

"Of course, Grand Neilem." I remember that I wanted water and walk over to the tray. I change my mind and pour a glass of prickly pear juice.

I wish I could re-do the exchange. It could have been more professional.

Let it go. Focus on the task at hand.

The recruitment cannot be processed by porta. Like most confidential documents the reports may only be accessed from the computers in Grand Neilem's office.

I choose the large screen above my desk, leaning forward for the retinal scan, and the report opens. The C1 potentials are listed by age. I swipe to see their test scores—academic, martial, and medical. Qualitative reports from Protector Nem and the other instructors are featured as well, along with their recommendations for continuation or redistribution. None of this is new information—I have spoken with each of the instructors at length. There are videos as well, though I have already reviewed them.

Most of the C1 potentials will remain at this base. Only three of them—two male, one female—will be leaving the base tonight. I sign off on the decision, staring at the photograph of the girl. She has light green eyes and a small, pointed chin. A kind child, from what I saw. Her understanding of teamwork made me hopeful initially, but her athletic performance was weak and her academic scores were only average. And Protector Nem caught her speaking with the other recruits on two occasions. There is no place at this base for soldiers who cannot follow orders.

I process her redistribution, along with the others, wondering why I am bothered by it. She will be placed in an environment better suited to her personal development.

Where? Another base?

I frown, wondering where the thought came from. My job is recruitment for this base—the redistribution itself is not my concern.

It would be illogical to send her to another base. If she is not suited to be a cadet here, she is not suited to be a cadet anywhere.

She might respond better to a different cohort and different instructors.

But teamwork was her strength, not her weakness.

Another sector then.

There are other sectors, of course. Seira is large but even so, there is only room for so many bases along the wall and so many protectors to patrol it. I know that some Seirans work in agricultural development and manufacturing, though what exactly they do is unclear. I imagine that they develop and test new technologies or supervise the artificial intelligence, though this is speculation only.

I look at the girl's small face and hope that one of these sectors is a better fit for her. It's an odd feeling and I hurry to close the report.

I am reviewing a resource request from engineering when Protectors Jace and Onyx return.

They speak with Grand Neilem in low voices while I focus on the resource request and try not to strain my ears. If they wanted me to be privy to their conversation they would have invited me to join them.

I draft my list of follow-up questions for engineering and then stare at the calendar on my porta until it is time for my weekly status update with Grand Neilem.

I join the others at the main desk, sitting across from the Grand. Protectors Jace and Onyx flank her, as usual, portas in hand to record any action points.

It is the same routine every week. I spend most of my time observing the other teams, serving as Grand Neilem's eyes within the base. Mostly I interact with the P4s in strategy and leadership, the P3s in weapons engineering, the P2 training masters and professors, and the P2s charged with sports and culture; however I also spend one day a week with the P2 unit commanders, observing the training of new P1s, and twice a month I meet with P3 Protector Zaphyr, the head of the medical ward and medical training.

I used to think that after I completed my apprenticeship I would spend more time in meetings with the P5, perhaps shadowing Grand Neilem or learning more about how her seconds support her.

Of course, with Protectors Jace and Onyx in good mental and physical condition; they have no need for me yet. I am a spare, nothing more.

Not that I mind spending time away from the P5s. I have excellent working relations with the other teams. Considering the frigidity of

Grand Neilem and Protector Onyx toward me, I can honestly say that I enjoy my time with the other teams more. But I feel at times that there is more that I could be doing.

I have already sent electronic notes, but I walk through the details of the week's observations with Grand Neilem, sifting through the mundane for information that she might find useful or interesting. I talk about the new long-range micro-missile that is being piloted, one that utilizes heat-based targeting to improve accuracy. Next, I update her on the C1 recruitment, and am just starting to discuss the upcoming base qualifiers when the lights dim and the screens that line the walls flash to life. All of them.

Grand Neilem's head snaps up, and she rises to her feet. To my surprise, she raises her arms and presses her hands together in front of her face. Protectors Jace and Onyx do the same.

I jump to my feet, following them in the sign for deference. For a P5, there is only one body that demands this sign of respect.

Five faces appear—one per screen, repeated until their faces fill all two dozen screens. A pattern of faces.

I feel my heart begin to pound. These are not the delegates or junior delegates that sometimes visit the base, or even the committee members they serve—we have been called into a meeting with Seira's council. The leaders of the Administration.

I know them all, of course. The council members appear regularly in national broadcasts. One of them I even met in person, back in my first year as a cadet. My eyes are drawn to one of his images now.

Seira's Chief Medical Officer is a few years shy of fifty. I know this because I have read his career summary recently. His, and all of the council members'. Councilman Naru is handsome still, with black hair that he wears short and oiled. A closely trimmed black beard lines a square jaw. He is the most charismatic of the council members, with an easy confidence that makes him seem almost approachable. On screen, anyway. Face to face, the power of his person is overwhelming. It isn't negative energy—only intense—but I remember feeling as though he had pulled all the oxygen from the room. When Councilhead Aries retires as councilhead, I suspect it will be Councilman Naru who takes his place.

In his late seventies, Councilhead Aries is the oldest member of the council, though Councilwoman Cyrus is only a few years his junior. They both streak their hair with lines of gold instead of hiding the grey, though this is the only visible sign of aging they permit—they have had their wrinkles removed, of course.

Councilwoman Cyrus and Councilhead Aries have other physical similarities—they are both tall and thin, though the councilhead has pale skin and light blue eyes, while Councilwoman Cyrus has dark skin and the hair on her head that is neither grey nor gold remains a deep, inky black.

Next in age comes Councilman Xander, who is in his late sixties and sports a long, dark blue ponytail. I have a feeling that he expects that he will be chosen as the next Councilhead—he has voted in support of Councilhead Aries' proposals for the entirety of his career.

I always group the three of them together—Councilhead Aries, Councilwoman Cyrus, and Councilman Xander. Because of their age, perhaps, or because of the quiet warmth they exude. Councilhead Aries in particular has a very relaxed manner; he is almost jovial. Councilwoman Cyrus, always serene, is dignified, and unhurried and graceful. I enjoy listening to her speak. Councilman Xander is the quietest, but seems kind. I feel calmer when they speak.

I doubt anyone feels calmer when Councilman Naru speaks.

I catch movement out of the corner of my eye and turn my head to glance at one of the screens displaying Councilwoman Myrrsa. Though her eyes are fixated now on Grand Neilem, I cannot shake the odd suspicion that she had been watching me. It is a fanciful thought. I should not be thinking it.

I turn away before I am caught staring, hiding my face behind my hands, which remain pressed together in front of my eyes. But almost immediately I find my eyes drifting to another of Councilwoman Myrrsa's screen images.

The fifth member of the council, Councilwoman Myrrsa, is more difficult to read. She is beautiful, with long black hair and amber eyes. Her light brown skin remains unmarked—I doubt she has even had it corrected. But then, she is the youngest member of the council at only forty-four. She doesn't speak very often—and even when she does, it is almost impossible to guess at her personal opinion. She remains a mystery.

Both her and Councilman Naru were elected to the council by the age of twenty—which means that the council itself has remained unchanged since I was born.

From behind my hands I scan the faces again—one, two, three, four, five. Repeat once, twice, thrice, four times, almost five. A fraction of five.

"Grand Neilem. Protectors." It is Councilhead Aries speaking.

At the acknowledgement, Grand Neilem and her seconds lower their hands, though they remain standing. I follow suit, wiping my hands as discreetly as I can against my pant legs. Even with a screen and hundreds of miles between us, the perceived proximity of the council members has me perspiring.

"Sorry to trouble you unexpectedly, but we have a code I7."

I can feel the tension in the room thicken.

Code I7. I know this.

It is treason.

Two of the screens turn black, images of Councilwoman Myrrsa and Councilman Naru replaced by a man and a woman I do not recognize.

The woman has pale skin and green hair. She appears to be around fifty years old. The man is younger, maybe thirty. His skin is dark and his closely cropped black curls have been dusted with pink.

Something is off about them. Something physical. They look healthy enough, of course, but they lack the muscle tone I am used to seeing on protectors. Are they medics, perhaps? Or professors?

"Unfortunately," continues Councilhead Aries, "it involves two committee members, making this a crime not only against Seira, but also against the council itself."

Committee members.

I stare at their faces again, memorizing the lines, the colours.

The one hundred women and men that serve on the committee report directly to the council. They are tasked with carrying out the orders of the councilhead and the council members, and charged with preservation of Seiran virtues.

The Administration depends on the committee members to thrive, just as the committee members depend on the delegates and junior delegates that serve the committee. The council leads, but they could do little without committee members to carry out their orders.

Treason is a horrific charge. Treason among committee members...it is unthinkable.

My eyes sneak over to Grand Neilem, to see how she is responding. The shock I feel seems to be mine alone—there is something in Grand's face that tells me that this, or something similar, has happened before. I glance at Protectors Jace and Onyx. Impassive as always. I can read nothing.

"We have intelligence that they may be moving through your territory—a stolen Lacewing, abandoned as it began to lose power, has been spotted northeast of your base."

I look now to the other council members. Councilhead Aries looks grim and calm, but I detect a hint of worry, panic almost, bubbling behind Councilman Xander and Councilwoman Cyrus's eyes. Only Councilman Naru seems relaxed, though Councilwoman Myrrsa, as always, is as stone. Her face is even more impenetrable than Protector Jace or Protector Onyx's.

"It is of utmost importance that they are apprehended."

"Of course, Councilhead," says Grand Neilem, speaking at last. "We will deploy every P1 excluding the standard skeleton crew that is required to defend the base."

"With due respect for protocol," Councilwoman Cyrus says, speaking in her quiet, clipped voice, "kindly deploy every fifth-year cadet that is competent, as well."

Grand Neilem's shock is visible. I expect mine is too.

"I—yes, of course." Her throat moves, as though she is swallowing her objection.

I have never heard of an instance where undesignated cadets were deployed north of the border. This must be a true state of emergency.

"Although—will we not—"

"Higher-ranked protectors as well," interrupts Councilman Xander. "As many as can be spared. Exclude only medics and weapons engineers."

"And you must remain at the base, of course," says Councilhead Aries. "But your seconds will take command in the field."

"Of course, Councilhead," says Grand Neilem. "Although, I wonder at the necessity. Our drones will detect—"

"They won't," says Councilwoman Cyrus. "Not this time. The two committee members will need to be tracked manually—on foot, and through aerial means."

Grand Neilem nods, though this too seems to elicit surprise. "Yes, Councilwoman. And our orders, upon sighting?"

"We want them stunned," says Councilwoman Cyrus. "If they elude you past 2100 hours, however, you will need to seal the line."

"Seal the—of course, Councilwoman."

"Oh, and one more thing," says Councilhead Aries, speaking pleasantly, as though ordering a luncheon rather than writing an execution. "Under no circumstance is any cadet or protector to speak with or approach the targets. Upon confirming a visual they are to fire a blue flare. Should they succeed in stunning one or both of the targets, they are to deploy a green flare. A special task force will be on standby for extraction."

"Understood, Councilhead."

He nods and smiles, his relaxed demeanor a stark contrast with the tension emanating from Councilman Xander and Councilwoman Cyrus.

It seems personal.

They are the council. Treason IS personal for them.

Is that it? Or is there something—

"I know you won't let us down." The screens cut out before the audio, leaving the councilhead's words to resonate in a suddenly dark room.

20

The South

Events advance at an alarmingly rapid pace. We are prepared for this, of course. Beyond the P1s, who exist within units led by P2s, select training masters, professors, even strategists belong to an emergency response unit.

Each unit reports to either Protector Jace or Protector Onyx. Grand Neilem calls the P2 unit commanders and P4 strategists together. I stand at attention in this room of women and men, most of them decades my senior, and await instructions.

"Your seconds will take command in the field," the councilhead had said. He used the word "will", not "may". It was an order.

I will get my chance.

It comes at the end of the meeting—an afterthought. It's not a full unit, only four dozen protectors, but they are mine to command.

Protectors Jace and Onyx are leading mass coverage with full visibility. In the off chance that the aerial sweeps drive the traitors eastward, I am to lead my units to the easternmost point as quickly as possible and then melt into the background, moving north. The stealth unit, Grand Neilem calls us.

We'll be taking the blades, of course. Slim, electric, and fast, the blades are ideal for aerial transport at extreme low altitude.

I push down my excitement. It would be unbecoming. I try for grim, and then catch sight of myself in the reflection of a darkened screen: I look as though I am about to be sick. *Not grim, then. Just try to look competent and prepared.*

And we are prepared. We have trained and trained with no real opportunity to test ourselves. Contests, after all, are for entertainment. This is real.

When I arrive at the launch strip I find cadets running back and forth with equipment and supplies, while protectors—my protectors—ready themselves for departure. The excitement in the air is palpable.

"So, ready to catch a fish?" Corvus grins at me, no attempt at professionalism.

"I think you've got that phrase wrong," I say, grabbing the meal replacement bar he passes me, unwrapping it, and taking a small bite.

"You wound me," he says, pressing a hand to his broad chest. "I know my history, Sie. People used to catch fish. Elium showed me pictures."

I swallow too quickly and choke a bit. Corvus hands me his water flask. "Yes," I say once I can speak again. "But I don't think it was a hunt the way you're thinking of it."

A C5 appears with my equipment, including two long-range stunners and a set of flares.

"Thank you," I say, taking the stunners and sliding them into the built-in straps on my pant legs. The flares I tuck into the side pouch of the small pack she hands me. The helmet she has brought me is sleeker than the ones I last trained in and lighter—I wonder what material they ended up using. I slip it on and swipe the air to test out the holodisplay, and quickly scan the new options. It looks as though they have managed to incorporate all of my requests. I lower the face shield for just a moment, to ensure functionality, before retracting it again.

Inside the pack she has brought me I find two large flasks of water, three more meal replacement bars, sun-saving lotion, remote-activated light spheres and knockout bombs, and medical glue. I look over at the cadet, standing at attention now that her hands are empty. She stares from me to the blades, back to me again.

And the cadets? Do they feel prepared?

"Are you in my unit?" I ask her.

"No, Protector Sierra. I will be serving under Protector Jace." The words tumble out, rushed. She is anxious. "Do you have everything you need, Protector?"

"Yes, thank you. You may return to your unit."

She turns and runs full speed for the door.

Corvus whistles. "Lucky us."

I glance around and am relieved to find that only full-fledged protectors remain in the room. No cadets, no trainees.

"I am sure she will be a credit to her unit."

He raises both eyebrows. "Can you imagine us at that age?"

"Don't start. It was an order given by the councilhead himself." The earpiece on my helmet hums to life. I wave Corvus away and unmute the microphone.

"Sierra here."

"Unit present and equipped?"

"Yes, Grand Neilem."

"Good. You have permission to deploy."

"Thank you, Grand Neilem. We will be out of the base in T minus 3 minutes."

"And Sierra?"

"Yes, Grand Neilem?"

"We do not want to seal the line."

"Understood, Grand Neilem."

I mute the microphone and turn to find Corvus watching me. I am opening my mouth to relay the information when he grabs me by the belt and pulls me in for a kiss.

I allow it. But only for a second, and then I push him back.

"What do I always say about romantic gestures in public?"

"Um, do it often, it improves morale?"

I turn away, but not quickly enough to hide the smile that has wormed its way to the surface.

"Protectors." I do not have to speak loudly. As soon as I turn to the group there is silence. Every protector stands at attention, helmets on, weapons stowed.

"It's a standard two-directional sweep. We'll be flying east to start. When I give the command to break, the first eight blades will move north: four in a slow sweep, the other four accelerating to a designated midpoint and beginning a slow sweep from there. The last four blades will move northeast in an expanding U-shape, and again half of these will start their sweep immediately, half will accelerate to the specified coordinates and sweep north from there.

"Each blade will carry four protectors—two teams of two. One team will drop to the ground, while the remaining two protectors will stay in the blade—aerial but low. The mission is stealth over speed. Pilots, use haste to hit marks one and two, but move north *slowly*. Your heat sensors will not be helpful. Use your eyes. We have a lot of ground to cover.

"Ground teams—you will set off a blue flare upon sighting the targets, a green flare to signify that you have successfully stunned them. Decide now within each team of two who is responsible for the flares and who will be on comms. Relay of the events as they unfold is mandatory, so that I may redirect reinforcements as necessary. Do not approach the targets, do not speak with them. This is a direct order from the councilhead. Questions? Good. Let's go."

I turn to see Corvus watching me with a troubling look in his eyes.

"What?" I ask, checking my equipment one last time. I turn on the secondary channel. "Test. Number off as soon as both teams of two are on the assigned blade and ready for take-off."

"I know you're going to say we shouldn't hope for action, but Sie, active command looks good on you."

I mute my mouthpiece. "You're incorrigible."

"Yes. You want to fly with me?"

"Fine."

CORVUS IS A VERY SKILLED PILOT, probably because flying is one of those rare non-athletics-based activities that he has decided is worth learning. Irritatingly, he also seems to have a natural knack for it, which has led him to master it in an absurdly short time.

The truth, though, is that mastery is not necessary to operate the blades. Most protectors could safely fly one after a short demonstration.

Along with being fast and silent, what makes the blade so incredible is the incorporation of echolocation technology. You cannot crash a blade—the plane's software commands this function. With no opportunity for human involvement the Administration has sensibly eradicated the possibility of human error.

Where a pilot such as Corvus makes a difference is in terms of speed. Echolocation has successfully improved usability and reduced risk, but the usage causes a lag. It's minor, but with a truly skilled pilot the plane's command function activates less frequently, and the overall speed can increase two, even threefold.

I buckle myself into a seat in the back and press my thumb into the oval-shaped button on the side of my helmet.

A map of the area lights up the air in front of me: the red outline of the blades, the green dots representing the protectors in my unit. Other units are visible, but displayed in a soft, semi-translucent grey. Visually muted so as not to be a distraction, I assume, but present so that I can see if anyone under my command starts to cross into Protector Jace's section.

I drag three fingers in a downward motion and the map shifts. The vital signs for each member of my unit appear, the data transmitted from sensory pads in their uniforms to my holodisplay in real time.

P5 equipment has its perks.

"On my command."

I count down departure for each blade. Though we are the last to leave the base, we have soon pulled too far ahead. "Slow down, Cor."

I ignore the overdramatic sigh from the front of the blade and keep my eyes on the holodisplay. I watch the small red symbols representing the blades move eastward, giving the occasional command to other pilots to increase or decrease speed.

"Unit break in T minus one minute." I wait, my eyes on the holodisplay, until everyone is in position. "On my count, protectors: three, two, one."

The first eight blades turn north. The rest of us shift direction until we are flying northeast. "Blades 1, 2, 3, and 4, slow. Ground teams prepare to drop." I count it down for them and watch as two green dots fall from each of the four blades.

I check the coordinates for the blades flying northeast. "Blades 9 and 10, slow. Ground teams prepare to drop." I wait for a moment, watching the coordinates on the holodisplay. "On my count, ground teams: three, two, one."

Two more sets of green dots separate from their blades. I drag three fingers downward and check the vital signs for all protectors on the ground. All normal.

I mute my microphone and notice Corvus passing the controls over to one of the other protectors.

"What are you doing?" I ask, fastening a fuel pack to my waist.

Corvus grins and grabs the other fuel pack. "Figured you'd want to be on the ground."

"You're the best flyer. You should stay with the blade. Hold on." I open the holodisplay and check the coordinates for the teams still flying at full speed. I wait one minute, two—then open the back hatch. Sand and sparse desert trees and shrubs fly past our eyes.

"I should stay with you!" Corvus says, shouting to be heard over the sound of the wind.

"Quietly," I mouth to him. "This is a stealth mission."

"What?" he shouts back.

I scowl at him and signal to the other two protectors that they are to remain with the blade.

I check my holodisplay again, then unmute my microphone. "Blades 5, 6, 7, and 8, prepare to slow. Ground teams ready to drop." I pull up the coordinates and watch as they approach the midpoint. "On my count, protectors: three, two, one."

Now it's our turn. "Blades 11 and 12, prepare to slow. Ground teams ready to drop." I wait, my eyes on the holodisplay as we approach our destination. "On my count." I turn off the holodisplay. "Three, two, one."

I mute my mic and jump.

We freefall, hurtling toward the ground for an exhilarating second until the fuel packs activate, exactly one foot from the ground.

"So wasteful." Corvus stretches out, hovering just inches above the sand. "But so effective."

I cut the power and fall to the ground. "Fuel, used responsibly for rare and necessary occasions—"

"—is not the enemy, but lack of individual ownership for the preservation of common resources."

I glare at him, and he floats toward me until our faces touch. I lift my head up for the kiss, breathing him in. One breath, that's all I allow myself. Then I roll to the side and jump to my feet, activating the holodisplay.

"Time to go," I say, examining the distribution of the twelve blades and the twenty-four protectors on the ground. I unmute my microphone and narrow my connection.

"Blade 3 ground team—advance two miles east before moving north."

"Understood, Protector Sierra."

Corvus and I set off at a comfortable pace. We have nine hours, according to the council's timeline. It would be unwise to burn through our physical resources too early.

I look down at the sand. It is different here; lighter both in colour and consistency. Grey-beige particles, disturbed by our feet, float upward and I wonder if it's even sand at all. It looks greasy and toxic. Another danger of the North.

Not that we're in the North, technically. This is Seiran-patrolled land. It is just that usually it is drones that do the patrolling, not us.

I try to remind myself of the hazards that exist here, beyond the wall, but the sun is shining and my partner is beside me, and it just feels like a beautiful day.

"You know," Corvus says, glancing over at me after several

minutes. "I was just thinking how sad it would be if we didn't have a chance to go for our daily run together."

"You should be grateful I make you run."

He waves lazily at me in response.

"You wouldn't have the stamina to spar if you didn't."

"Sure I would."

"Okay, perhaps you could spar for the duration of the match. But what if poor cardio cost you the victory?"

It's an old argument. Luckily, what Corvus lacks in ambition he makes up for with untethered competitiveness. If it is a game, he wants to win. His career, though...this is a matter that has never concerned him.

I check the holodisplay every fifteen minutes. The teams relay status every twenty.

We keep running. There are more trees here, though they remain small, and long grasses that graze the tops of our boots. The land shifts, climbs, opens. And then I see it. The grey expanse. It takes over half the sky and I don't know if I have ever seen anything so beautiful before. Even though I know that if we were closer we'd see through the shine to the grease that leaches onto the shore. Would the white surf bring the skeletons of mutated sea creatures? I'm not certain. Perhaps the chemicals have chewed through the bones by now. Perhaps there is nothing to see but dirty water. But we're not close. And though the sea is toxic and filled with death, at this distance it's unblemished. And unparalleled.

Remember your orders. I replay the councilhead's words in my head. *Think of the danger the targets must represent. To Seira. To those of us seeking to apprehend them.*

This is not a test.

This is a mission.

This is combat.

But this morning's urgent meeting feels very far away right now. I am north of the wall watching the sunlight sparkle on the eastern ocean, with my own unit to lead, and with Corvus beside me. I could blame this giddiness on the overload of Vitamin D, but it would be a lie. We are covered head to toe in long- and short-wave ultraviolet blocking fabric, so cholecalciferol can hardly be considered a key factor.

I call for a short rest after one hour has passed, and a meal break two hours later.

Eventually the sun begins to lower in the sky, though the temperature remains hot. I am starting to tire, and I can see the steps per minute decreasing among all ground teams. I call for another break.

Corvus walks across the scraggly, beige grass to a tall, multi-limbed cactus, retracting the face shield on his standard-issue helmet as he does so.

"Look, Sierra, it's like you. Succulent. And dangerous."

"You're not funny."

He plucks a white flower and brings it to me. "I'm kind of funny."

"We're not supposed to disturb the native flora," I say, though I accept the flower and raise my face shield to look at it more closely. It is surreal to think that something this intricate was created without human assistance.

We are forbidden from bringing organic materials back into the base, of course, so I lay it back on the cactus before settling down on a charred log and activating the holodisplay. The green dots are spread across the map in nice, neat rows. The ground team immediately west of us has moved too far east, and one of the blades is too far west—I will need to reposition them after the break—but overall it has been a well-organized, well-executed sweep.

I cannot measure success by acquisition of the targets, after all. They may not even be in our territory. I glance at the grey dots that represent Protectors Jace and Onyx's units. Like us, they move slowly and systematically. I assume that they, too, have found nothing. There are no clusters, after all. No merging of individual dots into a pack.

We sit in silence a few moments, watching as our shadows grow longer. We should lower our face shields again. The dark vision feature will be initiated soon.

"Okay. Time to go." I get to my feet and am brushing the dust from my uniform when an urgent message flashes. I open up the holodisplay and unmute my microphone.

"Blade II ground team, come in."

There is no reply.

"Blade II ground team, come in."

Still nothing. I pull on my pack and catch Corvus' eye. "We need to move," I say, and take off westward.

"What's wrong?" Corvus is immediately beside me, zipping up his bag as he runs.

I wave him away, already dialing Grand Neilem and her seconds.

"Yes, Sierra. Do you have an update for me?"

"Blade II ground team has lost comms. Their vital signals went black but have since reappeared and are within the normal range. PI Corvus and I will be there in minutes, but I'm sending you their coordinates. It is unclear yet whether this is a technical failing or an indication of stress."

I don't bother discussing a third possibility, not with healthy vital sign readings. If the issue is not our connectivity, then I suspect they have been stunned, or taken hostage. And though we are north of the wall, there is no risk of us encountering savages, not with drones programmed to pick up body heat.

Which means that the Blade II ground team might have located the targets.

"Thank you, Sierra. Protectors Jace and Onyx, have your units on standby."

"Understood, Grand Neilem." Their voices are almost synched, like a recording with a minor echo.

I redirect the channel to the protectors in my unit, and relay the same message before unmuting the microphone.

"Blade II ground team, come in," I try again. There is still no response.

"Do you think it's them?" asks Corvus.

"I don't know."

As we run, I wonder how the targets are blocking the heat signal. It will be something interesting to discuss with Elium when we return to the base.

We enter a new microclimate and I find my view obscured by the sudden abundance of low, scraggly desert trees. If it wasn't for the alert flashing in the right corner of my vision, I don't know that I would even have seen the canyon.

The ground is firmer here, clay laced with tree roots giving stiff but precarious footing as we weave our way down the cliffside. From the holodisplay, it looks like the Blade II ground team was walking along the path inside the canyon when the comms cut out.

That or they fell.

Corvus spots the bodies first. He pulls me down behind a bush, pointing to two figures lying in the sand up in the distance.

From the way that they've fallen, there can be no doubt. They've been stunned. Corvus knows it too. He is sliding a blue flare from his back when I shake my head at him.

Our instructions are to set it off once we've seen the targets.

In silence, I pull up the holodisplay and select the messaging function. A twist of my hands and a keyboard appears.

Two members of my unit stunned.

Vitals fine.

Targets not yet sighted.

Continuing the search.

I add the location coordinates and send it to Grand Neilem and the other P5s. It will be up to the Grand to decide when to alert the Administration.

I switch to map view, but with the weirdly abundant flora my visuals are limited.

I start making my way slowly and carefully down the cliffside. My blood is pumping harder now, from the exertion, I tell myself, though more likely it's the prospect of the chase. The prospect of winning.

The ground team is still unconscious when we reach them—a man and a woman, just a few years older than us.

"Did you call for an extraction?" Corvus asks in a whisper, bending down and physically checking their vital signs. I don't know why he bothers when their information is transmitted from the sensory pads in their uniforms directly to my holodisplay.

I shake my head, my eyes darting from large boulders to a cactus, to the sparse, brown desert trees. Just as I am wishing there was better visibility, the wind stirs and dust floats up, obscuring the air.

They could be here still, hiding. “We can’t,” I whisper. “It will give away our position.”

The immediate area around us has been cleared of footsteps—but they would not have had time to have covered their tracks for long.

“So, we are going to...” Corvus raises an eyebrow. “You’re going to leave me to watch them while you continue to track the targets.”

“Hmm? Oh, yes. We cannot leave them unprotected.”

“But then you’ll have nobody to—”

We notice the shadow at the same time. I look up, my heart sinking as the medic helicopter drops toward us.

So much for stealth.

Though the new models are almost silent, they cannot fly close to ground level like the blades can. The targets, wherever they are, will have seen the helicopter approach.

“Protector Sierra.” The words are being transmitted directly to the speakers in my helmet. A name and a P3 apprentice ranking flash at the corner of my vision. It’s one of the young protectors recently assigned to the medic unit—the first apprentice that the medical ward has accepted since my own cohort. “Permission to extract?”

“Yes, thank you, Protector.” I wonder why she is here. Councilman Xander had specifically indicated that medics were to be excluded from the mission. Surely Grand Neilem wouldn’t have disobeyed an order from the Administration.

The helicopter lands, and the P3 apprentice and a regular P1 protector jump out.

Or maybe only the fully trained medics were asked to stay at the base. Maybe Grand Neilem is only allowing this girl north of the wall because she is a trainee. Which is logical. Our medics have gone through years of training. We cannot afford to lose them.

So, it is better to risk a child?

A protector.

She does look young, though, as does the P1 assisting her. They move swiftly and competently, securing oxygen masks over the faces of the two protectors and then sealing the zero-gravity cases around, over, and then finally under the two unconscious bodies.

We watch in silence as the cases float up and drift over to the helicopter.

The two protectors make the sign of deference and turn to leave. I cannot help myself.

"Tell Lyra and Elium to take good care of them."

The girl smiles. "Of course, Protector Sierra."

So, they're not in the field, then.

Why does it matter? You have a mission. Focus.

Corvus flashes me a grin. "So, I guess I'm coming with you now."

I scan the ground in front of me for signs of disruption—footprints swept away in a hurry, a weapon or a personal item dropped and left behind. "This is a matter of state security, not a leisure activity. Act more—"

"Sombre?"

"Focused."

"Yes, Captain."

It doesn't take long to locate footprints. We find them only a few dozen feet away from where the two protectors had been stunned, and set off at a run.

Corvus pulls one of the stunners from its holster and sticks the blue flare in its place. He resumes running with the unholstered stunner in his hand. I do the same.

The footsteps lead us farther west along the canyon, and then back up the opposite side of the cliff, still in a westward direction.

I pull the terrain map up again on my holodisplay and scan for hazards—areas with low visibility, precarious footing.

"Cor," I say, frowning at the image in front of me. "Move away from the edge. This area had a rockslide—"

He's already slipping. I see him disappear over the side and it is as though the oxygen has been kicked from my lungs.

I lunge forward in time to watch him land with contest-worthy precision on a narrow ledge just ten feet down. A few feet to the east and he'd have fallen to the rocks below. Whether the ledge continues, forming a secondary path parallel to and below the cliff edge, it's difficult to see. A big, jagged boulder sticks out from the side of the cliff immediately west of Corvus.

And if he'd hit that on the way down?

"How'd I do?" asks Corvus, tipping forward into a handstand. "Top marks?"

"I—you—" I half crawl, half slide down to meet him, not sure if I want to kiss him or shoot him.

He pulls me into his arms before my feet even hit the ground. "I'm sorry," he says, holding me so tightly that I could not attack him even if I tried. "I didn't intend to do that. I mean, I meant to land beautifully, but not to fall."

I pull back from him just enough that I can look up into his face. "Don't— You have to be more careful, what—"

I only see the edge of the stunner poking around the boulder half a second before it fires. I leap forward, pulling Corvus back behind the rock as I lash out with my front leg, kicking the stunner out of the attacker's hand before moving back into cover myself.

I poke the tip of my stunner around the side of the boulder and fire blindly—once, twice, but I can already hear footsteps receding down the path. As I pull my arm back behind the boulder a shot fires past me. I fire a third time before sneaking a peek. I catch them in profile as they turn left, leaving the path for the cover of another boulder. It is only a second, but it is enough.

"It's them," I tell Corvus, slipping past the boulder onto the path they'd taken. "They're heading back down into the canyon. Send the flare."

My eyes are on the holodisplay. I can see the targets virtually now. My sensors are picking up the shapes of their bodies, if not the heat that would have allowed us to pinpoint their location from the base. "They have made it down into the canyon and are running west. They are in the open. Did you send the—"

As I'm speaking, the sky above us explodes in blue. When I look around for Corvus, I realize that he's ahead of me, sprinting down the path after them. "Wait—Cor!"

He shoots a grin backward at me and keeps running. I pick up the stunner that the traitor dropped and pop it into my pack before racing after him.

We're heading down into the canyon now. I check the holodisplay but the targets seem to be obscured among the trees once again.

We take cover behind another boulder and scan the area. I spy a low point, and hand signal to Corvus that we are going to advance.

The sand explodes around our feet—bullets, I register with shock. Actual bullets.

I dive into the trench. Half a second later Corvus lands beside me. "Are you okay?" I ask him.

"That's real ammunition, Sie," he says, staring at me with wide eyes.

"We could wait for the Administration," I say. "Did you see where it was coming from?"

"The third tree from the right."

"That's really close, Corvus—too close."

"Good," he says, pulling out his second stunner.

"We're under orders not to approach or speak—"

"Yes, Captain. Are we going or what?"

It's not enough for me, to locate them, and he knows it. I want them stunned and ready for extraction when the Administration arrives.

We move out simultaneously, but in opposite directions, shooting as we move to our second marks—another boulder for Corvus, another trench in the sand for me. It is too shallow—I have to lie completely flat.

I catch Corvus' eye and make the signal. He nods, and begins shooting at them from behind the boulder. I find the targets once again using the holodisplay and fix their location in my mind.

Then I dig a hand into my pack and pull out the KO bomb. I launch it and duck back down. Then I grab both stunners and fire at the tree.

Once, twice, three times—and I drop back down to the ground, hoping that Corvus has done the same.

My helmet muffles some of the sound—but the bomb is still loud enough to make my ears ring. The dust is everywhere—so thick I can barely make out the edge of the trench. Even on my holodisplay the picture is blurry. I dig a finger into my ear, willing the ringing to stop.

The dust settles enough for me to see Corvus as he peeks his head around the boulder, and sprints toward the tree.

I could tell him to stand down. This is my command. But we are so close.

I follow him, a stunner in each hand. A few steps out I catch sight of the body of the woman—lying prone. I look for the man and see the gun pressed against Corvus' head.

"This is unnecessary," I say, speaking as calmly as I can, though every muscle in my body is telling me to attack. "The Administration will be here shortly. There is no need to hurt this protector."

"I'll take the head start," the man says, walking backward, pulling Corvus with him. "Drop to the ground, hands over your head, or I will shoot him." He does not sound menacing, though. He sounds frightened. This man does not want to hurt Corvus—of that I am certain.

My hands are shaking now, though I do not release my stunners. "The life of one protector does not take precedence over my duty."

The man shakes his head. "I saw you on the cliff." The gun wobbles as he speaks. "You and him—"

"We do not negotiate with traitors." My voice is firm. Even. It's a lie.

"Trai—" The man lets out a bark of a laugh. "Do you know what they're intending to do? How many hundreds of thousands—"

I feel my body go limp and the stunners slip from my fingers. I try to look for Corvus but my body does not seem to be mine to control. My eyes pass upward as I fall to the ground. *The sky—someone has blotted out the sun.*

21

The Waste

THEY CHOSE NOT to risk a fire that night. Since most of the food that remained, rice and dried chana and lentils, needed to be boiled, their supper consisted of the last of the soybeans they'd brought from the Barrow and some of the dubious-looking meat from the bandits' supply.

It wasn't the first time she had eaten meat. The rations they had found in the cart had included several strips of dried beef, which the group had consumed before they were half a day's walk from the Barrow. Meat seemed to be a delicacy for the others. On Sam's part, she had found the beef overly salty.

Seems like a poor use of resources.

Didn't stop you from eating it.

To be social.

You're not that social.

I prefer artificial.

You prefer survival.

The meat pilfered from the skags, however, was so tough and

stringy that Sam thought they were probably burning more calories chewing than they were gained from the meat itself. Mostly it made her thirsty. Luckily there was still plenty of water.

In her tent that night it wasn't dreams that Sam dreaded for once but the sound of horses. She lay there staring at a patch of starlit sky visible through a hole in the canvas, counting. There were eight stars. Eight was not a number she liked, so she added the lines of the tent. Eight stars, four sides to their finite world. Twelve was a better number.

She reached out to stroke her knives, which she laid out in a row beside her boots while she slept: one, two, three. She repeated the count, the action, and wondered if she should name them. Northerners did things like that. Charis had called her crossbow Fury. Adder's knives were Lady and Rogue. His two remaining knives, anyway. He'd donated one to Sam, a beautiful blade. It made her two homemade shanks, selected from the collection of extra weapons Dot and Shya had managed to amass before they left the Barrow, look particularly primitive. They were sharp and lethal, but she certainly couldn't throw them with any accuracy. Of course, she had one of the crossbows they'd salvaged after the first attack. *One ancient crossbow and two rusted bolts. Not much of an improvement.*

She reached out and picked up Adder's blade. Maybe she'd just name the one. But what? All she could come up with were stupid adjectives. Stabby the Knife was not the name of a great weapon.

She counted the stars again, the edges of the rip. Quickly while she inhaled, slowly while she exhaled. Repeated it. The burn on her wrist still throbbed, quiet but relentless. Her shoulders and her arms ached too. She wondered whether they would be purple by the morning.

The tent rippled but it was only the wind. Sam glanced over toward Jackal and wondered if he was awake. Usually she could hear him breathing. When Adder was out, anyway. The latter tended to mutter in his sleep. It was very distracting.

She wondered what would happen if she reached over and touched him. Just to see if he was awake. Or to check that he was alive. It was unsettling, this shape beside her that she couldn't hear or see. Would he pull her toward him, if she did? Would she pull away from him? She wouldn't, so he couldn't, so they wouldn't find out.

It wouldn't be a betrayal. Not really.

Of course it would.

She wished the bandits would attack already, if they were going to. If she was going to have to fight to the death, she might as well spare herself the ugly waiting room that was her inner dialogue.

Inhale to six.

I want a bath.

Exhale for twelve.

Or one dreamless sleep.

Inhale to six.

I want to go home.

Exhale for twelve.

Inhale.

Exhale.

They weren't sparkles. Why had she thought they were sparkles? They were stars, of course, floating up out of the container in Xenia's hand.

Sam looked at Xenia's face, frozen mid-laugh, and reached out tentatively to touch one of the stars.

"Don't worry," said Shale. There was something wrong with her face paint. The skeletal lines were faded and streaky. And where was the yellow string? "They won't burn you. They're cold, see? Like she is."

The star fizzled when she touched it. Sam examined her fingertip and found frost. "We're not here for her."

"Hands out, lover." Shale smiled at her, but dark droplets trickled from the corners of her dark brown eyes. "Whatever you catch, you keep."

Electric lights flickered on, began pulsing. Music followed, growing faster and faster. Xenia laughed, turned, and ran.

They followed her into the party, sprinting past naked dancers and huainas wearing assault rifles.

"Hurry up!" Sam shouted back at Raina. "Or we'll lose her!"

Again, again, again.

Raina stopped, bent down, and tugged at the silver vines that were growing out of the ground and up her legs. "It's the damn irons."

Sam looked forward again. Had she lost Xenia? She started running.

"Sam!" Raina was screaming now.

Through the tangle of bodies Sam saw a flash of white-blonde.

"Wait!"

Sam spun to avoid a group of huaina and raced to catch up with her friend.

Xenia looked back at her. "Where's Raina?"

"I—" Sam frowned, glancing over her shoulder. "I had her. I think I lost her."

"You do that a lot." Xenia's face was changing with the pulsing light. Fresh paint over smooth skin on the strong beats was stripped to bone on the weak. Bits of paper kept most of the dirt contained.

Not paper. Skin.

"Anyway, come on." Xenia took her hand. Flesh to bone, then flesh again. She smiled. Plump lips. Then a wide skeletal grin. "We're almost at the climax."

Sam let herself be led up onto a stage full of dancers. Naked dancers, to be precise, with golden body paint and elaborate masks. When she turned to Xenia, confused, she saw that her friend was also naked.

"Your turn, ladki," she said.

"No, no, I don't—"

Xenia grabbed her shirt and pulled downward. "There, isn't that better?"

Sam looked down at the green uniform, the alphanumeric code on her chest. "I—"

"Come on, Sierra." Her voice was low, sultry. She winked at Sam. "Protect me."

A rope ladder swung by. Without looking, Xenia reached out a hand and snatched it from the air. Then she began to climb.

Sam glanced around, confused. "If we're looking for Raina, shouldn't we go back to the party?"

Xenia stopped climbing. Taking one hand off the rope, she beckoned to Sam. Her long, slender fingers turned to bone. The light pulsed and it was still bone. Xenia stared down at her hand. Shook it once, twice. "No matter," she said. "The rest of me is still fine."

With that she turned back to the ladder and resumed climbing. Sam followed, as she always did.

Up, up, they went. By the time Sam reached her nest, the sounds of the party had grown distant.

"Hi," she said to the green eyes that peered down at her. "I didn't mean to disturb you."

Orange ears flicked down toward her. Then, with a begrudging meow, Frank moved aside to give her space.

"Thanks," she said, pulling herself up onto the platform. "Where's Xenia?"

"Up."

Sam was reaching for the metal panel in the ceiling when she felt something smacking her ankle. She looked down to see Frank batting at her with a large, velvety paw.

"Pat me first."

"I'm in a hurry."

He turned sulkily away.

"Okay, fine." She climbed back down and ran her fingers through his thick orange fur. He rolled onto his back and stared at her.

"Your stomach?"

"It is magnificent."

"Sure, but I've really got to go." She stared at Frank. Frank stared back at her. "Fine."

A minute later, covered in fur, Sam pushed up the ceiling panel and crawled up into the tunnels. "Xenia?"

"This way."

"Jackal?"

Sam followed the sound of his voice. "Jackal?" She turned a corner but there was no one there.

"Is that daylight?"

Sam looked down. "Frank! Go back to the factory. This is no place for cats."

He licked his paw and flicked his tail. And then with a sigh as if to say that he was weary anyway, he turned and lumbered back the way they'd come.

Once he was out of sight, Sam began searching the tunnel walls. There it was: not daylight, a peephole. She bent down and peered inside.

"Just come back with me," Xenia was saying, her voice quiet and calm, although Sam could see that the hand that was gripping Cassio's arm was trembling. "We can sort this out tomorrow, on the outside."

"He's a domestic, a compound spy!" Cassio pointed at Hakuund with the knife.

"Shh, Cass, keep your voice down, we—"

She'd seen this before. Over and over. But he always arrived before she had time to call out. Sam watched Xenia crumple to the ground. Then she watched Cassio stab the guard and gather up his sister's body. "Xen, Xen, wake up, Xenia, please."

Sam looked away from Cassio. She didn't want to see this, not again. Instead she looked toward the door, where Jackal and a second Sam had appeared. "What about Raina?" Sam watched herself ask Hakuund. "Was she here?"

"She, she... It wasn't me," said Hakuund. "She was here but it wasn't me."

"We need to go," said Jackal.

"It was Fin's fault, he told me. Why would he tell me?"

"Sam, we have to go," said Jackal. He reached for Cassio's arm.

"I can't leave her," Cassio said. The words began to reverberate, echoing off the compound walls, through the tunnels.

Sam pushed away from the peephole. She didn't want to witness this, or what came next. What always came next.

"What about me, Sierra?"

Sam spun around. "Corvus?"

"Do you want to forget me?" He sounded young. Not Corvus yet, just Vireo.

"No." Her voice was a whisper. "I don't want to forget you."

"Come find me, then." The words came out thick, layered with new voices. Raina. Xenia. Anna. All the girls she couldn't name.

“Tick tock, love.” Sam spun to find a skeleton at her shoulder. She waited for the flash of light, for muscle and skin and eyes to appear. She waited but this time Xenia stayed dead.

Sam reached for her hand. Where was that spark? That star? She could put it back. She could fix it all, if only she could put the spark back.

Her hand touched cold, hard bone. Sam pulled her fingers away. They were covered in a white powder.

When she looked back at Xenia, there was nothing but dust.

22

The Waste

WHEN SAM DRAGGED herself from her tent the next morning, exhausted and hungry, Shya already had the fire going.

"Might as well eat," said Dot, adding rice to the lentils. "If they find us, they find us. No point being so starved we can't shoot straight. We'll make extra, though, so we can eat it cold on the go for our midday."

"Yum," said Adder. "Cold mush. The excitement will keep me incentivized all morning."

The corners of Dot's lips twitched. "Go walk the perimeter, Adder."

"What? I just got—"

"Now, Adder."

He tore off his black, dusty coat and flung it at Dot's feet, narrowly missing the rice and lentils. "Guard that. If I die on scout duty, I want you and Sam to fight for it."

Eyes high for dramatic effect, he spun around and strode off, only to smash his shin on a piece of dead wood. Without looking back he screamed a curse, shook out his leg, and then jogged off to where Jackal stood guard less than two dozen feet away, bow out, eyes scanning the horizon.

The three women watched him go, shaking their heads.

"You must miss Ava's cooking," said Jackal when he returned to the fire, his hat in one hand. Sam watched as he dusted it off, shook it once, and then bent forward to position it on his head. He did it the same way every morning. Like a dance. She enjoyed the ritual, for some reason.

"I, uh. Why? It's the same ingredients."

Jackal stared at her. "We don't even have salt. Or spices."

"Salt's not really that good for you."

"Sure it is."

"No. I mean, yes, a small amount is vital for fluid balance and transmitting nerve impulses and such, but overconsumption increases your likelihood of developing heart disease or having a stroke. Oh, and I guess they used to fortify table salt with iodine, but obviously that doesn't happen anymore."

"What's iodine?" asked Skye, crawling out of her tent. "Hurry up with that, Shya," she added. "I'm starved."

Shya straightened her spine and looked loftily down at the rice and lentils she was stirring.

"It's a mineral that's important for brain development," said Sam.

"So, you're saying the reason so many Northerners are idiots is that we don't have this iodine?" asked Shya.

"And who used to put it in the salt?" asked Skye.

"The government did." Sam began taking down her tent. Jackal moved to help her. "You can get it naturally from certain foods though."

"Does your government do that, in the South?" asked Shya, looking up from the cooking pot. "Add iodine to your salt?"

"Yes, but it's actually unnecessary since we started infusing agricultural soil with minerals," said Sam. "Also, we get a multi-vitamin, but of course there's debate over the true absorption level of supplements."

"She speaks another tongue," said Skye to Shya. "Very pretty. We should learn."

"That kind of stuff's not going to matter," said Shya. "Not to us, anyway."

"But we're going south," said Skye.

"Yes, but not to steal their iodine."

"Just to get Anna back."

"Right," said Shya. She smiled at Skye. A sad smile. It made Sam wonder whether the two of them were starting to bond, now that Charis was gone. They hadn't had much in common, before. Now they shared grief. And guilt.

Skye sat down beside Shya and rested her chin on the other girl's shoulder. "I'm really, really hungry."

"Jit taow, Skye. I can't make rice cook any faster."

They ate quickly, and in silence. Further proof of their collective unease.

They started out at a good pace, but by midday the wind was pushing the sand and dust upward, blurring the landscape. They huddled behind the cart, trying to shield their small rations of cold rice and lentils from the swirling dust, but the wind kept changing directions. Sam thought she ate more sand and ash than rice, in the end.

Could do with some ruins now, couldn't you? Ghosts notwithstanding.

But there had been none for miles. Nothing but dust. Their boots sank down into it, a foot deep in places, sometimes more, and still more dust coloured the wind in greyscale: a dehydrated beige. There must have been a recent burn here. She wondered what had sparked it. Lightning, probably.

Maybe not. Maybe it burned a hundred years ago and no rain has come to break down the ash, grind it to powder.

"At least they won't be able to find us, through all this!" Adder shouted as they resumed walking. That was what Sam thought he said, anyway. Between the noise of the wind and the bandana that covered his mouth, it was hard to understand even Adder's sharp enunciation.

"Is that true?" Dot asked Dash, who shook his head.

Dot stared at him for a moment, then pitched her voice louder. "Fan out!"

"No," said Dash. "Even a dozen feet is too far now. Too easy for someone to get lost."

Dot looked at Jackal, who only shrugged.

"Okay, fine," she said. "Stay tight! Eyes out, though!"

Even when the wind slowed, they maintained a close formation. The heavy winds could come back suddenly, Dash had warned them. Sam thought that most of them looked relieved to stay close to one another.

The illusion of safety. Scouting is better.

Except for the wind.

We could create an auditory system.

Poorly thought out. You can barely hear each other over the wind.

It made them twitchy, this watchfulness. A dead tree loomed up out of the haze and arrows were drawn, crossbows loaded.

Amazing no one has actually shot the flora today.

And lucky.

Sam stared up at the dead tree, spiked at the top like a giant meat-skewer, and wondered how much force it would take to knock it over. It was nothing but a husk, really. The wildfires had burned away the soil, the roots, leaving it hollow and unsteady against the wind. Untethered.

If trees were sentient, what would this one remember?

It was the wrong line of thinking, Sam realized as she clambered over one of the many charred logs that littered the ground beneath the tree. She'd just be creating more graveyards.

They were so busy peering through the sand for signs of bandits that they almost missed the woman.

She was lying on the sand beneath a trio of dead trees, her legs hidden behind a boulder and a handful of leathery desert shrubs. In the temporary calm, they saw her large, pregnant belly heave upward as though she was gasping for air.

Or as if she's in labour.

Adder raced forward, Sam close on his heels. The wind surged suddenly, pushing them onward as dust devils reared up around them. Sam reached the woman just a second after him, in time to catch sight of the woman's bloated, dead face before the snake slithered from her body.

"Stay still!" called Dash into the wind, prompting Sam to freeze, her hands already midway to the knives in her boots. Surprisingly, Adder obeyed as well. The snake seemed to hesitate, swaying. Deciding where to strike first. Who to strike first.

Sam's brain was just starting to wonder whether the wind would push Dash's shot wide, and also what exactly the formula was to determine the amount of wind necessary to move an object based on its weight, when an arrow sank into the snake's meaty flesh. It hissed and jerked to the right, bringing it within swinging distance of Sam. Her hand twitched, but a lifetime of obedience kept her from reaching for the blade in her boot. Even though she didn't actually know Dash all that well, or whether his advice was sound.

Perhaps it didn't matter. Perhaps trust was simply a choice.

Then a second arrow hit. And a crossbow bolt. And then another. None of them missed.

The wind changed directions and the sour smell of rotting flesh hit them like a tidal wave. Beside her, Adder turned and retched.

"Good thing," he said, wiping his mouth with the back of his hand and then pulling his kerchief back up over his face, "that no one's a crap shot. Or wants us dead."

It was a good point, Sam realized as she pulled up her own kerchief, looking from the dead snake to the group, and the trajectory the arrows and crossbow bolts would have followed. As she turned back toward the woman, sand and ash blasted her in the eyes. She ducked her head, blinking furiously.

The next person to reach them was Skye. There were tears running down her face, smearing the kohl around her large, dark eyes, as she knelt beside the dead woman.

"Wait," called Sam into the wind, grabbing her by the shoulder. "There might be more." Her words, muffled by the kerchief she wore and pushed eastward by the wind, seemed to have no effect on the other girl.

Skye shrugged her off, putting her hand on the dead woman's stomach. "But her baby."

"There was no baby," said Jackal as he and Dash caught up. "Just the snake making it look like that. Right, man?" he asked Dash, who couldn't have missed the hint in his voice.

"Probably not."

Jackal shook his head at Dash, but the latter just shrugged.

"What was she doing out here?" asked Skye, who didn't seem to notice, or at least didn't care, that the wind was whipping her long black dreadlocks against her face. "And are you sure there was no baby?"

"There was no baby," said Jackal firmly.

"It's weird, isn't it," said Adder. "Her being here, by herself. And recently," he added, pulling his kerchief up higher over his nose.

Jackal had yanked an arrow out of the snake and was starting to clean it in the sand when he stopped. Putting one hand up against his forehead in a doomed attempt to shield his eyes from the sand that swirled around them, Jackal squinted past the woman, toward the rocks. "That a spring?"

"Ooh!" said Adder. "Hey Dot! We can fill the canteens!"

"Good find," said Dot to Jackal as the rest of the group caught up with them. Beside her, Shya already had the cart door open and was pulling out empty containers. "Okay, then," Dot continued, pointing her crossbow up at the sky. "Everyone who's not filling water, eyes up and bows out!"

The others moved into position. Everyone but Sam.

"Sam?" Dot scanned the hazy horizon again before glancing back at her. "You okay?"

"Sorry." Sam frowned, looking at the little oasis as if seeing it for the first time. She traced the shape of the shrubs with a finger, then stepped back and counted the trees. Three above the girl, one in the distance. The one they had walked past.

I'm probably remembering it wrong.

You aren't.

It's probably a coincidence.

It's not.

"Right," Sam said, turning away from the spring. It didn't matter, either way. They weren't stopping here, after all. "The water."

"Oh, can someone get a fire going?" Adder called out. "Or do you think it's too windy?"

"We're not making camp yet, Adder," said Dot. "Quick fill-up and go. I want another mile before we—wait, what's he doing?"

They all stopped and looked where she was pointing. Dash, who had been kneeling in front of the woman, beside Skye, was moving over to the snake.

"Hey," Adder called out. "You courting that meat, or what?"

Dash looked over to them as Skye stood up and began walking back toward them. "We pray for all lives. Even the ones we take."

"Huh," said Adder. "We don't."

"Well, you might think about doing so," said Dash.

Skye looked to Dot. "We need to burn her."

"Why, though?" Adder asked Dash.

"Respect," he said, pulling out his arrow and wiping it clean in the sand.

"But it killed that girl and her—it killed that girl."

"Maybe. Or maybe she was dead when it got here. But either way, it's a snake." Dash stood up and put the clean arrow back into his quiver. "It does what snakes do." His hand shot out to grab a stick tossed by the wind.

He looked at the stick. So did Sam. The shape was wrong, she realized.

Dash sprang forward, reaching the cart before the next bolt arrived, disappearing into the air where he'd been standing only seconds before.

Sam followed, jumping back against the cart as two bolts bounced off the metal above her head.

Right. No cliff. They're all around us this time.

Sam loaded her crossbow, wishing it was a proper weapon and not a rickety piece of garbage.

A skag rode by on a small tan horse. Then another. These bandits were wearing red kerchiefs, too, though she couldn't see well enough to make out the markings. A different pack, perhaps. Or maybe not. Sam wasn't sure. It didn't matter.

There were only three of them, but they were mounted and had no cart to slow them down.

They circled the group, riding in the open.

Because they can.

Because they don't need to hide.

With every step their horses' hooves sunk deep into the soft, powdery earth, generating thick clouds of dust that swirled all around them, obscuring their movement.

Her first shot went wide. The crossbow pulled left. Sam reloaded and shot again, aiming to the right of the target. As she pulled the trigger the wind surged, knocking her shot wide a second time.

More crossbow bolts thudded into the cart, and the dead trees above them.

Somewhere a horse screamed with pain. The next scream was human. A skag, Sam thought, though she wasn't certain. The wind had worked itself into a fury. The trees above them were creaking with the strain, and she couldn't see more than a few feet in front of her face.

Maybe their god is listening after all. Maybe it's an angry god.

Or if it's the god of wind, maybe this is joy.

She wasn't really sure how the whole god-thing worked, to be honest.

Then a woman screamed.

"Shale?" The first time Sam said her name it slipped out of her mouth like a prayer. The second time it was a scream. "Shale!"

The wind slowed and the dust started to fall.

"Shale!" Jackal was screaming her name now, too. And Skye.

Sam could see the others—their silhouettes, at least. There was Jackal, a few feet away. And Dash. Adder and Dot came into view, then Shya and Skye. Dark mounds on the ground told Sam that two of the skags were dead.

And thirty feet away, racing northward at a pace no human could match, was the last mounted bandit, and Shale. From the way that she lay slumped over his horse, Sam couldn't tell if she was dead or alive.

As one, bows and crossbows aimed, and as one they seemed to realize the danger. With perfect visibility and a consistent terrain and less wind and proper weapons, they could hit the bandit from this distance. Right now the chances of hitting Shale were too great.

Sam started running after her, but even as she dug deep into her reserves to push herself harder, faster, she knew it was hopeless. Still, she kept running.

She tasted salt on her lips and realized that she was crying.

There was someone else, she realized, someone standing amidst the sea of dead wood and dust. A figure coming from the north, toward the spiked tree they'd passed on their way down.

Before Sam could comprehend what she was seeing, the figure raised a crossbow and shot the skag in the face.

The horse reared up, sending dust outward in a thick, hazy cloud, and both the skag and Shale slid off its back. For one terrifying moment Sam thought it might trample Shale with its hooves. Then the horse came back down on all fours and, freed of the burden of a rider, leapt over a fallen log and disappeared.

The wind swept northward, pushing the dust back toward the creaking, swaying tree, and giving them a better view of Shale's slight frame. Coughing, she climbed to her knees, and then her feet.

Twenty feet behind her, on the north side of the tree, stood a familiar figure—shoulders thrust back, chest puffed, crossbow pointing at the sky in cocky triumph.

"Well," called Charis into the wind. "Say what you want about me, but my timing is fu—"

They looked to the sky, thinking it was the crack and boom of a lightning storm. By the time they looked back it was too late. Even Charis knew, from the way her face froze. And then the full force of the dead tree came crashing down upon her.

"Charis!"

There were so many voices screaming her name that Sam couldn't distinguish one from the other.

"We have to do this together!" said Dash, shouting into the wind.

Shya and Skye had already reached the tree.

Dash ran to Skye, wrapped his arms around her and carried her back, away from the fallen tree. Away from Charis. "Stop!"

Skye screamed curses at him. Shya was already down on her knees, shoving futilely at the dead wood.

Dash looked to Jackal and Dot, who'd caught up with them. "They'll crush her," he said, struggling to contain Skye. "We have to time it—lift it straight up."

Without speaking, Dot ran to Shya and pulled her slim figure back from the tree.

"Spread out!" shouted Dash. "We lift upward on three."

As soon as Shya and Skye saw the others crouching down beside the dead tree, they stopped trying to fight their way to Charis and rushed to grab a spot.

"On three!" called Dot.

Sam slid her hands under the burnt tree trunk, closed her eyes against the onslaught of dust and ash, and tried not to calculate the probable weight of the dead tree, considering its size and moisture loss, versus the combined strength of the eight people trying to lift it.

They would kill her, if they didn't execute this properly.

If she's still alive, you mean.

"One. Two. Three!"

As one, they lifted upward. The tree didn't move.

"Again!" shouted Dash.

Dot looked around. "Ready? On three! One. Two. Three!"

This time the tree rose up an inch.

"Hold!" Dot's voice was raspy with the strain. "Don't let it drop! Shya, get ready to pull her out."

"No!" Sam's arms were straining under the weight. "If she has damaged her neck or her back you can't move her!"

"Fine," said Dot. "Up and toward me on three. One. Two. Three!"

They moved the tree up another inch and then pushed it toward Dot in slow, steady steps.

"Tell me when we're clear of her!" said Dot.

"Clear!" called Shya.

"Slowly!" said Dot. "Lower on—jit!"

The dead tree was already coming back down.

It landed with a thud, sending a cloud of dust up into the air.

"Everyone okay?" Sam heard Jackal ask, though she couldn't see him, couldn't see anyone. Someone was coughing uncontrollably.

From around the dead wood, nine voices responded.

Wait. Nine?

"Charis?" There was a tremor in Skye's voice.

A cough was choked off midway. "I'm alive," croaked Charis.

Someone let out a slow, shuddering sigh.

"Where are you?" asked Shya. Gone was her usual poise, and her anger. This was pure, undiluted fear.

"I dunno, man," said Charis, as the dust began to fall.

All around Sam, the shapes of her friends began to appear. One of the shapes climbed slowly to their feet.

"Keep talking, I'll find you." It was Shya, walking along the log, crouched over so her hand was grazing the top of the wood. Another figure stood and stumbled toward Shya: Skye.

As though they'd been commanded to do so, the rest of the party moved back from the fallen tree, to give them space.

There was a shuffling sound followed by a flicker of light, and the dust settled on the extraordinary image of Charis, who was pulling herself up onto two short, thick logs that lay perpendicular to the fallen tree trunk. She squirmed until one formed a backrest and draped her knees over the other, all while holding a smoke in one hand. Hasha, by the smell—the Barrow's heinous tobacco and cannabis blend.

"These guys," she said, gesturing to the two logs beneath her. They must have taken the brunt of the impact from the falling tree. "My new best friends."

Extraordinary planning, to dive down between two fallen tree trunks.

Or luck.

Nobody's that lucky.

Corvus' face flashed by, the dark blue eyes laughing at her.

Some people are.

Until they're not.

Skye burst into hysterical laughter, while Shya sank to the ground.

"Where did you get that?" she asked her sister, shaking her head in amazement. "And how—how are you here?"

"I followed you," said Charis, taking a deep inhale of the hasha.

"We had a day's head start," said Shya. "Unless the People of the Phoenix—"

"No, they held me alright," said Charis. "But damn, you lot are slow."

"Not that slow," said Shya.

"And this," said Charis, twirling the smoke in her ringed fingers, "I found on some horse-faced dead dudes, along with some Blue."

The collective shock would have alerted Sam to the severity of the narcotic even if she'd hadn't heard of it already. From what Ava had told her, taking Blue enabled you to move at an accelerated rate for days. Users didn't sleep or eat—which was a decided advantage in a city like the Barrow where work was scarce and sleep left you vulnerable to predators. Often, though, the euphoria moved to uncontrollable mania, ending in cardiac arrest. Hence the name: Blue, for the colour of their lips.

"The skags had Blue?" asked Dot. "And you didn't find it, Shya?"

It was Shale that answered. "We did," she said, her voice cold. "We left it behind on purpose."

"Not the hasha, though," said Shya. "We didn't find that."

"They must have hid it real good," said Skye, between gasps of laughter. "Where'd you—Charis, baby, where'd you..." The tears were rolling thick down her face now. She stumbled forward and sank to her knees, burying her face in Charis' lap.

And in that moment of calm a whinny sounded. Then another.

Sam froze. They all did. She caught Jackal's eye and saw the panic she felt mirrored on his face.

There were three fresh riders, racing toward them. One of the skags screamed something unintelligible at the sky and the other two took it up, turning it into a war cry.

Sam looked to her bow, left lying on the sand sixty feet away, near the cart. Not that it mattered. She was out of bolts.

No, there was only one thing to do.

After quickly checking that the blades were secure in their sheathes, Sam sprinted toward the closest bandit. Or rather, where they would be in five seconds.

Up close, the horses were even smaller than she'd thought. Some part of her brain registered that this made perfect sense. The smallest of the species were often the most resilient.

The rest of her brain was busy taking in the speed, height, and angle she'd need to reach the horse's rider.

The skag was gripping the horse with his thighs so that he was half sitting, half standing. He twisted his body, firing back toward the group, and moved to load another bolt, his horse continuing to race toward Sam.

She leaped upward, her hands outstretched to grab his arms, though whether she thought to knock him backward off his mount or pull him down toward her, she hadn't quite decided.

Sam's body snapped back with the contact. Her arms screamed as she hung by the man's forearms, her legs dangling dangerously close to the horse's hooves. Sam ducked as his crossbow slipped out of his hands and sailed past her face, disappearing into the dust.

The horse reared upward. As it came down on all fours, Sam swung her body back around behind the man. Gripping the horse with her knees as she'd seen him do, she pulled out one of the substandard blades and sank it into his shoulder.

The man screamed and jerked the reins. The horse reared again, wildly, out of control. Sam pulled out the knife and stabbed again, only to find herself beating him with the broken handle.

"Jit!"

She started to slide backward off the horse and dropped the handle, wrapping her arms around the bandit's neck.

Maybe he didn't realize what was happening in time. Or maybe he did and simply couldn't disentangle his hands quickly enough from the reins he'd grabbed to keep from falling. Either way, Sam's arms had locked in the chokehold before the blows came. She ducked her head and burrowed it into his back as he struck at her arms, her hands.

Sam felt the direction shift as the horse, galloping once more, started to move away from the circle. She gripped more tightly with her thighs and wondered dimly what kind of brain damage she was suffering from the whiplash.

Less than he was, anyway. The hands grasping at her arms were panicked. He was out of air.

She waited. His body hadn't even gone completely limp before she pushed him from the horse, sliding forward to take his place.

She let out a cry, though whether of relief or victory she wasn't sure.

"Okay, go back!" she called out.

The horse kept running.

Sam's legs were beginning to go numb. She took the reins and pulled on them gently.

The horse did nothing.

She pulled on the reins more firmly, and barely had time to throw up her arms before she found herself flying through the air. She hit the sand with her hands as she landed and rolled forward.

Don't get trampled. Don't get trampled.

Sam scrambled to her feet, hands out. The ground shifted beneath her once, twice. She focused her eyes just in time to see the horse turn and race away. Ten more seconds and it, like the crossbow, like the man, like her friends, had disappeared into the dust.

23

The South

I WAKE up in a room that I do not recognize. I sit up, looking around for Corvus, but I am alone. I pull needles and tubes from my hands and my chest and shift my legs off the side of the small, hard bed. I get to my feet slowly, hesitantly, waiting for my brain to process pain, numbness, stiffness, anything. It is unnecessary—I am unharmed. Odd. I am clearly in the underground medical ward, usually reserved for patients who have undergone severe trauma or come into contact with deadly contagions.

I reach the door—and find it locked. I look for a PCB—but there is none.

Very odd.

"Hello?" I call out. "P5 Sierra. I am conscious. May I please see my assigned medic for release?"

There is only silence. Perhaps they are busy with other urgent cases. I return to the bed and sit. I wish they had thought to leave me a spare uniform. Perhaps the medic gown is a subtle message. I should try to rest while I wait.

Some time passes, and a panel in the wall opens up to reveal a food tray. There is stew, millet bread, and a green sweet.

I eat slowly, trying to assess myself for the physical ailment that has me under such scrutiny, but I truly feel well. Only worried. I want to see Corvus. I am confident that he is uninjured, but I will feel better once I actually see him.

I place the empty tray back in the receptacle and the panel closes slowly. I watch the lines disappear into the wall. If I hadn't been alerted to its presence, I would never have guessed it was here.

That makes me wonder. *What else is hidden in these walls?* Without a more productive way to pass the time, I begin a systematic search. Floor to ceiling, inch by inch; eyes, ears, hands. I cannot reach the top, of course. There is no chair in this room, so I try and drag the bed to the wall, but find that it is bolted to the floor. *No matter. Eyes only, then.*

It takes some searching to find the first camera, but once I do, the other three are easy to locate. It's a relief, to know that I am being watched. It makes me wonder, though, why it has taken so long for a medic to come speak with me. If they know I am awake, what are they waiting for?

THERE IS ANOTHER MEAL, and then eventually I sleep. In the morning —*is it morning? Or night? I cannot be sure*—there is another tray, but I have no appetite. I eat a few bites of porridge and take my vitamins, then place the tray back in the receptacle.

I want to shower. There is a toilet stall and hand sanitizer, but no shower or sink.

I go through my morning exercises, slowly at first, and then more quickly. I feel a bit sluggish today, and tired, but not ill. I do not need to be here.

I have decided that I must have come into contact with an unknown toxin during the mission, a plant perhaps that is potentially dangerous to humans. Or perhaps all of the protectors who went north of the wall are being quarantined as a precaution. This would explain why I have yet to see a medic. I must be low-risk compared to the others.

Of course, if most of the base is under quarantine, it would seem more sensible to allow us to self-isolate in our rooms, for logistical reasons. Perhaps just my unit was exposed, then. Maybe there was something hostile in the eastern region where we conducted our search.

Or maybe it is the opposite and my exposure was the highest, and they are taking precautions to ensure that I do not infect any of the medics.

I am stretching when a door panel opens and a medic enters. I have seen her a few times before, but I cannot remember her name. She is older, perhaps close in age to Grand Neilem, and is rarely in the main medical ward. I wonder if she has been permanently assigned to the underground rooms.

"Hello," I say, as the door closes silently behind her. "P5 Sierra. What is the status on P1 Corvus?"

The medic does not respond, but begins to take my blood pressure.

"Excuse me." I look down into her face. "Protector, I apologize, but I do not know your name."

Avoiding my eyes, she takes my hand and turns it over. I watch her clean the skin on my arm with an antiseptic wipe, at a loss for words. I breathe out as the needle sinks into my vein. One vial. Two. She sticks them into a portable machine, and I watch the familiar numbers and letters flash by. My training never called for me to learn the meaning behind the codes. A P5 is expected to be familiar with all base systems and protocols, but in-depth technical knowledge in all areas is not feasible. Today, though, I find myself wishing for words—any words. Spoken, written; I need something to break the silence.

She holds the cotton pad to the skin and then wraps a small bandage around it. I cannot resist trying one more time. "Protector, are there any messages for me from Grand Neilem?"

She watches the machine for another moment, until the numbers slow and halt. Then she picks it up and stands. Seconds later the door opens. She steps through, and the door closes behind her.

I can feel myself becoming frustrated. There is something else, too, but I do not name it. I breathe out deeply and slowly, and settle myself on the floor.

Visualization. A visualization will help. Patience is a virtue.

I try, but cannot hold anything in my mind's eye. My thoughts keep slipping to Corvus, to the gun pressed against his head. I drum my fingers on the floor, a small protest against the silence. The sound is muted and small.

The food receptacle opens, and I stand to find only a small dish containing two more green sweets. I sit on the bed and eat them as slowly as I can.

The silent, empty hours are unnerving me—I need an activity but there is nothing here.

I go through an old routine—poses learned as a cadet. The old, remembered movements are comforting. When I finish, I try visualization again, but I cannot seem to block out my thoughts. My mind stays in this room, housed in the knowledge that something is wrong.

And Corvus—what of Corvus?

I lie back on the floor and stare up at the ceiling.

I could do some core exercises.

I find myself wanting another sweet.

Enough. Moderation is a virtue.

I run through a series of exercises once, twice.

At the end I find that I am tired—not only physically, but mentally.

Is it night? Should I sleep?

I try to count the day's meals, but I'm having trouble remembering.

I am just settling myself back down on the small, hard bed when the door opens a second time. On reflex, I jump up and stand at attention.

My relief is so strong that I only now realize how worried I have been. "Protector Jace, Protector Onyx," I say, trying to keep my tone light and conversational. As though I am not unbathed and wearing only a dirty medic gown. "I am pleased to see you. May I request a status update on the mission, and on Protector Corvus?"

"You may follow us," says Jace, no trace of a smile or even of recognition on his broad, dark face.

"Of course," I say, looking to Protector Onyx. His face is impassive, and though he meets my eyes I cannot reach him.

I want to say more, but something in their demeanor tells me to hold back.

I follow them out of the room and down a cold, white tiled hallway. The doors we pass, marked only with pale silver alphanumeric codes, are shut. The small screens, placed at eye-level, speak to high security.

I consider asking if I can stop in my room to shower and change into uniform, but decide against it. They can see the state that I am in. There is no need to state something so obvious. If they have chosen to keep me in my present condition, there must be a reason.

I am relieved when they bring me to a room with a shower. I fill a bucket and rinse the sweat and grime from my hair and body. I am so filthy that it feels almost pleasurable to wash. There is even a uniform —clean and pressed. It's not one of my mine, though. I run my hand along the smooth fabric, distracted by the absence of the P5 code. I feel younger without it.

I brush my hair and tie it back before stepping out of the lavatory. Protectors Jace and Onyx are waiting for me. Wordlessly they continue down the empty hall. I follow, like an apprentice following my training masters, or a cadet my professors. *Or a child following her designates.*

At the end of the hall a medic holding a paper file rushes past us. He gives a cursory nod to Protectors Jace and Onyx. He doesn't look at me.

We turn the corner and I look back in time to see him open a door into a room filled entirely with screens. Then we turn down another corridor. And another.

We reach a dead end, where a man and woman I do not recognize stand at attention. They are dressed in uniform, but not the green uniform of a protector.

I know this.

These are screen people, not real people.

Screen people.

Don't worry, they're not really here.

Protector Onyx completes an iris scan in front of a screen that I cannot see, and what I thought was solid wall slides away to reveal a doorway. Without speaking, Protector Jace gestures for me to enter. I do. They stay behind.

Those are police.

Protectors. Not police.

They are wearing the police uniform.

They cannot be. The police are in Ankev.

This room is large and dimly lit. I turn back to look for Protectors Jace and Onyx and find that the door has already closed silently behind me.

I breathe out, slowly, and walk toward the only structure I can see —a large table with four shadowy figures seated around it.

As I approach, overhead lights flash on. The brightness blinds me. I stop, waiting for the flashes of light and dark to settle so that I can make sense of the scene before me.

"Sierra," says a man's voice. The black spots writhe and then swim away and I find myself face to face with Councilhead Aries.

My hands shoot forward, pressing together in the sign of deference. "Councilhead." I glance around the table and swallow. "Councilman Xander. Councilwoman Cyrus. Grand Neilem. How may I be of service?"

"Sit, please," says the councilhead, gesturing at the chair on the opposite side of the table.

"Thank you, Councilhead." The legs scratch loudly against the floor as I pull out the chair, making me cringe.

He smiles at me and leans back in his chair. "Thank you for your support, Grand Neilem. Please, do not let us keep you from your duties any longer." Though he is speaking to the Grand, his eyes do not move from my face.

"I—thank you, Councilhead."

I want to look at Grand Neilem, but do not dare look away from the councilhead. I hear her chair moving, and her footsteps as she crosses the room. The sound grows faint and then disappears altogether before anyone speaks.

"So, Sierra," the councilhead continues, leaning forward, his hands folded on the table. "You directly disobeyed state orders."

My throat goes dry. "I—I… No disobedience was intended, Councilhead."

"Hm." He smiles at me, but it is a different smile than the one that I am used to seeing in state broadcasts. The aura of calm that he normally projects is absent. The pale blue eyes that stare back at me are cold, angry even. "The orders were clear, were they not? 'Under no circumstances is any cadet or protector to speak with or approach the targets.'"

"I—it was unintentional, Councilhead, I—"

"Traitorous words are a virus, Sierra. It is imperative that they are not spread."

"I—they—" My tongue feels gummy. I cannot seem to put words together.

"What did they say to you and the Pi?"

"Councilhead, I—I cannot be sure… He was not coherent, the meaning—"

"The words, Sierra. What were the words."

"I don't know," I whisper.

"You don't know." His eyes are more than cold now—they are hostile, dangerous.

"It—he didn't…" The words are swimming away from me. *Not just the words—there's something important here. Something you're forgetting.*

"I—oh! I recorded it!"

"You—" The councilhead stops. "You recorded it?"

I nod and then clear my throat. "It's a new function, a pilot—my helmet. I requested… I—I thought it might be useful, for training purposes, to have a record…"

"I see," he says, leaning back in his chair. He gestures, and an earpiece that I hadn't realized he was wearing flashes gold. "Councilhead Aries here. Please bring me Protector Sierra's helmet. And—

they what?" His voice snaps, and then he stops and forces a smile. "Thank you, P3. Send them in as well, of course."

The councilhead watches me, clicking his fingers against the tabletop. It is unnerving, to see him unnerved.

No one speaks.

Councilman Xander and Councilwoman Cyrus watch me as well. Aries, Xander, Cyrus, Naru, Myrrsa; the constant names. Each transition I lose who I am—but I always know who they are.

Or, I thought I did. Councilhead Aries, cheerful and kindly. Councilman Xander, with his ready smile, and the inky blue-black ponytail. Councilwoman Cyrus with her dark skin and relaxed, graceful confidence.

Faces and names and mannerisms I associate with order, with safety. *Why do I repeat myself? It is one and the same.*

I realize that I am sweating. The room shouldn't be hot—the underground floors that house the armoury are always cold. I look at the councilhead. No sweat.

Maybe he can't sweat.

Maybe he had his sweat glands removed.

Can he do that?

Perhaps they are more advanced in Ankev.

But would he want to? Sweat is a healthy cooling method.

It is more likely that the room is not actually hot. Just you.

I am trying to discreetly wipe my face with the sleeve of my uniform when the door opens again.

The medic that refused to speak with me earlier enters carrying my helmet. She brings it to me, makes the sign of deference to our leaders, and exits.

"Please," says the councilhead. He is smiling again. His normal smile, the one from the broadcasts.

"Thank you, Councilhead," I say. I have to fight to keep from slurring my words. I must be more tired than I realized.

I activate my helmet and flick my fingers to open the menu display. It only takes a second to find the recording option. I sync it with my last activation.

I hear my breathing, ragged with panic. Footsteps, muted by the soft ground. A pause, and then an intake of breath.

"This is unnecessary. The Administration will be here shortly. There is no need to hurt this protector." My voice echoes out of the recording—tinny but clear.

"I'll take the head start. Drop to the ground, hands over your head, or I will shoot him."

"The life of one protector does not take precedence over my duty."

"I saw you on the cliff. You and him—"

"We do not negotiate with traitors."

My words come out forced, clipped. The lie is poorly done.

"Trai—"

The laugh that is not a laugh, then:

"Do you know what they're intending to do? How many hundreds of thousands—"

Then the thud of bodies hitting the ground. This time, though, I hear the plane landing.

"That's enough, thank you, Sierra," says the councilhead.

I turn off the playback function and look to him and the other council members.

They look—it's not quite happiness. There's a more precise word. *Why can't I think?*

"You're quite right," says Councilhead Aries. "Incoherent, meaningless words."

Relieved. They look relieved.

"Psychosis," says Councilwoman Cyrus to the councilhead, speaking for the first time. "It was suggested by some of the committee members. We should look into a diagnosis."

"Agreed," says Councilman Xander. He looks at me now. "Mental illness of this type—it's a terrible affliction. We'll ensure they receive the support they require."

"And the Pi...was he wearing a similar device?" asks Councilwoman Cyrus.

I shake my head. "No, Councilwoman. He only had the standard-issue helmet."

Councilman Xander turns to the councilwoman, a frown on his

face. "You think there was a private exchange before the P5 arrived?" He speaks quietly, but my hearing is good.

"It's a risk, Xander. You know how I feel about risks."

I don't hear the door open, just the sound of footsteps.

Councilhead Aries looks past me.

"Councilhead. Xander. Cyrus. I hope I haven't inconvenienced you."

I stumble out of my chair and press my hands into the sign of deference, though Councilman Naru simply grins and claps me on the shoulders. "Have a seat, child. There's no problem here, I'm sure."

As I sink back down into my chair, I look past Councilman Naru to the two women behind him: the familiar silhouette of Grand Neilem, and Councilwoman Myrrsa.

The five are here.

Councilwoman Myrrsa bows her head toward the other council members and takes the seat that Grand Neilem offers her.

"We wanted to congratulate Grand Neilem in person," says Councilwoman Myrrsa. I find myself staring at the silky, dark green cloak that hangs over her shoulders. It reminds me of something, though I cannot remember what.

"It—"

"I know, I know, you said it wasn't necessary," Councilman Naru says to the councilhead, settling himself into the chair beside me. "But we couldn't resist. It has been an exciting and a successful few days. We wanted to see it through."

"Successful, yes," says Councilman Xander. "But not executed to standards. There was a breach of conduct."

Despite the heat, I feel a chill run up my spine.

Councilman Naru laughs. "A small matter, now that the traitors have been apprehended—don't you think?"

Councilhead Aries tilts his head upward. I look over my shoulder and realize that Grand Neilem is still here.

Of course she is. She hasn't been dismissed, has she?

"What were our orders to your protectors?"

"Do not, under any circumstance, speak with or approach the targets," she says.

"Do not, under any circumstance, speak with or approach the targets," repeats Councilhead Aries. "Young Sierra here, and a P1 under her command, disobeyed both orders."

Councilman Xander leans over, his eyes on me. "And how does your base typically respond to a direct breach of orders, Grand Neilem?"

"Obedience is crucial to order, and order to security and well-being. Disobedience of any kind must be met with fair and logical discipline."

She speaks as though reading from a textbook. *Of course she does. This is in the first-year virtues textbook.*

"Now, now," says Councilman Naru. "We saw the aerial visual recording. The P1 ran in first. As his commanding officer, Sierra here was obligated to remedy his error."

"By following him?" says Councilman Xander.

"By taking control of the situation," says Councilwoman Myrrsa from across the table.

"So, you're saying it's the P1 that should be disciplined?" asks Councilwoman Cyrus.

The P1. They mean Corvus.

"I—" My throat catches as I try to speak.

"Naturally," says Councilman Naru. "The Administration invests heavily in our P5s. The training here Sierra has undergone... Grand Neilem, you have mentored her. She is capable of exercising sound judgment, no? If not, I should be surprised that you permitted her to pass through her apprenticeship."

"Of course, Councilman," says Grand Neilem. As unwell as I feel, I don't miss the slight and neither does she. "P5 Sierra has been an exemplary protector."

"And the P1?" asks Councilwoman Myrrsa.

Grand Neilem hesitates. "Less...exemplary."

"There you have it," says Councilman Naru, getting to his feet. "Problem solved."

"I—"

"Sierra, did you have something to add?" asks the councilhead.

Six heads turn to face me. A bead of sweat drips from my forehead onto my nose.

"Cor—The P1 did not mean to...to..." *What was I saying?* I cannot seem to keep my intention clear.

"You did not order him to advance," says Councilman Naru. "The P1 acted of his own initiative."

"We just... We wanted to stun the—the targets." Every word is a struggle to push out. I am so tired. I just want to sleep. "We—he did not mean to get so close."

"Irrelevant." Councilwoman Cyrus looks at me. "I assume you communicated the directive to him earlier, did you not? Or did you not brief your unit properly?"

"Yes—no. I did."

"We need to see some consequences," says Councilman Xander. "Fair, reasonable consequences. Of course, as his commander, you can accept the P1's errors as your own—"

"Which would provide a poor example to the P1," interrupts Councilwoman Myrrsa.

"Exactly, exactly," says Councilman Naru. "And besides, disciplinary action involving a P5...it just doesn't reflect well on the base leadership, does it? Grand Neilem?"

I hear the click of Grand Neilem's boots as she steps forward. "It would be unacceptable, Councilman. A P5 who requires such action cannot remain a P5."

"It might even bring into question the Administration itself for supporting the development of flawed leaders, don't you think?" Councilman Naru is looking at the councilhead now.

Councilhead Aries studies Councilman Naru for a moment, and then nods. "Excellent point, Councilman." The pale blue eyes turn back to me. "Did you want to accept his error as your own, Sierra?"

I can feel their eyes on me. I open my mouth, close it, and then drag my sleeve across my forehead. Councilwoman Cyrus wrinkles her nose and I cannot blame her. I feel disgusting.

Explain it to them.

We thought they had been stunned.

The KO bombs were disorienting.

Corvus is a good soldier.
He has never been good at obeying orders, though, has he?
He was under my command. His error is my error.
What will you be, if not a P5?
But it's Corvus.
Who would you be?
Even before I shake my head, I hate myself.

24

The South

Time splits. My breathing is slow, ragged, my movements so sluggish I wonder that I am able to make it to the door without falling. The council is still conversing, but someone has erected a noise barrier. Vowels and consonants float by, untethered. They don't form into words. Like oil and water—the sounds don't touch.

Someone is guiding me out of the room. It is Grand Neilem.

"Grand—" I turn toward her, and realize that she is speaking into her headset.

Past the open door. The statues come to life and split apart—Protector Jace takes me by the elbow and begins leading me down the hallway. I look over my shoulder and see Protector Onyx following Grand Neilem back into the meeting room. The police haven't moved from their posts on either side of the door.

Maybe they are the statues.

Can we have that many statues?

I don't see why not.

It just seems excessive, I suppose.

I stumble and Protector Jace catches me by the arm. A brief check-in. I think he looks concerned, but I can't be sure. We resume our trek down the corridor. Protector Jace is not aggressive, but the movements are too fast. I stumble a second time. Then a third. Then the world flips and cuts out on me again.

I WAKE up in a pile of drool. Something is pressing down on me, heavy. I roll to the side and my neck muscles scream out in pain. I must have slept at an odd angle.

The dread hits me first, before the memory. I half climb, half fall out of the bed. I need to see Corvus.

But will he want to see me?

I am still in medic. I cross to one of the cameras, smooth back my hair, and paste on a pleasant smile. "P5 Sierra here. Ready to return to active duty."

The answer comes in the form of a breakfast tray. Or, I thought it would be breakfast. The selection of melon stew and grilled cactus suggests it is rather a midday meal, or supper. I pick up a piece of cactus and then put it back down. I still do not seem to have an appetite.

Corvus has never cared about breaking the rules. Or fought the consequences.

You're speaking of child's play. This is different. The council is involved.

I take my vitamins, washing them down with date juice.

Who could be more fair, more reasonable than the five? They are unparalleled—it is why they have been chosen. There is no need for concern.

I eat an orange sweet and then force myself to finish half of the stew. The last thing I want to do is elongate my stay in the medical ward by sending back an uneaten tray of food.

At least my illness from the prior day has passed. I do some slow stretches, and then begin to work my way through a series of simple poses. I am building up to punches and kicks when the medic enters.

"Good afternoon, P5 Sierra," she says, smiling at me.

I smile back, relieved that she is not repeating the silence of the previous day.

She stays only long enough to check my vitals and take a blood sample.

I resume my exercises, and am almost finished when a glass of juice and a second orange sweet appear in my receptacle. Perhaps my blood sugar level was low.

The medic returns. This time she carries a bundle of clothing under one arm. She takes more blood and leaves again.

After dressing I relax with a few gentle stretches. My anxiety has dissipated. Everything will be fine. Besides, we captured the traitors —there is cause for celebration.

"P5 Sierra," the medic says, as the door opens on her a third time. "Thank you for your patience. You are now well enough to return to your quarters. Please permit me to lead you out of the medic wing."

It seems strange, that I should need a guide in my own base, though as we weave our way through unfamiliar corridors, I find that I am grateful for the assistance. We do not pass the meeting room or the lavatory where I showered yesterday. I wonder if I could find them again on my own.

It is with relief that I arrive up on the main floor. I glance back, curious, and watch as the elevator door disappears into the wall. Only the security screen and the tiny alphanumeric code of P3xM give any indication that the wall behind me is anything other than a wall.

"Sierra!" Lyra appears instantly, clothed in her P3 medical coat, a worried look on her small face.

She takes my hands in hers. "Are you...well? Any after-effects of the stunning?"

I smile across at her. "I feel fine, thank you. Though I'm eager to see Corvus. Do you know if he has been released yet?"

She shakes her head. "I haven't seen him. I figured he was downstairs with you."

Elium walks out of an examination room, Lyra's concern echoed on his pale face.

I look up at him and smile. "Do not worry, I am well. Just heading back to my quarters."

I turn back to Lyra. "Maybe he has already been discharged."

"He...you mean Corvus?" Elium fiddles with his dark blue ponytail. "I haven't seen him. Did you know the council's been here, though? All five!"

I nod. "I met with them."

"Right. Of course," says Elium. "So, what happened? With the mission, I mean."

"You don't know?" I look from Elium to Lyra.

She shook her head. "They called it off, of course, but they haven't announced anything officially. And it's been a few days."

"I assume you and Corvus were involved?" asks Elium. "If so, they might have just been waiting until you were well enough to give your statements."

I nod. "We were. So that makes sense."

We continue speaking for a few minutes, but my thoughts keep flicking back to Corvus. I need to find him.

I say my goodbyes and make my way through the corridors to our quarters. It is crowded in the hallways, and I feel as though the protectors and cadets I pass are staring at me. More than usual. I smile and nod as they speak my name or share a greeting. Some of the young cadets still make the sign of deference when they see me, though it's not necessary. A P5 I may be, but I am only a second, not a grand.

I speed up when I reach the corridor outside our quarters.

What are you going to say to him?

It doesn't matter. It's Corvus. I will know when I see him.

I enter the code, my heart pounding, and swing open the door.

The room is empty.

This is good, I tell myself to ease the disappointment.

I find my porta and turn it on. The screen flashes with unread messages but I ignore them, going instead to the P1 files. I pull up Corvus' record: his cadet examination marks; the results of his medical exams; his sexual health history; his living arrangements; his designation as a P1; a list of minor transgressions and temporary docked pay or reduced free time. It's all there and none of it is recent.

Take a shower. Change into your own clothing. You will see him soon enough.

There is still glitter on the bathroom floor. I step on it as I pull off the borrowed clothes and stuff them in the laundry chute.

Once I'm inside the shower stall I slide the bucket under the tap and press the button. Water gushes down for exactly ten seconds. I stare at it for a moment. The colours seem wrong. Distorted and over bright. My brain is processing sensory input in flashes, like a photograph. My movement is jerky too. Like a marionette.

Where have all the transitions gone?

Strange thought.

I pick up a cup, dunk it in the bucket, and dump the warm water on my head.

Is he back yet?

You would have heard him.

Unless he came in while the water was running.

That seems improbable.

When I have finished, I select the maximum airdry option, closing my eyes as the hot air hits my body and hair. I forget to brace, and have to grab at the shower bar to keep from being knocked off my feet. Perhaps I should have selected a gentler option today.

I put on a fresh uniform and look at myself in the small, oval mirror above the sink. Bloodshot eyes stare back at me. I lean forward, examining the tiny red specks that dot my waxy, bloated cheeks. No wonder Lyra and Elium looked concerned.

I search through my cosmetics until I find a skin powder and some eyeliner.

Neither succeeds in making me look less corpse-like.

You just need to sleep.

I need to speak with Corvus.

I open the lavatory door hesitantly. No Corvus.

I sit on the bed, hugging my knees to my chest, and wait. Time passes. The supper bell chimes, but I can't seem to motivate myself to move.

The lights dim automatically as the sun sets. I do not override them. The room soon fades from dim to dark.

I MUST HAVE FALLEN asleep at some point, as I wake to simulated sunlight still fully clothed in the previous day's uniform.

I squint at the luminescreen for a moment and turn to Corvus' side of the bed, knowing even before I do that it will be empty.

Where is he? Still in medic?

A light flashes in the meal receptacle box beside the door. I am hungry, and bring the meal tray immediately to my desk. There is even a blue sweet on my tray—a nice touch after yesterday's ordeal—as well as the day's vitamins.

After I finish eating I place my tray back in the box and look around my room. I take out my porta, but do not turn it on. Though I am physically well, my head feels cloudy. Simple tasks first.

I enter the lavatory and take another shower. It is self-indulgent—I will need to skip bathing for the next two days in order to avoid exceeding my water quota. I hope the shower will help to clear my head. It doesn't.

I have just finished brushing my teeth when the familiar notes chime—a base broadcast. I approach the PCB, now featuring a close-up of Grand Neilem's face.

"Good morning, valued protectors, cadets. Let us begin today, as all days, with the words of thanks."

I watch her face: her eyes, the shape of her lips as they form each word, the teeth behind the lips. I barely hear the words at all.

The rhythm of her speech changes. I strain my ears to listen.

"...councilhead himself has asked me to congratulate you on a successful mission. Special thanks to Protectors Jace, Onyx, and Sierra, for leading the advance. As a thank you, the Administration has benevolently provided us with a special feast for tonight's supper, which will be followed by music and dancing."

Grand Neilem pauses as she waits for the excitement to subside. I assume, anyway—alone in my room, I hear nothing, of course.

Now that the words of gratitude are over, I seat myself on the floor and lean back against my bed. I wonder if I will be excused from active duty today. More sleep might be helpful.

"...inspired by our very own engineering department. Additional prototypes will soon be available. Stay tuned for the next national broadcast, when the council members themselves will discuss the rollout."

I stare at my toes. Wiggle them once, twice. I am wearing the rest of my uniform—I must have forgotten my socks in the lavatory.

I giggle. It sounds odd, like somebody else's laugh.

"...been hard at work. They have requested for seasoned protectors—particularly those who have participated in the contests before—to join them at one of their upcoming training sessions. Bring a timed challenge of your own creation, and prepare to score them at the end! For further details, contact—"

My shirt is inside out, as well. I take it off, but toss it on the floor beside me instead of putting it back on. I roll onto my back and stare up at the ceiling.

"Hello, ceiling," I whisper, and giggle again.

Stop laughing.

You stop laughing.

You were worried.

I don't think so.

There was—you've forgotten—

"—congratulate Pi Corvus, who has accepted a permanent transfer to another base. They are grateful for the opportunity to learn from him. Corvus' incredible athletic and martial abilities are well known—"

I sit up.

Transfer.

The words are falling.

Permanent.

I try to catch one, hold the meaning.

"...more contests than almost any protector in the history of this base."

Transfer?

"...hearty congratulations to Pi Corvus for this exciting promotion."

Promotion.

The words click into place. I reach for my shirt and pull it on again, only to realize that it is still inside-out. I yank it off and drag myself to my feet. I am unsteady.

Why am I unsteady?

I walk into the lavatory, pulling the shirt over my head. The momentary blindness throws my balance off even more and I bounce off the door frame.

Why am I here?

"Socks. I need socks."

I pull them out of the fresh laundry receptacle, try to pull them on while standing and end up on the floor.

What am I doing?

"Shoes."

I find my shoes beside the bed and am heading for the door when I remember my porta. I crawl onto the bed to grab it off my pillow, drop it, pick it up again, and fall headfirst back onto the bed.

"TIME S'IT?"

Silence.

Obviously. Nobody's here. Nobody. No body.

I flip onto my back and stare up at the ceiling, then the lumine-screen, which is casting a deep yellow glow suggestive of early evening. There is something in my hand. I look down.

"Hello, porta."

It does not respond.

Because you haven't unlocked it.

I press my hand onto the screen and watch it light up. The entire day has passed. The rest of the base will be finishing up at the feast by now. I look over to the box beside the door. Wait. Look at my porta again. There are messages, probably, but I do not click on the mailbox icon.

A flashing light draws my eye to the meal receptacle box.

A supper tray. Excellent.

The food is incredible: steaks of artificial beef; a rack of artificial lamb; roasted peppers and corn; millet bread; and pomegranate—real pomegranate.

You shouldn't be hungry.

Why? I haven't eaten in hours.

It's a distraction. You were after—it's important—Cor—

Ooh, more sweets.

They are purple this time. I appreciate the variety. Variety always makes for a more pleasant experience.

I look at the door, wondering if Corvus will come back before the dancing starts.

Corvus.

Grand Neilem's announcement. What had she said?

Promotion—that's a good thing. Not discipline—promotion. I should find her, thank her.

There was more.

I don't remember.

Try.

I make my way to the lavatory and splash water on my face. I look better than I did earlier, though my eyes look odd. Darker.

Am I wearing coloured contact lenses?

I touch my eyeballs.

Nope.

Coloured drops, maybe?

Maybe. But when would I have—?

"Transferred."

The words hit me suddenly.

Who said it?

I can't remember, but they sound true.

"Transferred."

As in—away from me.

I need to find Grand Neilem. If she wants to promote Corvus, there are ways to promote him within the base. A role in training cadets. Something less structured, of course, but perhaps if he were paired with a more responsible, more organized P2—

Why would they promote him?

I pull up Corvus' file again on my porta. Nothing has been added

—nothing about the mission, nothing about his transfer. It's odd, I think. But I am not certain. My brain is too muddled.

Find Grand Neilem. There are solutions—better solutions.

I leave my room and make my way down the corridor toward Grand Neilem's office. I want to jog, but my legs seem stuck on this plodding pace.

I keep getting distracted. Symbols on doors, voices, other cadets. Everyone is moving in the same direction. I wonder why.

"The Grand," I whisper to myself. I repeat it over and over, as my feet start to take me to the canteen or through a door that looks interesting.

I am sweating when I arrive at her office.

I knock once, twice, but nobody answers.

Minutes pass—or at least I think they do. I did not bring a timekeeping device. Eventually I turn away, make my way back down the stairs. I miss the bottom step and stumble, catching myself before I fall.

The corridors are empty.

There's something though—something unusual.

Violins. Piano.

Why is there music?

I follow them to a room I don't recognize. Tiny stars light the dance floor, where coloured dots move in perfect synchronicity.

Am I inside a holodisplay?

I swipe at the air and move closer. The dots become larger, and human shaped. I see faces, happy faces.

This is nice.

"Protector Sierra, congratulations." A woman smiles at me.

I smile back, though I cannot seem to remember who she is, or why I am being congratulated.

A star twinkles in front of me. I reach out hesitantly.

Don't burn me, little star. You tiny, tiny ball of gas.

It's warm, but not hot. And smooth.

What are you, fake star?

I swipe upward, but nothing happens.

I swipe again. There was something that I needed. What was it again?

A cadet passes by with a tray full of orange sweets. I take one, and am just unwrapping it when I feel a hand on my wrist.

"Protector Sierra." Grand Neilem takes the sweet out of my hand and replaces it with something hard and cylindrical. A glass of prickly pear juice.

"I am surprised to see you up, Protector. Do you feel quite well?"

"Quite well. Welllll.... Well."

My tongue is a snake. It won't stop moving.

Slither. Slither.

"Thank you, Grand Neilem."

Better.

She is leading me somewhere. We step into a corridor and Protectors Jace and Onyx appear.

"Hello," I say. I should include their titles, but my tongue is getting larger. I don't want to risk sounding unprofessional.

They are walking quickly, and I find it difficult to keep up. I stagger, and Grand Neilem takes my arm.

How pleasant, for her to be so supportive.

Usually she is so cold.

Cold, cold, cold, cold.

Doesn't matter, if she's cold. She's not your support person.

Corvus is my supp—

I stop.

"Corvus," I say. "I came to find you. Corvus—"

"Ah yes." She stops and smiles at me. "We are all very pleased for Protector Corvus. It was quite a promotion."

"But...discipline. They wanted discipline."

She waves it off. "Small matter. They can sort that out at his new base. A docked stipend for a few weeks, perhaps, or limited base privileges. Really, Sierra, not something you should be thinking about." Grand Neilem smiles again and moves to resume walking.

Something's pushing against my throat. There's a hum somewhere.

Shh. Everything's lovely. It's a beautiful night.

The hum grows louder. It sounds like a voice. Like a scream.

I grab Grand Neilem's arm. "But—but...transferred. I want—I need—he's my—"

Grand Neilem smiles again. Though the smile seems hostile suddenly.

Don't be absurd. Grand Neilem is the best. This night is lovely. We are lucky to be treated so by the Administration.

"Surely, Sierra, you aren't suggesting that your personal feelings for a protector take priority over the national interest? Protector Corvus has valuable skills that will improve the quality of training at one of our smaller bases. We are beyond pleased to have one of our protectors so honoured."

She glances down at my hand, still on her arm. I feel my fingers go slack.

"I want..." I can't find words. Where are my words?

Protector Jace takes my arm, and I find myself once again swept along with them.

"Please rest tomorrow—take two days if you need to," Grand Neilem says. "There is no hurry to return to active duty; your health takes precedence."

She has stopped walking again, and I realize that we are outside my quarters. Protector Onyx enters the code and the door slides open.

He knows my code?

Of course. All rooms must be accessible—what if you were to fall, or become ill? It would be unsafe, otherwise.

"Have a restful night." Protector Neilem is placing something in my hand. I look down and realize that it is the sweet she took from me earlier.

Oooh, she turned it purple.

It was always purple.

Wasn't.

"Thank...you." I pop it into my mouth and step into my room. The colours start to swirl around me. I take one step, two, and watch the ground lunge at my face.

Something catches me before I hit the ground, picks me up, and places me on the bed.

I am alright.

I try to speak, but my lips won't move.

Well, I can't move my body, but I am fine.

I hear footsteps receding.

"...increase her dosage? It was high to begin with."

"Exactly. She shouldn't even have been conscious yet."

"I could confirm with medic—"

The door slides shut, silencing the voices.

There are too many voices. There are words in my brain but nothing fits into boxes.

Words are lovely. Boxes too. Everything is lovely.

Corvus—they've taken him.

It's wonderful! It's for the good of the nation.

I don't care. I need him.

Shh. Why don't you sleep? It's a beautiful night. Look at the pretend moonlight.

I'll get him back.

Sleep. Sleep is lovely. Everything is—

25

The South

My body wakes in pieces. My eyes first. Then my fingers and my toes. Limbs follow, but one by one, as though I have been dismembered and then crudely sewn back together; I may be intact but the connections have been severed. I roll my head back, forth, back again. Wait for the heaviness to fade.

Daylight streams out from the luminescreen. I am just not sure which day it is.

I reach out at random until one of my hands connects with the cold metal of my porta. I pull up the day's messages and realize that a whole day and a night have passed.

There are many messages: quarterly reports from the training masters; resource requests from engineering and the medical ward; congratulatory notes on the success of the mission from other protectors.

The mission. It seems so long ago now.

There is also a note from Grand Neilem, sent early this morning.

Dear Sierra,

I hope you are recovering well. The weaponry used for aerial stunning is quite a bit more intense than a shot from a close-range stunner. I understand that the after-effects can be quite disorientating.

Let me congratulate you a second time on your success during the recent mission. The Administration has conveyed to me their gratitude for your leadership. The base is appreciative as well, of course—your success is our success, and each victory for the base is a victory for Seira. We are honoured by the Administration's trust in us—in our competence, our efficiency, and of course your discretion. Your conversation with the council, needless to say, is confidential. As is the small matter of P1 Corvus' breach of protocol. His promotion is more to our credit, and it benefits the nation to focus on achievement, rather than the mistakes we make along the path to excellence. I understand that the protector in question was a personal friend of yours, however, I trust that you value the good of the nation over the comfort of any individual protector.

I suggest you take at minimum today and tomorrow to rest. Please visit the wellness centre for a deep tissue massage. I would suggest some gentle stretching and meditation before you engage in your usual training routine or return to active duty.

Neilem

I READ THE NOTE ONCE, twice. There are points that I am missing. I read it again, when I am less groggy. Of course, the message is designed to disappear ten minutes after it has been opened; standard protocol for anything restricted to P5s.

I slide out of bed and walk to the bookshelf. Wedged between *A Seiran's Guide to Virtue* and a historical text on the nation's most influential council members is the double-sided slate. I stare at my name beside Corvus' and the scores underneath before erasing them.

We are tied at one hundred twenty-three.

I repeat it to myself a second time, and then a third, committing the score to memory. He'll be so disappointed if we have to restart our competition.

Returning to my bed, I copy the first two paragraphs onto the slate. I stare at the words, wondering if I am breaking protocol. P5 messages are intended to be deleted—is it dishonest to make a copy? I slide the slate under my bed.

I will erase it this evening.

Hoping it will help to clear my head, I follow Grand Neilem's instructions and visit the wellness centre. I assume the deep tissue massage was both pleasant and relaxing—I fell asleep almost immediately.

I awaken to the scent of clary sage and the familiar notes of Chopin's nocturne Op.9 No.2. One of the wellness attendants arrives and leads me to a warm mineral pool. I soak for twenty minutes, still half-asleep, dress, and head to the meditation tent.

I move carefully through a set of easy poses. Every time I reach for my thoughts I stumble, so I try to focus on breathing. When that doesn't work, I start to count.

Inhale for six.

Memories edge past the numbers, overexposed and sepia-toned like an old photograph. Corvus backlit by the evening sun, a cactus flower in hand.

Exhale for twelve.

The traitor with his gun pressed to Corvus' head.

Inhale for six.

Our voices during the standoff. The change in Councilhead Aries and Council members Cyrus and Xander's demeanor as they listen to the recording.

Exhale for twelve.

Grand Neilem and her seconds at my door.

The fragments begin to cycle, accelerating, growing more vibrant. I can taste the dust from the KO bomb, feel the sweat on my face as I am brought before the council.

I sit back and look up at the sky. These are my memories—I should be able to touch them, rearrange the pieces, trace the patterns.

It's past time for the midday meal. Unwilling to face the clamour of the canteen, I return to my room, where a tray awaits me. It is an ordinary meal today—stew with potatoes, squash and green beans, a big chunk of millet bread. I push the dish of purple sweets aside. I have had enough sweets lately. Enough coddling too.

I fall asleep at my desk, and wake several hours later to a headache and a spasm in my lower back. So much for that massage.

I am standing up to stretch when it hits me.

The tightness starts in my stomach, so intense I wonder if I am going to vomit. It travels up to my chest and outward through my limbs until my fingers shake and my lungs tighten. Air is moving through my body but I can't catch my breath. I wonder if I am in cardiac arrest.

I crouch down, taking slow, deep breaths, willing my body to calm.

There are tears streaming down my face.

I watch them drip onto my hands as the pain intensifies. It is as though I am being hollowed out; scraped clean like a cadaver before disposal.

The images come piecemeal—eyes, smile, hands. My brain fixates on one item at the time. The perspective is too close, the picture out-of-focus.

Body, then pictures, then understanding.

Corvus is gone.

This is loss. Grief. I have words for it now.

I say them again. *Corvus is gone.*

My body understands, even if my brain is in denial.

Get him back.

It is a permanent transfer.

I will request it as a favour.

You come second to the good of the nation—you know this.

I will ask to be transferred too.

Silence.

Can it be done?

I don't know.

I climb up off the floor and walk to the lavatory. I stare at my reflection. It is nothing but red. Red eyes. Red nose. Red cheeks.

Fix it. You are a P5. Look like it.

I splash cold water on my face and tie my hair back into a neat ponytail. Then I return to my bedroom, where I drink an entire glass of juice, warm and sticky, saved from my midday meal tray. I straighten my uniform and am about to leave when I pause, drop to my stomach, and pull the slate out from under the bed.

I re-read Grand Neilem's message once, twice, before tucking the slate back out of sight. I pull on my boots, grab my porta, and start off at a jog for Grand Neilem's office.

"Sierra." Grand Neilem does not quite succeed in hiding her surprise. "Please, come in. How are you feeling?"

"I am well, thank you, Grand Neilem," I say, following her to her desk, where I take the seat across from her. I place my porta on the desk, and fold my hands over my knees as if this might stop her from noticing how they tremble.

"Excellent news." She smiles, though the smile does not reach her eyes. Of course, it never does.

"I would like to make a proposal."

"A proposal."

Be calm. Speak slowly.

"P1 Corvus has been transferred to another base in order to improve the quality of their martial training program." *Too fast. You're slurring.* I take a calming breath before continuing. "In order to measure the success of the intervention, I request to be transferred as well. I can conduct a baseline survey, monitor the situation, and measure the results in order to determine which variables are impacted by his presence. The learning could then be applied to the current training curriculum for cadets as well as to a refresher workshop for protectors. When P1 Corvus and I return—"

"Protector Corvus has been transferred permanently, Sierra." Grand Neilem speaks slowly, patiently, as though to a young cadet or an invalid.

I straighten in my seat. I am neither. "In that case I request a permanent transfer as well. I believe that I am underutilized in this position. With two seconds, my role often seems superfluous. Naturally, if I were needed back at this base I could return, at least on a temporary basis—"

"Your request is denied, Protector." Grand Neilem laces one hand into the other and leans forward. The body positioning is meant to convey sympathy—there is a diagram to that effect in one of the newer textbooks on effective communication and empathy. I detect no empathy. "This base has invested heavily in you. I am sorry that you feel underutilized, although I think your recent leadership during the northern mission certainly proves otherwise."

"I could—"

"We can certainly expand your role. Perhaps I rely on Protectors Jace and Onyx too heavily. We will adjust your workplan. If in the end you still feel underutilized, I, well...the council has long been interested in your progress. I believe Councilman Naru wanted you to gain a few more years' experience, but he may reconsider..." Grand Neilem hesitates, sees the confusion on my face, and sighs. "There is the potential for an internship in Ankev. I could look into whether the council would be open to hurrying along the timeline."

"An internship...with...with the council?"

"I believe it would begin with the junior delegates, with the potential to expand to the senior delegates, and the committee. Beyond that, I have no additional information."

I open my mouth and then shut it again. Grand Neilem smiles—genuinely, this time. *How unusual.* "The Administration wants you to thrive, Sierra. It will not squander your potential. Whatever you need for your physical and mental growth and emotional well-being we can—"

"What if I need Corvus for my emotional well-being?" I have interrupted her. It is against protocol.

Do not apologize. Lift your chin. Level your gaze.

"PI Corvus is a protector." She emphasizes the rank, as though it diminishes his value. "You are a protector. You serve the nation, not yourselves. I am surprised that I have to remind you of this." Her voice remains pleasant. Mine must, as well.

I smile politely, though I feel as though my teeth are grating on metal as I do. "My apologies, Grand Neilem. I am simply seeking a solution that will please all parties."

She looks incredulous. "You are not involved in this decision, Sierra. This came from the council."

"I—" I stop. Something doesn't fit here.

"Why don't you rest. We can speak about your new workplan when you return to duty tomorrow."

I swallow and stand. "Thank you, Grand Neilem." I make the sign of deference, and leave her office.

"This came from the council."

It is inconsistent, I think.

There have been too many words—I cannot keep track. I need to write this down.

I AM STANDING in front of my door before I realize that I have forgotten my porta on Grand Neilem's desk. I jog back through the corridors, enter the secure area, and climb the steps back up to her office.

I am standing outside her door about to knock when I hear voices.

"—speaking about the PI. Corvus."

I stop. Grand Neilem's voice is loud—too loud. I realize with a shock that the door to her office has not been fully sealed.

"I would like you to augment her comfort measures."

She is speaking about you. You should leave.

I should, but I don't.

"All of them?" It is Protector Onyx who is speaking now.

"No. I do need her to be at near-optimal functionality. Cut the BlissX—but increase her regular SSRI by thirty percent."

"I assume since she rejected the morning's sweet—"

"No more sweets, Onyx. Adjust the dosage in her vitamins."

"This solution is still short-term." A third voice—Protector Jace.

"As is separation-loss. She will recover," says Grand Neilem.

"And the slate?" asks Protector Onyx.

"Keep an eye on her, by all means," says Grand Neilem. "But I am not concerned."

"It's subversive," says Protector Onyx.

"She was probably just too heavily medicated to process the information, and wanted the chance to read it properly a second time," says Protector Jace.

"Copying out confidential messages is a clear—"

"As I said, Onyx." Grand Neilem lowers her voice, but I can still hear every word. "Continue to monitor her behaviour. But I am not concerned."

"Is the Administration?" Protector Onyx's silky voice has grown louder, harsher. I step away from the door, one step, then two. "I find it odd that the P1 is penalized for subversion while Sierra is entirely—"

"Are you questioning the—"

I retreat to the bottom of the stairs, and make for the corridor. The conversation I have just overhead—

It wasn't meant for you.

What is an SSRI? And BlissX?

I need facts. And because this is the least confusing question, I find myself walking to the library. The bottom floor is busy, but I follow the books up and up to the second highest balcony, where the medical texts are kept. Accessible only to P3s and above.

An enormous skylight slathers the books in light. My head is hurting and I find it difficult to focus as I pull book after book off the shelves, scanning indexes until I find SSRI in an old, frayed copy of *A History of Pharmaceuticals.* BlissX isn't referenced.

I read the short description once, twice, before climbing back down to the main floor.

This is not complicated. Selective Serotonin Reuptake Inhibitor—it increases the level of serotonin in the brain.

To make you happy.

Exactly. This is a good thing. The Administration—

No. To make you think you are happy. Even if you aren't.

I need to think. I walk back to my room and pull on training clothes. I will go outside where I can focus.

Before I leave I pull the slate out from under my bed and read the message one more time.

"*...conversation with the council, needless to say, is confidential. As is the small matter of Pi Corvus' breach of protocol. His promotion is more to our credit, and it benefits the nation to focus on achievement, rather than the mistakes we make...*"

I relax my face into a calm, pleasant expression, and wipe the slate clean before sliding it back into the bookshelf. I tie my hair into a ponytail and leave my room.

I eschew the meditation tent for a patch of empty field. Away from people. Away from ceilings and walls and structures that conceal cameras. I scan the sky for drones—but it is quiet outside this evening. A sharp contrast to the noise in my head.

I sit cross legged on the warm sand. There are too many half-completed phrases. Too many inconsistencies. I need to organize the pieces, code them.

I try to start chronologically: the desert, the altercation with the traitors, the medical ward, the council...I think of Councilhead Aries' cold blue eyes and shudder. I lose the thread and try again. And again.

Start with the pieces that matter. With Corvus, and with...with....

The fact that they're watching you?

I trace circles in the sand with my finger. Light at first, then I press deeper. It's colder below the surface. *We have always been under surveillance. It is important for our safety.*

The tracker is, perhaps. And everyone knows the common areas are under surveillance. But a camera in your quarters? Couples quarters? What possible reason—

I have been ill. It is unsafe to be alone when you are ill.

If they thought you were physically at-risk, they would have left you in medic. Besides, they wouldn't install cameras on a case-by-case basis. It makes no sense. Everyone is ill at some point. They would be standard issue.

I stop. *So that means—*

Everything you have said and done. Every moment with Corvus.

If the cameras have always been there, there are probably regulations surrounding their usage.

Meaning?

Meaning they only monitor the screens when our safety and well-being are in question.

Your safety and well-being... And the fact that they have been drugging you?

There was no ambiguity in Grand Neilem's response. "C*ut the BlissX—but increase her regular SSRI by thirty percent.*"

The sweets. She'd referenced the sweets. And the vitamins.

You knew the sweets had physiological side effects.

The purple and blue ones, sure. But how often did we receive those? Or the orange ones? A few times a year maybe. This is different.

And the yellow?

There is no physiological effect with the yellow sweets. They don't generate feelings of euphoria, or...or...we just take them before bed...

And you sleep well, don't you?

I close my eyes. How many yellow sweets have I had in my lifetime? One a night, until it became two. Then three. I have been sleeping much better since I started taking three sweets before bed.

And the vitamins...

I swallow.

Serotonin has many benefits. The textbook noted that SSRIs have been used to treat depression and—

I don't have depression.

A mood boost, then.

To make us think we're happy when we're not.

Happiness is a good thing.

When it is real. And what else is in the vitamins? What else are they altering?

It is best not to make assumptions.

They're watching me. They're drugging me. And they're lying to me about Corvus.

I close my eyes.

"I find it odd that the P1 is penalized for subversion..." Amidst the blur-

riness of the past few days, Protector Onyx's words are clear in my memory.

Penalized. Not promoted. Penalized.

Because of you.

So why did they lie? Why did they say—

You know why.

I do know, too. It was right there in Grand Neilem's note. "*It benefits the nation to focus on achievement, rather than the mistakes we make along the path to excellence.*"

So why did they lie to me? I'm a P5—

Maybe they think you're fragile. Weak.

Maybe they think I'll try to help him.

Can I help him? How would I even find him?

My hands are shaking again. I press them into the sand in front of me and open my eyes to the dying sun.

You're a P5. Use it.

Use it. How?

You have access to everything—records, files...

Not everything. Or I would have known about the cameras, the drugs.

Start with what you do know.

What I do know. I know...I know that I have clearance to read everything linked to my porta and the central machines.

Which means...

Which means there is another system, one that I cannot access on my porta.

If there was another system I would know about it. I'm a P5.

But they don't see you as a P5, do they? Not really. Protectors Jace and Onyx knew about the drugs in your vitamins, in the sweets. They knew there were cameras in your quarters. They were watching you. Grand Neilem trusts them to watch you.

So, where then?

Grand Neilem's office.

I bend over until my forehead touches the sand. Take one deep breath, then another. Action points. What are my action points?

Get the drugs out of my system.

Find a way to linger in Grand Neilem's office after she has left.

She would not leave me unsupervised in her office. This plan is flawed.

You are overthinking it. Do it while she's there.

I consider it. I have every right to explore the information accessible with my P5 clearance. Have done so, in fact, on my porta. I'd just never thought to do so in Grand Neilem's office.

Because you thought the information would be the same? Or because you've been disinclined to spend more time in Grand Neilem's presence than is absolutely required?

It doesn't matter why. What matters is that I have a plan. Go to the Grand's office. Look up Corvus' records and see if there is more information—his current location, for one. Find a reason to go to him.

And do...what, exactly?

I take another deep breath. Negative thoughts are not helpful.

I stand and start walking, away from the setting sun, away from unwanted thoughts. My head hurts. Perhaps I will stop by medic for a pain reliever.

I am halfway to the medic wing before I realize what I'm doing.

No pain relievers. No sweets. No vitamins.

I need a clear head. Even if it means ugly thoughts.

Subversive thoughts.

The sound of hundreds of forks and knives scraping against hundreds of plates tells me that it is suppertime in the canteen. I walk past it, toward my quarters, thankful for the empty corridors. I am already so tired I doubt I could form a coherent sentence.

Tomorrow I will face the world. I will follow my agenda and complete the tasks assigned to me. I will be pleasant and calm, and when nobody is watching me I will find out where Corvus is and how to get to him.

26

The South

PRICKLY PEAR JUICE, sorghum porridge with date syrup as a sweetener, millet bread and a small bowl containing one more vitamin than usual.

I glance to my left, where Grand Neilem sits between Protectors Jace and Onyx. The three of them are engaged in a conversation I cannot hear. For once I am glad that the head table faces the room. There is no one seated across from me to notice as I slip the entire stash of vitamins into the sleeve of my shirt.

After breakfast I return to my quarters to brush my teeth. As I spit, I let the vitamins drop into the sink, watching as they hit the grate, bounce once, twice, and then drop down into the pipes below.

There is no response when I knock on Grand Neilem's door. I check my porta and realize that she is scheduled to be off base today. No details are provided. My fingers swipe to the protector files, as they have been doing since Protector Jace returned my porta to me this morning. There is still no new information on Corvus' file.

I start to leave and look back at the security screen. Do I have authorization to enter alone? If not, will attempting to pass security trigger an alarm?

Familiar footsteps alert me to the arrival of Protectors Onyx and Jace before they come into view.

I paste a pleasant smile on my face. "Protectors," I say, nodding to them. "I hadn't realized Grand Neilem would be off base today."

"Until 2100 hours, we expect," says Protector Jace, as Protector Onyx steps past me and completes the iris scan. "Did you need something from the office, or were you hoping to speak with her?"

I could do it—walk past them to my little desk, open the files I need. But I feel their eyes on me and know that they will be watching what I do. Without Grand Neilem to pull their attention there is no chance of a private moment.

"It's subversive," Protector Onyx had said about the slate. What would he say to me combing through Corvus' records?

I need to tread carefully. The Grand has already warned me away from asking more questions.

"I was merely hoping to touch base on the week's priorities. I can speak with her when she returns."

I duck my head respectfully toward him and start down the stairs, trying not to dwell on the impossibility of my poorly-formed plans to gain access to Grand Neilem's confidential records.

Is this caution? Or just fear?

There's another word. I shake my head but it seeps in anyway.

Paranoia.

Unsure of what else to do, I continue to weapons engineering, as per my usual schedule.

"Protector Sierra!" P3 Tarik takes my hand in greeting. Her eyes are purple today, a soft lavender to match the dye that streaks her long, blonde ponytail. "It's lovely to see you out and about again. I trust you're well?" As usual, Tarik does not wait for me to respond, but is already leading me back to her workstation. "Congratulations on your mission success, and of course, on Corvus' promotion. You must be so pleased."

The words, though well-intentioned, seem to slip like fingers into my ribcage.

"Thank you, I am happy to serve the Administration." My voice is light, at least.

Grip. Twist. Wring.

Just wait. Wait for Grand Neilem to come back. Wait for her seconds to stop watching you. Wait for the three of them to become immersed in their problems, their meetings, their plans for the future. When their eyes are off you, then you can search for the information you need. Until then, act normal. Complete your day's tasks.

"How did the prototype work out? Was it comfortable? Any glitches?" Passing me her porta to hold, Tarik picks up a helmet, similar to the one I wore on the mission, and slips it onto my head. "Bring up the holodisplay, please. I've moved it from two to three dimensional—is it helpful, do you think? Or distracting?"

I stare at the lines. They are too bright. As they shift and move from square to cube, I feel my stomach roll. "I'm not certain," I say. "Let me train with it for a few days."

"Of course." She pulls it off and hands it to me, smiling. "Oh! And here." She begins attaching something to the sleeve of my uniform, just above the elbow. "The voice-activated tranquilizers you wanted. As discreet as we could make them." Finished, she steps back. As her gaze moves from the pins on my sleeve up to my face, her smile fades.

"Is this—is this not what you had in mind? Protector Lyra said that you were hoping for a weapon to deploy in the event that two assailants attacked you from opposite sides. I thought—well, we thought—"

The air is stuck—I cannot seem to exhale. The memory of our last training session is so powerful that I can almost smell his sweat. I fight to keep my eyes open and my expression pleasant as vomit hits my tongue and I choke it back down. To think that I will never touch him again, never hear his voice, it is unbearable.

"Your prototype sounds very promising," I manage finally, though the sound is tight, strangled.

Protector Tarik doesn't notice. "I have given you ten," she continues, "so you can try out five shots in each direction. I haven't really had time to play around with it yet, so please take precautions when testing it out. But yes," she looks at me solemnly, "I have ensured they activate in one direction only—they cannot backfire into the wearer. And oh!" She looks around, hands on her hips. "And the voice activation. Where is...? Oh right." She laughs and steps forward to take something from my hand. Her porta.

She types in a code. "You can say it, or tap it rhythmically. The tapping was Protector Lyra's idea." She blushes a bit as she says Lyra's name. "It will deploy one tranquilizer in each direction. It's a bit cumbersome, of course, but then—"

"It's fine for piloting purposes. Thank you."

I need to leave.

I excuse myself and make my way out of engineering.

The corridor is even brighter. I miss a step once, twice. The space between the floor and my feet seems to be off.

The canteen is nearby. I stop in and obtain a glass of prickly pear juice. It doesn't assuage the pounding in my head, and the sugar makes me feel nauseous. I barely make it back to my room in time to vomit again.

I sit back on the cold, hard cement of the lavatory floor and close my eyes.

Acknowledge the pain. Now let it go. Think.

Yesterday's plan was weak, childish. I knew it then, I know it now.

Grand Neilem does not want me to look into Corvus' whereabouts. That much is clear. As long as I report to her, I—

I sit up. The internship in Ankev. Members of the Administration go where they like. Not just the council, either. Even the committee members that support them, even the delegates that report to the committee members, even the junior delegates below them. What information could an intern access?

You always wanted to rise to the top.

This isn't about me.

Convenient, though.

I ignore the last thought and try to focus. If Grand Neilem and her seconds are my obstacle, the logical move is to remove them, or to remove myself from a situation where they have power over me.

There is no reason to remain at this base. Grand Neilem, Protectors Jace and Onyx, they will never divulge Corvus' whereabouts verbally. And the information will surely have been shared directly with Ankev.

So, go to Ankev. I'm sure someone will have the information you need. It might only take five or so years to gain the seniority to access the information.

Panic pushes up against my lungs, tightening.

Maybe my first plan was better.

What, gain Grand Neilem's trust, obtain access to the files? You've been working for her for years and have made minimal progress. Can you wait ten years to make her inner circle? Fifteen?

There has to be a faster way.

Something flickers behind my eyes. Not a full memory, just a flicker. A medic disappearing into an underground room filled with screens.

There are screens throughout the main medical ward. Why have a full room of them locked away in the basement where most of the medics don't go?

Are those computers connected with the system in Grand Neilem's office? It is possible. Either that or it is another system entirely. But in either scenario the Grand, as the senior-most protector at the base, would be able to access the system, and might be using it to transmit or file information.

I try to focus on the image in my head. The medic's face is gone. I cannot even remember if they were young or old, male or female.

I push at the memory, but it's faint, colours and sounds flitting in and out so shakily I cannot be certain what I am remembering and what my mind is fabricating.

Focus on what you know.

It was not Grand Neilem or Protectors Jace or Onyx. Which means that whoever it was, they have lower security clearance than I do. Which means I should be able to access the room.

You couldn't access anything in the underground wing when you were there.

I was under investigation then. I am not under investigation now.

Another question pushes up. I shove it back down.

Or maybe it's not a question.

I lean over the toilet just in time as I begin vomiting again.

THE MEDICAL WARD IS EMPTY. I close my eyes against the lights and take a breath, willing the nausea to lessen.

There is a schedule on one of the large screens mounted on the wall, but the print is blurry. I approach more closely and stare at the letters as they vibrate and dance. It takes a moment for the current event, highlighted in red, to come into focus. *Weekly P3 Medic Team Meeting*.

Of course. I should have known—I attend these meetings most of the time. Often new biotech is discussed or modelled.

I avoid the meeting room and make my way to a back corridor. Slip through a secure door and down a second corridor. It takes me a moment to find it again, but eventually the flash of silver catches my eyes. I trace the alphanumeric code with my fingers to be sure. *P3xM*.

It's time to see whether my clearance has been fully restored.

I press my hand to the screen and wait. *One. Two. Three.*

The elevator door appears, opening soundlessly. With one glance behind myself, I step in, and press *S*.

The descent is brief, though it makes my stomach heave. I breathe slowly out of my mouth and press a knuckle into my temple.

I should have waited until tomorrow.

I shake off the thought and stagger into the dark, white-tiled hallway. A smell hits my nose, familiar though I don't remember noticing it the last time I was here. Like antiseptic, but flowery. I gag, but my stomach must finally be empty, as nothing comes out.

Once again there is no one in sight. I look right, then left. My memories are not clear enough to guide me. I select left at random. Then right. Then left again.

It was between the lavatory where I showered and the meeting room where I met with the council. Of course, I don't remember where either of these rooms are located.

I am starting to sweat, despite the cold.

Think. A lavatory cannot be that difficult to locate.

I stop and close my eyes, listening for the sounds of running water.

Nothing.

I make my way to the next corridor and do the same. On the fourth attempt I hear it.

I follow the sound to the lavatory. Leaning against the door, I contemplate the corridor in front of me. It is one of these rooms, I am sure of it. I search my memory but the image I'm seeking ducks and weaves and dances around, so instead I go about it in the clumsiest way possible—I approach the first door and press my hand to the security screen, which for some reason is rectangular shaped.

Nothing happens.

I wait, wondering if this was a mistake, if I have triggered an alarm somewhere. I wipe my forehead with the back of my hand and try to slow my breathing. *I am a P5. I have the right to go where I wish.*

I lift my hand again, and then realize my mistake. I step closer to the screen and open my eyes wide for the iris scan.

A second later the door opens and I step inside.

It is identical to the room they held me in. So is the room next to it. I find an office, too, and then cross the hall to find more private rooms.

For patients.

For prisoners.

What matters is that they are empty.

Midway down the hallway is a door with the alphanumeric code P3HST. Even before I complete the iris scan I know that I have found it.

I wait until the door closes behind me, and then scan the corners of the room.

No cameras. Odd.

The stale air and blue lights bring on a fresh wave of nausea.

I collapse into the nearest chair and stare at the closest screen. There is a light blinking at me. I bend forward and squint at the words. *Identification code.* A timer appears beside the message, a countdown of 60 seconds that flashes to *59*, then *58* as I stare at it, frozen.

Identification code.

I have a code, of course. I received it when I completed my apprenticeship as a P5, though I have never used it. My fingerprints give me access to the PCBs and my porta.

It was simple, though. A name, a designation, and a short numerical code that I selected.

I type in *SierraP5* and then pause. I squint at the timer—*41 40 39.*

I stare at the numbers on the keypad and type in 3426.

The message *Incorrect* flashes in red. We're down to thirty seconds now.

I type in *SierraP53618*. I know before it flashes red that it will be incorrect.

Twenty-five seconds

Twenty-four

Twenty-three.

I stare at the numbers. I was right the first time, I know I was. I like these numbers because they can be multiplied to make twelve; and added together they total fifteen, which is divisible by the first number, three.

Twenty seconds.

Nineteen.

I start typing it in again, and then pause. Deleting what I have entered, I flip the letters into numbers. "S" is the nineteenth letter of the alphabet. "I" is the ninth...

The screen blinks green and I let out a deep breath. I squint at the timer, now frozen. Two seconds remained.

A menu appears in front of me and I lean forward, willing the letters to come into focus. It's my name, and a pleasant greeting.

So, I have access, officially at least. If only I'd known this room existed. Did she simply forget to brief me? Or was the omission deliberate?

I select "Records" and am about to scroll through the list of protectors when a bubble pops up. *Would you like to view recent entries only?*

I select yes.

The first name that pops up is my own. My heart starts to beat faster as I scroll past the photograph and try to focus my eyes on the report in front of me. I cannot seem to absorb full sentences. Words and fragments jump out, in a scrambled order.

*Cleared by the council...Obsessive behaviour...Error of judgment... Repeated insistence...Obsession with...Best interest...Inability to accept...*P*i Corvus...Slate...Confidential message...Potential subversive.... History of exemplary...Model...Council...*

At the bottom, a green status bar swims up for the forefront. In bold block letters, the single word: *Monitor.*

I realize I have been holding my breath. I let it out slowly.

Process it later. You're here for Corvus.

I return to the previous screen. The next name, of course, is his.

His eyes stare at me, laughing, from the photograph. The smile is restrained, of course. Feigned solemnity. I stare at his face and feel as though I might be sick again.

Later. Absorb it later.

I scroll past the photograph. *Bare minimum...physical specimen... attitude...support from his year-mates...incident alpha...*

The report is long. I scroll down farther until I find it. Lean forward to focus on the final line, the green status bar.

Terminated.

My breath sticks to my lungs. I stare at the screen, scrolling upward to the final paragraph.

Breach of protocol...Potentially subversive...Likely a juvenile disregard... Request of the council...

I see the word again: *terminated.*

Read it again.

I press my hands to my head and breathe deeply, pushing my panic down.

Later.

I am starting the paragraph again when an alert flashes up. The letters jump and settle into a familiar pattern: *Sierra.*

Subversive...Grand Neilem's specific instructions...Evident distrust... Medic records lab...

Then the big, block letters on the green bar: *Terminated.*

I stand and hear a crash behind me. I whirl around only to realize that it is my chair, which I have accidentally knocked to the ground.

I look back to the screen, willing the letters to rearrange themselves. To tell me that I have misunderstood.

I don't hear the door open. Only the footsteps.

They come at me from both sides, slowly, stunners raised.

"Is there a problem?" I ask, trying and failing to keep my tone light.

Talk them around.

It won't work.

What else are you going to do, fight them?

I...

This is absurd. You cannot attack a fellow protector. It is wrong. And you do not even have a weapon.

"You are unwell." Protector Jace's voice is calm, even. "Let us proceed upstairs where one of the medics can take a look at you."

"I..." Excuses, tactics come to my lips, die. "What did you do to Corvus?" The words are sluggish on my tongue. I barely recognize myself as the speaker.

"Forget the PI," says Protector Jace, taking a step toward me. He looks concerned. He looks like he wants to help me. "Understand? Just let it go. It's over. You need to focus on yourself."

I step back, bumping into the screen behind me. The pain in my head roars, slicing across both temples and I have to fight to keep from closing my eyes as the room swims in front of me. "Over," I repeat, my voice a whisper. "You mean terminated. Like you are going to do to me."

"Okay, enough talking." Protector Onyx is smiling. Not a feigned, friendly smile, either. He is enjoying this.

"There's no need for those," I say, nodding at the stunners. I am stalling. I know it, they know it.

To what end? They have stunners, you have—

I cross my arms. Let my finger find the pin. They wouldn't think to look for it, of course. It's nothing they've ever seen.

The first two tranquilizer darts shoot out as expected, one in each direction, both hitting their mark. The eight that follow are a surprise. A glitch I would have found if I'd taken Tarik's design to the training ring and tested it on dummies.

It happens so quickly that neither Protector Jace nor Protector Onyx register fear or even surprise as they fall.

27

The Waste

"WELL, THIS IS...NOT OPTIMAL." Hands on hips, Sam squinted into the swirling dust and spun, slowly, as though she might see something important. As though the wind's onslaught wasn't coming from all directions at once. As though the sand didn't blend into the sky.

She fell to her knees and scanned the ground for tracks, but the wind had already swept the sand clean. She closed her eyes to listen, but could hear nothing beyond the whistle of the wind.

Choosing a direction at random did not seem particularly wise. But then, neither did lying down and waiting to die of thirst.

Maybe don't wait quite that long, then. Maybe just wait for the wind to settle.

She sat down in the sand, her back to the sun. It felt hotter than usual, probably because she had lost her hat at some point during the fight. And even then, the actual temperature was much hotter still —the wind always made it seem cooler than it was.

She reached up and touched the top of her scalp. Would her entire head burn? Or just the line of skin that showed along her part?

To pass the time, she listed the heat-related illnesses from least to most severe. Heat cramps came first, causing muscle spasms, usually in the legs or abdomen. Electrolytes or water helped, along with light stretching or massage of the afflicted area. Obviously, moving to a cooler environment was essential.

Next came heat exhaustion. Symptoms could include a headache or nausea, even dizziness, along with cold, clammy skin. The treatment for heat exhaustion was similar to that for heat cramps, although for some reason that Sam couldn't remember it was dangerous to consume water or juice too quickly.

Heat stroke was life-threatening. Weirdly enough, sometimes those with heat stroke actually stopped sweating—their skin turned dry and red instead. Sam had always found this to be a confusing symptom.

Confusion, right—that's another symptom. And vomiting and seizures.

Always a good idea to call for medic if you're having a seizure.

Of course, you might be too confused to remember that.

Sam touched her neck with the back of one grimy hand. Her skin felt warm, but not sweaty.

Fine so far, then. I will continue to monitor the situation.

Unless you were sweating earlier and have forgotten—possibly because you're suffering from confusion.

I'm fine. I just need some water.

By the time darkness fell her thirst was almost unbearable.

She lay down on her back and closed her eyes against the dust that threatened to settle on her eyeballs.

So, that's it, huh? We're going to die in the Waste after all.

Almost like we never left.

Maybe we didn't. Maybe this whole time we've just been dreaming as we die.

So, it was all just a subconscious projection?

It makes sense, if you think about it. We've been dying of thirst. Needing water, dreaming of finding—

The rain.

Raina.

And Ava?

She symbolizes family, of course. The outdated idea of unconditional love between parent and child. Unconditional means forgiveness.

And Jackal?

Little obvious, isn't it? Someone to put you back in your skin. To give you distance. Hope, even.

And Adder? Why would I dream up someone that irritating?

Someone irritating who likes you when you're surly. Who plays off your words. Who do you think—

I am not attracted to Adder.

Obviously. But maybe you crave his stupid banter.

Okay, okay. Enough.

I could keep going.

I didn't even know that obese cats existed.

Maybe they don't.

Sam sat up and squinted into the dust. Then she climbed, wobbling, to her feet and reached her arms up to the sky to stretch out her aching back.

Okay. I've changed my mind. Better to die walking.

Head down and hands up to protect her eyes as best she could, Sam started walking.

This way, huh?

It felt right.

Did it, now.

Less wrong, then.

This all seems very scientific.

It's the Waste. I just wish I had a god to pray to.

You shut your mouth.

The body of the skag had been covered so completely by dust that she wouldn't have found it if she hadn't tripped over it.

She flipped the skag onto his back and dusted off his face. He was younger than she'd thought. Maybe a year younger than her.

Or five. If the Barrow ages you prematurely, how do you think time works in the Waste?

The skags don't live in the Waste—Dash said.

And you just vacationed in the Barrow. Still got scars, though, didn't you?

She rummaged through his pockets until she found it.

Sinking down into the sand, she pulled the top from the water skin and tried to drink slowly, carefully—she couldn't risk spilling a single drop.

She meant to ration it. Instead she emptied the entire skin.

With a sigh she tossed it back down onto the sand beside the man and stood back up. Hands pressed to her forehead, Sam spun in a slow circle, straining her eyes as she searched for light, or a tendril of smoke from a campfire. She would have settled for being able to see the horizon.

In the distance something howled.

Sam shivered and bent back over the body at her feet.

There wasn't much to take, not when his crossbow had been lost in the struggle. There were a couple of bolts; another heavy metal ring; more dried meat. A poor haul.

Does killing a skag and looting his body make you a skag?

It was a good question. She took it all anyway.

If the horse threw him first, it was reasonable to suppose that she'd been heading in the right direction after all, and should continue along the same trajectory. Reasonable if the horse had been running in a straightish line, anyway. Which it might have been.

She heard another howl and took out one of her knives. Was it the same creature? If so, was it following her? If not...she swallowed and tried not to imagine how many might be out here. Circling. Waiting.

Another howl. Then another.

Sam took out her second knife and spun around, expecting to see yellow eyes, teeth.

Nothing.

She could handle one, probably. But two?

She strained her ears, but could hear nothing now beyond the shrieking wind.

She was starting to sweat, despite the chill of the desert.

Good. Fear adds a lot of flavour, I've heard.

Please, shut up.

The howling began again. She counted at least three distinct sounds.

Suddenly she started coughing uncontrollably.

How much sand and smoke could brutalize her lungs before they started impacting her ability to run and fight?

Wait.

Smoke.

Sam sniffed the air.

It was definitely smoke. Her party? Or more skags?

There were voices, now. Did she detect familiar notes? Or was that the dehydration speaking?

"Sam!"

She tried to call out, but only managed a second coughing fit. "Here!" She walked forward, pushing into the wind, toward the voice.

"Sam!" It seemed to be coming from the other side, now. She switched directions. "I'm here!"

"Sam!"

Another direction entirely. Sam spun, feeling the panic rise in her throat.

A howl sounded, and she understood. It had been an illusion, then. A desert dream.

She crouched down and took a low breath. Readied her weapons. Waited for them to close in.

"Sam!"

Her head snapped up. A familiar, sunburned figure stepped into view.

Sam stood up. "Dot?"

"Sam!" Dot pulled her into a one-armed hug. Her other hand, Sam saw, remained firmly on her crossbow.

"This is a dream."

Dot stepped back and raised her dusty eyebrows. "Well, that's flattering."

"Pardon me?"

"I mean, that you'd choose me to rescue you."

"Oh, um..." Sam said, feeling silly. As she spoke the wind shifted, slowed. From swimming in sand, she found she could now see five, then ten feet in any direction. "That's a good point. If this were my subconscious I would be seeing—"

"You're okay," said Jackal, jogging toward them. "Sam, I—"

"Hurrah, you're alive!" Adder came into view too, along with Dash.

Knives still in her hands, Sam squinted into the haze. "Something howled."

"Hmm? Oh, that was our new pal." Adder reached up as if to tousle Dash's straight black hair. Without looking at him, Dash reached out and gently deflected Adder's outstretched arm.

"Best way to keep from losing each other," said Dash.

"But—did it have to be a wolf sound?"

Dash shrugged. "It carries."

Sam checked behind herself, the hackles on her neck still raised, as though she could smell a fight. "There were more...I heard—"

"He taught us, obviously," added Adder. "Did it worry you? I figured you'd know it was us, if you heard it. Since, you know, anything that howled either moved north or died out ages ago. Right, Dash?"

"You talk too much."

Adder pressed a delicate hand to his dusty chest. "You wound me. You really do."

As the air cleared, Sam saw that Dot was bleeding from a cut on her arm, and both Adder and Jackal seemed to have taken a few fists to the face.

More shapes appeared in the distance. She counted three small silhouettes and the looming shadow of the cart.

"Is everyone okay?" asked Sam.

The others looked at each other.

"Shya..." There was a slight tremble in Dot's voice, but she squared back her shoulders and continued. "Shya got hit."

"She's alive." Stress lines deepened on Jackal's sun-browned face. "She's in the cart. We patched her up with the supplies we have, but..."

"It's not enough," said Adder. "And that's not all of it." He ran a hand through his black hair, pulling at the dusty strands until the ends stuck up. "The water got hit too. One of their explosives."

"Shya's injured. And we have no water." Sam stared at him.

"Two skins," said Dot. "That'll last—"

"A few hours," said Dash.

"So, we pretty much found you so that we could all die together," said Adder. "That's nicer, isn't it?"

Sam waited until the others had caught up, her thoughts racing. It was a risk. But there didn't seem to be much of a choice.

She was surprised, and touched, when Shale raced ahead of the others and pulled her into a hug. "Let's stop almost dying, okay?" she whispered into Sam's ear. "I know I've been a ghost lately, but that doesn't mean—I don't keep a lot of friends. Don't make me lose another one."

Sam hugged her back. She couldn't find the words she was looking for, so she said nothing. Just held the redhead's tiny frame, feeling undeserving. Feeling guilty.

"Unfortunately," said Dot from behind them, "that spring wasn't—"

"It's not a spring," said Sam, speaking over Shale's shoulder. "I think it used to be, but nothing we can get at."

Adder stared at her. "And you know this."

Sam nodded, the decision made. "I think I know this."

"You wanna explain?" asked Charis as she and Skye joined them with the cart. Sam was surprised they'd managed to pull it at all without a third pair of hands. In addition to the dents and scratches, the cart was leaning dangerously to one side, and only two wheels seemed to be functional.

"It looks like an area I came through on my way north."

"But you're not sure." Charis looked shaken. Shaken but not teary, Sam noticed. The attitude was gone, replaced by steel. And anger. And a twitchy, combative vibe.

Maybe this is how she processes fear.

Or it's the Blue.

She looks murderous. Does Blue make you violent?

"I was coming down off a lot of...stuff. So, no, I'm not certain. But if it is, there's a...a safehouse. Of sorts. It's close by, but I'm not positive exactly how to get there."

"They took you in last time?" asked Dot.

"They...did. Yes."

Adder raised an eyebrow at her. "You're being cagey. Why are you being cagey?"

"Good enough," said Charis, rapping her knuckles on the side of the cart. "Which way?"

"I need to get back to the—the non-spring spring," said Sam. "I know the last thing you probably want to do right now is backtrack, but—"

"Uh, Sam?" said Adder. "It's just right there." He pointed back the way they'd come. "Like five minutes if we walk slow. Maybe less."

"Oh." Had she tried screaming? She couldn't remember. The wind would have swallowed her cries, anyway. Probably. Or maybe she'd just spent the last few hours picturing a lonely, arid death, when all she'd needed to do was breathe from the diaphragm and holler.

Back at the clearing she saw the bodies of the remaining bandits, looted and laid out in a row. No horses, though. It seemed they had all fled.

The woman's body was hidden under a pile of sand. They'd tried to cremate her, apparently, but after the wind had put out the fire three times Skye had decided that the gods wanted the woman buried instead. It was a kinder fate than the skags would see. If you thought the body mattered, that is.

Sam stared at the shrubs and then closed her eyes, trying to ignore the fact that eight other people would die if she got this wrong. She could feel their impatience weighing on her. How much time did Shya have? Days? Hours?

Not just Shya. Without water none of us have time.

Focus.

Her memories were patchy and internally focused. Sweat, panic, grief—this was what she remembered. What of her surroundings?

Work harder.

There had been a place like this, she was certain. It was where she'd stopped to drink. Sam dug a knuckle into her temple, willing herself to remember.

Ah. There you are.

She had been on her knees, drinking and deciding whether to give up. There were definitely rocks and shrubs—she'd counted them, traced the lines they made against the horizon. And then she'd gotten up and walked...where?

Feeling self-conscious, Sam knelt on the ground, trying to match the picture in her mind with the ground in front of her. The lines, shaky, shimmered, slipped, fell into place. Like tracing a diagram by placing transparent paper on top.

"This way," said Sam.

You think.

No point killing morale. Better if they believe I'm certain.

Except that you're not. But go ahead, lead them to their deaths.

They'll die here anyway.

Maybe. Or maybe you're just making decisions you have no right to be making. Again.

28

The Waste

"How long?" asked Jackal, thirty minutes after they'd set off in a vaguely northeastern direction.

"Five minutes, maybe. Or an hour?"

"Right."

"Or we've missed it. Or he's gone."

"He?"

Sam nodded. "He was a friend of Ava's."

Jackal didn't say anything, just continued walking beside her, a worried look on his face.

Of course he looks worried. He should be worried. And there's nothing wrong with being quiet. It's better than cluttering the silence with useless chatter.

"So, is it weird that we haven't found it yet?" Adder called from behind them, where he was pulling the cart with Dash and Charis. "I mean, what are we even looking for? A shack? A tree fort?"

"Look for light, silly," said Skye, who was walking so close to Charis that she tripped her, twice. "Always look for light."

"She's right, actually," said Sam. "Though he doesn't always light the torch. And it's low, his house. In this dip you can't really see, not until you fall into it."

Which we should have by now.

Or we will, soon.

Or we've missed it. Or we're miles away and you're remembering it wrong.

29

The South

THE SECONDS TICK by as I stare at their crumpled bodies. I wait for the rise and fall of their chests. A minute passes. Then two.

It was an accident.

Later—process it later.

I need to call a medic.

You need to run.

The word *terminated* hovers in the blurry space between my mind and my eyes.

I gather up all my shock, denial, terror, and stuff it down. Then I squint at the screen until letters and colours settle back into words and maps. A wave of nausea hits and I turn and vomit on the floor. I take a deep breath and check the clock on the wall. I have another twenty minutes until the P3 medic meeting finishes. Somehow it took less than thirty minutes to destroy my life.

It doesn't take me long to access the base security functions.

Plan it out. Simple steps.

I don't look at their faces as I take Protector Jace and Protector Onyx's stunners and slide them into the straps on my pant legs.

The main floor is still empty, as expected. I hurry to the fifth operating room. My eyes flicker to the disabled camera as I enter the room and rush over to the cupboards. I know the contents well, so even with blurred vision and nausea it doesn't take me long to locate antiseptic, a localized freezing agent, and a surgical blade.

A murmur of white noise tells me that the meeting has ended early. I drop the freezing agent and wipe antiseptic on the knife and my armpit. On second thought, I stuff a thick bandage into my mouth.

The noise grows. Biting into the gauze, I take a deep breath and begin the exhale as I slice into the soft skin in my armpit. The pain is so sharp that I feel as though I have punctured a lung, though I can see that the cut is shallow. A second cut, then I dump the remaining antiseptic on my finger and reach in.

I can discern footsteps now. I stuff more gauze into my armpit, pull my shirt down, dump the supplies and the bandage into the trash, and stride out of the room.

"Sierra!" Elium's grin quickly turns to an expression of concern. "You don't look well."

"It's nothing," I say, trying unsuccessfully to move past him. "Gastrointestinal problems, that's all." Despite my best efforts the words come out strained and sluggish. "And a headache."

"Great meeting." A young, blond medic comes up behind Elium, patting him on the back. "If you would like another set of hands for the trials, please keep me in mind."

Elium turns pink. "Sure. Uh, thank you. I will let you know."

I try to sneak past him as they're speaking, but Elium takes me by the arm and ushers me to a seat in a nearby station. "I was hoping you'd be there today," he says, pulling a small dish and several bottles down from an upper shelf. "I thought you'd be interested in—"

"Sorry, Elium, I really need to—"

He passes me a dish of pills and then pulls something circular and white from his pocket. *An arm band?*

"What's this?" I ask, trying not to squint.

"I have been waiting to show you. I had to work with engineering, of course, and I don't know that it replicates exactly what they had, but so far it seems to have the same effect."

"El—"

"The trickiest thing was dropping body temperature without triggering symptoms of hypothermia, so the majority of the perceived decrease is just that—a perception. The blocking of the transmission of heat, rather than an actual reduction."

I close my eyes against the lights in an attempt to focus.

"It's how they avoided detection."

The word *traitor* sticks in my head. I open my eyes. "The targets. Of course." An idea occurs to me. I try to keep my voice light. "I'll take it to the engineering lab for a closer look."

"Great." Elium's smile fades. "But, oh, can it wait until after the trials? We have them scheduled—"

"I'll have it back to you by supper, Protector." I see Elium stiffen slightly as he realizes that for the first time in our friendship, I'm pulling rank.

He hands it to me. "Of course."

I stand, and try to hand him back the dish of pills.

"Oh! Right. So, take this one to reduce the gastrointestinal symptoms. These two should give you some relief from the headache." He points to a big blue pill. "If you're having trouble sleeping, take this." He smiles at me, and I realize that I am already forgiven for overstepping. "These, of course, are just your regular vitamins, in case the gastrointestinal issues have led to an absorption issue. Which might explain your headache."

I slip the pills and Elium's arm band into my pocket as soon as I leave the medical ward.

The launch strip is empty when I arrive. Which is lucky, as blood is now dripping through the gauze.

The ground tilts beneath me. I stagger to regain my balance and then vomit on the concrete.

I squint at the number on the blade in front of me and then start making my way slowly down the line. Too slowly. My panic mounts as the seconds tick by.

It's the last blade, of course, the one farthest from the entrance. The one that's unlocked, with the tracker disabled.

"Protector Sierra!"

I turn to see a young protector hurrying toward me.

My fingers twitch toward the stolen stunners.

The protector is female and young, maybe eighteen years old. "May I be of assistance?" She beams at me.

"Thank you, Protector." I speak slowly in an effort not to slur. "I am—"

"You're bleeding." She's looking down and I follow her gaze to find that a trail of blood has been shadowing my progress through the launch strip.

"It's nothing." I push my lips into a smile. Judging by the uncertain look I receive in return, I suspect it is not terribly convincing. "I will patch it up on the blade." There are medical supplies onboard—that at least is true. Medical kits, emergency rations. Things I am going to need.

"I thought the next test flights were—"

"Tests are best conducted at unexpected moments," I say. The nausea is bubbling up. I need to move. "If you'll excuse me."

"I—"

"Protector," I say, nodding to her.

She makes the sign of deference and stands back, looking chastised.

I stagger into the blade and up to the pilot's seat. At least it is darker in here—the lights are muted, meant to guide, not blind.

The protector waves at me and hurries over to the control panel. The roof above me disappears and I kick the blade into motion, rising up out of the base.

"I guess there is only one possible direction." I laugh, and then choke back a sob. *Later.*

Once the blade's course has been set, I switch the piloting to auto and lurch into the back supply area. I find glue in the medic kit and seal the cut in my armpit.

Then I stuff the medic kit and some water-purifying tablets into one of the standard-issue, waterproof backpacks, along with juice and water, meal replacement bars, a lighter, a blanket, and a small tent. I search for a fuel pack but cannot find one. Perhaps they have not yet been refilled.

I return to the cockpit and check the coordinates, then pre-set a course to take the blade north, then west, then south, and then east until it arrives back at the base. Then I manually disable the blade's memory function and sit back, watching the map as we move farther and farther north.

I check the coordinates one last time and decrease the altitude until the blade is flying as low to the ground as possible.

Then I make my way back to the rear of the blade. I secure the backpack and then, holding tightly to a stabilizing bar, I open the door.

A few shrubs and low desert trees poke up, breaking the monotony of the charred earth beneath me. As the blade slows to turn, I jump.

I slap the ground as I land, on instinct. Then for several long minutes I continue to lie, prone, where I've fallen.

The other drop plays and replays in my mind. I see him hovering above me. I can almost taste the kiss.

Corvus.

The word *terminated* sounds in my mind and I find myself rifling through my pockets for the pills Elium gave me. I catch sight of the armband and activate it, although I expect I am far enough north to be out of range.

Too far to be tracked and hunted down.

As a traitor.

I pull out the handful of pills and have them halfway to my mouth before I stop. Drag myself to my knees and then my feet. Throw them backwards.

Something rips through me—something that wasn't there before. Born of fear maybe, or grief. I scream, and my voice is deep and ragged. Like an animal. Anger. Real anger.

They don't give us words for this, so I just keep screaming. I scream until my voice gives out and I sway on my feet. Hollowed out, I turn and make my way deeper into the North. The wind picks up and sand swirls around me, blurring the line between earth and sky. My lungs grow thick with grit. I lower my head and push onward.

The sun lowers and then sets to my left. The moon rises, though I cannot see stars for the dust.

I find rocks shrouded by shrubs and tall, dead trees, and stop to drink. It looks like a fine place to die but instead I get back up and keep walking. I pick a tree in the distance and walk toward it. Then another. Then I stop watching the horizon.

I walk without thinking, without planning.

I walk until I don't care if they find me.

I walk until I don't care about surviving the night.

I walk until the sun rises—not in the sky, but low, in the dirt.

Fire.

And a red door.

30

The red door gleamed at them long before the rest of the cabin came into focus, illuminated by a torch in the sand.

It had always struck Sam as arrogant, though if it were someone other than Epa she might have been more charitable with her adjectives. Called it bold or temerarious, instead. But really, what was Epa saying, leaving this bit of fire untended on his doorstep? Did he think his house couldn't burn?

It wasn't the only building in the pit to survive the Decline, though the others had long since been swallowed up by dust. Now they were just bumps in the horizon; big, looming shadows that ate the light, like the black holes in space. Abandoned, though Sam had suspicions that Epa crept through them sometimes. Perhaps there were hidden doors or tunnels. Or maybe he slithered down the chimneys like a snake.

A tall, goggled figure in a brown cloak opened the door before she had a chance to knock.

"Sierra?"

Sam made to speak and choked on a mouthful of dust.

"Oh, right. You wanted Sahara." Epa slid his goggles onto his forehead and looked down at her, an odd, triumphant look on his face.

"Samarra." She saw herself as he must be seeing her—dirty, bruised, and desperate—and had to fight the urge to apologize.

"Close enough."

"This the guy?" asked Charis. Sam looked over to see that the others had stepped forward, a mix of hope and suspicion on their dusty faces.

"This is Epa. He found me before," said Sam, "and, er, saved me."

"Looks like it didn't stick," he said. "You need my help again, eh?"

"We...do," said Sam.

"Our water got exploded," said Adder. "And we have injured."

"We need her seen to," said Charis. "Now."

"Of course, of course," said Epa. "Although, there is a matter of—"

"We'll give you whatever we can," said Dot. "Please, can we get her inside?"

Epa watched them, his face impassive. He wouldn't refuse them, Sam knew. It was a meaningless display of power from a lonely old man.

Kindness won. Or curiosity, perhaps. Avarice, definitely. "You got injured, eh?" Epa glanced toward the cart. "In there?"

Charis and Dot lifted Shya out of the cart. Her body was limp; her long black hair, grey from the dust, hung over her face in sweaty clumps.

Jackal moved to help and Charis bared her teeth at him. She carried her sister herself as they filed through the door and followed Epa down a long, dank corridor to the living room. He shed the cloak as they walked, revealing a tall, though slightly stooped frame, and long brown hair streaked with grey. He shook out his cloak before tossing it onto a chair as they entered the main living space.

Sam eyed the cloak as she passed, wondering if it was a coincidence that he had returned home only minutes before their arrival. Wondering if he had been watching them.

The main living space was lined with bookcases displaying weapons, clothing, dishes, even books, though Epa could not read. Sam's eyes rose immediately to the top shelf on the back wall.

Her bag was there, along with the standard issue Seiran blanket and a small tent. Even her clothes had been folded up and carefully stacked on the shelf, a white armband on top. She didn't see the stunners. Epa had hidden them, probably.

She had understood when he took the medical kit, and she hadn't begrudged sharing her food and the water-purifying tablets, of course. But the other items he had pilfered as trophies. Her payment to him.

For a second, she almost thought she could smell it—the residue of Seira on these items she had left behind. A lingering detergent, or maybe it was the waterproofing spray on the tent. Except that it was impossible, of course. She couldn't smell them from this distance. A trick of her subconscious. Memory clinging to one sense and confusing the others.

She found herself wanting to climb up and touch her old things, to prove that her past was real, though she'd pulled on new clothes and a new name. She didn't, of course. Epa was particular about his things.

"Here," said Epa, using the first torch to light a second one, which he placed in a metal bin in the small room off the main living space. The sickroom, as Sam thought of it, though only because it was the room she had slept in.

Charis carried her sister inside and Dot helped lay her flat. The others crowded uselessly around.

Shya's eyes fluttered open. She took in the room, the faces looming over her, and closed her eyes again. Sam looked from Shya's pale, sweaty face to the strips of fabric that they'd wrapped around the wound on her leg. The blood was already soaking through.

"Do you still have the antiseptic? And the antibiotics?" asked Sam. "There should have been a sealant, too, I don't—"

Epa turned and glared at her. "Out."

"I'm sorry, but no," said Sam.

"Think you know better than me, girl?"

"These are southern items. I know them better than you, yes."

He stepped forward, looking down at her. His mouth was angry, his eyes hurt.

"Fixed you up, didn't I?"

"You kept me alive while time fixed me. Kind of. And I'm grateful.

You know that. This is not the same thing." Sam crossed her arms and glared up at him. "I am not leaving."

Epa stepped back, examining her, a stubborn look on his broad face.

"You're wasting time," said Charis. Though she spoke slowly, her voice shook with barely suppressed rage. "Stop wasting time."

"You can stay," Epa said to Sam. "The rest of them, out." He turned to his table of supplies. "Room's too damn small for an audience, shint's sake."

Shale and Dash backed out, followed by Skye, Dot, and Adder.

Sam felt a hand on hers and flinched before realizing it was Jackal. He was looking at her questioningly. She nodded at him, and he followed the others out as well.

Only Epa, Sam, and Charis remained.

"It's her sister," Sam told Epa. "Just let her stay. Please."

He glared at Charis. "Fine. Sit," he said, pointing to a small stool beside the bed.

"Girl, grab me water and clean cloths."

Sam said nothing while Epa cut away the fabric that surrounded the lesion on Shya's leg and washed the area. Instead she spent that time searching through the shelves. She found the antiseptic, antibiotics, and sealant she'd brought from the base arranged carefully on a bottom shelf. There was even a roll of gauze, still.

Begrudgingly, Epa allowed Sam to sanitize the area and seal the wound. She tried to involve Charis by giving her the job of syringing liquid antibiotics down her sister's throat, but the huaina's hands were shaking too badly.

By the time they were done, Shya was sleeping. Charis sat beside her sister, shifting uncomfortably every few seconds. It was as though her skin didn't fit properly anymore. Epa had left. "To get water," he'd said.

To rummage through the cart, more likely.

Sam watched the two sisters, a heaviness in her heart that had nothing to do with infection or fever or doomed rescue missions.

"She gonna be okay?" asked Charis, too loudly. She had stripped down to a sleeveless shirt, giving Sam full view of the black symbols that twined up her left arm and down her collarbone, meeting in a swirl on her shoulder blade. Huaina branding.

"I don't know." Sam turned away and busied herself with the cleanup. "I think so. She could have used a blood transfusion."

Not that any of them know their blood type.

Or know that they have a blood type.

Or know whether they carry the human immunodeficiency virus or any other northern infections.

Charis looked at her blankly.

Sam sighed. "She should be."

Charis nodded, letting out a slow, shaky breath, and rummaged in her back pocket until she found another hasha smoke. She dropped it, picked it back up, dropped it again, and cursed loudly.

"Uh, that's not—"

"What?" asked Charis.

"You shouldn't smoke in a sickroom," said Sam, struggling to keep her voice even as she crouched down, picking up a blood-soaked rag that had fallen to the ground. Judgment wouldn't be helpful here.

I should be wearing gloves. Why didn't I ask Epa for gloves?

There had been a pack of them in the medical kit she'd brought north with her. Single-use biodegradable medical gloves that were probably sitting, useless, on one of his shelves.

Charis stared at the hasha smoke, still lying on the floor. "Fine." She took something else out of her pocket and began fiddling with it. "I'm glad you didn't die."

Sam was so taken aback that she froze, staring at the bit of bloody cloth in her hand.

"Thank you," she said. "I'm glad that tree didn't crush you."

"Yeah, me too," said Charis.

Sam stood up and placed the cloth in the basket that Epa had left by the door. She'd boil the rags later. Or he would. Someone would.

"What's that in your hands?" asked Sam.

"What? Oh." Charis flipped over her hand to show the small, flat circular device that she'd been playing with, her palm shaking so badly that it took Sam a moment to figure out what it was.

"Is that a compass?"

"One of Dash's buddies showed it to me. Tells you where's north, see?" Charis pointed at the top of the compass. "Kinda like the one Dot has. It's how I found you guys."

"But Dot's porta—her compass doesn't point north. It's different."

Charis nodded, shoving the compass back into her pocket. "But mostly it had us walking south-east. So I guessed. Got lost near morning, but then I saw—I saw something." She reached out to stroke her sister's hair—missed, tried again, missed a second time, and gave up.

"You saw something?"

"What? Oh. Smoke. I saw smoke from your campfire."

"Well, it was nice of him to give it to you."

Charis looked at Sam, confused. "Who?"

"Dash's friend," said Sam.

"Oh naw, he didn't. Nicked it," said Charis. She took her rings off and laid them on the bed beside her sister.

"Right," said Sam. "I need water, you need water?"

When Charis didn't answer, Sam left the sickroom. Only Dash and Jackal were present in the living area. The former was asleep on a couch, the latter crouched down in front of one of the bookcases, examining some of Epa's curios. He stood up when she entered the room.

Too tired and dehydrated to answer questions, Sam walked past him to the kitchen, rummaged until she found the tin she used to use as her cup, and filled it with the lukewarm water from the stove. She glanced back to see if Epa was watching, lurking from a corner somewhere, and then downed a second cup. She refilled it a third time and carried it over to Charis, who accepted it wordlessly.

"How's she doing?" Jackal asked when Sam returned to the living area and flopped down on a long brown couch.

"Okay, maybe. I don't know. It's as much as I could do." The failure of those words tugged at her. "We'll have to wait and see. Where are the others?"

"Outside."

"Outside." Sam stared blankly at Jackal. "What—it's the middle of the night. Why are they outside?"

Jackal crossed his arms and leaned against the wall. His head almost touched the ceiling. "Dance party."

"Dance—are you—is this a joke?"

"Skye traded the skag rings for mushrooms."

"Mushrooms. Why would that—" Sam stopped. Sat up straight, then closed her eyes and slumped forward, sinking her head into her hands. "You mean the northern kind of mushrooms. The ones that poison you." She let out a groan. "Why would they—we're on a mission!" She looked up and glared at Jackal.

He looked unperturbed. "And Shya might die. And we might too. Guess this is their way of saying they ain't dead yet."

"By poisoning themselves."

"Yep."

"That is really stupid."

"Yep."

"You seem very unworried."

Jackal gave her a wry smile. "We all cope how best we can."

"You're not high on mushrooms."

"Yeah, well, I'm older. And you shoulda seen me after Anna disa—after they took her."

Sam looked down, her eyes settling on the V on her wrist. The skin was still wet and oozing. *Will it ever heal?* "Where would Epa have even gotten the mushrooms from? It's not as though they grow in the Waste."

"Looks like your man collects all manner of things."

"He's not my anything."

"I can tell. Reckon you want to get out of here as fast as you can." Jackal's eyes were on hers, not intrusive or aggressive, but she felt suddenly too visible. Overexposed. "But I figure Shya's not gonna be able to move tomorrow. Might as well let them have some fun. They'll sleep it off. We'll head out the day after."

Sam sighed but nodded. It was not as though her being scandalised was going to un-drug her friends.

"Wind's died down. Want to sit outside with me, make sure nobody wanders off and gets lost?"

"Fine."

31

Without the wind to blind and bully them, it was almost peaceful outside. The stars blazed overhead, with a nearness and clarity she'd missed living in the smog of the Barrow. Under the moonlight the dust looked like fallen snow. Not that she'd ever seen snow. But she had seen photographs.

Only the large, hulking frames of the empty houses disrupted the brilliance of their view; the mausoleums of the Waste.

Only if there are bodies beneath the floorboards.

Maybe there are.

Though she couldn't see the others yet, she heard singing and laughter coming from the other side of the cabin.

"This way," said Jackal, reaching for her hand.

"I have a better idea," Sam said, flushing. She led him to the side of the house, where the metal husk of an old car had been parked beside Epa's shed. After checking to make sure that Epa wasn't watching, she climbed onto the car, and then pulled herself onto the roof of the shed. From here she was able to make her way up onto the roof. Jackal followed her up, of course. Swiftly, and with his own long-limbed, wiry sort of grace. Together they climbed up to the peak of the roof, where they could sit and watch with an unobstructed view.

Someone had planted a torch in the sand. Skye, Dot, Shale, and Adder were dancing around it, arms flung out, legs spinning, singing.

"Hey, hey, they cried bullshit on the day."

It was the same song she'd heard at the factory party during the solstice. The leitmotif of her suicide mission, it seemed.

She thought of Xenia, covered in paint and laughing, and felt incredible sadness. It seemed impossible that someone so bright could have been snuffed out so quickly.

Like Corvus.

The familiar ache ran up her spine and along her jaw. She waited as the heaviness of guilt followed. The faithful companion to her grief.

She looked down at her friends, dancing. She watched Shale spin by, a flurry of auburn hair, her body lithe and graceful even in this state, and Dot, bouncing up and down, her face raised to the stars, and understood.

"It looks like fun," she said in a small voice.

"You never seen anyone on mushrooms before?" asked Jackal.

Sam shook her head, then frowned. "Well, I might have. You Northerners are always on something."

"Mushrooms are a funny one, though. The happy part doesn't always last."

Soon only Dot and Shale were still dancing. Skye was wandering around, reaching out to touch, and sometimes taste, flora only she could see. Adder had sat down beside the torch and was deep in conversation with himself.

"So, I can guess how you ended up here," said Jackal after a few moments.

Sam glanced over, traced his face in the dark. "I needed help, stumbled upon the cabin."

"And he helped you."

"Yes," she said, though the words tasted bitter in her mouth. "He gave me shelter, and food and water once mine had run out."

"In exchange for your things."

Sam nodded. "All my things. Gave me some castoffs to wear. Sent me in the direction of the Barrow with Ava's name and as much water as I could carry."

"You sound upset he sent you off."

Sam shrugged, then leaned back, her hands on the sharp edge of the rooftop. "I was angry when he threw me out. I wasn't ready." One girl alone in the desert—skinny and pale, sweating and shaking with the shock of withdrawal that had only just started to come down from its peak. No weapon and just enough food and water to make it a race against starvation and fatal dehydration. It was luck that nothing predatory had found her—a different role of the dice and she would have been just another bloated body lying in the Waste, waiting for the sand to bury her.

She watched as Adder stood up, staggered past Shale and Dot, and began vomiting profusely in the sand.

"At the same time, though, I was also worried—" Sam swallowed. Breathed out slowly. "I thought he might not let me leave. He asked me to stay, at first. I didn't know if it was really a choice."

"As his girl?" Jackal frowned. "Old guy like that..."

"I'm not sure," said Sam, wrinkling up her nose. "Maybe. Maybe not. He likes control, Epa. He's like a spider. He thinks that anything that stumbles into his home belongs to him."

"How'd he know Ava?"

Sam shook her head. "He never said. Neither did she."

"You asked?"

Sam looked at him, as her face stretched into the unfamiliar shape of a smile. "Are you making fun of me?"

He grinned back at her—a true smile. It opened up his face, and showed how handsome he actually was, beneath the dust and the sadness.

"No," said Sam. "I didn't directly ask. Obviously." She laughed.

Adder's head snapped up. He looked up toward the roof and then fell flat onto his back. From there he curled into the fetal position, hiding his head under his arms as though protecting his skull from an onslaught of blows.

"What—is he okay?" asked Sam, leaning forward. "Adder!"

"He'll be fine," said Jackal. "Probably just thinks you're a demon coming to take his soul, or something."

Sam stared at him, open-mouthed. "He what?"

"Mushrooms," he said. "Least he's young and healthy enough. Probably won't have a jammer or anything."

"A jammer."

"Heart pain, the kind that'll kill you."

"That's a possibility?"

"Sure. He'll probably be fine, though." He peered down at the torch, where Shale had sat down, her knees pulled tight to her chest. "Shale we might need to get inside. Sweating like that ain't good—she'll get the chills any minute."

He turned to her and grinned again. "Least nobody's pissed themselves."

32

The sun was rising by the time they managed to convince Shale to come inside, pink sky interlaced with blue, like pictures Sam had seen once of an underwater coral reef before the shores of Seira went dark.

Dot and Skye followed soon after, and Adder last of all, a twitchy, hunted look in his eyes. They slept on the couches and on blankets on the floor. Epa even took Sam's own blanket down from the shelf and gave it to her, though whether it was intended as a kindness or a way to remind her of who she was and where she came from, she wasn't sure. Probably the latter. Epa was fond of manipulation.

Sam lay on the floor, wishing she were anywhere else.

At least you're not dying of dehydration.

There is that.

"Sam."

Sam rolled over to see Charis leaning against the doorway to the sickroom. From the light streaming through the dirty window behind her, it looked to be midmorning.

"She's awake." There were dark circles under Charis' eyes and her words were heavily slurred. The older girl was crashing, Sam realized —from the Blue, from exhaustion, from the emotional upheaval of the last three days.

Sam slipped out from under the thin, tan blanket and made her way across the body-strewn floor and into the sickroom.

"I hear you patched me up," said Shya from the bed, her voice rough from disuse.

"I tried." Sam felt Shya's forehead with the back of her hand, wishing she had a thermometer.

"You have my thanks." Shya coughed, and the smile she had been directing at Sam turned into a grimace of pain.

"Of course—I was happy to." Sam began unravelling the outer bandage. "You don't seem to have a fever." She gave the bandages a sniff, and examined the skin surrounding the wound for signs of infection. "And this seems to be healing okay."

Sam heard Charis let out a low, shaky breath, and busied herself winding the fabric back around Shya's leg.

"I'll get you something to drink," said Sam, leaving the two sisters to process the information in private.

Epa was in the kitchen. He watched as Sam took a cup of water and added a pinch of sugar and a shake of salt to the cup. "I suppose your friends will want to eat."

"We have food, thank you. I'll get it from the cart." Sam hated the way her voice sounded. Nervous. Pleading. This man had no power over her. Not anymore. "You're welcome to share in it, of course."

He sniffed. "Fine."

Sam gave the drink a quick stir and was turning to go when she felt his hand on her shoulder, pulling her back. His fingers slid up toward her neck, where he grasped the thin cord and pulled. The two copper charms appeared from beneath her thin black shirt. He caught them in his large, callused palm: a rectangle and a bird.

"So, I see you found my Ava," he said.

His use of the possessive set Sam's teeth on edge. "I did."

"She must have liked you, to have given you this."

Sam said nothing, just waited, the cup still in her hands.

"Thought she woulda given it to Raina."

"Raina's missing," said Sam.

Epa's hands stilled. He dropped the necklace and took her chin in his fingers, lifting her face up toward his. "What do you mean, missing?"

His voice was low, dangerous. Sam stifled the urge to drop the cup and shift into a fighter's stance.

"Girls have been taken from the North and sent south. We don't know why. It's why we're crossing the Waste."

"To find them."

"Yes."

Sam felt his fingers quiver slightly before he released her face and reached for the necklace again. He lifted it over her head and tucked it into his shirt pocket.

Sam's mouth went dry.

"Bring the girls here when you're on your way North again. Bring them to me. I'll feed them. No payment. And you can have your trinket back."

She didn't argue. Instead she nodded and crossed back across the sleeping bodies to the sickroom.

You could have fought him.

Don't be stupid.

Nine bodies to one.

Eight. Dash isn't here.

Fine, eight to one.

Are you counting Shya? Because—

It's one old man.

With blades up his sleeves and vials of poison in his pocket.

It's not just that.

He's Ava's friend.

You fear him.

She brought Shya her drink and then left the sickroom, wondering how much they'd overheard, if anything. Wondering why she felt ashamed.

The cabin felt too small, too stuffy. The headache that had been hovering threateningly at the edge of her skull was taking hold. If only she wasn't so tired. Sam rolled her head forward, relaxed her jaw, dropped her shoulders. None of it helped to release the metal vice that seemed to be squeezing her brain.

Will it pop, do you think? Like a rotten gourd?

You're slurring. Go to sleep.

The need to distance herself from Epa was stronger, however, so she made her way outside to the cart, where she found Dash hammering away.

"The axle?" she asked.

"Yep."

"Both of them?"

"Yep."

She picked up a second hammer, discarded at his feet, and moved to the other axle.

She supposed Epa must have brought him the tools.

Another favour to add to the tally.

They settled into a steady rhythm, losing the count only when Sam stopped to shake out her throbbing arms and shoulders.

Being crushed by boulders was unfortunate.

Don't worry. Soon you'll be dead and they won't trouble you anymore.

Hush. I'm having a nice time.

She was, in fact. Probably because she was beginning to enjoy Dash's company. A strong fighter who prioritized sleep over narcotics and felt no need for idle chatter—she was beginning to think they should have traded Adder in, as well.

After several minutes Sam put her hammer down and tried to delicately spit out the ash that had accumulated in her mouth. The spittle dribbled onto her lower lip and down her chin.

Pathetic.

She wiped her face with the back of her hand and glanced at Dash, who had been smart enough to take his kerchief outside with him.

He had stopped hammering and was watching her, though she couldn't read his expression.

"I guess you're used to all—all this," she said, and immediately wished she'd come up with something better to say. Or better yet, had maintained their pleasant silence.

Dash shrugged and resuming hammering the axle. "When you live as close to the Waste as we do, you learn to deal with it."

"Right," she said, and retrieved her hammer.

"It's not like this, in the South?"

"Oh, um, no. I mean, there were wildfires too, early on during the Decline, but not as many."

Dash pulled down his kerchief and turned his full body toward her, the hammer forgotten in his hand. "So, it got green again, then? Everyone always said it didn't, but—" He stopped as Sam started shaking her head.

"It's just desert," she said, hating how the brief shimmer of excitement was already fading from his dark eyes. "There was always a desert south of Seira, but it expanded during the Decline. So even after the ash washed away, not much grew back."

"Is there rain?"

"A little," she said. "But not enough. Not like there used to be."

He nodded. "It still rains in the Waste, sometimes. Just not this time of year. And when it does it's the wrong type—storms that bring too much water, too fast. My ancestors used to call them 'Cropkillers', because everything they planted would drown. Even the trees. Not the big ones—they were fine for a while. But the saplings kept rotting."

There was something in Dash's face. Almost as though they weren't speaking about the world his forebears had lived in. Almost as if it had been his world, too.

"When you can't grow anything..." He shrugged, and looked down to his hammer.

There was nothing to say, so Sam said nothing, just waited for Dash to continue. When he didn't, she picked up her hammer again. He joined her on the second strike.

When they had finished repairing the axles they moved on to hammering out the dents in the cart itself. Once the cart was functional again, they silently pulled out rice and lentils for the midday meal, as well as dishes and a fuel puck.

Still in silence, Sam and Dash prepared the meal.

Eventually the others woke, ate, went back to sleep.

Sam brought lunch in to Shya and found Charis drifting in and out in her chair. Charis eyed Sam, the food, and then staggered off to the living area, where she promptly fell asleep on the couch.

Maybe she trusts me now.

Or maybe she's just so tired that she doesn't care.

Or that.

That evening Sam and Dot went through the cart, picking out non-essential items. There wasn't much: an extra blanket, a few items of clothing, a dried plant Skye had insisted on bringing with them for luck.

"He's really going to want this crap?" asked Dot, surveying the small pile with a skeptical expression. "What use will he have for, say, this?" She picked up one of Shya's t-shirts, black and artfully ripped to expose the abdomen.

"I don't know," said Sam, laying the blanket flat on one of the bunks.

Dot had been uncharacteristically pessimistic all evening. Moody, even. An after-effect of consuming psychedelic mushrooms, perhaps, although Sam didn't actually know whether hangovers were part of the hallucinogenic experience.

Or maybe she's fretting about our impending doom.

Or she saw you up on the roof last night with Jackal.

Sam lined up the edges of the blanket and began to fold it. "As far as I can see, the more useless the better for Epa."

All we did was talk—and anyway, Dot and Jackal are not in a relationship. She would have no justification for jealousy.

This isn't Seira. And even Southerners aren't that sensible when it comes to intimate partner selection. Not really.

It was supposed to be an outdated cultural norm, jealousy. That was what she had been taught as an adolescent. They had discussed it as part of their unit on sexual health and consent.

But she didn't really believe that it was a learned behaviour. Something persisted, deep down at the chromosomal level—some residue of primal instinct that all the education in the world hadn't been able to quell.

Dot frowned. "He's a weird dude."

"Yes."

Which means that she'll see me as a threat, even if I'm not. And despise me.

You could just talk to her, you know.

"I get the feeling he'd like to cut me up and put my bits on his shelf, you know?"

"Oh no," said Sam. "He's not harmful like that. I mean, if you died of natural causes he might do that, but he wouldn't actually murder you. Is that reassuring?"

Dot stared at her for a second and then burst out laughing. "Nope."

Sam found herself joining in. It felt good, even though the imagery of Epa practicing taxidermy on them was horrible and morbid. Or perhaps she was only relieved that Dot wasn't angry with her.

They gathered up the goods and shut the door to the cart.

"Anyway," said Sam. "We might need him on our way back north."

"On the way back, eh?" Dot grinned at Sam. "So optimistic."

"I just don't think we should—what's the term you use? Burn bridges? Even if I'd like to." Sam took a deep breath. "And speaking of, there's something I wanted to clarify, just in case you misunder—"

Just then Epa appeared in the doorway, a smile on his face. "Gifts? You shouldn't have."

"A thanks for your hospitality," said Dot. "We were in a sore spot."

"You were." He eyed them for a moment and then gestured behind him. "There's enough water here to last you all a few days."

Sam looked at the pile of containers and said nothing. He must have spent hours at the spring. It was constant, what he had access to —but not fast or plentiful. She felt herself softening toward him.

"Thank you, Epa." Sam picked up a container of water and began lugging it back to the cart.

"And how long's the haul to the border?" she heard Dot ask.

"Depends. I'm guessing you don't just want the border, you want the station."

Sam's pace quickened.

"That's right. We want the base—er, station. The big building."

"If you leave early tomorrow, you'll reach it mid-morning on the fourth day. Samarra," he continued, as Sam approached for a second container. "I filled the basin in my room. And there's powder. You should wash."

"Thank you," said Sam, though an ugly feeling crept up her spine and settled along the back of her neck. "I'll let the others know."

"Oh, there's hardly enough for the group. Not with all the drinking water you're taking from me. This little treat is just for you." He picked up a large container of water and held it out for her to take.

Sam nodded, keeping her eyes on the container to hide her repulsion. She moved to take it from him, but it didn't budge.

"Samarra," said Epa.

She looked up at him, her face expressionless.

"Say thank you."

"Thank you." He released the container and she turned away, hauling it back toward the cart.

Dot, coming toward her, offered a sympathetic smile that only made Sam feel worse. As Sam moved to walk past her, Dot put a hand on her arm.

"Were you saying something, before?"

Sam shook her head and kept walking. She'd lost the stomach for confrontation. "I don't remember."

The others were already in bed when they returned. She crept past them to Epa's bedroom, despising him and his forced dependence but unwilling to create conflict over such a small matter. Because there were no easy refusals with Epa.

She walked straight to where she knew the basin would be, lain atop the dresser. She refused to look at this man's space, as though his mouldy, predatory presence might be absorbed through her eyeballs. Not that it mattered. She'd seen the room before.

She lowered her face to the water, using the clean rag he'd left out for her to scrub the grime from her face.

Patting herself as dry as she could with the wet rag, Sam raised her eyes to the mirror she'd been avoiding since she'd entered Epa's room.

Would they even recognize me in Seira? she wondered, staring at her thin, sunburnt face, the bags under her eyes, at the bruise along one cheek. She brought up a hand and poked at it gingerly. Fresh, though it was already dark purple. From her fight with the skag, perhaps.

She untied her loose braid and let the gnarled, greasy strands of hair fall forward. Bits of dust and ash had turned her black hair grey, making it look as though she had aged decades since she last saw her own reflection. It had only been a few weeks, of course. In a very different room, in a very different home, with a very different idea of her own life expectancy. She wondered if they were okay, Geo and Jem. And then she wondered what it had been like for Adder, growing up with them.

Don't shine nostalgic lights on the Barrow. Geo and Jem are outliers. Most people don't live long enough to know their grandchildren.

But some do.

More die from contaminated water, or pneumonia or some mutated virus or STI. Or they're robbed and murdered by huainas.

Sam found the jar of powder and poured a tiny amount into her open palm.

In the South, children were raised to love their country above all else. To be loyal to Seira. In the North, people were loyal to their families, their friends.

She worked the powder into her hair, soaking up the worst of the grease. Maybe that was all that bound these strange pairings. Dot and Shya. Charis and Skye. Maybe friendship and love didn't need commonality. Maybe all that mattered was a history of loyalty.

Her hands drifted down from her head to the water basin. She let the rest of the powder float on the greasy water, like sea foam in a city flooded with sewage. She was tired. She should try to sleep.

Returning to the living room, Sam found a blanket and curled up in a corner between Adder and Jackal. Adder was already asleep, though he kept muttering and twitching. Jackal's eyes were closed, but Sam knew him to be awake.

She thought about crawling in with him. To be warm, to feel momentarily safe— She sat up and looked at him, and then lay back down. She hated the idea of Epa seeing her, making inferences, thinking he knew anything about her. He already knew too much.

33

"Sorry, am I distracting you?" Corvus crossed his arms and leaned against the wall of the shooting range, a grin on his face.

Sam turned to glare at him, and then stalked down the range and yanked her knife from the target. "You give yourself too much credit."

"Credit? Isn't that blame?"

"To someone else, maybe. You take everything as credit."

That smile again—something between a smirk and an invitation.

Sam faced the target again. Closed her eyes.

Breathe in. Breathe out.

The knife is an extension of my hand. We are smooth and fluid and fast, like a rushing stream.

Holding the target in her mind, she lifted her arm back and then snapped it forward.

"That's more like it." Corvus strode down the range to the target and pulled the knife free. "My turn," he said, and untied the girl. She fell to the ground in a graceless heap, the blood pooling outward on the cold, cement floor of the firing range.

Sam frowned. "She had a name. Do you remember?"

Corvus shrugged, busy tying himself to the target. "Come help me with this, would you?"

"Of course." She jogged down to meet him. "I hate doing this," she said quietly in his ear.

"I know. But they need a show."

Sam looked up at the crowd, the smiling, cheering faces. She waved back and they screamed in response, stomping their feet and waving red swaths of fabric.

"Of course," she said. "But isn't there another way?"

Corvus lifted his chin for a kiss. Sam stepped forward, pressing her lips to his.

"You know there is," he said.

"Raina."

Corvus gave a subtle nod—the most he could manage with the ropes binding him. "She'll trade with me. You know she will."

"I know." Sam looked up at the crowd again. It was mostly cadets. Would they wait?

"Just be quick."

"Okay."

"And kiss me one more time."

Sam scowled at him. "You are becoming greedy."

"I am repeating a successful strategy."

She laughed and kissed him one more time.

"Now go," he said.

She took the knife and sprinted up the range. Yanking open the door, she—

"Time to wake up, Sam." Dot's voice tugged her upward.

Sam tried to force her eyelids open. Failed. Tried again. This time Epa's living room came into focus. The pale light streaming in through the windows that told her that it was not yet dawn.

"I'm awake," she said, her voice creaky. She rolled onto her side, trying to shake the taste of the dream. Too much death. There was always too much death when she slept.

She helped the others stack Epa's blankets in a corner and collect their things.

He was already outside waiting for them when they reached the cart.

"Thank you," said Sam when she reached him. "You've saved my life twice now."

He smiled, as she'd known he would. Nothing pleased him more than favours owed. He leaned in. "Just bring the girls here. Remember. Raina and the others." He reached out and took her hand. "Promise me."

Sam forced her lips into a smile. "I will try."

He frowned slightly at that, but released her hand.

"You," he said as Shale moved to walk past. "You won't mind leaving a small token, will you?" He passed her a knife.

Shale took it wordlessly, looking at him, then down to the knife. To Sam's surprise, she separated a lock of auburn hair from the base of her neck and sawed it off. She passed it to Epa with a smile and a wink.

As the party marched south, Sam stole a look at Shale's face. The smile was gone. What remained flickered between rage and disinterest.

Shale caught her watching and shrugged, her nonchalance so convincing that Sam wondered whether her previous impression was correct after all. "Not the first time it's happened."

Sam nodded and turned away.

A moment later she felt Shale's small hand slip into hers. "It's a small price to pay," she said. "He's a shady one, but we'd be dead without him. Without you."

Sam nodded. They had needed rescuing. Still though… "It would have been nicer if he had been, well…nicer."

"Or at least good looking," Shale said, and laughed. Her real laugh, like wind chimes in the morning. But prettier.

Sam brightened, hearing it. Shale had been acting more and more like her old self. The sadness was still there, and the heaviness, but Sam was grateful that the other girl's spark hadn't died with Xenia.

"Makes you wonder how Ava could stand him, huh?" asked Shale. "Not that there was a lot of choice, out here."

Sam stopped.

"Hey! Give a little warning next time," said Charis, who had to step to the side to avoid walking into her.

Sam still hadn't moved. Shale pulled her hand out of Sam's and brushed dusty hair out of her face. "What's wrong?"

"Everything that you just said," said Sam. "Was he—were he and Ava—really? And what did you mean by 'out here'?"

Shale looked like she regretted having spoken. "Jit taow. I thought Ava woulda told you." She sighed and took Sam's arm in hers. "Keep walking or Charis will lose her shit again."

"Epa and Ava were together?"

"Well, yeah. For a bit, anyway. They came to the Barrow together. With Raina."

Sam's arm jerked. "You don't mean—Epa's not Raina's father?"

"He is. At least from how it looked. I mean, I was a kid, but they seemed like a family."

"Wait—you and Epa knew each other from before? Why didn't you—"

Shale was already shaking her head. "I never actually met him. This was before me and Ava got close. But I was at the factory a lot back then, so yeah, I saw him."

Sam's head was reeling. "And Ava and Raina used to live—live *here*?"

"I think there used to be more water or something. Anyway, a bunch of people all left and came to the Barrow. Then, I guess, Epa came back."

"And Ava chose him." Sam thought of Epa's hands—his large, long fingers—and shuddered. "Why?"

"She was really young," said Shale. "And I don't think he was like that, before. I think living out here's turned him into a creep."

"I thought you said you were a child." Sam didn't mean for it to sound like an accusation, but it came out like one nonetheless.

The wind stirred, grabbed Shale's laugh, bitter this time, and threw it behind them. "I got a great memory." She pulled her kerchief out of her back pocket and tied it over her mouth and nose. "Nothing ever fades."

Maybe it was the euphoria of evading death by bandit or dehydration. Maybe it was relief at Shya's quick recovery. Maybe it was the fact that they'd had a good night's sleep. Whatever the reason, the party was in good spirits that day.

Dot permitted the fire to burn after the evening's meal had cooked. They didn't need it for warmth, of course. It was cooler in the evenings, but it certainly wasn't cold. It was an emotional warmth they sought, Sam supposed. The sociability that comes from shared resources.

Fire is pretty.

And broadcasts your exact location.

It's still pretty.

They were far enough south now that another skag attack was unlikely, but Dot had decided that she and Dash should still walk the perimeter, ranged weapons out and loaded. Just in case. The rest of the party sat around the fire, sharing the remainder of the liquor and meat they'd pilfered from the bandits. Adder and Charis had stabbed theirs with crossbow bolts and were roasting them over the flames. It was technically hygienic, Sam supposed—the fire sanitizing the bolt as it heated the meat—but she still waved it away when Adder offered to share. It was no different than hunting with a crossbow, not really, but Sam couldn't shake the image of those same bolts slicing into the meaty flesh of the snake they'd found. It was tangled up in her memory with the bloated face of the woman and the smell of putrefying flesh.

"Glad Epa didn't get these," said Shale, passing the skin to Sam with a wink.

Sam took a sip of the venomous brew before passing it to Jackal beside her. He chuckled and she felt her skin grow hot.

"What?"

"It was a tell."

"What was?"

"That face. When you drink."

Sam leaned back on her hands and looked up at him. "You can't tell me that Northerners actually like the taste of this stuff."

"No. That's why you don't let it sit on your tongue."

"I'm sorry?"

He tipped his head back and seemed to pour the alcohol straight down his throat. "'Down the hatch.' That's what we say."

"Down the—you mean like a hatch on an aircraft?"

Jackal chuckled again and passed the moonshine to Skye. "Don't know. It's just something we say."

"Down the hatch."

"Down the hatch. But you gotta say it before you drink."

Sam shook her head, though she couldn't help laughing too.

"Here, practice," said Shale as the skin came around again.

"Down the hatch." Sam tried to imitate Jackal and found herself coughing and gasping for breath.

"You okay there, Southerner?" asked Charis from across the circle.

It could be Sam's imagination, but she thought the tone was slightly warmer than it had been.

"You sound like you're drowning," said Adder. "It's very attractive."

"I'm okay," Sam rasped.

"Good," said Adder. "Because I think we should talk through the plan."

There was a general murmur of assent. Shya stood up. "Dot should be here."

Charis caught her wrist with one hand. "You. Girl who almost died. Sit. I'll spell her."

"You're so sweet, my love," said Skye, running a hand up Charis' leg as the huaina jammed the remains of the jerky she'd been gnawing into her mouth and got to her feet.

Shya settled herself back down, rolling her eyes as she stretched out and then re-crossed her long legs. Though whether the eye-roll was in response to her sister's protectiveness or Skye's overt display of affection, Sam couldn't say.

"There isn't really a plan to walk through," said Sam, once Charis had reloaded her crossbow and left the fire. "Which has been the problem from the start."

"Oh, enough with your 'we're all going to die' bit," said Adder.

Skye stopped drinking long enough to nod emphatically, her black dreadlocks bouncing. "It's a bit of a downer."

"But in all likelihood we *are* going to die."

"Maybe that's the difference." Shale leaned over and tucked a strand of dusty black hair back behind Sam's ear. "Between us. In the Barrow, likelihood is you die before you're born. Or soon after."

"Definitely before you're up and running," said Adder.

"Or when you have babies." Skye was still now, her voice a whisper.

"Or when you get shot with a crossbow." Shya gave Sam a quiet smile.

"We get used to not dying," said Jackal.

Adder laughed. "It's why there are so many damn cults. Everything starts to seem like magic."

"It is different in the South?" There was something in Shale's voice. Not resentment. A touch of longing, maybe.

Do you blame them?

They don't know what you give up, in the South. How much the Administration takes.

More than they've lost?

Sam looked around the circle. She didn't actually know how many of them had living parents, or siblings. How many friends of theirs had died early, how many lovers.

"Okay," said Dot as she joined the circle, laying her crossbow down on the sand and settling onto a low boulder beside Skye, who passed her the skin of moonshine. "I hear we're going over the plan."

Sam sighed and pressed a knuckle into her temple. This conversation was giving her a headache. "There is no plan."

"Well, that's bleak," said Dot, taking a sip and then passing it over to Shya. "Hey Skye, go spell off Dash, would you?"

"Why?"

"Because he might be useful with this stuff."

Skye made an indignant sound, but untangled her skirts and got to her feet. After slowly and dramatically brushing the ash from her shirt, she picked up Dot's crossbow and headed off into the darkness. Sam thought she heard something about "the gods" and "destiny," but couldn't be certain as the wind surged for a moment, fanning the flames of their little fire higher and pushing the smoke eastward.

"That was fast," said Adder as Dash appeared only seconds later. "Is that why they call you Dash? Do you literally run everywhere?"

Dash ignored him and placed his bow in the sand before taking the space Skye had vacated. "Any real questions?" he asked.

"Actually, yes," said Sam. The moonshine reached her again, but this time she only pretended to drink before passing it to Jackal. She needed to focus. "Are you sure we won't see bandits again?"

Dash rolled a kink out of his neck and then stretched his arms. "I don't think so. We're getting too close to your wall."

"And bandits don't go there?"

"They think it's held by spirits. At the wall and in the sky."

"Well, that's a bit nuts," said Dot. "And what do you mean the sky? They think the crows are haunted, too?"

"Do you hear crows?" The skin reached Dash. He sniffed at it and then passed it to Dot, looking mildly disdainful. "No birds in the Waste." He walked to the cart, found a container with water in it and took a rationed sip, and then returned to the fire.

"Then what did you mean by spirits in the sky?"

"Oh," Sam said, when Dash gestured for her to explain. "Sorry. They're machines that fly. Like, um, like the shells of the cars you see in the Barrow. Except, they work."

Around the fire heads were shaken and eyebrows raised. Nobody accused her of lying, but it was clear that they didn't really believe her, either. It reminded Sam of just how badly outmatched they were.

"Actually," said Sam. "We—I mean the girls—should start riding in the cart tomorrow...in case of survei—in case their machines are watching. And it's not just visual—they'll have audio on us once we're within sight of the wall. Sound, I mean. They'll be able to hear our conversations."

Dot took a piece of jerky and began chewing at the edges. "You know how that sounds, right?"

"So, we're just going to be lying there in the cart, in silence, waiting," said Shya.

"There's the ropes," said Dot. "So, should be we can walk, as long as we're tied together. Still no talking, though."

"That's...better?" asked Shya.

Dot took a long swig of moonshine, passed it to Shya, and then went back to her dried meat. "At least we'll be awake."

That was the worst of it, of course. The part they'd all been dreading. The Vauns had supplied sedatives and a crudely illustrated note that made it very clear that the women were meant to be unconscious when they reached the border.

"Do you need the drugs?" asked Dash. "You can't just pretend to be asleep?"

Sam shifted, pulling her knees up to her chest and locking her arms around them.

What, you don't want to lose face in front of your new friends by jumping up and pacing the sand?

Often, anxiety can be diffused with mindfulness.

Which you are not practicing.

I feel the sand beneath me, I smell the smoke from the fire, I taste—

That's great and all, but if you don't answer them soon you're going to look very strange.

"We'll be scanned as we enter," said Sam. She could picture it now, the intel coming through to the screens in the Grand's office. "They'll be able to tell from our heart rates whether we're sedated." She could fool it, maybe. It would require deep meditation and a level of mental discipline she had spent a lifetime strengthening. And still she might fail. And even then...

It was Shya who spoke next, the skin of moonshine forgotten at her feet. "So, we take less. Enough of the stuff to fool the machines, but not so much that we actually pass out."

"Unless they look inside the cart."

"And you don't know if they do?"

Sam shook her head. "I don't. I don't even know if the carts themselves pass through the border. We might be moved to a train or, or something else, in which case we definitely will not be able to fake sedation. But a reduced dosage is still a good idea. Just enough to keep us unconscious through the border."

"And then we'll wake up," said Shya.

Sam nodded. "And then we'll wake up."

"How much is less?" asked Shale.

"I don't know."

Dot spoke up. "We'll reach the wall mid-morning on the fourth day, Epa said. That gives us two days to figure it out."

"I don't like it," said Charis, appearing suddenly behind Dot and causing her to jump and flail for her crossbow. "I thought the whole point was to be able to leap out of the cart and stab whoever took Anna and all the others."

"Jit taow, Charis! You're supposed to be on lookout!"

Charis nudged her way between Shya and an irritated Dot. "Decided I didn't want you making plans without me." She nodded toward Shale. "Send her to keep watch. Not going to add much value here, anyway, are you?"

Sam felt Shale stiffen beside her.

"Okay, enough," said Dot. "You got issues with the team, talk it out now or get over it." She shot Jackal an imploring look.

Jackal stood up and retrieved his longbow. "Fill me in after," he said and walked out into the darkness.

"That is the whole of our plan, though, isn't it?" asked Shya after a moment. "Get delivered. Get vengeance. Grab Anna and the others, if we can, and get out of there." She lifted her chin, letting her long black hair slide down her back until it touched the ground. She didn't bother saying that this was a best-case scenario. She didn't need to. They all knew it.

"Well, yes," said Sam. "But being unconscious at the border isn't —the border's not the problem. We just need to pass the scanners, and a visual check, maybe." Something important dawned on Sam. She looked at Dot. "The rings that Dash's people gave us, and the necklaces...have we checked their condition recently? Because knives and crossbows will give us away if they look inside the cart—we'll have to hide them. Which means that we won't have them with us if we're transferred from the cart to another form of transportation at the border."

"Checked yesterday," Shya answered for Dot. "They're fine."

Sam nodded, wondering if the others were realizing as she was how much feebler their plan would have been if they hadn't had the luck of being captured by the People of the Phoenix and gifted toxic jewelry. "Then we can wake up anytime between the border and when we get delivered to the actual buyer. And then, yeah. Leap up and, you know—" Sam's right arm released her knees long enough to make a stabbing gesture, before returning to their locked position.

An uncomfortable silence spread around the circle.

It was Dash who spoke first. "That's it? That's all you have? What about the buyer? What do we know about him?"

Six heads turned to face Sam. "I...I know as much as any of you." She swallowed. "I knew my division, much farther south, and I knew my base. I visited another base, once, but really, that's all I know of Seira."

"That's bav," said Charis. "You just hid inside two buildings your whole life?"

"Well...we weren't actually trapped indoors, but basically, yes. We don't get to move around in the South. It's not like that."

Dash looked at Sam. "So, we don't know the buyer. Do you at least know if the carts come north again?"

Sam shrugged, or attempted to. She was so tense that her shoulders were already almost as high as they could go. "I would assume they do, but I don't know for certain."

Shale grabbed her hand, gently but firmly. Sam looked down, surprised, to see that she had been tracing triangles in the sand.

"And you won't be a giveaway?" Her voice was quiet, relaxed, but the tension in the air told Sam that the others had been waiting to ask this question as well. "They won't recognize you?"

Sam swallowed. "No. The two people who had high enough authorization to receive the shipments before—they're both dead."

"So, who had the next highest authorization?" asked Shya.

"That would have been me."

"You feel pretty important, huh?" asked Charis. "You're not there, obviously. Who's next?"

"It's not like that. To be a second—a special guard to the base Grand and next in line for leadership—that takes a lot of training. You can't just replace a second."

"So?" asked Charis. "Get to the point, Southerner."

"So, the protocol—not that it's ever used, because three P5s don't just disappear, or die, that never happens—but the official protocol is to have a senior P5 apprentice from another base move over and undergo an expedited program." More confused faces. "To train them quickly."

"And these people from other bases—they won't recognize you?" asked Dot.

Sam shook her head.

"Well, that's good—"

"No," said Sam. "I mean, I don't know. I don't know if the Administration publicized my escape." She could see it—her face flashing across the screen during a national broadcast, the word *traitor* stamped above her head. "Maybe, maybe not. Even if they did, this person will only know my face from pictures."

"Easy," said Shale. "We cut your hair—"

"No—"

"Don't fret, Sammy," said Adder. "You'll look great bald."

"Please don't call me that again. And what I mean is that there's no point. In the South we change hair colour, eye colour. It's easy. And we do it all the time. It's like changing clothes."

"You change eye colour?" asked Shya. "That's—that's not possible."

"It's just a contact lens," said Sam. "Plastic you put on your eyeball."

Dash shook his head. "No wonder the skags think you're demons."

"Yeah," said Adder. "Also now I get why the South is so aggressive. If I had plastic on my eyes I'd be pissy too."

"It doesn't—it doesn't hurt, Adder. And the point is that unless you can make me gain or lose a hundred pounds or lose a limb, the idea of a disguise is useless." She was a liability. They all knew it. "If I'm identified, I'll tell them I was kidnapped. It won't help me, but the rest of you will be able to stay on mission." She thought they'd look relieved—grateful, maybe. But her plan of self-sacrifice hadn't elicited much of a response. Only Dash was nodding at her, a look of grim satisfaction on his face.

For the rest of them, she wondered if the danger was becoming too real. Did they want to back out? Did she?

Maybe that's why we work in packs. If nobody voices their doubts aloud, we'll all just keep going.

Die together. Die alone. Same outcome.

There was only ever going to be one outcome here.

"So, if the cart goes all the way to the buyer, we jump out, kill them, grab Anna and the others, pop back in the cart, and go home?" asked Dot after a moment.

"And if the cart gets unloaded at the border, and if we're sedated so we don't get caught, we'll get dumped in some other cart or whatever, and *then* we'll jump out and kill them, blah blah, but have no way to get home," said Charis.

"Maybe don't kill them—" said Dash.

"Sorry if that hurts your feelings," said Charis. "But we're here to murder those slime-eating—"

"All," finished Dash. "Keep some alive to help you get out. Take hostages."

"That," said Shale, "is not a bad idea."

"Assuming we pass inspection at the border," said Sam.

"And still have our cool little weapons," added Adder.

"And what about us?" asked Dash.

"What about you?" asked Charis.

"If they take you, but turn back the cart at the border, do they turn back the guards?"

"Oh," said Dot. "Right. Sam?"

"They'd want the guards out of the South as soon as possible," said Sam.

"So, what then?" asked Dash. "We take the cart and wait for you in the Waste?"

"That's unacceptable." Adder waved his hand dismissively, a piece of jerky clutched in his fingers. "We'll say we have orders to meet the buyer."

"On what grounds?" asked Sam.

"To make sure we're getting the right price, of course," said Adder.

"That's not going to work. The Vauns have no power in the South, the Administration—"

"Depends how badly they want the girls," said Shale. "That's bartering, Sam. It's not about who has more stuff. It's about who wants it more. My guess is, whoever's taking the girls wants them real bad."

"Yeah," said Adder, though he was staring confusedly at his fingers; apparently he'd forgotten the jerky was there. "Also, hang on—we had rope this whole time? We just walked through, like, a dozen sandstorms, and we had rope?"

34

The next morning after breakfast Dot and Shya went into the cart to unearth the colourful scarves and clothing they'd brought with them from the Barrow. In sombre silence they traded their dusty t-shirts for colourful tops or dresses and braided ribbon into their hair. Just six girls dressed for the solstice on their way to a compound party.

Too bad we don't have the masks.

Economical of the Vauns to remove them. Why make new masks every solstice when you can re-use the old ones?

It would have been convenient when we passed the border.

Technically it was the environmental choice.

Then Dot passed the compass that was not a compass to Jackal, and the women entombed themselves within the cart.

There were four triple bunk beds, although the term bed was generous. They were really just metal grills with thin pads on top. And because storage units had been built under each set of beds, there was minimal vertical space between bunks. They couldn't sit up properly, and floor space was so tight that two women couldn't pass each other without finding themselves on intimate terms.

And there are only six of us. Imagine it with twelve.

At least our supplies are organized.

Yes, the storage units make for a pleasant voyage.

The jolting and bumping of the cart also triggered nausea, induced headaches, and left bruises on their bruises. Of all the forms of transportation that Sam had encountered, this was without a doubt the most disagreeable. At least they didn't fear death by heat exhaustion. There were downward-sloping vents, designed to generate airflow whilst keeping out the rain, and cool air flooded the cart at the hottest part of the day, triggered by some predetermined threshold. Southern witchery, Charis called it.

"Can't have the goods spoiled," Skye replied. "No one wants a mouldy peach."

The first morning they started with a third of a dose. Shale, Shya, and Dot blacked out for close to three hours—a half hour longer than Charis and Skye. The lethargy lasted another four. Sam felt nothing.

"What do you mean, nothing?" slurred Dot, when she awoke to find Sam tracing patterns on the roof of the cart with her finger.

"I think my body responds differently to pharmaceuticals," said Sam, tapping her fingernail against one of the thin streams of light that had managed to filter through the grills on the side of the cart. "Drugs, I mean."

"Different...how?"

"I think I need a lot of drugs to see an effect."

"Well, try more then."

"I will. Hey, check your dexterity. Your movement, I mean. Mime opening the clasp on your ring."

She heard sounds of mild effort and lazy frustration. "Jit...I'm drooling," said Dot after several minutes.

"How well do your fingers work?"

"They don't."

"Okay. We'll try you on a quarter dose."

"Whatever. You cut it. Since you're all perky. I'm gonna...I'm gonna nap...just for a minute."

"Is it a southern thing?" asked Dot that evening, as they readied themselves for what was hopefully the last experimental sedation. "Are you so pumped full of drugs this garbage does nothing to you?"

"I don't think so," said Sam, trying to stretch within the pod-like confinement of her bed. "I mean, yes, we are. But I think it's just me."

"Always gotta be special, huh," said Charis, who was passing out their pills.

"And you always got to be a bully." Shale's voice was a purr; the tone she used to seduce or antagonize.

"And you always got to be a—"

"Enough, Charis," said Shya. She sounded exhausted, though whether it was from the drugs or the living conditions, Sam wasn't sure.

"Hey, pup, I don't need you—"

"Enough! Charis!" There was the rustle of movement and then a roar of pain. Sam assumed Dot had tried to sit up, and had hit her head on the metal grate above her.

"Okay," said Dot a moment later in an overly patient voice. "I know we're all tired. And—what was that word you used, Sam?"

"Claustrophobic."

"Claustrophobic. That's what's making us lash out. And fear. But we chose to be here. We all chose this. Because we want our friends back, or because we want to gut somebody for what they done to us or people we love. This means that even though we're different, we got something important in common."

"We're also all stunners," said Skye.

"Thank you, Skye, for saying something nice. Even if it's totally off topic."

"You're welcome, love. Oooh, maybe we could all talk about our deepest darkest—"

"I have an idea for something we could do that would be, um, productive," said Sam. "While we're waiting for the drugs to kick in."

"Holy Ba'al I hope it doesn't involve sharing our feelings," said Charis as she climbed into her own bunk. "No offense, babe."

"It's a—a sort of mental training," said Sam. "I'll talk through a possible scenario. Try to imagine yourself doing the actions as I describe them."

"Is this a southern, brainwashy thing?" asked Shale.

"Yes, but no. Well, it's southern. But I think it's helpful. Not everything they taught me was wrong." The truth of the statement made the words reverberate in her skull. "Just most of it."

Skye giggled. "Imagine she's actually a southern spy. And this is a really long plot to kidnap us."

"There are so, so many easier people to kidnap," said Shya. "Nobody would choose us. Well, I mean, they did choose me. But they didn't really know me."

"You're sneaky with those blades, sis."

"Thanks, Char."

"Okay," said Sam. "Imagine you are on a mountain. There is no earth beneath your feet, only rocks..."

THE SWEET ZONE seemed to be somewhere between a fifth and a sixth of a dose. The blackout lasted an hour, with hearts beating slow and steady for three more. Movement was possible but slow after the first hour, functional after the second, close to normal after the third.

To see similar results, Sam required a full dose.

With the sedation quandary solved, they decided to switch to walking alongside the cart the next morning, their hands roped together.

"Try to look like you have been doing this for weeks," said Sam, briefing them from inside the cart. "Don't make eye contact with the men or each other."

"Why not? I want to know if they're secretly enjoying it," Charis said, glaring at the doorway where Adder, Jackal, and Dash stood, and eliciting indignation and disgust in return.

"Because if our body language is off," said Sam, "it will be evident even in a quick, five-to-ten-second video feed."

"Right, so, we can look at them as long as we're throwing angry glances," said Skye, with a mock pout in Dash's direction.

"In theory, yes," said Dot. "But please don't. Unless you're a really good actor."

"I'm a—"

"No, Skye." Dot looked them over. "Shale, you strike me as someone who can play a part."

"Not sure if that's a compliment, Dot."

"Me, either. Actually, Shya is pretty good at controlling her face. Sam, you're not bad. As long as you're not pretending to be a Northerner, from what Jack says. Charis—you're mad all the time anyway, so that's actually fine. You know what? Actually, it's just Skye that's not allowed."

"Ha," said Adder, pointing a dusty finger at her.

"And you," said Dot. "Jackal and Dash are fine. They're always hard to read."

"But—"

"Maybe you shouldn't talk at all, Adder." The corners of Dot's mouth twitched upward.

"Seems safest," said Shya.

"But what if I look really cross."

Dot shook her head. "Like Shya says, better safe than sorry."

"I won't even look at you. I'll just mutter under my breath. Can I mutter under my breath?"

Dot glanced across at Sam.

"You can mutter under your breath," said Sam. "Until we're within sight of the wall. Then you'll need to be silent."

As she spoke, the air seemed to grow heavier. Adder looked at her, the playfulness suddenly gone from his face. Skye reached out for Charis, and all around the cart hands grabbed for knives, bows, bolts.

Because if Epa was correct, they would reach Seira the following day.

35

"You're talking different," said Shale, her fingers gentle as she combed them through Sam's tangled, greasy hair that evening.

They were alone in the cart, Sam sitting cross-legged on the floor, Shale kneeling behind her. Everyone else was outside, roped together by the fire. The remaining bunks were covered with the last of the rations and the drugs to be cut for the next day.

They had to be close now. Sam had been staring at the horizon all afternoon, certain with every footstep that the wall was going to appear in the horizon, slicing land and sky, past and present. Not that they could see very far with the dust.

"I...It's..."

"Just wanted to let you know. I'm not pulling at strings." Shale's voice was low, little more than a whisper. "We've all got our secrets."

It was an easy out. If she wanted it.

We probably won't live past tomorrow.

Clutching at intimacy, are we?

Clutching at my friend. And I'm tired of secrets.

"It's like the closer we get to the border, the more I'm becoming the old me."

Shale separated a section of hair and began braiding. "That a bad thing?"

"Not for me, maybe. But for you—for anyone else..."

"Don't think too much about it. My mom—" Shale went quiet for a moment, though her hands kept moving, winding the braid along the crown of Sam's head. "I have memories of her. Nothing grand or beautiful. But there's a—a sweetness there. Can't explain it better than that. And then I remember being on my own. I don't know if she died or left me or what—and the things I—we do what we have to. It's not who we are."

Sam felt her heart beating faster. Truth, from Shale, was an intimate gift. Not one that she deserved.

"We dance ahead of the reaper,'" said Shale. "That's what Xenia liked to say. It's not always to stay one step ahead, either. Sometimes we're two steps, three steps away. Still the same dance." She pinned the braid. "Kohl?"

"If you want," said Sam. It seemed silly to her, in truth. But then makeup always had.

Shale sighed. "Look at me."

Sam turned so that she faced the older girl. Shale's wavy auburn tresses had been pulled into a long braid that hung heavy over one shoulder.

"It's not about how it looks, lover. The point is, there's gonna be a lot of marks on our bodies that we don't choose." Shale held up the kohl. "This is a choice. I can line your eyes or draw—I dunno, a goat on your forehead. Or do nothing. It doesn't matter. Just decide what you want."

"I—okay. Yes. Just my eyes, though. Not the goat," said Sam, closing her eyes and lifting her face up toward Shale.

"Pity," said Shale as she leaned in and slowly dragged the kohl along Sam's eyelids. "I do a great goat. Now look up."

As Sam stared upward at the ceiling, the bottom half of her vision filled with Shale's large brown eyes, her tiny nose, the plump red of her lower lip. Sam felt the coolness of the kohl as Shale lined her lower lids. "Can I ask—what happened with Charis?" Immediately Sam wanted to backpedal. Shale didn't like questions. It was a matter of respect. "You don't need to answer that."

"It's okay," said Shale, after a moment. "After all, we're probably gonna die tomorrow."

Sam lowered her eyes from the ceiling to her friend. "We might not."

"Then I can always kill you," said Shale with a crooked smile, handing Sam the kohl. "Do me."

Sam looked from the kohl in her hands to Shale, kneeling in front of her. Despite the shadows and the dust and the fatigue, Sam thought that Shale looked younger, somehow.

Maybe it's the honesty of the conversation.

Or maybe she wasn't that much older than you to begin with.

Shale closed her eyes and Sam leaned in, holding the other girl's head with one hand as she gently traced the kohl along first one eyelid, then the other.

"The man who took me in after I lost my mom, he took in a lot of kids. Girls, mostly, a few boys. All pretty. They called him the Handler. He got us young, so the debt we owed him... We had to work it off, he said."

Sam wanted to cover her ears. She hadn't wanted to know this.

"It wasn't just our bodies, though it was that too. He had us spy on huaina. And steal. It's how I ended up meeting Ava." Shale's tone lightened. "I was watching some huaina who used to visit a girl living in the factory." Feeling that Sam had finished, Shale opened her eyes and looked up to the ceiling.

Trying to keep her hand steady, Sam lined the lower lids. "She caught you sneaking around?"

"It got harder to hide after awhile," said Shale. "One of those sicknesses went around, the kind that make you shit until you die."

"Oh."

"Yeah. So, suddenly there was a lot of empty space at the factory. And Epa had just left, so maybe she was looking for, I dunno, distraction or something."

Finished, Sam placed the kohl on the bunk beside her. "So, Charis..."

Shale stayed on her knees, her eyes moving from the ceiling to the kohl on the bed, to Sam's face. "One of the gangs I was watching had lookouts, kids they'd recruited."

"Charis."

"Yeah. She caught me. Gave me to the men."

It wasn't just sadness on Shale's face. The anger was old. Deeply rooted.

Say something.

It's too heartbreaking. Everything I want to say sounds false.

It's not.

It's still insultingly insufficient.

Of course it is. Say it anyway.

"I'm so sorry."

"It's how it works, in the Barrow. If they'd found me, Charis woulda been punished the same way. So, it wasn't her fault, not really." There was a long pause. "But I hate her anyway."

"What happened to the man?"

"Which one?"

"The one who—"

"Oh, him. He was stabbed to death not long after."

"Oh. By one of the huaina he was spying on?"

"No, by some of the kids."

"The kids."

"Yeah. A bunch of them. I was out, on a job." She exhaled, slowly. "Wish I coulda seen it."

"And Ava—"

"Ava's always had an eye out for the screw-up," said Shale. "Maybe she shoulda had more kids, but after Epa..." She made a face. "Guess it kind of turned her off it, huh?"

Sam pictured Epa's face, his sunken cheeks, his hunched, lumbering walk, and tried to imagine him as a lover. And a father.

"So, he just left Raina, then," said Sam.

"Yeah. She was wee, though. Probably didn't really remember him."

"Doesn't," said Sam, with a frown.

"Sure," said Shale, though Sam heard appeasement, not agreement in her tone. "My guess is he probably tried to get her and Ava to go back to the Waste with him. Getting Ava to go somewhere she don't want to, though..."

"And he didn't try to take just Raina?"

Shale let out a low whistle. "Try to take Ava's girl? She'da murdered him. Even if she had to follow him out here to do it."

Sam nodded, trying to keep the sadness off her face. Not knowing why she suddenly felt so lonely.

"Poor Ava," said Shale. "Everyone keeps disappearing on her."

"Maybe we'll get back to her. With Raina."

Shale nodded, but her thoughts seem to have drifted. She reached forward to pick the kohl up off the bunk. "Hard to believe it was only a few weeks ago we were doing this with Xenia."

Sam felt something tighten in her chest. "I miss her. I know it's nothing to how you feel, but I do, I miss her all the time."

Shale's eyes were wet as she passed the kohl to Sam. "Write her name, for me?"

Sam nodded. "Where?"

The redhead turned her tiny frame around and lowered her shirt so that her shoulders and the top half of her back were bare. "Somewhere they won't see," she said.

Sam looked at the pale, smooth skin, the bird bones beneath, and started writing. "It's next to your heart," she said after a moment. "The other side of your heart, anyway." She looked at her handiwork, at Xenia's name stark against Shale's white skin, and felt an overwhelming surge of envy.

To have lost someone, and be blameless. To wear their name as a token of your love. It felt like a fairy tale, the kind of northern story where you die a hero and your ghosts are young and beautiful and greet you with open arms.

Even if there was life after this one, Corvus wouldn't be waiting for her. His story was over, and she would always be the villain.

The last bit of light was fading. Sam could barely see Shale as the other girl pulled her shirt back up and turned around to face her.

"Did you know we don't have parents, in the South?" asked Sam.

"I heard it. Didn't know how it could be true, though."

"They make us in a lab. I wonder, though... Maybe we're missing something."

"What do you mean, missing?"

"That ability to sacrifice ourselves for someone else. Maybe we don't have that kind of loyalty."

"Is that bad?" asked Shale. "That sacrifice, it's a raw deal, Sam."

"Did you...I mean, sorry, I don't need to ask."

Shale laughed. "Girl, I am giving you free reign today. If we survive this, I probably won't let you ask me another question until the day I actually do die. So, you might as well keep going."

"I just wonder...did you want that? To be a mother?"

It was the wrong question. Sam knew it immediately.

"It doesn't matter," said Shale, her voice flat. "I can't. The Handler —he... I got, by one of the clients. The Handler got rid of it. But the damage he did, I can't have them now."

Sam wanted to say something, but the coldness in Shale's voice held her back.

"I always wondered if it was an accident, or if he did it on purpose. The damage, I mean." Shale took the kohl from Sam, who'd forgotten she was still holding it. "I'm lucky I didn't bleed out." Her voice lowered to a rumble—the sensual purr that Shale used to feign intimacy when she was actually pushing you away. "I've always been lucky when it comes to not-dying. The rest of it, though... Anytime something seems good, it gets taken away."

"I understand losing someone you love," said Sam, but Shale was already climbing to her feet.

"Let's go see about that fire, huh?" she asked before she left the cart.

Before Sam could collect herself enough to follow, Dot's large frame filled the doorway. She stepped into the cart and pulled the door closed behind her.

"Sam?"

"I'm here. Did you need help finding something, or—"

"Nope. Already found her."

"You were looking for me?" Sam wasn't sure whether she should sit or stand, so she just stayed on the floor.

"Yeah."

Nobody spoke for a moment. Then they both started to speak at once.

"Did you want to go over the—"

"Shya said she talked—"

They both stopped.

"You go," said Sam.

"Thanks." It was the hesitation in Dot's voice that told Sam what was coming. "Shya said she talked to you awhile back. About Jack. About me."

Sam nodded, then remembered that Dot might not be able to see. "She did, I—"

"Just let me talk for a minute, okay? Best if I just say it all at once."

Sam traced the shadowy lines of the cart with her eyes, and waited. The bunks. The walls. The ceiling.

"It's always been Jack, for me. And I've never been what he wanted. And that's fine. That's him and this is me and that's just what it is." Dot shifted in the doorway. "And maybe you don't see him the way that I do. You might not notice it, because he's quiet, but he looks after people. He always put Anna first, about everything. And it's funny, because he's been alone so much. Not alone, alone—there was always people who wanted him, and they'd come around for a bit, but it never seemed to stick. Not for him. I don't think—I don't think he's fallen in love, much. And maybe it was fine when he had Anna—she had lots of lovers but she and Jack were the family. Then came us. Then came the rest of the world."

Dot took a deep breath. "So maybe there's something between you. Maybe not. But it's probably our last night. And I don't want him to be lonely."

Sam stopped tracing patterns and looked over at Dot, though she couldn't see more than her silhouette. It made Sam grateful for the darkness. Dot's words were raw enough.

"So if it's me that's stopping you. Don't let it be." Without waiting for a response, she opened the door and stepped back out into the night.

With Dot gone the cart seemed somehow smaller, the night colder.

Sam stood up.

It's a bad idea. No matter what she says.

36

Jackal got up from the fire and walked over to meet her as she stepped down from the cart.

"Sorry," he said as he began wrapping the heavy rope around her hands. She watched him, silently. Then her eyes slid to the fire and the shapes huddled around it.

Shale sat alone. The rope that bound her hands snaked along the ground to where Dash and Adder pretended to keep guard. The two men were deep in conversation, Sam noted, though oddly it was Dash speaking while Adder listened in silence. Behind the fire, the dark hulk of the tents stood sentinel. She assumed that Charis and Skye occupied one, Dot and Shya the other.

Well, there are your choices. It's all laid out for you nicely in vignettes.

How did she want to spend her last night? With a lover, a best friend, a new friend, or alone?

"Well," said Jackal, standing up to his full height. "Do you—"

Sam leaned forward until her forehead rested on his chest. Jackal stopped speaking and slid his hands up her arms.

"I'm surprised everyone's not getting drunk," said Sam, her voice light.

"All out of brew."

She felt his words reverberate through his chest. "Good. Clear heads tomorrow."

Are you smelling him?

I like the way he smells.

He's covered in sand. And sweat.

So am I.

Neither of you have bathed in weeks.

"Do you want to come sit by the fire?" asked Jackal. "There's rice, still."

"No." Sam's voice was a whisper.

Jackal pulled away from her slightly and looked down at her face, his eyes searching. "Do you wanna come with me?"

SHE MADE it to the tent. She even kept it at bay when his hands went to her lower back and her lips met his. She pulled his shirt off, then her own.

And then she panicked.

"Are you okay?" he asked as she crouched down, her hands pressed against her head and the voice that screamed at her.

She nodded, and then remembered that he probably couldn't see her. "Yes."

"Is this about tomorrow?"

An easy out.

"No."

She heard the rustle of fabric and kept her head down as he moved to sit down beside her. He laid one of the blankets across her shoulders. "Is this okay?"

"Yes."

He sat beside her in silence, while she focused on breathing.

"Is there someone else?" he asked after a few moments.

The tears came hot and fast and unexpected.

"There was." Sam's throat ached as the words clawed their way out. "He's dead now."

She braced herself for questions.

"What was his name?"

Not the question she'd been anticipating. "Corvus." Oh, what a long, long time it had been since she had said that name aloud.

"Corvus."

"It was my fault." Her voice was robotic, belying the tears that were now pooling into the crooks of her arms and spilling onto her legs.

"Did you want him dead?"

"No." *No, no, no, no, no.*

"Then maybe you caused it, but it wasn't your fault."

She wanted out of her body. Out of her head.

"Feels like a betrayal, don't it," said Jackal. "Being alive when they're not."

She squeezed her eyes closed, though she wasn't sure why she bothered. It didn't help to drown out her thoughts. It never had.

"I'm so tired of living with it."

"At least you are." His voice was thick, heavy with sadness. "Trying, I mean. Anna always said any night your demons don't win is a good night."

The wind intensified, rattling the tent. Sam looked up. Through the rents in the fabric she could see the fire pulsing higher.

She wanted to move. She wanted to take the sand and scrape off her skin, leave it to fossilize in the desert. Grow new cells, maybe.

Or maybe just bleed out.

That's not you, and you know it.

So, I'll go out swinging, then.

She smiled. *Better.*

"What do you need?" he asked.

She didn't bother with words this time.

Her tears mixed with the dust on their skin and she wondered if he tasted salt on her mouth.

37

"Well," said Dot at the same time that Jackal spoke from the doorway.

"Well—"

"This is it, kids," said Adder, squeezing past Jackal into the cart.

Dash stepped up to stand beside Jackal. "May we all have quick wits and faster hands."

"And luck," said Shale. "We're gonna need a lot of that."

"And luck," said Dash.

"Everyone got your shiny baubles?" asked Adder.

Six pairs of hands held up rings, bracelets, necklaces. Their knives and crossbows had been wrapped up in old clothing and hidden in the drawers beneath the bunks, where they could easily access them after passing through the border. Hopefully.

"No talking once we start moving," said Dot for the third time that morning. "Unless you can lie perfectly. Even then, limit it."

"No pretending. Be the character."

"This isn't a game, Skye."

"Enough talk," said Charis. "Let's get to it, snake boy."

Adder took the pills they'd cut before breakfast and went bunk to bunk, passing out the precise amounts they'd decided upon.

"I love you, sis," said Shya. "And Dot."

"I love you, too," Charis said. "And you, babe."

Sam slipped a hand over the side of her bunk, felt Shale reach up and squeeze her fingers.

"And yours, Sammo," said Adder, passing her a small piece of paper with the pill inside. "Our teeny tiny heavyweight." To her surprise, he leaned over and gave her a peck on the cheek. "I'm glad we didn't accidentally kill each other on the solstice." He grinned as she fumbled for a reply. "Now let's break into your house and make a mess."

She reached out as he turned away, caught his hand, gave it a squeeze. Then she turned her eyes to the doorway, where she felt Jackal watching. Felt the memory of the morning's kiss on her lips. She traced the silhouette of his face, his shoulders, the edges blurred by the force of the early morning sun.

She placed the pill on the bunk beside her, next to the small skin of water. A moment later the cart began to move. With nothing else to do, her eyes shifted to the roof of the cart and she began to count.

NOBODY SPOKE. Nobody moved. Even as the first hour rolled into a second, and then a third. Even though the cart protected the privacy of their movements, if not their words. It may have been mental preparation. Perhaps it was fatigue. Probably it was fear.

Even though they were expecting it, Sam wasn't the only one to jump when Jackal pounded on the side of the cart. Three times, to signify that they could see the wall. Twice again an hour later to tell them that they were approaching the border. At the second signal, each girl inside the cart wordlessly swallowed a pill. Without knowing what she would wake to. Or if she would wake at all.

Sam imagined she could hear the hum of electricity and pictured scanners processing their cart, the six bodies inside, the men who appeared to be transporting them. Her chest continued to rise and fall slowly, like a metronome.

She imagined alarms sounding, triggered by a secret barcode on the underside of her tongue, or carved into her fibula, and was grateful for the calming effect of the drugs that were overriding her system. Anxiety, longing, none held sway.

Younger versions of herself seemed to crowd in around her, like a sequencing challenge or a game of connect the dots.

How did I end up here?

She saw their faces, their disappointment.

All that training.

All that work.

And this is how it ends.

She'd let them down. She'd let so many, many people down. Corvus' face swam up. Back when he was Vireo, and Ash, and all the others in between. The multi-him smiled at her, trusting her. His mistake.

Several minutes passed, and then she heard voices. Sunlight was replaced by the cold constancy of electric bulbs and the ground beneath them evened out, from rocks and dirt to concrete.

Then the slow, mechanical descent of an elevator.

Six of us. Three of them. Nine in our party. Twelve bunks.

You shouldn't be counting. You should be unconscious.

And I will be, any second now. Let me count.

Four wheels, plus the two spares was six. One poisoned ring on her right hand. One poisoned bead in her paper necklace.

Two weapons. That's a bad number.

It's better than zero.

It's still a bad number.

Count your fists, then. And your feet.

Ah, six. Yes, that's better.

You're still counting.

The cart slowed and then came to an abrupt stop.

Black out.

Get through the border.

Pass the inspection.

Wait while the cart moves to the final destination.

Or they dump us onto a train.

Or something else. Maybe trains are outdated now. A lot can change in a year.

Just look at us.

The door to the cart opened. Sam closed her eyes.

Work. Please work.

Her dosage was over five times higher than what the other girls had taken. It had worked when they tested it. What was different this time?

My active sympathetic nervous system.

That would not alter the potency of the sedative.

It changes my body chemistry.

Of course it does. Why didn't we think of that?

The footsteps were light, quiet. Too light and quiet to belong to Grand Neilem. Of course, she'd known that it was highly improbable that the Grand would process a shipment herself. But losing all your seconds on one day was also highly improbable. It had been a gamble.

Two steps, a pause. Then a beep.

The beeping moved from the top of the opposite set of bunks to the bottom, to the bottom of hers. Then to Shale. Then to her.

The scanner beeped once, twice. Then stopped.

Silence.

Sam could feel her body shrugging off the calming effects of the drugs. Her heart started to pound, faster.

She couldn't do it anymore. Slowly, lazily, as though she were half-asleep, Sam opened her eyes just a slit.

Then all the way.

The P5 was beside her bunk, large, grey eyes wide with shock, her mouth already whispering Sam's name.

Her old name.

"Sierra?"

Lyra. *Her* Lyra. Her ally since the day they became cadets. When Sam was Sora and Lyra was Starling. Just little birds.

Play through the scenario. You fled north, yes, and then were kidnapped by a southern compound who had no idea who you are.

She opened her mouth to speak, and then stopped.

Don't do it. Don't—

It's Lyra.

Don't do it, Sierra!

"Lyra."

"Sierra—how...?"

"We don't have a lot of time, Lyra." Sam spoke softly. She didn't think there was audio surveillance here, in the base, but it was always possible. "Someone in the South is having girls and women in the North kidnapped. We need to follow the trail. My friend, her daughter was taken—"

Lyra stepped back, shaking her head. "No, no, you have been misinformed. These are Southerners. They were stolen from the labs as infants, we have agents that track them down and—" Lyra's voice was defensive, the cloak of the lie pulled tight around her shoulders.

"That doesn't make any sense, Lyra." Sam reached out and took her small, pale hand. The other one, the one holding the scanner, fell limply to her side. "Even if that were true, if babies were taken—Look at these girls—they're all different ages. And if they had trackers in them the Administration would have retrieved them years ago. And there are babies everywhere in the North—why would anybody steal them?"

"I—I cannot listen to anything you say."

"Look at them. They've been drugged. Why drug them if this is an honest mission?"

"To reduce stress."

"Lyra—"

She shook off Sam's hand. "You've been branded, Sierra! They said you stole intel and brought it to enemies in the North, I—"

"Another lie, Lyra."

"What do you mean, a lie? Sierra, you disappeared. And Protectors Onyx and Jace were killed by— They said it was you. That you killed them."

Sam forced her voice to be calm, reassuring. "We have a duty to others, Lyra. Don't we? We have a responsibility to report unlawful behaviour. Kidnapping is a heinous crime."

"Sure, but—"

"You can help. Just process us the way you've been told. Send us on. We'll take care of it from there."

"But I—"

"You didn't recognize me," said Sam. "You...you thought I was dead."

Lyra's eyes welled up. "I didn't know what to think. You were just gone, Sierra. First Corvus, then you."

"Corvus—Corvus didn't disappear, Lyra. The Administration killed him."

Lyra shook her head again.

"They did. I found out, and then I had to run. Protectors Jace and Onyx tried to stop me, but it was an accident—the darts were supposed to stun."

"It was an accident."

"It was. I didn't want to leave you, or Elium. There was an internship in Ankev... But you look well, Lyra. You're a P5, obviously. That's —that's wonderful! I mean, I'm surprised—protocol is to bring in seconds from other bases, but you're an excellent choice, of course."

Lyra gave a sad smile. "Thank you. I miss being a medic, though. It was better."

Sam nodded. "It's not that great, is it, being a P5."

Lyra shook her head.

"Grand Neilem always hated me," said Sam.

"Hate is unproductive."

"I know, but she hated me anyway."

Lyra seemed to remember the other five girls for the first time. She glanced down at Shale, and then over to Dot, Shya, Skye, and Charis. None of them had so much as stirred.

"Why would they take girls?" Lyra's voice was a whisper.

"There are things in Seira that aren't what they seem," said Sam. "Please believe me."

"Corvus was transferred," said Lyra, but her tone was doubtful, unsure.

"I hacked into the offline system in lower medical." Sam's voice shook. "His name, his picture, and the word 'terminated.'"

"Terminated." Lyra took a step closer, her eyes searching Sam's.

She almost believes you. She wants to believe you.

"I was next, I—"

Sam's words were drowned out by the sound of voices outside the cart. She heard Adder cry out in pain.

"Call them off," said Sam. "Call them off, Lyra."

Lyra shook her head, tears streaming down her face as her eyes flickered to the scanner in her hand. And Sam understood.

"You called them."

"Before you woke up."

"Lyra—"

Her tone was robotic as she pulled out the syringe. Someone who didn't know her as well as Sam did might have missed the sadness underneath. "It's protocol, Sierra, directly from the councilhead. You're a traitor to Seira."

38

When Sam opened her eyes next, she was alone in a concrete box. Body unbound, still in her solstice clothes. She looked at her hands, the dirt under her fingernails, and the ring on the middle finger of her right hand.

Yes.

She rolled her neck, feeling for the ridges of the beads.

Two for two, then.

When the medic entered her cube fifteen minutes later, Sam didn't hesitate. In the swift motion she'd practiced, she undid the clasp on the ring and blew the powder into the medic's face.

The bead she twisted off as she ran forward, and jammed it into the mouth of the guard that waited outside her door.

She looked around herself and felt nauseous.

The sheen of the walls, the floor, the ceiling was disorientating. Was it a screen? She looked back to her cube but the doorway was gone. There was nothing but gently swirling metallic shapes, symmetrical and beautiful the way the inside of a machine was beautiful.

She scanned the walls, looking for some sign that her friends were here. They had to be here.

Why? They're the shipment. You're a traitor.

Could she lift the guard, use his hand on the security screen, his eyes for the iris scan?

Footsteps sounded in the distance, to the left of her. She ran her hands along the walls, looking for a door handle, an alphanumeric code, a security screen, anything. The footsteps grew louder.

Run.

She turned to her right and sprinted down the corridor. Took a left. Then a right. The lights made it hard to tell how fast she was moving, and she soon lost track of the turns she'd taken.

Is this real?

She stumbled, misjudging the depth of the floor, caught herself, and raced down another corridor.

Am I in a holodisplay? Some kind of virtual prison?

The hallway ended in a T. Sam ran left and skidded to a stop in front of a glass wall.

It was a virtual holodisplay. It had to be.

She was staring at a hall of sorts, though planters had sliced the room into a series of pathways. The walls were painted a pale, earthy green, and the lighting was pleasant and dim.

Women dressed in soft cotton robes walked slowly, three by three, along the paths. Not speaking, not looking at one another. A manufactured calm, she knew, from the relaxed, neutral expressions on their faces, the glassy shine of their eyes.

Most of them flawless—perfect hair, perfect teeth. Skin unmarked by sun or scratch or laugh line. But against the muted colours of the room the black ink of homemade tattoos shone garishly bright on the arm of one woman, the neck of another.

Southerners and Northerners, both. And almost all of them visibly with child.

"No." Her voice was a whisper.

Row after row of women passed by. She stared at their faces. And then at one face.

An old memory. Running down a cold hallway. The climb through the vents. A hand in hers, before the other girl followed a strange medic through a door.

"Iris?"

Sam stepped closer to the glass, but the woman on the other side didn't so much as glance over.

"Iris!"

Sam hit the glass with one palm, and then the other.

"Iris!"

She was screaming so loudly she didn't hear them approach. There was only the cold pain of the needle.

39

The first thing that Sam became aware of, when she became aware again, was that she was lying on a plush bed. The second thing she noticed was that the room was green—not the calm green of dried grass but a bright, emerald green. Heavy curtains had been drawn to reveal a three-dimensional holodisplay. It was the sharpest picture Sam had ever seen. Big, beautiful multi-story buildings. Agro-cylinders. All with the shine that told her that they were absorbing and harvesting the rays from the hot evening sun. In front of the holodisplay was a table set with fruit, mesquite cakes, and a jug of prickly pear juice.

And she wasn't alone.

Sitting in a high-backed, cushioned chair beside her bed was Councilman Naru.

"Ah, Sierra." He smiled. "Awake at last."

He looked unchanged from the last time Sam had seen him, his build powerful, his skin unlined, his teeth white and straight, the black hair on his head and the closely cropped beard unmarred by so much as a single strand of grey.

You've grown used to the Barrow. This is what aging looks like in Seira.

"Councilman—"

"Ah ah, have a drink first, my dear." He went to the table, poured a small glass of juice, and carried it over to her. "Slowly. Don't want you getting sick, now."

Obediently she took a small sip.

"Sorry about that first room—yikes, that must have given you a scare." He chuckled as he sat himself back down, careless of the beautifully crafted indigo suit jacket that had been slung over the arm of his chair.

"Course, you repaid that scare to the poor medic and her guard."

"I—"

"Drink." He pointed at the cup. The forearm beneath the crisp white shirt sleeve was heavily muscled, the skin tanned. It reminded her that he'd been a cadet once, and then a protector.

Sam took another sip. Something glinted down near his wrists. Cufflinks, she realized.

"Neat little devices," said Councilman Naru. "Where did they come from?"

It took Sam a moment to realize that he was referring to the weaponized jewelry they'd been gifted by the People of the Phoenix. "A tribe—"

"Never mind, that can all wait." He cocked his head, looking at her wrist, and then shook his head. "You've had quite the adventure."

Sam looked down at the raised, pink "V" on her wrist. Bits of it had scabbed over, though it still oozed in places. The skin felt different, though. Tight. Someone had treated it. She took a closer look at her hands, the clean white nails, and put a hand up to her hair. Breathed in the subtle scent of earth apple. Someone had bathed her while she was unconscious.

"Where are my friends?" It was impertinent. Sierra would never have asked it. Sam didn't care.

"So, they are your friends, then? You know, I couldn't get a word out of them. About you, I mean. They told me their names, the mission, blah blah, but nothing about you."

"Are they—did you hurt them?" The words came out a whisper.

"Hurt them? What a thing to say. They're being processed, I would assume."

Sam's hands started to shake. "What does that mean, processed?"

"Deep breaths, my dear. Would you like some calming tea?"

"No drugs," she said.

"Oh." He looked genuinely surprised. "Well, then, give me the juice." He reached over and took the cup from her. "I'll ring for a fresh batch." He put the cup on the nightstand, picked up his porta, and swiped through a few screens before placing it back down on the nightstand beside the juice.

They were wolves, she realized. Small, golden cufflinks in the shape of wolves.

He caught her eyeing them and winked. "Like them? They were a gift from Myrrsa on our anniversary."

"I—" Sam stopped. She needed to stay on track. "My friends—"

"This loyalty you have." He shook his head. "It's a great trait, Sierra, but oh, you did take us for a ride. If I'd had any notion that you might skip the border...well, we would have handled things differently, wouldn't we?"

"I was marked for termination."

"Yes, well, that was Grand Neilem overstepping." His brows creased. "Had to speak rather sternly to her about that. There's a form, you know, with approval required by the council. Skipping protocol, like that—"

"So, I wouldn't have—"

"We would have sorted it out, of course. The timing was just unfortunate. Like today! If I had been in Ankev instead of visiting the western seaboard...but anyway. No matter. We've got you here, nice and comfortable, instead of in one of those horrible little cubes that Councilhead Aries favours."

"He's coming for me." Sam's left hand twitched instinctively toward her neck, her right thumb to her middle finger where the heavy metal ring had rested. The weapons that she'd used and discarded. Her only chance.

"Calm down, my dear. Oh, look. Your new juice is here." Councilman Naru walked over to where a box on the wall was gently blinking. "Did you want a mesquite cake, too? No?"

"He branded me a traitor," said Sam. "Lyra, at the base—"

"Oh, yes, we can work around that too, of course. Special reconnaissance for us in the North." He winked at her. "The role of double agent is highly valued by the Administration."

"But Councilhead Aries—"

"My apologies, I should have told you immediately." His easy smile settled into a sombre expression. "There's been a tragedy. A horrible accident."

It was off, somehow, his look of sorrow. A mask that didn't quite fit.

Sloppy.

No, he's not trying to deceive me.

"He was riding in one of the newer Lacewings. There was some kind of mechanical error—it crashed just minutes after takeoff."

"Is he—"

"Dead? Oh yes. The pilot too, unfortunately, but that couldn't be helped. Just minutes after your little friend alerted us to your presence."

Sam felt her throat go dry. She glanced to the corners of the room.

"Oh, don't worry. No cameras in here. These are my private quarters, you see. You're quite safe here." He smiled at her and then stood up again. "If you're not having a mesquite cake I think I will."

Sam closed her eyes.

None of this makes any sense.

Process it later. Focus on what's urgent. For some reason he wants you alive. For now, anyway. What about the others?

She tried again. "My friends, where are they?"

"Hmm?" The councilman bit into a mesquite cake. "Delicious. I love when they add dates, you know?" He looked at her face and placed the rest of the cake back on the table. "Alright," he said, dusting the crumbs off his fingers. "One moment." He walked back over to the nightstand, picked up his porta again, and began swiping. "Ah. So, the males have been processed for manual pollination, and the females for insemination." He returned the porta to his table a second time and smiled at her.

"Insemi—you mean—" She stopped. Took a deep breath. "How is this happening? It's barbaric."

He frowned at her. "Is it? You found the prenatal gardens. The carriers—the birthing mothers, that is—they seem quite content, do they not?"

"Content? They're drugged."

"Yes, well, artificial emotions are still valid emotions, Sierra."

"And why—" Her voice gave way to a whisper. "Why do we have them? Why do we need birthing mothers when we have artificial gestation?"

"Yes, about that." He walked back to the table, picked up the mesquite cake, took another bite, and then wandered over to the holodisplay. "Our forbearers jumped the gun a little on that announcement."

"They couldn't produce infants?"

"Oh, no. They could. And did. They created healthy, normal little humans. Even the aesthetic modifications worked—eye colour, hair colour, height—whatever was in style." The mesquite cake finished, Councilman Naru licked his fingers and then tucked his hands into the pockets of his tailored indigo pants and surveyed the screen. "It just didn't last. Cancers, autoimmune diseases, heart problems, the issues were endless. And that was only physical health. The mental wellness, ouch. Big issues there." He smiled at her. "Turned out it was easier to stick with old-fashioned in-utero gestation. Which is where your Northerners came in handy."

"But I saw—" The memory was already flimsy, Iris' face blending into Raina's into Xenia's. "I thought I saw—"

"Ah. Yes. Well, we don't tell you what triggered mass infertility in Seira. We should, of course. I've voted to include it in first-year curriculum numerous times." He looked back towards the holodisplay. "It was a pesticide. When the drought came, they allowed a new, untested pesticide to be used. Idiots."

"And it rendered us sterile."

"It killed most people, actually."

"Why didn't they test it properly?"

"Greed, some people say. Our ancestors let the merchants rule. Others argued we were at the tipping point of famine and that it was necessary. Either way, the consequences were immediate and they were dire."

"There are always some, though, that come through these moments untouched. Though not common, there are girls born in Seira every year who still possess the ability to carry a child. Between five and ten percent nationally. Only slightly more than the percentage of the male population capable of passing on genetic material through sperm."

"Iris."

"Hmm?" He turned to look at her.

"Iris was there. I—she was with me at my division."

"Ah, yes, well, then, she would have been transferred here after the medical examination."

Sam felt like she was going to be sick. "She's been here ever since?"

"Given the best food, gentle exercise, lots of companionship—"

Sam just shook her head. "And the insemination—"

Here she saw him hesitate for the first time. "Some of the council and committee members, well... The councilhead saw it as a rewards system. Not me," he said. "I preferred the clinical donation methods. What they did—well, it never seemed right to me."

It was too much to process. Sam stared at the holodisplay, waiting for the pieces in her head to click together. In the corner, something moved.

Was that a Lacewing Jet?

She squinted.

That's not a display. That's a window.

"So, I have parents," she said. An unwilling mother. A father who justified rape in the name of national interest. "Was she southern? Or a Northerner? Is she even still alive? Does she—" Sam paused, waited for her breathing to slow, for her voice to return to normal. "Does she remember me?"

"She does." Sam's head snapped to the opposite wall, and the woman who had soundlessly entered the room.

Councilwoman Myrrsa had always been difficult to read. Sam's eyes raced over the councilwoman's black hair and light brown skin, and the dark purple dress that she wore, flecked with gold so that you couldn't help but notice her bright amber eyes. Eyes that gave nothing away. The enigmatic council member. Ever elegant. Always poised.

She was carrying an armload of clothing, and bent down to place the items atop the other nightstand before turning to face Sam, her beautiful face composed except for the slightest quiver in her chin.

"Your father thought it best," she said, "that I avoid all contact. Lest I give it away."

Sam's eyes felt full to bursting. She looked back at the councilman, still standing in front of the window.

"It was for all our sakes, Sierra," he said. "If Myrrsa had been found to be a carrier—well, she would have been confined to the gardens. Council member or not."

"I thought you said it was a good life."

"It is!" He walked back toward Sam and seated himself once again in the chair beside the bed, facing her. "For a regular Seiran. Not for a councilwoman. Just like it wouldn't have been good enough for you." He flashed her a smile. "Luckily, being Seira's Chief Medical Officer has its perks."

"He attended to me during labour and delivery," Councilwoman Myrrsa explained, seeing Sam's confusion. "And during the prenatal and postnatal period, of course. Officially, we said—"

"That you had a concussion." Sam had read about it. Myrrsa had been in an accident soon after being elected to the council. She'd been unable to leave her home for almost a year, as all bright lighting, whether natural or electric, had caused her severe pain; screens in particular had been problematic.

It was clever. Very clever. No screens meant no video calls, no photographs, no witnesses.

Something else clicked in Sam's memory. Two voices, two black heads seen from above. "The day I left the division. You were there."

Councilman Naru clapped his hands and leaned back, shaking a finger up at Councilwoman Myrrsa. "I told you she was sharp."

The councilwoman took a small, measured step forward. "We watched your progress with pride. Everything you accomplished—we couldn't be there, but we were watching, always. And now that you're back, and Aries is gone—"

"It's a new day for Seira." The councilman leaned forward and took Sam's hands gently but firmly in his. As Sam's brain roared, she found herself focusing in on his hands. Large and warm, with clipped fingernails, and smooth, unmarked skin the same light brown shade as her own.

It was too much. She pulled her hands away. Forced herself to sit tall, speak with a full voice.

"I want my friends back."

"Sure." He spoke softly, as though she were a wild beast that might startle and flee. "Myrrsa?"

She frowned. "Your porta's on the nightstand, Naru."

"I've done a lot of overriding today. Better use your codes."

She sighed and pulled out a porta from one of the folds in her dress.

"Not just the ones I came south with," said Sam. "The ones we came to...to..."

"To rescue?" His chuckle was kindly, but the sound lashed at Sam. "I suppose we can look into that. Within reason, of course."

She met his gaze and understood. It was a carrot, a bribe. Sam could pluck a few flowers as long as the garden continued to thrive.

But how many? Are you going to choose Raina over Anna? What about Dash's people?

What about Iris?

"Sierra." There was a break in the councilwoman's tone. She looked like she wanted to approach Sam, to touch her.

Hadn't Sam imagined this, since living in the Barrow? Hadn't she wondered what it would be like, to have a mother?

A real mother. Not like this.

She focused her eyes straight ahead. A prisoner's passive aggression—refusing to look at either of them. It was a poor substitute for hiding. She did it anyway.

There was silence. Sam began tracing the windows with her eyes.

"Get some rest," said Councilwoman Myrrsa after Sam had reached her third count of twelve. "We'll process these eight to start with. In the morning we'll look into identifying the woman you came for."

"And my friends. We all came for somebody."

There was a silence pregnant with decision. She was asking for more than they had planned to give.

"And your friends, too," said the councilman, at last.

"Thank you." Sam kept her eyes on the window, holding the tears back, waiting for them to leave.

Councilman Naru patted her shoulder and stood up. "And we'll talk about the future, eh? It's a new start for Seira, Sierra, a new start. And you're going to be a big part of this new beginning."

"Samarra."

"What's that?"

"It's Samarra now."

He clapped her on the shoulders again and made to join Councilwoman Myrrsa at the door.

A thought occurred to her. Such a small detail and unimportant. But for some reason she needed the answer. "You were at the base before my designation."

The councilman turned back. "I was."

"Did you tell Grand Neilem to choose me?"

"I told the Grand that she needed to take on *an* apprentice. The choice was obvious."

"We didn't have to meddle," said Councilwoman Myrrsa. "You excelled. As we'd known you would."

Councilman Naru took the councilwoman's hand in his. "Because you were born to excel. And Seira will benefit." He punched in a code and a door materialized in the wall. "Beholden, duty-bound, in gratitude."

Sam kept her chin up, her face composed, until the wall closed soundlessly behind them. Even then she sat frozen, unwilling to permit entry to the emotions that clawed, desperate against the walls in her mind. Instead she reached outward, needing to touch something tangible, found the clothing that Councilwoman Myrrsa had brought. Sam pulled it onto the bed, the fabric pooling, inky, onto her lap, finer material than she'd ever touched before. There were shirts, dresses, pants, all in deep, bold hues. And underneath it all, a scarlet cloak.

"Beholden, duty-bound, in gratitude." Sam's voice was a whisper in an empty room.

ACKNOWLEDGMENTS

There are three experts who were instrumental in helping to shape the Waste. Thank you to Dr. Ellen Whitman, forest fire research scientist with Natural Resources Canada; Dr. Barry Smit of the University of Guelph, expert in climate change, environment and resource use and global change; and Dr. Mathieu Bourbonnais of the University of British Columbia Okanagan, formerly a wildland firefighter with the Alberta Wildfire Rappel Program and Parks Canada. I will be forever grateful to you for answering my numerous and pesky questions about wildfires and re-burns, both the current reality and the more abstract "what if" situations.

Thank you to my editor, Melissa Frain, whose insightful and hilarious feedback improved this story exponentially. Melissa, you're a genius. My writing would be mud pies without you.

A massive thank you to the amazing Lena Yang for coming in mid-series and creating such beautiful covers. Lena—you're incredible. Thank you for putting up with my horrible ideas.

I said it with *The Wolf and the Rain*, but I want to mention it again here. Russ Foxx, body piercing and modifications expert, thank you for taking the time to answer numerous questions on the subject of body branding.

For helping me to better understand some of the martial aspects, thank you to Christopher Gagne of the International Krav Maga Federation (IKMF), Toronto.

I'm very fortunate to be surrounded by a bubble of brilliant friends and family members. If I start naming names I'll never stop, but to those of you that read advanced copies, or let me pick your brain on everything from the title to cover design to marketing to martial arts or psychology, thank you. This book is better because of you.

This book was written and re-written over eighteen particularly turbulent months—through three moves, two provinces, during pregnancy and those first delirious post-partum months. I couldn't have done it without my husband and my parents. Thank you for taking care of me emotionally and physically. For watching the babies so I could write. For buying me my weird late-night writing snacks. For still loving me when I was sleep deprived and crazy. I couldn't have done it without you three.

ABOUT THE AUTHOR

Tanya Lee holds a B.A from the University of British Columbia in literature and political science, and an MSc.(Planning) in international rural planning and development from the University of Guelph. With a focus on international development and human rights, Tanya has worked on counter-trafficking, safe-migration, and maternal and child health projects in India, Nepal, Mexico, and various countries in Africa. She also acts in independent films, particularly those with a focus on human rights and gender equality.

Her first novel, *The Wolf and the Rain*, was the 2019 IndieReader Discovery Award Winner for best YA fiction, received a bronze medal at the Wishing Shelf Book Awards, and a silver medal at the Readers' Favorite Book Awards (young adult sci-fi category), is a B.R.A.G medallion honoree, and was shortlisted for the Whistler Independent Book Awards. She currently lives in B.C. with her husband, her two young children, and a belligerent 23lb orange tabby named Frank.

Visit Tanya's website at: Tanya-Lee.com to sign up for the official mailing list and receive a **free bonus chapter**, set six months before *The Wolf and the Rain.*

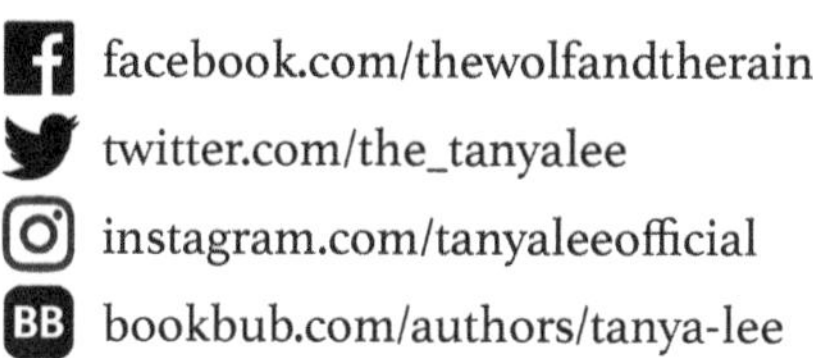

BOOKS BY TANYA LEE

The Wolf and the Rain Trilogy

The Wolf and the Rain

The Thief and the Waste

The Crow and the Smoke (2021)

www.ingramcontent.com/pod-product-compliance
Lightning Source LLC
Chambersburg PA
CBHW020457310726
48979CB00016B/2698/J
* 9 7 8 1 7 7 5 3 9 2 9 5 8 *